#1 *New York Times* Bestselling Author

LINDA LAEL MILLER

WILD ABOUT HARRY

HARLEQUIN
BESTSELLING
AUTHOR
COLLECTION

If you purchased this book without a cover you should be aware that this book is stolen property. It was reported as "unsold and destroyed" to the publisher, and neither the author nor the publisher has received any payment for this "stripped book."

HARLEQUIN®
BESTSELLING
AUTHOR
COLLECTION

Recycling programs for this product may not exist in your area.

ISBN-13: 978-1-335-40619-4

Wild About Harry
First published in 1991. This edition published in 2021.
Copyright © 1991 by Linda Lael Miller

Stone Cold Surrender
First published in 2004. This edition published in 2021.
Copyright © 2004 by Brenda Streater Jackson

All rights reserved. No part of this book may be used or reproduced in any manner whatsoever without written permission except in the case of brief quotations embodied in critical articles and reviews.

This is a work of fiction. Names, characters, places and incidents are either the product of the author's imagination or are used fictitiously. Any resemblance to actual persons, living or dead, businesses, companies, events or locales is entirely coincidental.

This edition published by arrangement with Harlequin Books S.A.

For questions and comments about the quality of this book, please contact us at CustomerService@Harlequin.com.

Harlequin Enterprises ULC
22 Adelaide St. West, 40th Floor
Toronto, Ontario M5H 4E3, Canada
www.Harlequin.com

Printed in Spain

CONTENTS

Also by Linda Lael Miller

HQN

Painted Pony Creek

Country Strong

The Carsons of Mustang Creek

A Snow Country Christmas
Forever a Hero
Always a Cowboy
Once a Rancher

The Brides of Bliss County

Christmas in Mustang Creek
The Marriage Season
The Marriage Charm
The Marriage Pact

The Parable series

Big Sky Secrets
Big Sky Wedding
Big Sky Summer
Big Sky River
Big Sky Mountain
Big Sky Country

McKettricks of Texas

An Outlaw's Christmas
A Lawman's Christmas
McKettricks of Texas: Austin
McKettricks of Texas: Garrett
McKettricks of Texas: Tate

Visit her Author Profile page on Harlequin.com,
or lindalaelmiller.com, for more titles!

WILD ABOUT HARRY

Linda Lael Miller

For Jim Lang,
who married the girl with snowflakes in her hair,
thereby proving what a smart guy he really is.

Chapter 1

Amy Ryan was safe in her bed, drifting in that place where slumber and wakefulness mesh into a tranquil twilight, when she distinctly felt someone grasp her big toe and wriggle it.

"Amy."

She groaned and pulled the covers up over her head. Two full years had passed since her handsome, healthy young husband, Tyler, had died on the operating table during a routine appendectomy. She *couldn't* be hearing his voice now.

"No," she murmured. "I refuse to have this dream again. I'm waking up right now!"

Amy's toe moved again, without orders from her brain. She swallowed, and her heart rate accelerated. Quickly, expecting to find eight-year-old Ashley's cat, Rumpel, at the foot of the bed playing games, she reached out and snapped on the bedside lamp.

A scream rushed into her throat, coming from deep inside her, but she swallowed it. Even though Tyler was standing there, just on the other side of her blanket chest, Amy felt no fear.

She could never be afraid of Ty. No, what scared her was the explicit possibility that she was losing her mind at thirty-two years of age.

"This can't be happening," she whispered hoarsely, raising both hands to her face. From between her fingers, she could still see Tyler grinning that endearing grin of his. "I've been through counseling," she protested. "I've had grief therapy!"

Tyler chuckled and sat down on the end of the bed.

Amy actually felt the mattress move, so lifelike was this delusion.

"I'm quite real," Tyler said, having apparently read her mind. "At least, *real* is the closest concept you could be expected to understand."

"Oh, God," Amy muttered, reaching blindly for the telephone.

Tyler's grin widened. "This is a really lousy joke," he said, "but I can't resist. Who ya gonna call?"

Amy swallowed and hung up the receiver with an awkward motion of her hand. What *could* she say? Could she dial 911 and report that a ghost was haunting her bedroom?

If she did, the next stop would be the mental ward at the nearest hospital.

Amy ran her tongue over dry lips, closed her eyes tightly, then opened them again, wide.

Tyler was still sitting there, his arms folded, charming smile in place. He had brown curly hair and mischievous brown eyes, and Amy had been in love with him since her freshman year at the University of Washington. She had borne him two children, eight-year-old Ashley and six-year-old Oliver, and the loss of her young husband had been the most devastating experience of Amy's life.

"What's happening to me?" Amy rasped, shoving a hand through her sleep-rumpled, shoulder-length brown hair.

Tyler scratched the back of his neck. He was wearing slacks and a blue cashmere cardigan over a tailored white shirt. "I look pretty solid, don't I?" He sounded proud, the way he used to when he'd won a particularly difficult case in court or beaten a colleague at racquet ball. "And let me tell you, being able to grab hold of your toe like that was no small feat, no pun intended."

Amy tossed back the covers, scrambled into the adjoining bathroom and frantically splashed cold water on her face. "It must have been the spicy cheese on the nachos," she told herself aloud, talking fast.

When she straightened and looked in the mirror, though, she saw Tyler's reflection. He was leaning against the doorjamb, his arms folded.

"Pull yourself together, Amy," he said good-naturedly. "It's taken me eighteen months to learn to do this, and I'm not real good at sustaining the energy yet. I could fade out at any time, and I have something important to say."

Amy turned and leaned back against the counter, her hands gripping the marble edge. She sank her teeth into her lower lip and wondered what Debbie would make of this when she told her about it. *If* she told her.

Your subconscious mind is trying to tell you something, her friend would say. Debbie was a counselor in a women's clinic, and she was working on her doctorate in psychology. *It's time to let go of Tyler and get on with your life.*

"Wh-what did you want to-to say?" Amy stammered. She was a little calmer now and figured this figment of her imagination might give her an important update on what was going on inside her head. There was absolutely no doubt, as far as she was concerned, that some of her gears were gummed up.

Tyler's gentle gaze swept her tousled hair, yellow cotton nightshirt and shapely legs with sad fondness.

"An old friend of mine is going to call you sometime in the next couple of days," he said after a long moment. "His name is Harry Griffith, and he runs a multinational investment company out of Australia. They're opening an office in Seattle, so Harry will be living here in the Puget Sound area part of the year. He'll get in touch to offer his condolences about me and pay off on a deal we made the last time we were together. You should get a pretty big check."

Amy certainly hadn't expected anything so specific. "Harry?" she squeaked. She vaguely remembered Tyler talking about him.

Tyler nodded. "We met when we were kids. We were both part of the exchange student program—he lived here for six months, and then I went down there and stayed with Harry and his mom for the same amount of time."

A lump had risen in Amy's throat, and she swallowed it. Yes, Harry Griffith. Tyler's mother, Louise, had spoken of him several times. "This is crazy," she said. "*I'm* crazy."

Her husband—or this mental *image* of her husband—smiled. "No, babe. You're a little frazzled, but you're quite sane."

"Oh, yeah?" Amy thrust herself away from the bathroom counter and passed Tyler in the doorway to stand next to the bed. "If I'm not one can short of a six-pack, how come I'm seeing somebody who's been dead for two years?"

Tyler winced. "Don't use that word," he said. "People don't really die, they just change."

Amy was feeling strangely calm and detached now, as though she were standing outside of herself. "I'll never eat nachos again," she said firmly.

Ty's gentle brown eyes twinkled with amusement. When he spoke, however, his expression was more serious. "You're doing very well, all things considered. You've taken good care of the kids and built a career for yourself, unconventional though it is. But there's one area where you're really blowing it, Spud."

Amy's eyes brimmed with tears. During the terrible days and even worse nights following Tyler's unexpected death, she'd yearned for just such an experience as this. She'd longed to see the man she'd loved so totally, to hear his voice. She'd even wanted to be called "Spud" again, although she'd hated the nickname while Tyler was alive.

She sniffled but said nothing, waiting for Tyler to go on.

He did. "There are women who can be totally fulfilled without a man in their lives. You aren't one of those women, Amy. You're not happy."

Amy shook her head, marveling. "Boy, when my subconscious mind comes up with a message, it's a doozy."

Tyler shrugged. "What can I say?" he asked reasonably. "Harry's the man for you."

"*You* were the man for me," Amy argued, and this time a tear escaped and slipped down her cheek.

He started toward her, as though he would take her into his arms, then, regretfully, he stopped. "That was then, Spud," he said, his voice gruff with emotion. "Harry's *now*. In fact, you're scheduled to remarry and have two more kids—a boy and a girl."

Amy's feeling of detachment was beginning to fade; she was trembling. This was all so crazy. "And this Harry guy is my one and only?" she asked with quiet derision.

She was hurt because Tyler had started to touch her and then pulled back.

"Actually, there are several different men you could have fulfilled your destiny with. That architect you met three months ago, when you were putting together the deal for those condos on Lake Washington, for instance. Alex Singleton—the guy who replaced me in the firm—for another." He paused and shoved splayed fingers through his hair. "You're not cooperating, Spud."

"Well, excuse me!" Amy cried in a whispered yell, not wanting the children to wake and see her in the middle of a hallucination. "I *loved* you, Ty. You were everything to me. I'm not ready to care for anybody else!"

"Yes, you are," Tyler disagreed sadly. Quietly. "Get on with it, Amy. You're holding up the show."

She closed her eyes for a moment, willing Tyler to disappear. When Amy looked again and found him gone, however, she felt all hollow and broken inside.

"Tyler?"

No answer.

Amy went slowly back to bed, switched out the light and lay down. "You're losing it, Ryan," she muttered to herself.

She tried to sleep, but images of Tyler kept invading her mind.

Amy recalled the first time they'd met, in the cafeteria at the University of Washington, when she'd been a lowly freshman and Tyler had been in his third year of law school. He'd smiled as he'd taken the chair across the table from Amy's, and she'd been so thoroughly, instantly besotted that she'd nearly fallen right into her lime Jell-O.

After that day, Amy and Tyler had been together every spare moment. Ty had taken her home to Mercer Island to meet his parents at Thanksgiving, and at Christmas he'd given her a three-carat diamond.

Amy had liked Tyler's parents immediately; they were so warm and friendly, and their gracious, expensive home practically vibrated with love and laughter. The contrast between the Ryans' family life and Amy's was total: Amy's father, one of the most famous heart surgeons in the country, was a distant, distracted sort of man, totally absorbed in his work. Although Amy knew her dad loved her, in his own workaholic way, he'd never been able to show it.

The free-flowing affection among the Ryans had quickly become vital to Amy, and she was still very close to them, even though Tyler had been gone for two years.

Alone in the bed where she and Tyler had once loved and slept and sometimes argued, Amy wept. "This isn't fair," she told the dark universe around her.

With the morning, however, came a sense of buoyant optimism. It seemed only natural to Amy that she'd had a vivid dream about Tyler; he was the father of her children and she'd loved him with her whole heart.

She was sticking frozen waffles in the toaster when Oliver and Ashley raced into the kitchen. During the school year she had trouble motivating them in the mornings, but now that summer had come, they were up and ready for day camp almost as soon as the morning paper hit the doorstep.

"Hey, Mom," Oliver said. He wore a baseball cap low on his forehead and he was wearing shorts and a T-shirt with his favorite cartoon character on the front. "Kid power!" he whooped, thrusting a plastic sword into the air.

Ashley rolled her beautiful Tyler-brown eyes. "What a dope," she said. She was eight and had a lofty view of the world.

"Be careful, Oliver," Amy fretted good-naturedly. "You'll put out someone's eye with that thing." She put the waffles on plates and set them down on the table, then went to the refrigerator for the orange juice. "Look, you two, I might be home late tonight. If I can't get away, Aunt Charlotte will pick you up at camp."

Charlotte was Ty's sister and one of Amy's closest friends.

Ashley was watching Amy pensively as she poured herself a cup of coffee and joined the kids at the table.

"Were you talking to yourself last night, Mom?" the child asked in her usual straightforward way.

Amy was glad she was sitting down because her knees suddenly felt shaky. "I was probably just dreaming," she said, but the memory of Tyler standing there in their bedroom was suddenly vivid in her mind. He'd seemed so solid and so *real.*

Ashley's forehead crumpled in a frown, but she didn't pursue the subject any further.

Fortunately.

After Amy had rinsed the breakfast dishes, put them into the dishwasher and driven the kids to the park, where camp was held, she found herself watching for Tyler—waiting for him to come back.

When she'd showered and put on her best suit, a sleek creation of pale blue linen, along with a blouse, she sat on the edge of her bed and stared at the telephone for what must have been a full five minutes. Then she dialed her best friend's number.

"Debbie?"

"Hi, Amy," Debbie answered, sounding a little rushed. "If this is about lunch, I'm open. Twelve o'clock at Ivar's?"

Amy bit her lower lip for a moment. "I can't, not today...
I have appointments all morning. Deb—"

Debbie's voice was instantly tranquil, all sense and
sound of hurry gone. "Hey, you sound kind of funny. Is
something wrong?"

"It might be," Amy confessed.

"Go on."

"I dreamed about Tyler last night, and it was ultra-real,
Debbie. I wasn't lying in bed with my eyes closed—I was
standing up, walking around—we had an in-depth conversation!"

Debbie's voice was calm, but then, she was a professional
in the mental health field. It would take more than Amy's
imaginary encounter with her dead husband to shock this
woman. "Okay. What about?"

Amy was feeling sillier by the moment. "It's so dumb."

"Right. So tell me anyway."

"He said I was going to meet—this friend of his—Harry
somebody. Who names people Harry in this day and age?
I'm supposed to fall in love with this guy, marry him and
have two kids."

"Before nightfall?" Debbie retorted, without missing
a beat.

"Practically. Ty implied that I've been holding up some
celestial plan by keeping to myself so much!"

Debbie sighed. "This is one that could be worked out
in a fifteen-minute segment of any self-help show, Ryan.
You're a healthy young woman, and you haven't been with
a man since Ty, and you're lonely, physically and emotionally. If you want to talk this out with somebody, I could
give you a name—"

Amy was already shaking her head. "No," she interrupted, "that's all right. I feel foolish enough discussing

this with my dearest friend. I don't think I'm up to stretching out on a couch and telling all to some strange doctor."

"Still—"

"I'll be all right, Deb," Amy broke in again, this time a little impatiently. She didn't know what she'd wanted her friend to say when she told her about Tyler's "visit," but she felt let down. She hung up quickly and then dashed off to her first meeting of the day.

Amy often marveled that she'd made such a success of her business, especially since she'd dropped out of school when Tyler passed the bar exam and devoted herself entirely to being a wife and mother. She'd been totally happy doing those things and hadn't even blushed to admit to having no desire to work outside the home.

After Tyler's death, however, the pain and rage had made her so restless that staying home was impossible. She'd alternated between fits of sobbing and periods of wooden silence, and after a few weeks she'd gone numb inside.

One night, very late, she'd seen a good-looking, fast-talking man on television, swearing by all that was holy that she, too, could build a career in real estate trading and make a fortune.

Amy had enough money to last a lifetime, between Tyler's life insurance and savings and her maternal grandmother's trust fund, but the idea of a challenge, of building something, appealed to her. In fact, on some level it resurrected her. Here was something to *do,* something to keep her from smothering Ashley and Oliver with motherly affection.

She'd downloaded the program and signed up for a seminar, as well.

Amy absorbed all the sessions in the program. The voice was pleasant and the topic complicated enough that she had to concentrate, which meant she had brief respites from thinking about Tyler. Under any other circumstances, Amy would not have had the brass to actually do the things suggested by the program and seminar, but all her normal inhibitions had been frozen inside her, like small animals trapped in a sudden Ice Age.

She'd started buying and selling and wheeling and dealing, and she'd been successful at it.

Still, she thought miserably as she drove toward her meeting, Tyler had been right, she wasn't happy. Now that the numbness had worn off, all those old needs and hurts were back in full force and being a real estate magnate wasn't fulfilling them.

Harry Griffith smiled grimly to himself as he took off his headphones and handed them to his copilot, Mark Ellis. "Here you are, mate," he said. "Bring her in for me, will you?"

Mark nodded as he eagerly took over the controls, and Harry left the cockpit and proceeded into the main section of the private jet. Often it was filled with business people and assorted hangers-on, but that day Harry and Mark were cutting through the sky alone.

He went on to the sumptuous bedroom, unknotting his silk tie with one hand as he closed the door with the other. He'd had a meeting in San Francisco, but now he could change into more casual clothes.

With a sigh Harry pulled open a few drawers and took out a lightweight cable-knit sweater and jeans, still thinking of his friend. He hadn't been present for Ty's services two years before. He'd been in the outback, at one of the mines, and by the time he'd returned to Sydney and learned about Tyler's death, it was three weeks after the fact.

He'd sent flowers to Tyler's parents, who'd been like a second mother and father to him ever since his first visit to the States, and to the pretty widow. Harry had never seen Amy Ryan or her children, except on the front of the Christmas cards he always received from them, and he hadn't known what to say to her.

It had been a damn shame, a man like Tyler dying in his prime like that, and Harry could find no words of comfort inside himself.

Now, however, he had business with Tyler's lovely lady, and he would have to open this last door that protected his own grief and endure whatever emotions might be set free in the process.

Harry tossed aside his tie and began unfastening his cuff links. Maybe he'd even go and stand by Tyler's grave for a while, tell his friend he was a cheeky lot for bailing out so early in the game that way.

He pulled the sweater on over his head, replaced his slacks with jeans, then stood staring at himself in the mirror. Like the bed, chairs and bureau, it was bolted down.

Where Tyler had been handsome in an altar-boy sort of way, Harry was classically so, with dark hair, indigo-blue eyes and an elegant manner. He regarded his exceptional looks as tools, and he'd used them without compunction, every day of his life, to get what he wanted.

Or most of what he wanted, that is. He'd never had a real family of his own, the way Tyler had. God knew, Madeline hadn't even tried to disguise herself as a wife, and she'd sent the child she'd borne her first husband to boarding school in Switzerland. Madeline hadn't wanted to trouble herself with a twelve-year-old daughter, and Eireen's letters and phone calls had been ignored more than answered.

Harry felt sick, remembering. He'd tried to establish a bond with the child on her rare holidays in Australia, but while Madeline hadn't wanted to be bothered with the little girl, she hadn't relished the idea of sharing her, either.

Then, after another stilted Christmas, Madeline had decided she needed a little time on the "the continent," and would therefore see Eireen as far as Zurich. Their plane had gone down midway between New Zealand and the Fiji Islands, and there had been no survivors.

Harry had not wept for his wife—the emotion he'd once mistaken for love had died long before she did—but he'd cried for that bewildered child who'd never been permitted to love or be loved.

Later, when Tyler had died, Harry had gotten drunk—something he had never done before or since—and stayed that way for three nightmarish days. It had been an injustice of cosmic proportions that a man like Tyler Ryan, who had had everything a man could dream of, should be sent spinning off the world that way, like a child from a carnival ride that turned too fast.

"Mr. Griffith?"

Mark's voice, coming over the intercom system, startled Harry. "Yes?" he snapped, pressing a button on the instrument affixed to the wall above his bed, a little testy at the prospect of landing in Seattle.

"We're starting our descent, sir. Would you like to come back and take the controls?"

"You can handle it," Harry answered, removing his finger from the button. He thought of Tyler's parents and the big house on Mercer Island where he'd spent some of the happiest times of his life. "You can handle it," he repeated gravely, even though Mark couldn't hear him now. "The question is, can I?"

* * *

Amy had had a busy day, but she'd managed to finish work on time to pick up Oliver and Ashley at day camp, and she was turning hot dogs on the grill in her stove when the telephone rang.

Oliver answered with his customary "Hey!" He listened to the caller with ever-widening eyes and then thrust the receiver in Amy's direction. "I think it's that guy from the movies!" he shouted.

Amy frowned, crossed the room and took the call. "Hello?"

"Mrs. Ryan?" The voice was low, melodic and distinctly Australian. "My name is Harry Griffith, and I was a friend of your husband's—"

The receiver slipped from Amy's hand and clattered against the wall. Harry Griffith? *Harry Griffith!* The man Tyler had mentioned in her dream the night before.

"Mom!" Ashley cried, alarmed. She'd learned, at entirely too young an age, that tragedy almost always took a person by surprise.

"It's okay, sweetheart," Amy said hastily, snatching up the telephone with one hand and pulling her daughter close with the other. "Hello? Mr. Griffith?"

"Are you all right?" he asked in that marvelous accent.

Amy leaned against the counter, not entirely trusting her knees to support her, and drew in a deep breath. "I'm fine," she lied.

"I don't suppose you remember me..."

Amy didn't remember Harry Griffith, except from old photographs and things Tyler had said, and she couldn't recall seeing him at the funeral. "You knew Tyler," she said, closing her eyes against a wave of dizziness.

"Yes," he answered. His voice was gentle and somehow

encouraging, like a touch. "I'd like to take you out for dinner tomorrow night, if you'll permit."

If you'll permit. The guy talked like Cary Grant in one
of those lovely old black-and-white movies on the Nostalgia
Channel. "Ah—well—maybe you should just come here.
Say seven o'clock?"

"Seven o'clock," he confirmed. There was brief pause,
then, "Mrs. Ryan? I'm very sorry—about Tyler, I mean.
He was one of the best friends I ever had."

Amy's eyes stung, and her throat felt thick. "Yes," she
agreed. "I felt pretty much the same way about him. I-I'll
see you at seven tomorrow night. Do you have the address?"

"Yes," he answered, and then the call was over.

It took Amy so long to hang up the receiver that Oliver
finally pulled it from her hand and replaced it on the hook.

"Who was that?" Ashley asked. "Is something wrong
with Grampa or Gramma?"

"No, sweetheart," Amy said gently, bending to kiss the
top of Ashley's head, where her rich brown hair was parted.
"It was only a friend of your daddy's. He's coming by for
dinner tomorrow night."

"Okay," Ashley replied, going back to the table.

Amy took the hot dogs from the grill and served them,
but she couldn't eat because her stomach was jumping back
and forth between its normal place and her windpipe. She
went outside and sat at the picnic table in her expensive
suit, watching as the sprinkler turned rhythmically, making its *chicka-chicka* sound.

She tried to assemble all the facts in her mind, but they
weren't going together very well.

Last night she'd dreamed—only *dreamed*—that Tyler
had appeared in their bedroom. Amy could ascribe that to
the spicy Mexican food she'd eaten for dinner the previous

night, but what about the fact that he'd told her his friend
Harry Griffith would call and ask to see her? Could it possibly be a wild coincidence and nothing more?

She pressed her fingers to her temples. The odds against
such a thing had to be astronomical, but the only other explanation was that she was psychic or something. And Amy
knew that wasn't true.

If she'd had any sort of powers, she would have fore-
seen Tyler's death. She would have *done* something about
it, warned the doctors, anything.

Presently, Amy pulled herself together enough to go
back inside the house. She ate one hot dog, for the sake of
appearances, then went to her bathroom to shower and put
on shorts and a tank top.

Oliver and Ashley were in the family room, arguing over
which program to watch on TV, when Amy joined them.
Unless the exchanges threatened to turn violent, she never
interfered, believing that children needed to learn to work
out their differences without a parent jumping in to referee.

The built-in mahogany shelves next to the fireplace were
lined with photo albums, and Amy took one of the early
volumes down and carried it to the couch.

There she kicked off her shoes and sat cross-legged on
the cushion, opening the album slowly, trying to prepare
herself for the inevitable jolt of seeing Tyler smiling back
at her from some snapshot.

After flipping the pages for a while, acclimating herself
for the millionth time to a world that no longer contained
Tyler Ryan, she began to look closely at the pictures.

Chapter 2

The next day, on the terrace of a busy waterfront restaurant, Amy tossed a piece of sourdough bread to one of the foraging sea gulls and sighed. "For all I know," she confided to her best friend, "Harry Griffith is an ax murderer. And I've invited him to dinner."

Debbie's eyes sparkled with amusement. "How bad can he be?" she asked reasonably. "Tyler liked him a lot, didn't he? And your husband had pretty good judgment when it came to human nature."

Amy nodded, pushing away what remained of her spinach and almond salad. "Yes," she admitted grudgingly.

A waitress came and refilled their glasses of iced tea, and Debbie added half a packet of sweetener to hers, stirring vigorously. "So what's really bugging you? That you saw Tyler in a dream and he said a guy named Harry Griffith would come into your life, and now that's about to come true?"

"Wouldn't that bother you?" Amy countered, exasper-ated. "Don't look now, Deb, but things like this don't hap-pen every day!"

Debbie turned thoughtful. "The subconscious mind is a fantastic thing," she mused. "'We don't even begin to com-prehend what it can do."

Amy took a sip of her tea. "You think I *projected* Tyler from some shadowy part of my brain, don't you?"

"Yes," Debbie answered matter-of-factly.

"Okay, fine. I can accept that theory. But how do you ac-count for the fact that Tyler mentioned Harry Griffith, spe-cifically and by name? How could that have come from my subconscious mind, when I never actually knew the man?"

Debbie shrugged. "There were pictures in the albums, and I'm sure Tyler probably talked about him often. I sup-pose his parents must have talked about the guy sometimes, too. We pick up subliminal information from the people around us all the time."

Her friend's theory made sense, but Amy was still un-convinced. If she'd only conjured an image of Tyler for her own purposes, she would have had him hold her, kiss her, tell her the answers to cosmic mysteries. She would never have spent those few precious moments together talking about some stranger from Australia.

Amy shook her head and said nothing.

Debbie reached out to take her hand. "Listen, Amy, what you need is a vacation. You're under a lot of stress and you haven't resolved your conflicts over Tyler's death. Park the kids with Tyler's parents and go somewhere where the sun's shining. Sunbathe, spend money with reckless aban-don, *live* a little."

Amy recalled briefly that she'd always wanted to visit Australia, then pushed the thought from her mind. A trip like that wouldn't be much fun all by herself. "I have work to do," she hedged.

"Right," Debbie answered. "You really need the money, don't you? Tyler had a whopping insurance policy, and then there was the trust fund from your grandmother. Add to that the pile you've made on your own with this real estate thing—"

"All right," Amy interrupted. "You're right. I'm lucky, I have plenty of money. But work fills more than just financial needs, you know."

Debbie's look was wryly indulgent, and she didn't speak at all. She just tapped the be-ringed fingers of her right hand against the upper part of her left arm, waiting for Amy to dig herself in deeper.

"Listen," Amy whispered hoarsely, not wanting diners at the neighboring tables to overhear, "I know what you're really saying, okay? I'm young. I'm healthy. I should be… *having sex* with some guy. Well, in case you haven't noticed, the smart money is on celibacy these days!"

"I'm not telling you to go out and seduce the first man you meet, Amy," Debbie said frankly, making no apparent effort to moderate her tone. "What I'm really saying is that you need to stop mourning Tyler and *get on with your life.*"

Amy snatched up her check, reached for her purse and pushed back her chair. "Thanks," she snapped, hot color pooling in her cheeks. "You've been a real help!"

"Amy…"

"I have a meeting," Amy broke in. And then she walked away from the table without even looking back.

Debbie caught up to her at the cash register. "My brother has a condo at Lake Tahoe," she persisted gently. "You could go there for a few days and just walk along the shore and look at the trees and stuff. You could visit the house they used in *Bonanza*."

Despite her nervous and irritable mood, Amy had to smile. "You make it sound like a pilgrimage," she replied, picking up her credit card receipt and placing it neatly in a pocket of her brown leather purse. "Shall I burn candles and say, 'Spirits of Hoss, Adam and Little Joe, show me the way'?"

Now it was Debbie who laughed. "Your original hypothesis was correct, Ryan. You are indeed crazy."

It was an uncommonly sunny day, even for late June, and the sidewalks were crowded with tourists. Amy spoke softly, "I'm sorry, Deb. I was really a witch in there."

Debbie grinned. "True, but being a friend means knowing somebody's faults and liking them anyway. And to show you I do have some confidence in your reasoning processes, expect my cousin Max over tonight." She paused to think a moment, then her pretty face was bright with inspiration. "Max will wear coveralls and pretend to be fixing the dishwasher or something. That way, there'll be a man in the house, in case this Griffith guy really is an ax murderer, but Mr. Australia will never guess you were nervous about having him over."

Amy wasn't crazy about the idea, but she had neither the time nor the energy to try to talk Debbie out of it. She had an important meeting scheduled and, after that, some shopping to do at the Pike Place Market.

"I'll call you tomorrow," Amy promised, as the two women went in their separate directions.

Because she didn't know whether to go with elegant or simple and typically American, Amy settled on a combination of the two and bought fresh salmon steaks to be seasoned, wrapped in foil and cooked on the backyard barbecue. She made a potato salad as well, and set out chocolate éclairs from an upscale bakery for dessert.

She was setting the picnic table with good silver when a jolting sensation in the pit of her stomach alerted her to the fact that she wasn't alone.

Amy looked up, expecting to see Debbie's cousin Max or perhaps even Tyler. Instead, she found herself tumbling end over end into the bluest pair of eyes she'd ever seen.

"Hello," the visitor said.

Oliver, who had apparently escorted their guest from the front door, was clearly excited. "He sounds just like Hugh Jackman when he talks, doesn't he, Mom?" he crowed.

The dark-haired man was incredibly handsome—Amy recalled seeing his picture once or twice—and he smiled down at Oliver with quiet warmth. "We're mates, me and Hugh," he said in a very thick and rhythmic down-under accent.

"Wow!" Oliver shouted.

The visitor chuckled and ruffled the boy's hair. Then he noticed Ashley, who was standing shyly nearby, holding her beloved cat and looking up at the company with wide eyes.

"My name is Ashley Ryan," she said solemnly. "And this is my cat, Rumpel. That's short for Rumpelteazer."

Amy was about to intercede—after all, this man hadn't even had a chance to introduce himself yet—but before she could, he reached out and patted Rumpel's soft, striped head.

"Ah," he said wisely. "This must be a Jellicle cat, then."

Ashley's answering smile was sudden and so bright as to be blinding. She'd named Rumpel for one of the characters in the musical *Cats:* Tyler had taken her to see the show at Seattle's Paramount Theater several months before his death. Ever since, the play had served as a sort of connection between Ashley and the father she had loved so much.

"Harry Griffith," the man said, solemnly offering his hand to Ashley in greeting. He even bowed, ever so slightly, and his mouth quirked at one corner as he gave Amy a quick, conspiratorial glance. "I'm very glad to meet you, Ashley Ryan."

Amy felt herself spinning inwardly, off balance, like a washing machine with all the laundry wadded up on one side of the tub. She reached out, resting one hand against the edge of the picnic table.

Harry's indigo eyes came back to her face, and she thought she saw tender amusement in their depths. He wore his expensive clothes with an air only a rich and accomplished man could have managed, and Amy concluded that he was used to getting reactions from the women he encountered.

It annoyed her, and her voice was a little brisk when she said, "Hello, Mr. Griffith."

His elegant mouth curved slightly, and the ink-blue eyes danced. "I'm very glad to make your acquaintance, Mrs. Ryan. But since Tyler was one of my best friends, I'd be more comfortable having you call me Harry."

"Harry." The name came out of Amy's mouth sounding like primitive woman's first attempt at speech. "My name is Amy."

"I know," Harry answered, and, oddly, his voice affected Amy like a double dose of hot-buttered rum, finding its way into her veins and coursing through her system. Leaving her dizzy.

"S-sit down," Amy said, gesturing toward the picnic table.

"I'd like that," Harry replied. "But first I'd better tell

you that there's a man in coveralls out front, ringing your doorbell."

Debbie's cousin Max, no doubt. Although she knew intuitively that she wouldn't need protection from a make-believe dishwasher repairman, Amy was relieved to have something to do besides standing there feeling as if she were about to topple over the edge of a precipice.

"Please," Amy said. "Make yourself at home. I'll be right back." As she hurried into the house, she couldn't help remembering what Tyler had said, that she was meant to marry Harry Griffith and have two children by him. She was glad no one else could possibly know about the quicksilver, heated fantasies *that* idea had produced.

Sure enough, she found Debbie's cousin peering through the glass in the front door.

She opened it. "Max? Listen, you really don't need—"

"Can't be too careful," the balding middle-aged man said, easing past Amy with his toolbox in hand. Then, in a much louder voice, he added, "Just show me to your dishwasher, and I'll make short order of that leak."

"You do understand that the dishwasher isn't broken?" Amy inquired in a whisper as she led the way to the kitchen.

He replied with a wink, set his toolbox in the center of the table, took out a screwdriver and went right to work.

Amy drew three or four deep breaths and let them out slowly before pushing open the screen door and facing Harry Griffith again.

He had already won over both the kids; Ashley was beaming with delight as he pushed her higher and higher in the tire swing Tyler had hung from a branch of the big maple tree a few years before. Oliver was waiting his turn with uncharacteristic patience.

Amy had a catch in her throat as she watched the three

of them together. Until that moment, she'd managed to kid herself that she could be both mother and father to her children, but they were blossoming under Harry's attention like flowers long-starved for water and sunlight.

She watched them for a few bittersweet moments, then went to the grill to check the salmon. The sound of her children's laughter lifted her heart and, at the same time, filled her eyes with tears.

Amy was drying her cheek with the back of one hand when both Oliver and Ashley raced past, arguing in high-pitched voices.

"I'll do it!" Oliver cried.

"No, *I* want to!" Ashley replied.

Rumpel wisely took refuge under the rhododendron beside the patio.

"What...?" Amy turned to see Harry Griffith standing directly behind her.

He shrugged and grinned in a way that tugged at her heart. "I didn't mean to cause a disruption," he said. "I guess I should have gone back to the car for the cake myself, instead of sending the kids for it."

Amy sniffled. "Did you know Tyler very well?" she asked.

Harry was standing so close that she could smell his aftershave and the fabric softener in his sweater, and together, those two innocent scents caused a virtual riot in her senses. "We spent the better part of a year together," he answered. "And we kept in touch, as much as possible, after high school and college." He paused, taking an apparent interest in the fragrant white lilacs clambering over the white wooden arbor a few yards away. "I probably knew Ty better than most people—" Harry's gaze returned to her, and her heart welcomed it "—and not as well as you did."

Smoothly, one hand in the pocket of his tailored gray slacks, Harry reached out and, with the pad of his thumb, wiped a stray tear from just beneath Amy's jawline. Before she could think of anything to say, the kids returned, each carrying one end of a white bakery box.

Harry thanked them both in turn, making it sound as though they'd smuggled an important new vaccine across enemy lines.

"I guess we'd better eat," Amy said brightly. "It's getting late."

Oliver and Ashley squeezed in on either side of Harry, leaving Amy alone on the opposite bench of the picnic table. She felt unaccountably jealous of their attention, suddenly wanting it all for herself.

"Mom says you and Dad were buddies," Oliver announced, once the salmon and potato salad and steamed asparagus had been dealt with. He was looking expectantly at their guest.

Harry put his hand on Oliver's wiry little shoulder. "The very best of buddies," he confirmed. "Tyler was one of the finest men I've ever known."

Oliver's freckled face fairly glowed with pride and pleasure, but in the next instant he looked solemn again. "Sometimes," he confessed, with a slight trace of the lisp Amy had thought he'd mastered, "I can't remember him too well. I was only four when he...when he died."

"Maybe I can help you recall," Harry said gently, taking a wallet from the hip pocket of his slacks and carefully removing an old, often-handled snapshot. "This was taken over at Lake Chelan, right here in Washington State."

Ashley and Oliver nearly bumped heads in their eagerness to look at the picture of two handsome young men grinning as they held up a pair of giant rainbow trout for the camera.

"Your dad and I were seventeen then." Harry frowned thoughtfully. "We were out in the rowboat that day, as I recall. Your aunt Charlotte was annoyed with us and she swam ashore, taking the oars with her. It was humiliating, actually. An old lady in a paddleboat had to come out and tow us back to the dock."

Amy chuckled, feeling a sweet warmth flood her spirit as she remembered Ty telling that same story.

After they'd had some of Harry's cake—they completely scorned the éclairs—Amy sent both her protesting children into the house to get ready for bed. She and Harry remained outside at the picnic table, even after the sun went down and the mosquitoes came and the breeze turned chilly.

"I'm sorry I didn't make it to Ty's funeral," he said, after one long and oddly comfortable silence. "I was in the outback, and didn't find out until some three weeks after he'd passed on."

"I wouldn't have known whether you were there or not. I was in pretty much of a muddle." Amy's voice went a little hoarse as the emotional backwash of that awful day flooded over her.

Harry ran his fingers through his hair, the first sign of agitation Amy had seen him reveal. "*I* knew the difference," he said. "I needed to say goodbye to Tyler. Matter of fact, I needed to bellow at him that he had a hell of a nerve going and dying that way when he was barely thirty-five."

"I was angry with him, too," Amy said softly. "One day he was fine, the next he was in the hospital. The doctor said it would be a routine operation, nothing to worry about, and when I saw Ty before surgery, he was making jokes about keeping his appendix in a jar." She paused, and a smile faltered on her mouth, then fell away. She went on to describe what happened next, even though she was sure Harry already knew the tragic details, because for some reason she needed to say it all.

"Tyler had some kind of reaction to the anesthetic and went into cardiac arrest. The surgical team tried everything to save him, of course, but they couldn't get his heart beating again. He was just...gone."

Harry closed warm, strong fingers around Amy's hand. "I'm sorry," he said.

One of the patio doors slid open, and Amy looked up, expecting to see Ashley or Oliver standing there, making a case for staying up another hour. Instead, she was jolted to find cousin Max, complete with coveralls and toolbox.

Amy was horrified that she'd left the man kneeling on the kitchen floor throughout the evening, half his body swallowed up by an appliance that didn't even need repairing. "Oh, Max... I'm sorry, I—"

Max waggled a sturdy finger at her. "Everything's fine now, Mrs. Ryan." He looked at Harry and wriggled his eyebrows, clearly stating, without another word, that he had sized up the dinner guest and decided he was harmless.

In Amy's opinion, Max couldn't have been more wrong. Harry Griffith was capable of making her feel things, remember things, want things. And that made him damn dangerous.

"Mr. Griffith was just leaving," she said suddenly. "Maybe you could walk him to his car."

Harry tossed her a curious smile, gave his head one almost imperceptible shake and stood. "I've some business to settle with you," he said to Amy, "but I guess it will keep until morning."

Amy closed her eyes for a moment, shaken again. She

knew what that business was without asking, because Tyler had told her. This was all getting too spooky.

Harry was already standing, so Amy stood, too.

"It's been a delightful evening," he said. "Thank you for everything."

His words echoed in Amy's mind as he walked away to join Max. *It's been a delightful evening.* She wasn't used to Harry's elegant, formal way of speaking: Tyler would have swatted her lightly on the bottom and said, *Great potato salad, babe. How about rubbing my back?*

"You're making me sound like a redneck," a familiar voice observed, and Amy whirled to see Tyler sitting in the tire swing, grinning at her in the light of the rising moon.

She raised one hand, as if to summon Harry or Max back, so that someone else could confirm the vision, then let it fall back to her side. "It's true," she said, stepping closer to the swing and keeping her voice down, so the kids wouldn't think she was talking to herself again. "Don't deny it, Ty. You enjoyed playing king of the castle. In fact, sometimes you did everything but swing from vines and yodel while beating on your chest with both fists."

Tyler, or his reflection, raised one eyebrow. "Okay, so I was a little macho sometimes. But I loved you, Spud. I was a good provider and a faithful husband."

Instinct, not just wishful thinking, told Amy that Ty's claim was true. He'd been the ideal life partner, except that he'd thrown the game before they'd even reached halftime.

"Go ahead, gloat," Amy said, folding her arms. "You told me Harry Griffith would turn up, and he did. And he said something about discussing business with me tomorrow, so you're batting a thousand."

Tyler grinned again, looking cocky. "You thought you were dreaming, didn't you?"

"Actually, no," Amy said. "It's more likely that you're some sort of projection of my subconscious mind."

"Oh, yeah?" Tyler made the swing spin a couple of times, the way he'd done on so many other summer nights, before he'd single-handedly brought the world to an end by dying. Somewhere in that library of albums inside the house, Amy had a picture of him holding an infant Ashley on his lap while they both turned in a laughing blur. "How could your subconscious mind have known Harry was about to show up?"

Amy shrugged. "There are a lot of things going on in this world that we don't fully understand."

"You can say that again," Tyler said, a little smugly.

He still couldn't resist an opportunity to be one up on the opposition in any argument, Amy reflected, with affection and acceptance. It was the lawyer in him. "Debbie's theory is that you represent some unspoken wish for love and romance."

Tyler laughed. "Unspoken, hell. I'm telling you straight out, Spud. You're not going to find a better guy than Harry, so you'd better grab him while you've got the chance."

Only then did Amy realize she hadn't felt an urge to fling herself at Tyler, the way she had before. The revelation made her feel sad. "Doesn't it make you even slightly jealous to think of me married to someone else?"

Amy regretted the words the instant she'd spoken them, because a bereft expression shadowed Tyler's handsome features for several moments.

"Yes," he admitted gruffly, "but this is about letting go and moving on. Think of me as a ghost, or a figment of your imagination, whatever works for you. As long as you get the message and stop marking time, it doesn't matter."

"*Are* you a ghost?"

Tyler sighed. "Yes and no."

"Spoken like a true lawyer."

He reached out one hand for her, as he would have done before, but once again he pulled back. He didn't smile at Amy's comment, either. "I'm not a specter, forced to wander the earth and rattle chains like in the stories they used to tell at summer camp," he told her. "But I'm not an image being beamed out of your deeper mind, either. I'm just as real as you are."

Amy swallowed hard. "I don't understand!" she wailed in a low voice, frustrated.

"You're not supposed to," Tyler assured her gently. "There's no need for you to understand."

Amy stepped closer, needing to touch Tyler, but between one instant and the next he was gone. No fade-out, no flash, nothing. He was there and then he wasn't.

"Tyler?" Amy whispered brokenly.

"Mom?" Ashley's voice made Amy start, and she turned to see her daughter standing only a few feet behind her, wearing cotton pajamas and carrying her favorite doll. "Did Mr. Harry go home?"

Apparently Ashley hadn't heard her mother talking to thin air, and Amy was relieved. She reached out to stop the tire swing, which was still swaying back and forth in the night air.

"Yes, sweetheart," she said. "He's really a nice man, isn't he?"

Ashley nodded gravely. "I like to listen to him talk. I wish *he* was still here, so he could tell us a kangaroo story."

"Maybe he doesn't know any," she suggested, distracted. If Tyler had known what she was thinking earlier, had he also discerned that his widow felt a powerful attraction to one of his best friends?

"Sure, he does," Ashley said confidently as they stepped into the kitchen together. Amy closed and locked the sliding door. "Did you know they have yellow signs in Australia, with the silhouette of a kangaroo on them—like the Deer Crossing signs here?"

Amy turned off the outside lights and checked to make sure all the leftovers had been put away. The dishwasher showed no signs of Max's exploratory surgery. "No, sweet-heart," she said, standing at the sink now and staring out the window at the tire swing. It was barely visible in the deepening darkness. "I didn't know that. I guess it makes sense, though. Off to bed now."

"What about the story?"

Amy felt tears sting her eyes as she stared out at the place where Tyler had been. That was what her life was these days, it seemed, just a place where Tyler had been.

Harry sat on the stone bench beside Tyler's fancy mar-ble headstone, his chin propped in one palm. "Damn it, man," he complained, "you didn't tell me she was beautiful. You didn't say anything about the warm way she laughs, or those golden highlights in her hair." He sighed heavily. "All right," he conceded. "I guess you did say she was a natural wonder, but I thought you were just talking. Even the Christmas cards didn't prepare me…"

He stood, tired of sitting, and paced back and forth at the foot of Tyler's grave. It didn't bother him, being in a ceme-tery at night. He wasn't superstitious and, besides, he'd been needing this confrontation with Tyler for a good long time.

"You might have stuck around a few more years, you know!" he muttered, shoving one hand through his usually perfect hair. "There you were with that sweet wife, those splendid children, a great career. And what did you do? In the name of God, Tyler, why didn't you *fight?*"

The only answer, of course, was a warm night wind and the constant chirping of crickets.

Harry stopped his pacing and stood with one foot braced against the edge of the bench, staring down at the headstone with eyes that burned a little. "All right, mate," he said softly, hoarsely. "I know you probably had your reasons for not holding on longer—and that's not to say I won't be wanting an accounting when I catch up with you. In the meantime, what's really got under my skin is, well, it's Amy and those terrific kids."

He tilted his head back and looked up at the moon for a long time, then gave a ragged sigh. "We were always honest with each other, you and I. Nothing held back. When I laid eyes on that woman, Ty, it was as though somebody wrenched the ground out from beneath my feet."

While the damning words echoed around him, Harry struggled to face the incomprehensible reality. He hadn't been with Amy Ryan for five minutes before he'd started imagining what it would be like to share his life with her.

He hadn't thought of taking Amy to bed, though God knew that would be the keenest of pleasures. No, he'd pictured her nursing a baby…his baby. He'd seen her running along the white sand on the beach near his house in northern Queensland, with Ashley and Oliver scampering behind, and he'd seen her sitting beside him in the cockpit of his jet.

This was serious.

He touched his friend's headstone as he passed, and started toward the well-lighted parking lot. "If you know what's good for you, Harry," he muttered to himself, "you'll give the lady her money and then stay out of her way."

Harry got behind the wheel of his rented vehicle and started the engine. Nothing must be allowed to happen between him and Amy Ryan, and the reason was simple. To touch her would be to betray a man who would have trusted Harry with his very life.

Chapter 3

Amy didn't sleep well that night. She was filled with con-tradictory feelings; new ones and old ones, affectionate and angry ones. She was furious with Tyler for ever dying in the first place, and with Harry Griffith for thawing out her frozen emotions. She was also experiencing a warmth and a sense of pleasant vulnerability she'd never expected to know again.

After Oliver and Ashley had gone to camp, Amy didn't put on a power suit and go out to network with half a dozen potential clients as she normally would have done. Instead, she wore jeans and a pastel blue sun top and pulled her heavy shoulder-length hair back into a ponytail. She was in the spacious room that had once been Tyler's study, bal-ancing her checking account and listening with half an ear to a TV talk show, when the telephone rang.

Amy pushed the speaker button. "Hello?"

Harry's smooth, cultured voice filled the room. "Hello, Amy. It's Harry Griffith."

"I know," Amy answered automatically, before she'd had a chance to think about the implications of those two simple words. She laid down her pen and turned away from her banking, feeling vaguely embarrassed. She wanted to say something witty, but of course nothing came to mind; in an hour or a day or a week, when it was too late, some smidgen of clever repartee would come to mind in a flash.

"I enjoyed last night's visit with you and the children," he went on, and Amy leaned back in her chair, just letting that wonderful voice roll over her, like warm ocean water. "Thank you for inviting me, Amy."

Amy closed her eyes, then quickly opened them again. She needed to be on her guard with this man, lest she say or do something really foolish. "Uh...yes...well, you're very welcome, of course." *That was really brilliant, Ryan,* she added to herself.

"I'd like to return the favor, if I might. I've made an appointment to look at a rather unique house over on Vashon Island tomorrow, and I could really use some company— besides the real estate agent, I mean. Would you and Ashley and Oliver care to go out and offer your opinion of the place?"

Amy's heart warmed as she thought how her son and daughter would enjoy such an outing, especially when it meant close contact with Harry. She wasn't exactly averse to the idea herself, though she couldn't quite admit that, even in the privacy of her own soul.

"It would give you and me a chance to discuss that business you mentioned last night." That was the best attempt at setting up a barrier Amy could manage.

Harry sighed. "Yes, there is that. Shall I pick the three of you up tomorrow, then? Around nine?"

A sweet shiver skittered down Amy's spine. "Yes," she heard herself say. But the moment Harry rang off, she wanted to call him back and say she'd changed her mind, she couldn't possibly spend a day on Vashon. She would tell him she had to clean the garage or prune the lilac bushes or something.

Only she had no idea where to reach the charming Mr. Griffith. He hadn't left a number or mentioned the name of a hotel.

Feeling restless, Amy pushed the speaker button on the telephone and thrust herself out of her chair. So much for balancing her checking account; thanks to Harry's call, she wouldn't have been able to subtract two from seven.

Amy paced in front of the natural rock fireplace, wondering where all this unwanted energy had come from. For two years, she'd been concentrating on basic emotional survival. Now, all of the sudden she felt as though she could replaster every wall in that big colonial house without even working up a sweat.

She dialed Debbie's private number at the counseling center.

"I'm going crazy," she blurted out the moment her friend answered.

Debbie laughed. "Amy, I presume? What's happened now? Have you been visited by the ghost of Christmas Weird?"

Amy gave a sigh. "This is serious, Debbie. Harry Griffith just called and invited me to go to Vashon Island with him tomorrow, and I accepted!"

"That *is* terrible," Debbie teased. "Think of it. After only *two years* of mourning, you're actually coming back to life. Quick, head for the nearest closet and hide out until the urge passes!"

Rolling her eyes and twisting the telephone cord around her index finger, Amy replied, "Will you stop with the irony, please? Something very strange is going on here."

Debbie's voice became firm, reasonable. She had become the counselor. "I know a crazy person when I see one, Amy, and believe me, you're completely sane."

"I saw Tyler again last night," Amy insisted. "He was sitting in the backyard swing."

"Your deeper mind is trying to tell you something, Ryan. Pay attention."

"You've been a tremendous help," Amy said with dry annoyance.

Debbie sighed philosophically. "There go my fond hopes of writing a bestselling book, becoming the next self-help guru and appearing on TV."

"Debbie."

"Just relax, Amy. That's all you have to do. Stop analyzing everything and just take things one day at a time."

Amy let out a long breath, knowing her friend was right. Which didn't mean for one moment that she'd be able to *apply* the information. "By the way, thanks for sending your cousin Max over last night. My virtue is safe."

Debbie chuckled. "Too safe, methinks. Talk to you later."

Amy said goodbye and hung up. She went into the kitchen and turned on the dishwasher. Almost immediately, water began to seep out from under the door.

"Great," she muttered.

As the rest of the day passed, Amy discovered that her normal tactics for distracting herself weren't working any better than the dishwasher. She had absolutely no desire to contact prospective clients, make follow-up calls or up-date her files.

At two o'clock, a serviceman came to repair the damage Max had unwittingly done to the dishwasher. Amy watched TV, having no idea who the characters were or what in the world they were talking about. She was relieved when it was finally time to pick the kids up at day camp.

The announcement that Harry had invited the three of them to spend the next day on the island brought whoops of delight from Oliver and a sweet smile from Ashley.

After those reactions, Amy could not have disappointed her children for anything.

That night in bed, she tossed and turned, half hoping Tyler would appear again so she could give him a piece of her mind. Of course, she reasoned, he probably *was* a piece of her mind.

When the first finger of light reached over the mountains visible from Amy's window, Oliver materialized at the foot of her bed. He scrambled onto the mattress and gave a few exuberant leaps.

"Get up, Mom! You've only got four hours to get beautiful before Harry comes to pick us up!"

Amy pulled the covers over her head and groaned. "Oliver, children have been disowned for lesser offenses."

Oliver bounded to the head of the bed and bounced on his knees, simultaneously dragging the blankets back from Amy's face. "This is your big chance, Mom," he argued. "Don't blow it!"

Shoving one hand through her rumpled hair, Amy let out a long sigh. "Trust me, Oliver—while I may appear hopeless to you, I have not quite reached the point of desperation."

The words were no sooner out of her mouth when Tyler's accusation echoed in her mind. *You're not happy.*

The assertion would have been much easier to deal with if it hadn't been fundamentally true. Amy loved her children, and she found her work at least tolerable. She had good health, a nice home and plenty of money.

Those things should have been enough, to her way of thinking, but they weren't. Amy wanted something more.

By the time nine o'clock rolled around, Amy had put on jeans and a navy sweater. She wore light makeup and a narrow white scarf to hold her hair back from her face.

"Am I presentable?" she whispered to Oliver with a twinkle in her eyes, when the doorbell sounded.

Oliver had already rushed to answer the door, but Ashley examined her mother with a pensive frown and then nodded solemnly. "I suppose you'll do," she said.

When Amy saw Harry standing there on the porch, looking rakishly handsome even in jeans and a white cable-knit sweater, her heart raced the way it did when she was trying to get in step with a revolving door.

His too-blue eyes swept lightly over Amy, but with respect rather than condescension. "G'day," he said.

The children's laughter seemed to startle Harry, though he looked suavely good-natured, as usual.

"You sounded like Hugh Jackman again," Amy explained with an amused smile. She was grateful to the children for lightening up the situation; if it had been left to her, she probably wouldn't have been able to manage a word. "Come in."

Harry smiled at the kids and rumpled Oliver's hair. Then, as if he hadn't already charmed the eight-year-old right out of her sneakers, he bowed and kissed Ashley's hand. The effect was oddly continental, despite the child's diminutive size.

Minutes later, after making sure that Oliver and Ashley's seat belts were properly fastened, Harry joined Amy in the front seat.

"You're quite competent at driving on the right-hand side of the road," she remarked, strictly to make conversation, when Harry had backed the van out onto the quiet residential street. An instant later, Amy's cheeks were flooded with color.

Harry's grin could only be described as sweetly wicked. "I've spent considerable time in the States," he responded after a time.

Amy ran the tip of her tongue over dry lips. With Tyler, there had always been so much to talk about, the words had just tumbled from her mouth, but now she felt as though the fate of the Western hemisphere hung on every phrase she uttered.

Lamely, she turned to look out the window, all the while riffling through the files in her mind for something witty and sophisticated to say.

"Mom isn't used to dating," Oliver put in from the back, his tone eager and earnest. "You'll have to be patient with her."

Harry chuckled at Amy's groan of mortification, then sent a seismic shock through her system by innocently touching her knee.

"It's all *right,*" he assured her in his quiet, elegant, hot-buttered-rum voice. "Why are you so nervous?"

Why, indeed, Amy wondered. Maybe it was because she was really beginning to believe that a ghost had set her up for a blind date!

"Oliver was right on," she said after a few moments of

struggling to get her inner balance. "I'm not used to—socializing."

Harry grinned, skillfully shifting the van into a higher gear and keeping to the right of the yellow line on the highway. "Dating," he corrected.

Amy's color flared again, and that only amused him more.

"No wonder Ty was so crazy about you," he observed, keeping his indigo gaze on the traffic.

Foolishly pleased by the compliment, if mystified, Amy did her best to relax.

The lull obviously worried the children; this time it was Ashley who leaned forward to put in her two cents' worth.

"Once Mom went out with this dude who sold real estate," the little girl said sagely. "Rumpel bit his ankle, and the guy threatened to sue."

Amy shook her head and closed her eyes, beyond embarrassment. Then she risked a sidelong glance at Harry. "Rumpel has always been an excellent judge of character," she admitted.

Harry laughed. "All the same, I'll watch my manners when the cat's about."

The thought of Harry Griffith *not* watching his manners made a delicious little thrill tumble through Amy.

Presently they arrived in west Seattle, and Harry took the exit leading to the ferry terminal. He paid the toll and drove onto the enormous white boat with all the savoir faire of a native.

Ashley and Oliver were bouncing in their seats, but Amy made them stay in the van until the boat had been loaded. Their eagerness carried a sweet sting; riding on ferry boats had been something they did with Tyler. He'd taken them from stem to stern and, on one occasion, even into the wheelhouse to meet the captain.

The four of them climbed the metal stairway to the upper deck, Oliver and Harry in the lead, and then walked through the seating area and outside. The wind was crisp and salty and lightly tinged with motor oil.

While Oliver and Ashley ran wildly along the deck, exulting in the sheer freedom of that, Amy leaned against the railing as the heavy boat labored away from shore.

She was only too conscious of Harry standing at her side, mere inches away. He was at once sturdy as a wall and warm as a fire on a wintry afternoon, and Amy was sure she would have sensed his presence even in a pitch-black cellar.

"Have you seen pictures of this place we're going to look at?" she asked, and she sounded squeaky in her effort to keep things light.

Harry shook his head. "No, but the agent described it to me. Sounds like a terrific place."

Amy swallowed. So far, so good. "You'll be renting it, I suppose?"

"Buying," Harry responded. "My company is opening offices in Seattle. I'll be here about six months of the year."

Amy had a peculiar, spiraling sensation in the pit of her stomach. "Oh." She was saved from having to make more of that urbane utterance when Ashley and Oliver returned to collect Harry. They each took a hand, and in moments he was being led away toward the bow.

Wishing she'd had a chance to warn her son and daughter not to promote her like some revolutionary new product about to hit the supermarket shelves, Amy watched the trio stroll away in silence.

When Harry returned from inside, he brought coffee

in plastic cups. The kids had a cinnamon roll but, instead of eating it, they were feeding bits and pieces to the gulls.

"They're very beautiful children," he said. The sadness in his tone resonated inside Amy like a musical chord.

"Do you have any kids?" she asked.

Harry sighed and stared at the receding shoreline and city. "I had a stepdaughter once. She died with her mother in a plane crash."

Amy winced inwardly. Losing her husband had been torment enough. To lose Tyler *and* one or both of her children would have been unbearable. "I'm so sorry," she said.

Harry's smile was dazzling, like sunlight mixing with sparkling water early on a summer morning. "It's been a long time ago now, love. Don't let it trouble you."

"Have you any other family?" Amy wasn't to be so easily turned aside.

"My mother," Harry answered with a grin. "She's a Hun, but I love her."

Amy laughed.

"What about your mother?" Harry asked. "Is she beautiful, like you and Ashley?"

Once again, he'd used an invisible emotional cord to trip her. She tightened her grip on the railing and felt her smile float away on the tide. "She died when I was four. I don't remember her."

It seemed perfectly natural for Harry to put his arm around her shoulders. Amy felt comforted by the gesture. "You've had a great deal of loss in your life," he said gently. "What about your father? Do you have one of those?"

Amy nodded, squaring her shoulders and working up a smile. "He's a doctor, always busy. I don't see him much."

"Do I detect a note of loneliness?" Harry asked, letting his arm fall back to his side again. He seemed to know intuitively when to touch and when not to, when to talk and when to keep silent.

A denial rushed into Amy's throat. Lonely? She had her beautiful children, her friends, her job. "Of course I'm not—"

"Lonely," Harry finished for her, arching one eyebrow.

Amy sighed. "Okay," she confessed, "so sometimes I feel a little isolated. Doesn't everybody have moments like that?"

The wind lifted a tendril of Harry's perfect hair. "Some people have *decades* like that," he replied, leaning against the railing now, bracing himself easily with both forearms. "Even lifetimes, poor souls."

A brief boldness possessed Amy. "What about you?" she asked. But an instant later she wished she could call the question back because it made her look like such a naive fool. Of course a rich, handsome, sophisticated man like Harry Griffith would never be subject to such a forlorn emotion as loneliness.

"There were days—nights, more particularly—when I honestly thought I'd die of it," he confessed, looking Amy directly in the eye.

She didn't think Harry was lying, and yet she couldn't imagine him in such a state. He was obviously a jet-setter, and women were probably willing to wrestle in the mud for the chance to be with him.

He smiled. "I can see by your expression that you're skeptical, Mrs. Ryan," he teased.

Harry Griffith was as suave and handsome as Cary Grant had been in his youth, and Amy could well imagine him as an elegant jewel thief. "Well, it's just—"

He cupped her chin lightly in his hand and stroked her lips with the pad of his thumb, making them want to be kissed. "Being surrounded by people doesn't make a person immune to emotional pain, Amy."

She could feel herself being pulled toward him by some unseen inner force. Harry's mouth was descending toward hers, at just the right angle for the kiss she suddenly craved, but Oliver prevented full contact.

"Mom?" he shouted, tugging at her sleeve. "Hey, Mom? When we get to the island, is it okay if I go swimming?"

Amy pulled back from Harry. Her frustration knew no bounds, and yet she spoke to her son in reasonable tones. "Puget Sound is too cold for swimming, Oliver," she said. "You know that."

Harry reached out to rumple the boy's hair affectionately, an understanding grin curving his lips, and Amy liked the Australian all the more for being so perceptive.

Soon they reached the island, driving ashore in Harry's van. He brought a small notebook from the catch-all space between the front seats and consulted some hastily scrawled directions with a thoughtful frown. After that, he seemed to know exactly what he was doing.

Within fifteen minutes, they pulled up beside the kind of place northwest artists loved to sketch. It was a lighthouse, built of white stone, with a long house stretching out in one direction, its many windows sparkling in the sunshine. On the other side was a fenced courtyard, complete with rose bushes, stone benches and a marble fountain.

Amy drew in her breath. "Harry, it's wonderful," she said.

A perfect gentleman, Harry had come around to her side of the van. Perhaps it was an accident, and perhaps it wasn't, that her midsection slid the length of his when he lifted her down. "Then I'll have no choice but to sign the papers," he said, his mouth very close to hers again.

Oliver and Ashley were sizing up the lighthouse, heads tilted back, eyes wide.

"I'll bet you can see all the way to China from up there!" Oliver crowed.

Ashley gave him a little shove. "Don't be a dummy. You'll only be able to see Seattle."

An expensive white car came up the cobbled driveway and stopped behind Harry's van. A tall, artfully made-up woman with champagne-blond hair got out. She was wearing a trim suit in the palest pink, with a classic white blouse, and Amy suddenly felt downright provincial in her jeans and sweater.

"Mr. Griffith?" the woman asked, smiling and extending her hand. As she drew closer, Amy let out her breath. The real estate agent was strikingly attractive, but she was also old enough to be Harry's mother. "I'm Eva Caldwell," she added. Her bright eyes swept over Amy and the children. "And this must be your family."

Harry only grinned, but Amy was discomfited by the suggestion. No matter what her subconscious mind had to say through very convincing images of her late husband, Harry Griffith was not the sort of man to want a ready-made family. He was the type that married a beautiful heiress and honeymooned on a private yacht somewhere among the Greek Islands.

"We're just his friends," Ashley piped up.

"Very good friends," Harry confirmed, giving Ashley's shoulder a little squeeze.

Mrs. Caldwell jingled a set of keys, her smile at once warm and professional, and started toward the double mahogany doors leading into the addition. "The lighthouse, of course, was the original structure. The other rooms were built around the turn of the century..."

The inside of the place was as intriguing as the outside. On the lower level was a living room with beamed ceilings. It stretched the width of the house, and the wall of windows gave a startling view of the water. The floors were pegged wood, and there was a massive fireplace at one end, with brass andirons on the hearth and built-in bookshelves on both sides.

On the far side of the room was an arched doorway leading to a hallway. There were four bedrooms beyond that, the master suite with a natural rock fireplace of its own, and up a short flight of stairs was a large loft, offering the same view of Puget Sound as the living room.

There was a door leading from the loft into the lighthouse itself. The kids rushed up the spiral staircase ahead of Mrs. Caldwell and Harry and Amy, in their excitement to see China or, failing that, Seattle.

"A place like this ought to come with a ghost, by all rights," Harry remarked.

If he'd tossed Amy a leaky plastic bag filled with ice, Harry couldn't have startled her more. She stopped on the stairs and stared at him, feeling the color drain from her face, wondering if he somehow knew she was seeing things and wanted to make fun of her.

"Amy?" He stopped, letting Mrs. Caldwell go on ahead. She was still talking, unaware that her prospect was lagging behind. "What's the matter?"

The calm reason of his tone and manner made Amy feel silly. Of *course* he didn't have an inkling that she'd seen Tyler, and as brief as their acquaintance had been, she knew Harry was above needling another person in such a callous way.

"Nothing's the matter," she answered finally. Her smile felt wobbly on her lips.

Harry frowned, but then he reached out to her, as naturally as if they'd always been together. Just as naturally Amy took his hand and they climbed the rest of the way together.

In the top of the old but well-maintained tower was a surprisingly modern electric light.

"The lighthouse is still used when the weather gets particularly nasty," Mrs. Caldwell explained.

"I can see Seattle!" Oliver whooped from the other side of the little causeway that surrounded the massive, many-faceted lamp.

"He's apparently given up on China," Harry whispered with a slight smile and a lift of one eyebrow.

Amy felt just the way she once had as a kid at summer camp, when she'd fallen off a horse and knocked the wind out of her lungs. Remarkable that just a hint of a smile could have such an effect.

"Spend as much time looking as you'd like," Mrs. Caldwell said, holding out a single key to Harry. She gave him brief directions to her office, which was near the ferry terminal, and asked him to stop by before he left.

When Ashley and Oliver raced back downstairs to check out the yard, Harry and Amy remained where they were.

Amy read the sober expression in Harry's eyes as consternation. He frowned again, as though she'd said something he was forced to disagree with, and then pulled her close and kissed her.

The gentle, skilled prodding of his tongue made her open to him, and she gave an involuntary moan, surrendering even before the skirmish had begun.

Harry held her hips in his hands, pressing her lightly against him. He nibbled at her lower lip and tasted the corners of her mouth, and still the gentle conquering went on.

Finally, though, Harry thrust himself back from her. He was breathing hard as though he'd just barely managed to escape a powerful undercurrent.

"I'm sorry," he said, and although Amy knew he had to be talking to her, it was almost as though he were addressing someone else.

An apology was probably the last thing Amy had wanted to hear. She was still responding, body and spirit, to the kiss, still reeling from the way she'd wanted him. She cleared her throat delicately and led the way downstairs without a word, using the time with her back to Harry to regain her composure.

"What do you think of the place?" he asked sometime later, when the four of them had built a driftwood fire on the beach and brought a cooler and a picnic basket from the van.

"It's wonderful," Amy answered, feeling her cheeks go warm as an echo of Harry's thorough kiss tingled on her mouth.

Harry surveyed the beautiful lighthouse pensively as he roasted a marshmallow over the fire. "It's big," he countered.

Ashley and Oliver were running wildly up and down the beach, their cheeks bright with color, their laughter ringing in the salty air. Amy couldn't remember the last time she'd seen them enjoy an outing so much.

She put a marshmallow on another stick and watched it turn crisp and bubbly over the flames. "I imagine you can see the ferry lights from the living room at night," she said a little dreamily.

Harry ate the sticky marshmallow he'd just roasted, and Amy imagined that his lips would taste of it if he kissed her again. For a long moment she honestly thought he was about to, but then he started gathering the debris from their picnic on the beach.

Amy helped, and by the time they reached the real estate office, Ashley and Oliver were already asleep in the back of the van and a light rain was falling.

Waiting in the van, watching the windshield wipers whip back and forth over the glass, Amy felt sad, as though she were leaving the one place where she really belonged.

Chapter 4

Harry Griffith was not a fanciful man. He dealt in stark realities and played for very high stakes, and he hadn't done an impetuous thing since he was seven years old.

For all of that, he signed the papers to buy the lighthouse when he'd only meant to drop off the keys. He couldn't stop imagining Amy in the massive living room, reflected firelight glittering in her golden brown hair. Or in his bed, her trim yet lush body all soft and warm and welcoming.

If that wasn't enough to haunt a man for days, the mingled sounds of the children's laughter and the tide whispering against the shore were still echoing in his mind.

"I'm sure you'll be very happy on the island," Mrs. Caldwell said.

"I'm sure I will," Harry agreed, but he wasn't thinking about the view or the clams and oysters he could gather. He was obsessed with Amy Ryan, had been practically from the moment he'd met her.

Mrs. Caldwell smiled. "Do let me know if there's anything else I can do," she said. She and Harry shook hands, and then he turned and sprinted out into the rain to rejoin Amy and the children in the van.

Amy looked every bit as nervous and unsettled as he felt.

"I bought the house," he announced, the moment he'd closed the door and put the key into the ignition. Again Harry had taken himself by surprise; he'd definitely decided, only moments before, that he wouldn't mention the purchase to Amy until they knew each other better.

She seemed a bit bewildered, but there might have been just a glimmer of pleasure in those wonderful hazel eyes, too. Harry, who was usually such a good judge of people, couldn't be certain.

"You won't find a more charming place anywhere in the country," she said after a few moments of silence.

Harry glanced back over one shoulder at the sleeping children. "Do you think they'll wake up for dinner? We could stop somewhere on the other side…"

Amy shook her head. "Thank you for offering," she said softly, "but I think it would be best if I took them straight home. They've had a pretty full day as it is, and any more excitement would probably put them on overload."

Harry felt another new emotion: chagrin. Maybe he'd offended Amy by kissing her earlier that day in the lighthouse, made her wonder what kind of friend he could have been to Tyler. God help him, Harry had known better than to do what he did, but he hadn't been able to stop himself.

His vocal cords seemed to be on automatic pilot, yet another unfamiliar experience. All his adult life, except for those few whiskey-sodden days after he'd learned of Tyler's death, Harry had been in complete control of all his faculties. Now, suddenly, nothing seemed to follow its usual order.

"Tomorrow night, then?" he asked, before he could measure the words in his mind.

She smiled at him with a certain sweet weariness that made him want to give her comfort and pleasure. "Oliver and Ashley will be spending the day with Tyler's folks," she said, and he wondered if she expected him to withdraw the invitation because of that.

"But you won't be?"

Amy shrugged one strong but delicate shoulder. "I'd be welcome if I wanted to go. But I think both the kids and Mom and Dad Ryan need time to interact without me hovering around somewhere."

Harry rode the crest of foolhardy bravado that seemed to be carrying him along. "Fine. Then you'll be free to have dinner with me."

He sensed that she was carrying on some inner struggle, he was aware of it all the while he paid the toll and drove onto the Seattle-bound ferry, and the fear that she would refuse was as keenly painful as a nerve exposed to cold air.

"I'd like that," she finally said, her voice soft and cautious.

With some effort, Harry held back a shout of gleeful triumph—the sensation was rather like scoring the winning goal in a soccer match—and managed what he hoped was an easy, man-of-the-world smile.

"So would I," he agreed. "So would I."

Charlotte Ryan's voice echoed off the walls of Amy's closet as she plundered the contents for something suitable for that night's heavy date. Small, with sleek dark hair and inquisitive brown eyes, Charlotte was one of Amy's clos-

est friends. Tyler had always referred to her as "my favorite sister," subsequently making light of the fact that she
was his *only* sister.

She came out carrying a sophisticated silver-lamé sheath
with a gracefully draped neckline.

"This is perfect," Charlotte announced. "Which isn't to
say you couldn't give a lot of that stuff in there to the Sal-
vation Army and start fresh with a whole new wardrobe."

The glittery dress was expensive, and one of the few
garments in Amy's closet that wasn't a holdover from the
fairy-tale time before Tyler's death. She'd bought it a few
months ago for a banquet honoring her father and hadn't
worn it since.

"Maybe it's too fancy," Amy fretted. "For all I know,
we're going to a waterfront stand for fish and chips."

"With Harry Griffith?" Charlotte countered, laying the
dress carefully on the bed. "Not on your life, Amy. The
man is class personified. Mark my words, he'll be wearing a tux and holding flowers when he rings the doorbell."

Amy's heart rate quickened at the romantic thought, and
she was instantly ashamed of the reaction. Tyler would be
so hurt if he knew the depths of the attraction she was feeling for Harry Griffith.

Immediately her mind presented a counterpoint to its
own suggestion, reminding her that it had been Tyler who'd
told her she was supposed to marry Harry, even bear his
children.

It was all too confusing.

Charlotte was waving one hand back and forth in front
of Amy's face. "Yo, sister dear," she teased. "Are you in
there?"

Amy busied herself finding panty hose in her bureau

drawer. "How long is it supposed to take to get over…well, to get over becoming a widow?"

Her sister-in-law was silent for a long moment. Then she laid a gentle hand on Amy's shoulder. "I don't think there are any written rules about that. But I do know Ty wouldn't want you to spend the rest of your life grieving for him, Amy."

Tears burned in Amy's eyes and thickened in her throat. "I loved him so much."

Charlotte came around to face Amy and give her a quick hug. "I know," she said. "But, Amy, he's gone, and you're still young…"

"It's Ty's fault that I'm so hesitant to get into another relationship, you know," Amy sniffled. "Marriage to him was so wonderful, nothing else could possibly be expected to equal it."

Charlotte's eyes widened, and she chuckled. "That's the damnedest reason for staying single I've ever heard! You're scared of finding another husband because you were *too happy* the first time?"

"I know it sounds crazy," Amy insisted, pushing her bureau drawer shut with a thump, "but Tyler Ryan would be a very hard act to follow."

"Don't expect me to argue," Charlotte said, her eyes moist with emotion. "I loved my brother a lot. He was an original. But you can't just hide out in your career for the next forty years, waiting to join him in the great beyond. You've got to get out there and *live*."

"Who says?" Amy asked, but she knew Charlotte was right. Life was a precious gift; to waste it was the unpardonable sin.

Charlotte gave Amy a little shove toward the bathroom.

"Get in there and take a long, luxurious bubble bath. I'll drop the kids off at Mom and Dad's."

Amy sniffled one last time. "Thanks," she said hoarsely, giving her sister-in-law another hug.

Taking Charlotte's advice to heart, Amy filled the tub in her private bathroom, adding generous amounts of the expensive bubble bath her father had given her for Christmas the year before. She pinned up her thick hair and hung her long white terry-cloth robe on the hook on the inside of the door.

Amy stripped and sank gratefully into the warm, soapy water.

"Charlotte's right," Tyler announced suddenly, so startling Amy that she barely kept herself from screaming. "Harry is a classy guy."

Tyler, dressed in a vaguely familiar blue-and-white sweater, stood with one foot resting on the toilet seat, elbow propped on his knee, chin resting in his palm.

"You might have knocked or something!" Amy hissed, when she was finally able to speak.

"Knocked?" Ty looked downright offended. "We were married once, in case you've forgotten."

Amy sighed. "Of course I haven't forgotten. And what do you mean, we *were* married?"

Tyler shrugged and pretended a sober interest in the composition of the shower curtain. "You know. I'm here, you're there. And you've got a lot of time left on your hitch, Spud, so you'd better get your act together."

She started to rise out of the water, felt self-conscious, and decided to keep herself cloaked in the piles of iridescent bubbles. Then she narrowed her eyes. "Are you saying that you plan to go on to wherever you're going without me?" she demanded.

"The bargain was 'till death do us part,' darlin'. And don't look now, but death done parted us."

Amy felt a wrenching sensation deep within her, a tearing away that seemed decidedly permanent. "You've met someone!"

Tyler grinned. "It doesn't work that way on this side, Spud. And even if there were some kind of celestial dating service, I have too much work to do to take time out for a relationship."

He looked so real, as if she could reach out and touch him and he'd feel solid under her hand. She made no effort to do that, however, because the memory of the way he'd pulled back from her the other time was still fresh in her mind.

Amy leaned back against the blue plastic bathtub pillow and closed her eyes. "I'm hallucinating," she said. "When I open my eyes, you will be gone."

But when she looked again, Tyler was still standing there. "Are you through?" he asked a little impatiently. "I told you before, Amy...my energy is limited and I don't have time to play 'is he or isn't he?'"

Amy's mouth dropped open, and she closed it again.

"Harry's taking you to the Stardust Ballroom," Tyler went on. "He's very attracted to you, but he's also having some conflicts. It bothers him that you were my wife."

Amy waited, in shock.

"You've got to reassure Harry somehow, before he comes up with some excuse to go back to Australia and stay there. I'm counting on you, Amy."

There was an urgency in Tyler's tone that troubled Amy, but she had her hands full just trying to cope with *seeing* him. She blinked, that was all, just blinked, and when she looked again her husband's ghost was gone.

Relaxing in the bathtub was out of the question, of course. In fact, Amy wasn't sure she shouldn't call 911 and have herself trundled off to the pot-holder-weaving department of the nearest hospital.

She jumped up, grabbed her robe and wrapped it around herself without taking the time to dry off. The thing to do was call Harry and beg off from their dinner date. She could claim illness, since there seemed to be every possibility she was losing her mind!

The trouble was, Amy still didn't have Harry's number, nor did she know where he was staying.

But the Ryans might. Surely Harry had contacted Tyler's parents, since he'd lived in their home as an exchange student for six months, back in high school…

Amy was about to dive for the telephone when her eyes fell on the spray of white lilacs lying on her pillow. Their lovely scent seemed to fill the room.

The blossoms were Tyler's special signature. In the old days, before the great and all-encompassing grief that had practically swallowed Amy's very soul, he'd often cut a bouquet in the backyard and presented them to her in just this way.

Her eyes stung. "Oh, Tyler," she whispered.

Since she knew she'd obsess if she stayed home, Amy went ahead with the preparations for her dinner date. She applied makeup, put on the shimmery dress and did her hair up in a loose bun at the back of her head. A few tendrils of sun-streaked blond hair were left to dangle against her cheeks and neck.

She was in the den, pacing, when the doorbell rang.

Opening the door, Amy found Harry waiting on the step. He was wearing a tux, just as Charlotte had predicted, and he looked like an advertisement for some exclusive European wristwatch. In one hand he carried a delicate bouquet of exotic pink-and-white blossoms.

His blue eyes darkened slightly as he looked at Amy, then he smiled and held out the flowers, along with a long white envelope.

"You must surely be the most beautiful woman in the whole of the Western hemisphere," he said, his voice a low, rumbling caress that struck sparks in some very tender parts of Amy's anatomy.

"Come in," Amy said, sounding a lot more composed than she felt, stepping back to admit him. She admired the velvety pastel lilies for a moment, then turned the envelope over, as if its back might reveal its contents.

"Your dividend on Tyler's investment in the opal mines," Harry explained, his voice a bit gruff. He cleared his throat, but it didn't seem to help much. "Obviously I forgot to give it to you yesterday."

Amy hesitated.

"Open it," Harry prompted, closing the door.

She tore off the end of the envelope and slipped the check out. As financially secure as Amy was, the amount still came as a pleasant shock. It was enough to buy a decent house outright.

"Tyler must have made a very large investment," she mused.

"Actually, he put up the accumulated birthday money from his grandmother," Harry explained.

Amy went into the den and put the check between the pages of her personal journal. Harry stood with his back to her, in front of the stone fireplace, looking at the row of pictures on the mantel.

When he turned to face Amy, the thought flew into her mind that she could probably achieve some distance be-

tween them by telling Harry she'd seen Tyler on three different occasions. Odd that she was more frightened of this
living, breathing man than of a dead one.

"Shall we?" he said, offering his arm.

Amy couldn't bring herself to mention her hallucinations. "Just let me put these lilies in water," she said hastily, turning to hurry into the kitchen for a shallow bowl.

Floating in that fiery crystal, the flowers were so beautiful that they made Amy's throat swell.

There was a white limousine, complete with driver, waiting at the curb. Harry helped Amy into the backseat, which
was upholstered in suede of a smoky blue, and climbed in
beside her.

"I forgot to thank you for the dividend check," Amy said,
feeling awkward and shy again. She couldn't help remembering the kiss she and Harry had shared the day before;
just the thought of it made her go all warm and achy inside.

Harry gave an elegant shrug. "It's rightfully yours," he
said. Then he reached out and lightly entwined his finger
in one of the wisps of hair bobbing against Amy's cheek.
"Such a bewitching creature," he added, as if musing to
himself rather than speaking to her. "If a being as lovely
and magical as you can exist, then surely there must be
unicorns somewhere in this world as well."

Amy felt dizzy. "That's some line," she said, after a few
moments of being totally inarticulate.

He smiled. "Oh, it's not a line," he assured her suavely.
"I meant every word."

Amy believed him, although she knew she should have
had her head examined for it. Next, he'd be telling her
that no other woman had ever understood him the way
she did, and asking her to come to his hotel room to view
his etchings.

She ran the tip of her tongue over her lips. The gesture was quick, over in a second, but Harry followed it with his eyes, and it seemed that time stopped for a little while. That she and Harry were alone in the universe.

For all of the thrumming attraction she'd felt ever since she'd met this man, their second kiss startled her completely.

Harry tasted her lips expertly, as though they were flavored with the finest wine, sending little shocks reverberating throughout her system. He might have been kissing her much more intimately, given the responses the contact wrought in her, and when his hand cupped her breast, she gave a whispered moan and tilted her head back.

He sampled her neck, the tender hollows beneath her ear, the pulse point at the base of her throat.

Harry apparently remembered the driver, even if Amy, to her vast chagrin, did not. He drew back from her, smiled in a way that made her heart and throat collide at breakneck speed, and caressed her cheek with the side of his thumb.

He didn't have to say he wanted to make love to Amy; his eyes told her clearly enough.

Minutes later, when the limousine was purring at a downtown curb, the driver came back to open the door. Amy was grateful for the cool breeze that met her as she stepped out onto the sidewalk.

She was also enormously relieved, because the restaurant was not the Stardust Ballroom, as Tyler had predicted. That made things a little less spooky.

The place was shadowy and elegant, with candles flickering in the centers of the tables, and the atmosphere was intimate. Amy hoped the dimness would hide her bright eyes and glowing cheeks—it wouldn't do for Harry to guess how thoroughly he'd aroused her.

Amy had seafood salad and Harry had a steak, and they both drank a dry, velvety wine. When the meal was over, they danced.

For all that there were other couples around, the experience was another alarmingly intimate one for Amy. The way Harry held her close was in no way inappropriate, but the scent and substance of him excited her in a way nothing in her life had prepared her for. Her breasts and thighs were cushioned against the granite lines of his frame, and Amy's body was responding as though she were naked beneath him, in a private place.

He had guessed what was happening, evidently, for a half smile curved his lips. He gave no quarter.

His lips moved, warm, against her temple. "There's no going back now, love," he warned in a ragged whisper. "It's going to happen—tonight, tomorrow, next week."

Amy knew Harry was right, but as much as she wanted him, the idea of such total surrender terrified her.

He traced her mouth with the tip of one index finger. "So beautiful," he said.

"C-could we sit down, please?"

Harry led her back to their table and seated her with as much grace as if she'd been a princess.

She couldn't meet his eyes, and her cheeks felt as hot as the tip of the candle's flame. After all, she'd practically come apart in the man's arms, and all because of the way he'd been holding her.

Harry reached out to curve his finger under her chin. "We have time, Amy," he reminded her.

Amy was relieved when he didn't ask her to dance again, though. She wasn't sure how much intimate contact she could take without making an absolute fool of herself.

They had Irish coffee and then left the restaurant.

"I think I have a headache coming on," Amy lied, once they were settled in the limousine again. Inside, she was still quivering from the tempestuous desire he'd awakened in her.

Harry grinned. "We can't just go off and leave the driver, now can we?" he teased.

Amy glanced nervously toward the front. There was no sign of the chauffeur. "Maybe I could just take a cab..."

But Harry shook his head before she'd even finished the suggestion. "When I take a lady out," he said in his rich accent, "I always take her home again. Come here, Amy."

She was overwhelmingly conscious of Harry's aftershave, the softness of the suede seats, the gentle command in his dark blue eyes. She tried to think of Tyler and, to her utter frustration, found that she couldn't remember what he'd looked like. Although she would have testified in a court of law that she hadn't moved, Amy suddenly found herself in Harry's arms again.

He kissed her, that was all, and yet Amy felt herself melting like warm wax. For the first time ever, she actually wanted a man other than Tyler, and her emotions were as tangled as a string of garage-sale Christmas tree lights.

The tinted windows of the limousine provided a high degree of privacy; the fact that the driver could return at any moment lent the situation a sense of breathless urgency.

She heard the electric locks on the limousine's doors click into place, and that made her eyes go wide.

He did nothing more than kiss and hold her, and yet Amy felt like some succulent dessert. Everything seemed to be happening in slow motion, and Amy was helpless to stop the tide of fate. She was abashed to realize that, if Harry suggested heading straight for his hotel room, she would have agreed.

Suddenly, though, the locks clicked again, and Harry was sitting a respectable distance from her, looking as unruffled as if he'd just stepped from his barber's chair.

Amy, on the contrary, was in a state of blissful shock.

The driver got back into the car, and Amy heard Harry give him a familiar address—her own. The only emotion that exceeded her relief was her disappointment.

On the porch, Harry bent forward to kiss her lightly on the tip of her nose. "You were too delectable to resist," he told her. "I'll try to mind my manners a little better next time."

Amy's senses were still rioting, and she rocked slightly on her heels, so that Harry clasped her elbows to steady her. "You could come in and have coffee," she said, and then she bit her lip. She'd had virtually no experience at being a vamp, since she'd never been with another man besides Tyler.

His smile was sexy enough to be lethal, though there was an element of sadness in it, too. "If I came in tonight, Amy," he said, "I'm afraid I would want much more than coffee. And neither of us is ready."

With that, Harry kissed her on the forehead—it was a purely innocuous contact that left Amy feeling hollow—and walked away.

She had the presence of mind to turn the lock and put the chain on the door after he was gone, but just barely. She gave a little hiccuping sob when Rumpel appeared and wrapped her sleek, silky body around her ankles.

"Reowww," she said companionably.

In need of comfort, Amy scooped the small animal into her arms and hurried up the stairs.

All the while she was taking off her dress and washing her face and putting on cotton pajamas, Amy cried. She had turned some kind of emotional corner, and she knew there would be no going back.

Tyler's mother awakened her with a phone call at ten-thirty the next morning.

"Hello, Amy," Louise Ryan said warmly. "I'm calling to ask a very big favor."

Amy was only half-awake, and rummy from a night of alternate crying and soul-searching. "A favor?"

"John and I are leaving for Kansas, the first of next week…his side of the family is having a big reunion. We hadn't planned on going, but at the last minute we decided to live a little. And, well, we'd like to take Oliver and Ashley along on the trip, if you don't mind."

The breathless hope in her mother-in-law's voice brought a tender smile to Amy's mouth.

"Of course they can go, Louise," she said, marveling even as the words left her mouth.

The next few minutes were taken up with the making of plans; John and Louise planned to drive back to the midwest in their motor home, and they wanted to pick the kids up early Monday morning.

"Oliver tells me you've been seeing Harry Griffith," Louise said, when everything had been decided.

Just remembering last night's interlude in the limousine made color flow into Amy's cheeks, but she managed to make her voice sound normal. "I'm not *seeing* him, actually," she hedged. *You are, though,* challenged a voice in her mind. *And admit it, you'd like to do a lot more than that.*

"Harry is a wonderful young man," Louise said brightly.

"Yes," Amy agreed, keeping her tone strictly noncommittal. Despite the fact that she'd behaved like a teenager in the backseat of a Chevy the night before, she had a lot of reservations where Harry Griffith was concerned.

Amy swallowed, winding her finger in the telephone cord. She should tell Louise she'd been seeing Tyler, she knew that, but the risk was just too great. She depended on John and Louise Ryan—for all practical intents and purposes, they were the only family she had—and she didn't want them to think she was having a nervous breakdown or something.

"We'll bring the children home later this morning," Louise went on, apparently failing to notice the long lull on Amy's end of the conversation. "And thank you, dear, for letting us take them on the trip with us."

Amy said something ordinary, something she couldn't remember later, added a warm farewell and hung up. After she'd brushed her teeth and washed her face and generally made herself presentable, she went downstairs in shorts and a T-shirt to let Rumpel out.

She was having a much-needed cup of coffee when the doorbell rang, and when she reached the entryway, she found Harry standing on the step. He was wearing jeans and a Henley, and yet he managed to look as elegantly rakish as an old-time riverboat gambler.

"G'day," he said, leaning one shoulder against the doorjamb. "Is that offer of coffee still open?"

Amy hadn't prepared herself, mentally or otherwise, for an encounter with Harry, and she was caught off guard. She blushed, nodded, and stepped back.

"You know," Harry said with a grin, "it's perfectly charming, the way you do that."

"Do what?" Amy challenged. For some reason she couldn't have put a name to, she needed to contradict him.

"Color up like a naked virgin when the bathhouse wall has just collapsed," he answered. "Are the children about?"

Amy led the way into the kitchen. "No," she answered, grateful that her response only called for simple words. "They're with the Ryans, making plans for a trip."

Harry turned her when she reached for the cupboard where the mugs were stored, and she was trapped between his hard torso and the counter. He traced her mouth with the tip of one index finger. "Excellent," he said. "That leaves you with no rational excuse for refusing to fly to Australia with me tomorrow."

Chapter 5

Amy had every rational reason to refuse Harry's invitation to visit Australia with him. She *must* have rational reasons, she thought. It was just that she couldn't summon up a single one on such short notice.

Harry smiled his slow, knee-melting smile, only too aware, evidently, of her dilemma, then arched one eyebrow as if prompting her to produce a suitable answer.

"I don't have a visa for Australia," she finally said, flustered.

Harry outlined the edge of her jaw with a fingertip, sending fire racing through her system. "No worries, love," he said, his voice husky and low. "I can take care of that with a single telephone call."

Amy was trapped and she liked it, and the fact incensed her. "I can't just go flying off to another hemisphere with a man I hardly know!" she pointed out irritably.

He was so close, so solid, so warm. So male. "Ah," he

said wisely, "but you *want* to know me quite well, don't you, Amy?"

Coming from any other man, the question would have sounded insufferably arrogant. From Harry, it was the unvarnished, pitiless truth.

"Yes," she confessed weakly, before she could stop herself.

Harry touched his lips to hers, with the lightest brushing motion, and a fiery shiver exploded in the core of her being, flinging rays of sweet heat into all her extremities. In fact, it was a wonder to Amy that her hair didn't crackle.

"Yes," he agreed with a sigh.

They just stood there like that, for an eternity, it seemed to Amy, and then he kissed her forehead.

"I think I'd better go now," he said reluctantly. He laid a finger to her nose. "Pack for a warm climate, love, and bring something for a glamorous occasion."

Amy didn't ask how he'd know when to pick her up. There was something mystical about the whole thing, something preordained. When it was time to leave, Harry would simply be there.

After he was gone, Amy went out into the backyard and stood by the tire swing.

"Tyler!" she demanded in an anxious, self-conscious whisper. "Where are you? I need to talk to you right now!"

There was no answer but for a breeze that ruffled the bushes burgeoning with white lilacs and carried their scent to Amy like a gift.

"This is important!" she pressed, feeling desperate. She knew what was going to happen if she went to Australia with Harry Griffith, and she was terrified. After all, she'd never been intimate with another man, before Tyler or after, and she felt as shy as a virgin.

"What's that, dear?" inquired a pleasant female voice.

Amy looked up to see Mrs. Ingallstadt, her neighbor, peering at her over the fence. The older woman was wearing a gardening hat and wielding clipping shears.

"I was just—" Amy paused to clear her throat and to work up a smile. "I was just thinking out loud, Mrs. Ingallstadt. How are you?"

"Well, my arthritis is going to be the death of me one of these days, and my gall bladder is acting up again, but otherwise I'm pretty chipper. Tell me, dear, how are you?"

Well, Amy thought, *I'm seeing things and I think I'm actually going to get on an airplane and fly away to another continent with a virtual stranger. Other than that, Mrs. Ingallstadt, I'm just fine.*

"I've been keeping busy." Recalling Mrs. Ingallstadt's fondness for white lilacs, and how Tyler had occasionally charmed the old woman with a bouquet, Amy walked over to one lacy bush and broke off several blossom-laden boughs. Without saying any more, she handed the flowers over the fence to her friend and neighbor.

Mrs. Ingallstadt beamed with pleasure, and Amy realized, with some chagrin, that she'd hardly exchanged a word with the woman in six full months. After Tyler's death, Mrs. Ingallstadt had been wonderful to Amy, and to Ashley and Oliver as well. She'd made meals, baby-sat and listened patiently when Amy was overwhelmed with grief. That first dreadful Christmas, when it seemed there would never again be reason to celebrate, the thoughtful neighbor had come into Amy's kitchen, pushed up her sleeves and proceeded to bake sugar cookies with the children.

"I'll just take these right inside and put them in water," Mrs Ingallstadt said happily. "I don't know why I haven't planted a few lilac bushes of my own. My husband was allergic to them, you know, but Walter's been dead these twenty years and I don't reckon anything could make him sneeze now."

Amy's grin was probably a little on the grim side. *Don't count on it,* she thought.

Later that day, when she'd vacuumed the upstairs hallway and gone through her closet four times, all the while insisting to herself that she *would not* do anything so impetuous as fly to Australia with Harry Griffith, Amy got her suitcases from the guest-room closet and laid them on her bed. Open.

Even then, she told herself she only meant to pack things for Ashley and Oliver to take to Kansas.

Still, when Louise brought the kids home from Mercer Island in her shiny silver Mercedes, Amy had filled the luggage with her own best summer clothes.

She and Louise did the kids' things together. Louise Ryan was an attractive woman, tanned and obviously prosperous, and she was intelligent.

"How was your evening with Harry Griffith?" she asked, snapping the catches on Ashley's suitcase into place.

Color surged into Amy's face, and she didn't quite manage to meet her mother-in-law's gaze. She couldn't help wondering what Louise would think if she knew her son's widow was about to do something completely reckless and wanton.

"I like him," Amy finally replied. She was sure a greater understatement had never been uttered.

Louise smiled, her Tyler-brown eyes laughing. Her hair was a rich auburn color, frosted with silvery gray, and she claimed she was covered in freckles from head to foot. "A woman doesn't simply 'like' a man like our Harry," she said confidently, her gaze steady as she regarded Amy.

"She either finds him totally intolerable or can't keep her hands off him."

Guess which category I fall into, Amy thought ruefully, her face going warm again. "I guess Tyler liked him a lot," she hedged, picking up Ashley's suitcase and lugging it to the doorway. Its weight didn't justify the effort, however, and she had a feeling Louise knew that.

"Tyler thought the world of Harry Griffith. So do the rest of us."

As understanding and progressive a woman as Louise was, Amy still couldn't make herself confide that she was wildly attracted to Harry. The thought reverberated inside her mind, however, like the silent toll of some mystic bell. "He's a nice man," was all she said.

After Ashley and Oliver had left the house with their grandmother, bag and baggage, Amy felt as insubstantial as an echo, bouncing aimlessly between one empty room and another. Finally, she went to the phone and dialed Debbie's home number, knowing she'd get an answering machine because her friend would be at the clinic.

"Hi," Amy said with a stilted effort at normalcy, "this is Amy. I just wanted to let you know that, well, I've completely lost my mind. Harry Griffith invited me to fly to Australia in his private jet, and God help me I'm going to do it." Color flooded her cheeks, even though she was talking to a whirring mechanism and not another human being. "Actually, *do it* isn't precisely the phrasing I was looking for, although I'm a grown woman and responsible person and if I want to do—anything—oh, never mind!" Amy forcibly stopped herself from rambling, drew a deep breath and let it out again. "I'm going to Australia, but I don't want you to worry about me because I know what I'm doing."

She hung up before adding, "I think."

Harry arrived an hour later, looking like a *GQ* model in his elegantly cut navy-blue suit. When he saw her luggage sitting in the entryway, he arched one dark eyebrow and favored her with one of his nuclear grins.

"Let's go, love," he said, reaching down to take the handle of one suitcase in each hand. Rumpel purred and curled around Harry's left ankle. "You have, I presume, made arrangements for the cat?"

"Mrs. Ingallstadt will look after Rumpel," Amy said, and even as she spoke she could hardly believe she was really doing this crazy, impulsive thing. She had always been the practical type, the one who balanced her checking account to the penny and color-coded her sock drawer.

Harry's blue gaze drifted over her simple cotton print dress with unsettling leisure. "Mmm. Well, then, we're off."

They drove to the airport in Harry's rented van, and Amy gnawed at her lower lip through practically the whole trip. Once in a while, she even reached for the door handle in an impotent stab at making a run for it.

Harry seemed amused.

"I suppose you're used to women who do this sort of thing all the time," Amy said in stiff and testy tones, clutching at her anger as though it were a lifeline.

He chuckled. "What sort of thing is that, my lovely?" he teased, pulling the van to a stop next to a sleek jet that stood gleaming on the tarmac beside a private hangar.

"This is not at all like me," Amy insisted, when Harry came around to her side to help her down.

He made an answering sound, a low rumble in his throat, and then brushed her lips ever so lightly with his own. "Which is one of the many things that makes you so blasted appealing," he agreed with a philosophical sigh. For the first time, Amy realized that Harry didn't want this attraction between them any more than she did.

The idea was oddly painful, all things considered.

The pilot had already arrived and was in the process of a preflight check when Harry gave Amy a tour of the aircraft. There was a galley, glittering and efficient, and all the leather-upholstered seats were cushy and wide, built to swivel on their shiny steel bases. There was a bar, which didn't interest Amy—just the thought of combining liquor with altitude made her queasy.

"There are water closets back there," Harry said, gesturing toward a wide hallway at the rear of the cabin. "Take your choice."

For Amy, in those moments, curiosity was a refuge, a place she could scurry into and hide out from her fear of the inevitable. She ventured into the hallway and peered through two separate doorways.

Even though Amy's father was a heart surgeon, and she'd never known poverty in her life, those glitzy bathrooms came as a surprise to her, with their glass and marble.

Harry went past her with the suitcases, disappearing into yet another room. The master suite, no doubt.

The magnetism was powerful, and resisting it took a formidable effort, but Amy managed to grope her way back to the main cabin. She was standing behind one of the elegant seats, her fingers digging deep into the sumptuous upholstery, when Harry returned.

She smiled shakily. "You certainly have nice bathrooms," she said. The instant the words had left her mouth she longed to call them back, they sounded so silly.

Harry chuckled. "Yes," he agreed. His indigo eyes moved over her in a way that was, incomprehensibly, both arrogant and reverent.

Amy felt as though he'd deftly peeled her clothes away, and it seemed to her that the very air was pulsating with some elemental, unseen force—a power that emanated from Harry himself.

The intercom saved her from having to speak, which was fortunate because a troupe of heated fantasies had invaded her mind, crowding out all rational thought.

"The preflight check has been completed, sir," announced the pilot's voice, "and we have clearance for takeoff."

Harry walked over to the bar and pushed a button on a high-tech unit behind it, and his soul-searing gaze never left Amy once. "Fine," he said in a voice that was somewhat hoarse. "Thank you."

He crossed the cabin then and, smiling slightly, pressed Amy into a seat. The act of crouching beside her and fastening her seat belt was entirely innocent, and yet it left Amy feeling as though they'd engaged in half an hour of intense foreplay.

Harry took the seat nearest hers and fastened himself in. It was plain enough to Amy that he hadn't missed the significance of her bright eyes and flushed face.

Soon the plane was speeding down the runway. Harry held Amy's hand until they were aloft.

"There now," he said, unsnapping his seat belt and rising as casually as he might from an easy chair in his living room. "We're on our way. Would you like something to drink?"

Yes, Amy thought. *A double shot of the strongest whiskey you have.* "A diet cola would be nice," she said aloud.

Harry made no comment on her choice; he simply went about taking a can of soda from the refrigerator beneath the bar.

Amy unfastened her seat belt and thrust herself shakily to her feet. There was no going back now.

She crossed to the teakwood bar, which was bolted securely to the floor, and leaned against it, trying to look as though she did this sort of thing all the time.

"You must practically live in this plane, it's outfitted so well," she commented.

Harry was still behind the bar, and he handed Amy her cola. Then he grinned his endearing, soul-wrenching grin and said with a shrug, "I'm rich."

A nervous giggle escaped Amy, and she just barely kept herself from slapping one hand over her mouth. She'd never been more sober in her life, and yet she felt as though she were roaring drunk.

"Relax, Amy," Harry said, leaning forward slightly, bracing himself against the bar with wide-spread hands. "I'm not planning to heave you over one shoulder, haul you off to my bed and ravish you. When we make love—and we will, God help us—it will be because the desire is mutual."

Although Amy was relieved by this declaration, she was also damnably disappointed. And she certainly would have been better off without the caveman images Harry had just planted in her mind.

"Did you do that on purpose?" she demanded, only realizing she'd spoken the thought aloud when Harry laughed and answered her.

"Do what, love?" he countered, rounding the bar and laying his hands on either side of her narrow waist.

Amy swallowed hard. She was a modern woman, liberated and successful in her own right, but she couldn't help imagining what it would be like to be hoisted over Harry's shoulder like the willing captive of some sexy pirate. "Oh, God," she groaned.

Harry bent his head and tasted her mouth as though it were some rare and priceless delicacy, to be enjoyed at leisure.

Amy's heart began to pound and her breathing was audible.

Harry's lips strayed to her throat, the tender hollow beneath her ear. He took the glass from her hand and set it on the bar.

Amy's traitorous body was already preparing itself to receive him, already pleading for a fulfillment that had been denied it for over two years. "Oh, God," she said again, when Harry's hands cupped her breasts. His thumbs made her nipples go taut against the soft cotton of her sundress.

"Maybe," he speculated huskily, from the tingling space between Amy's shoulder and the base of her neck, "we'd better do something about this."

"D-do something about what?" Amy's voice trembled, like her body. The rumblings of an impending spiritual and emotional quake were making cracks in the wall she'd built around her innermost self, while, on the surface of her skin, a million tiny nerves quivered.

Harry touched the tip of his tongue to the corner of her mouth, and Amy had a melting sensation. In another minute, she'd be all over his shoes, like warm wax.

"About this attraction between us," he finally replied. Between light, teasing kisses, he added, "Amy, we're not going to have a moment's peace until we've made love."

The last of Amy's defenses crumbled then; she knew Harry was right. "Yes," was all she could manage to say, she was so overcome, so confused, so in need.

He lifted her easily, gently, into his arms and started toward the hallway and the one room Amy hadn't dared to explore earlier.

"Will the pilot know?" she asked warily.

Harry kissed the top of her head and chuckled. "No, love. Not unless you turn on the intercom."

The master bedroom was surprisingly spacious, even considering the luxurious proportions of that airplane. The floor was carpeted, the lighting dim, the air subtly tinged with Harry's very distinctive scent.

He set Amy on her feet at the foot of the bed and pushed a tendril of hair back from her cheek with a gentle forefinger.

"You're sure?" he asked.

She nodded, unable to speak, though every word in every dictionary in the world seemed to be waiting at the back of her mind, wanting to be part of some enormous declaration she couldn't begin to make.

He unzipped her sundress and eased the fabric down over her shoulders. When the dress was gone, Harry caught one finger under her bra strap and brought that down, too. She sucked in her breath and tilted her head back in surrender when he bent to sample her nipple as he'd tasted her lips earlier.

Tears trickled over Amy's temples and into her hair, not because she was ashamed or unhappy, but because it felt so wondrously good to give herself in this age-old way.

Presently, Harry bared her other breast and gave it proper and thorough attention, having tossed her bra aside. She was wearing only her satiny panties when he laid her on the bed.

The velvet softness of hundreds of rose petals cushioned her fevered flesh, and their lush scent perfumed the room. Amy was transfixed as she watched Harry strip away his clothes.

His body was lean and magnificent as he stretched out

beside her. Taking a handful of the scattered pink, yellow and white petals, he sprinkled them over her and then bent to kiss the places where they landed. As he did this, he took her panties down over her hips and thighs, and they were lost in the blanket of blossoms.

Harry covered Amy with petals, and with the touch of each one to her quivering skin, she wanted him more.

"Harry, please," she finally rasped in desperation.

He raised her knees and knelt between them. He burrowed and nuzzled his way through the blossoms that sheltered her most vulnerable place, then scored her boldly with his tongue.

Amy gave a primitive groan of welcoming surrender and arched her back. Harry held her taut bottom in his hands and drank from her greedily.

Delirious with a terrifying, sweeping pleasure, Amy tossed her head from side to side. One forearm rested across her mouth, muffling the soft cries of wonderment and glory that she couldn't hold back.

And still Harry consumed her.

Finally, with a shout of joyous desolation, Amy reached her climax.

Even as he lowered her back to the flower-strewn mattress, Harry kissed the insides of Amy's thighs and the smooth moistness of her belly. She was beyond speech, beyond thought; all she could do was lie there in Harry's arms, her head resting on his strong chest. As pieces of her soul gradually wandered back from the far reaches of the universe, where her shattering release had flung them, Harry lightly caressed her shoulder blades, the small of her back, her bottom, her thighs.

Presently, he laid her on her back and settled his powerful frame between her legs. It seemed to Amy that every muscle in her body had melted—she could not possibly respond to this final stage of Harry's lovemaking—but she longed to be joined with him. The desire was far more complex than mere physical need.

He paused at her entrance and looked deeply into her eyes, silently asking her permission.

Amy nodded, tilted her head back, and closed her eyes.

Harry moved into her in a powerful stroke that awakened all her satisfied senses to an even keener need than before.

Amy's eyes flew open again, in startled surprise, and her fingers rushed to Harry's hard, sun-browned shoulders.

"Do you want me to stop?" he asked quietly, his manhood buried deep within her.

"No," Amy whispered in a frantic rush, shaking her head.

He withdrew slowly, until their joining was almost broken, and Amy felt genuine despair. But then Harry took her forcefully and she was completely, joyously lost.

As her body convulsed beneath his in the final moments of Harry's conquest, her cries echoed off the back of his throat.

Moments after she'd settled back to the mattress, completely exhausted, Harry wedged his hands under her hips to press her closer still. With a low groan, he faced his own moment of utter surrender.

At least half an hour must have passed before either of them had the breath to speak.

"Rose petals, huh?" Amy said, staring up at the ceiling. "You were pretty sure of yourself, weren't you?"

Harry was propped up beside her on one elbow. With the fingers of his other hand, he caressed a responsive nipple. "I was pretty sure of *you*," he countered.

Amy was holding a lot of things at bay in those moments. Like reality, for instance. "The flowers were a po-etic touch," she said. "I guess you probably do that every time you bring a woman here."

He was silent for a long interval, during which he con-tinued to tease her nipples, each in turn, with skillful fin-gers. "I've brought women to this bed before, of course," he said finally, unapologetically. "But those rose petals were for you and you alone, Amy."

What a line, observed the left side of Amy's brain. *If this is a dream, don't let me wake up,* countered the whimsi-cal right side.

As if to prove his assertion, Harry gathered a handful of the bruised, fragrant petals and began to rub them lightly against Amy's breasts and belly.

She moaned helplessly as he lowered his mouth to her nipple, once again to drink from her.

They landed in San Francisco some two hours later and although Amy's knees were still wobbly from Harry's love-making, she'd managed to grab a shower in one of the fancy airplane bathrooms and put on evening clothes.

She wore a snowy-soft white jacket, with tiny irides-cent beads stitched to it to lend a subtle sparkle, a delicate camisole top, and black silk slacks.

As she and Harry descended the roll-away stairs to the tarmac, a pearl-gray limousine whisked to a stop beside the plane.

"Wow," Amy said. "You really know how to impress a girl."

Harry's grin was downright wicked. "You did seem pretty impressed," he agreed, and Amy knew he was re-ferring to her unbridled responses to his lovemaking.

She felt a little anticipatory thrill, because she knew she would return to Harry's bed that night.

They dined in a restaurant atop one of San Francisco's finest hotels, and since the requisite fog had somehow failed to roll in, the view of the harbor and the Golden Gate Bridge was unobstructed.

Amy had seafood of some kind—she would never remember exactly what—and she indulged in one glass of white wine. The sweet, pulsing daze she'd been wandering in turned to a feeling of giddy adventurousness.

She wanted to neck in the rear of the limousine while they were driving back to the airport, but she was too shy to make the first move, and all Harry did was hold her hand and look at her as though she were a poem he wanted to memorize. Or a puzzle he couldn't solve.

They had barely returned to the jet when two men in suits appeared. Harry obviously knew them, but they produced Customs badges anyway, and Amy showed them her passport. She was heart-stoppingly certain they were going to say she couldn't leave the country.

"Have a good flight," one of them said to Amy with a smile, while the other shook hands with Harry.

When the Customs agents were gone, Harry went to the cockpit to confer with the pilot. Amy strapped herself in and waited.

After a few minutes, Harry's voice came over the intercom. "Sit tight, love," he said. "The flight check has been completed and we're about to take off."

They'd been airborne almost half an hour when Harry finally returned to the main cabin. With a chuckle he unfastened Amy's seat belt and pried her fingers loose from the arm rests.

"You're as beautiful as a moonflower," he said, holding her close and burrowing into the soft skin of her neck.

"And despite the shower and that perfume you're wearing, I can still catch the scent of the rose petals."

He left her, just briefly, to dim the cabin lights and turn on soft music. Then Harry drew Amy into his arms and they danced, and for Amy that was almost as keenly erotic as lying naked in a bed of flower petals.

Emotionally, Amy was drowning. She thought of Tyler, in a desperate attempt to anchor herself to the only world she really knew, but suddenly he was only a sweet, fading memory.

The music went on and on, and Harry and Amy danced tirelessly. Then he took her hand and led her back to his bed.

Where before their lovemaking had had a fevered urgency, now it was leisurely and deliberate. Harry brought Amy to one release after another before he permitted her the final conquering she literally begged for, and the first light of dawn was sparkling on the blue waters of the sea when he finally allowed her to sleep.

The thump and lurch of landing brought her bolt upright in bed, her eyes wide. Harry was fully dressed, wearing charcoal slacks and a lightweight white sweater, his sleek, raven-black hair glistening in the morning light.

"Where are we?" Amy asked, pulling the sheets up under her chin even though she knew it was too late to hide herself from Harry.

"Honolulu," he answered, grinning at her rumpled hair and dazed expression. "We'll only be here long enough to refuel, do some maintenance and change pilots, so take your time getting dressed."

Blushing to recall how she'd behaved with this man, how she'd let him shape and maneuver her into every possible position for taking, Amy tried to get out of bed without letting go of the sheet. She wanted the blue terry cloth robe draped over a nearby chair, but Harry got to it before she did and held it out of reach.

"On second thought," he said, his dark blue eyes full of mischief and passion, "don't bother to get dressed at all."

Chapter 6

Amy settled into the airplane's big marble bathtub with a contented sigh. The intercom crackled out the announcement that the flight had been cleared for takeoff, and she gripped the sides of the tub as the craft hurtled down the runway and then catapulted into the air.

Some of Amy's bubbly bathwater slopped over onto the floor.

"They should have put a seatbelt in this thing," she muttered.

Harry's laughter came over the intercom, along with a few chuckles from the pilot.

"Push the white button on the panel, love," Harry told her. *"After* you get out of the tub."

Red in the face, Amy snatched up a towel and scrambled out. She could hardly get to the intercom panel fast enough.

Once Amy was dried off and dressed, her hair toweled and then combed into a casual style, she made the bed. The crushed rose petals had mysteriously disappeared, but their luscious scent lingered.

Amy ventured out into the main cabin. She sat contentedly at one of the windows for a long time, looking down on the clouds—giant cotton balls stretched thin—as well as the sea, just enjoying the view.

She was surprised when Harry showed up, carrying a tray. He'd brought her a gigantic fruit salad, a croissant and a little pot of special Hawaiian coffee.

Amy gratefully accepted the food, but her tone of voice was testy. "Do the rest of the intercoms on this plane have minds of their own, or just the one in that particular bathroom?"

Harry grinned and sat down in another seat, facing her. He was wearing jeans and a light yellow sports shirt, but he still looked elegant enough to play for high stakes in Monaco. "No worries, love. That's the only one with temperament."

Amy popped a juicy piece of fresh pineapple into her mouth and looked out at the sea.

"What are you thinking?" Harry asked softly at great length.

She sighed, gazing at him with bewildered eyes. "I guess I'm waiting for the guilt to strike."

He took a strawberry from her bowl and touched it lightly to her lips. Amy opened her mouth to receive the tidbit and felt a sweet tension begin to curl up tight within her.

"Why would you feel guilty?" he asked quietly.

Amy was practically breathless. She was going to have to talk to Debbie when she got back to Seattle, find out why a simple thing like having a man put a strawberry to her lips felt so much like a sweet seduction.

"Because of Tyler," she said lamely. "Oh, I know we

haven't done anything wrong." She wanted to tell Harry about her strange encounters with Ty, but she was afraid of the impression that would make.

Harry raised both eyebrows. "Well, then?"

"It's just that, well, I'd never been with anyone else—until you."

Resting his elbows on the arms of his chair, Harry made a finger steeple beneath his chin. He sat quietly, ready to listen, and if Amy hadn't already been crazy about him, that gesture would have done it.

"Instead of guilt," Amy stumbled on awkwardly, "I feel a sense of adventure and newness and excitement. Like, maybe I'm something more than a mother and an erstwhile wife."

Harry's dark brows knitted together in a momentary frown. "Maybe?"

Amy bit into a grape, chewing thoughtfully and then swallowing. "Tyler was a great guy," she finally said with a shaky sigh. "And God knows, I loved him. But I don't think it ever occurred to either of us that I should have an identity apart from being a wife and mother."

"Mmm," Harry said.

Amy laughed. "If you ever get tired of being a venture capitalist, or whatever you are, you could be a shrink. You listen very well."

He took another strawberry between his fingers and traced the outline of her mouth with the morsel until her lips parted. Just when Amy thought surely he was going to take her to his bed, he asked, "How would you like to try your hand at flying the plane?"

Although her first instinct was to draw back and shake her head no, Amy made herself nod.

Moments later, she was in the cockpit, in the copilot's

seat, wearing earphones and staring at the instrument panel in utter ignorance. The pilot had gone to the rear of the aircraft, and Harry was occupying his chair.

Over the next hour he taught Amy the function of most of the instruments and showed her how to gain and lose altitude. For a while, she was actually flying the aircraft herself, and the knowledge filled her with a kind of pride she'd never felt before.

Finally, however, Amy excused herself and left the co-pilot's seat to the man who had come on board in Honolulu. She found a book in Harry's room and settled into one of the comfortable seats in the main cabin to read.

Lunchtime came, and Harry clattered around in the galley, opening and shutting doors. A bell chimed, and he carried a tray forward to the pilot, then brought Amy a compact meal of Spanish rice and vegetables, along with a plate for himself.

They ate in comfortable silence, not needing to talk, and then Harry went back to the cockpit. Amy tidied up the galley, thinking that was the least she could do, since Harry had done the cooking, then returned to her book.

She was so absorbed in the story, a fast-paced spy thriller, that when Harry appeared, she was startled.

He took the book from her hands and set it aside, then unsnapped her seat belt. Again, Amy was electrified by a perfectly ordinary thing.

She knew what Harry wanted, and she wanted it, too, but the vamp in her made her offer a token resistance.

"What if I don't go to bed with you?" she whispered. Even though the blood was thundering in her ears, Amy hadn't forgotten the incident with the bathroom intercom, and she wasn't taking any chances on having the pilot overhear such an intimate conversation.

Harry ran his hands lightly over her thighs, easing her legs apart at the same time. "Then I'll have you right here," he said, his voice low, like thunder rumbling in a summer sky. After that, he kissed her, subjecting her to a preliminary conquering with his tongue. Then he bared her breasts.

"I'll go," Amy moaned, as he nibbled at her. "I'll go!"

Harry chuckled and lifted her legs, so that her knees rested over the arms of the seat. Then he opened the snap on her jeans.

"Harry," she pleaded.

He bent to nip at the crux of her womanhood and, despite the sturdy denim covering her, Amy felt the contact to the core of her being. She closed her eyes, loving the feeling of his hands cupping her breasts, and let her hips rise and fall as he bid them.

After tormenting her for at least fifteen minutes, he took her legs from the arms of the chair and relieved her of her jeans and panties, then put her back into position again. The first foray of his tongue tore a raw cry from her throat, but Harry granted no quarter. He slipped his hands under her bottom and then feasted in earnest.

When the first wave of satisfaction struck, Amy was grateful, because the sensations Harry was treating her to were so intense they were almost frightening. But that crest was followed by a second, higher one, and then a third.

As Amy shuddered with the volcanic force of her pleasure, she clasped Harry's shoulders in both hands. Her vision blurred and she cried out at the top of her lungs, but there was no helping that. She was totally out of control.

Her heart had almost settled back into its normal rate when he gathered her up and carried her to his bed.

The taking of Amy Ryan had only begun.

* * *

They landed in Fiji, then briefly, hours later, in Auckland, New Zealand, then in Sydney, where more Customs men came on board and inspected Amy's passport. Finally, they headed north again.

When Amy finally stepped off the plane, into a lush tropical climate, she was amazed to see colorful parrots flying free, as robins did at home in Seattle. The sea was as blue as India ink, lapping at sugar-white beaches, and a spectacular stone house loomed in the distance, as imposing as a castle.

"Where are we?" Amy asked, still in a fog from all the sweet, busy hours spent in Harry's bed.

He laughed and kissed her softly on the mouth. "Paradise," he answered. "The island is named Eden, and not without reason."

A Jeep was waiting at the edge of the private airstrip, and Harry flung the suitcases into the back with a practiced motion, then helped Amy onto the seat. The pilot was evidently staying behind to perform maintenance on the plane.

There was a working fountain in front of the house, and two Australian sheepdogs came bouncing across the yard, barking gleefully, to greet their master.

Harry took a moment to acknowledge the animals, then lifted Amy down from the Jeep.

"You'll be needing a bath and something to eat," he said, his accent sounding more pronounced than before. "Then you'll want to catch up on all that sleep I've deprived you of since we left Seattle."

An amiable housekeeper opened one of the stately double doors, and Amy stepped inside. She didn't notice much about Harry's house that first day, because she was too tired and distracted, and she was grateful when he led her upstairs to an airy suite filled with the distant sound of the tide.

He undressed her, like a child, and they showered together. Even as Harry tenderly soaped and rinsed her exhausted body, Amy could barely keep her eyes open.

At last, he wrapped her in a soft, giant towel and took her to bed. After pulling a T-shirt over her head, he tucked her under the covers and bent to kiss her forehead.

"Sleep well, love," he said.

Dimly, Amy was aware of Harry moving around the room, getting dressed again, and she wanted him beside her even though she hadn't the strength for even one more session of lovemaking.

"Harry," she whimpered, patting the mattress fitfully with one hand.

He chuckled. "No, love, not today. You're too tired."

Amy fought to open her eyes, marshalled all her strength to ask, "What about you? Aren't... you tired?"

Harry bent and planted a smacking kiss on her forehead. "On the contrary, my sweet little Yankee, I feel like I could take on the world with one hand lashed behind my back."

"Don't...go."

"Sleep," he ordered with mock sternness. Then he was gone and Amy slept.

The room was bright with sunshine when she awakened, alone in the big bed and fully rested. Her suitcase was nowhere in sight, but when Amy opened the top drawer of a beautiful antique bureau, she found some of her clothes neatly stacked inside.

Quickly she dressed. Beyond the glass doors leading onto the terrace, parrots made their raucous cawing sound and the tide recited its ancient, rhythmic poetry. After brushing her teeth, grooming her hair and applying lip gloss, Amy ventured out of the bedroom.

She was ravenously hungry and nervous because there was no sign of Harry in any of the enormous, rustic rooms that lay between his room and the kitchen.

The familiar housekeeper was there, stirring batter in a crockery bowl, and she greeted Amy with a gapped smile.

"There you are, then," the woman chirped gleefully. "If I hadn't seen you arriving with me own eyes just yesterday, I would have sworn you were nothing but a story our Harry had made up."

Amy was embarrassed, but she made an effort to be cordial. "My name is Amy Ryan," she said,

"Elsa O'Donnell," said the housekeeper, with a nod and a twinkly smile. "You'd be Master Tyler's widow, then. Oh my, but we was fond of that boy."

The reminder of her husband unsettled Amy a little. As much as she'd loved Tyler, she'd never responded to him in quite the way she did with Harry. She just nodded.

"Sit down," Elsa commanded good-naturedly, setting the mixing bowl aside. "I'll see about getting you some tea."

Amy glanced at the clock and saw that it was two-fifteen. She'd not only slept away the night, but a good part of the day as well.

By tea, Elsa meant a scone with jam and fresh cream, a plate of fruit, four delicate sandwiches and a pot of rich orange pekoe.

Amy consumed the repast as politely as she could, considering that she was famished, then asked shyly, "Is Harry around?"

"He's down at the beach, I imagine," answered Elsa, methodically putting away the ingredients of afternoon tea. "Headed straight for it after getting you settled yesterday, and was off to the water again this morning, right after breakfast."

Amy rinsed her cup and plate and silverware at the sink, then set them on the drain board. "If I walk down there, will I find him?"

"It's a big island," Elsa replied. "But I think you'll run across him. Just mind you don't go through the cane fields—there's snakes there."

Amy shuddered, but even the thought of snakes didn't dampen her excitement at being in a new place and, yes, the prospect of seeing Harry again had its attractions, too.

The sheepdogs joined her on the lawn, romping along beside her, and they were the ones who led her to Harry. He was in water up to his hips, examining the hull of a sleek sailboat, and his grin was as dazzling as the tropical sun.

"So then, Sleeping Beauty has awakened," he teased, making his way toward her. He wasn't wearing a shirt, just cutoffs dark and sodden and clingy with seawater. "Welcome to the land of Oz."

Amy, wearing shorts and a T-shirt herself, kicked off her sandals so she could feel the fine, pristine sand between her toes.

Harry met her on the beach, and his kiss, quick and innocent as it was, sent her senses tumbling in all directions, just as always. He curled two fingers under her chin and grinned again.

"If you're all rested up, love, I'd like to volunteer to wear you out again."

Amy laughed and twisted away from him, running toward the sparkling turquoise water. The dogs bounded after her, barking with delight at the game.

She and Harry splashed each other in the lapping tide,

and Amy felt as though all the grief had been erased from her past, leaving only the joy.

"Who else lives on this island?" she asked later, when the two of them were sitting on the beach, their feet buried in the sand.

Harry brushed a tendril of hair back from her forehead. "Just Elsa and her husband, Shelt. He's the gardener."

Amy lay back with a sigh, looking up at an impossibly blue sky. Exotic flowers bloomed at the edges of the cove, orange ones, pink, violet and white. Birds that would only be seen in pet stores and zoos at home chattered in the trees, crazy splotches of living color.

"This really is a garden of Eden," she said, recalling what Harry had said when they'd first arrived on the island. "I wish we could stay here forever."

Harry stretched out beside her and gave her a brief but tantalizing kiss. "There's no reason why we can't. Live here with me, Amy. We'll start the world all over again."

Amy blinked, and her throat tightened with emotion. "I can't do that," she said. "I have two children, remember? They need to go to school and spend time with their friends and with Tyler's family."

Harry shrugged. "We'd live in the States half the year anyway, love. We could hire a nanny to look after Oliver and Ashley here on the island, and the Ryans would be welcome to visit at any time. They know that." He paused, gazing pensively out to sea. "There are worse things than growing up in paradise, you know."

Deep down, Amy knew Oliver and Ashley would be happy here. They adored Harry, just as she did, and his island would seem like heaven on earth to them. When he got bored with domestic life, however, and wanted to return to the jet set, they'd be shattered.

Losing Tyler had been enough trauma. Playing Swiss Family Robinson for a few months or years, then being abandoned again, would crush Oliver and Ashley, maybe destroy their ability to trust.

"I want a ride in the sailboat," Amy announced, as much to change the subject as anything.

"Tomorrow," Harry promised. He seemed troubled, distracted.

That night, it rained as it can only rain in the tropics. The droplets were warm as bathwater, and Amy stood on the terrace outside Harry's room, her face turned upward and her arms outspread to welcome the deluge.

"You're daft," Harry accused, but he laughed and kissed Amy and soon he was drenched, just as she was.

When he finally hauled her inside the house and began toweling her dry, she saw that the bed was literally mounded with orchidlike blossoms. Some were pink, some white, but all were beautiful.

A sweet ache constricted Amy's throat, and she stood still while Harry peeled away her sodden clothes, then his own. Finally, he laid her on the bed of flowers and made slow, gentle love to her.

In the morning it was as though the rain had never fallen, so fiercely did the sun shine on the sea and the dazzling sand. Amy awakened slowly, cushioned in crushed petals, but this time when she reached out, Harry was beside her.

"When are we going home?" she asked, dreading the answer. If it hadn't been for Oliver and Ashley, she would gladly have agreed to live on the island for the rest of her life.

Harry rolled onto his side and kissed her breast. "Never,"

he replied throatily. "Consider yourself kidnapped, a one-woman harem."

"Just promise never to give me back," she whispered, "no matter how high the ransom gets."

Moments later, ransom was the farthest thing from Amy's mind. She was into unconditional surrender.

After a leisurely shower together, and an equally unhurried breakfast in the kitchen, Harry and Amy took the picnic basket Elsa had packed and set out for the nearby cove where the sailboat was moored.

"Take your clothes off," Harry ordered, when they reached the shore.

"Already?" Amy countered, eyeing him skeptically.

He laughed. "Yes. If you don't want to get them wet when you wade out to the boat." With that, Harry removed his cutoffs and T-shirt, rolled the garments up and secured them under the handles of the wicker picnic basket. Balancing that on top of his head, he stepped into the water, magnificently naked.

Amy was considerably more self-conscious about stripping, even though she knew they were completely alone on that magical beach. Nonetheless, she followed Harry's lead, took off everything and marched into the water.

After tossing the basket onto the deck, Harry vaulted over the side and reached down to help Amy in after him. The weathered old boards were smooth and warm from the sun.

Amy could have languished there for a while, but Harry gave her a playful swat on the bottom and said, "What's this? A mutiny before we even weigh anchor?"

Hastily, Amy rose and put her clothes back on, except for her shoes.

After a few minutes of busy preparation, they set sail.

"Where are we going?" Amy inquired, shading her eyes with one hand.

"That island over there," Harry answered, pointing.

Amy felt like an intrepid explorer. All her life she'd taken the safe and practical route, whenever a choice was offered. Now here she was in a foreign country, with a man she'd known only briefly, about to set sail in tropical seas.

So what if their destination was clearly in sight?

The water between Eden Island and its neighbor was so clear that Amy could see the reefs beneath the surface and the colorful fish that swam through intricate passages. When she saw a shark glide by, she drew back from the side of the boat, her mind filled with movie images.

Harry, who was working with the sails, smiled at her reaction. "What did you see, love? A great white?"

Amy felt the blood drain from her cheeks. "Do you mean to tell me that *Jaws* might be swimming around down there, at this very moment?"

Harry laughed. "A famous shark like that? Not likely, rose petal. He's living in the South of France and wearing sunglasses so his fans won't recognize him."

"Very funny," Amy replied grudgingly, peeking over the side of the boat again. The spectacle going on down there was just too good to miss.

When they reached the other island—if it had a name of its own, Harry didn't mention it—Amy was possessed by a remarkably pleasant feeling that she and Harry were completely alone on the planet.

The only sign that anyone else had ever visited the island before was a tree house wedged between two massive palms. Small boards had been nailed to the trunk of one of the trees to form a crude ladder, and the structure's thick roof appeared to have been woven from long, supple leaves.

"Yours?" Amy inquired.

Harry looked away. "I built it for my stepdaughter, Eireen. Unfortunately, Madeline—my wife—never gave the poor little thing a chance to be a child."

Amy touched his arm lightly, then pushed up nonexistent sleeves—she was wearing a T-shirt—and started up the ladder.

"Best let me go first, love," Harry remarked presently, when she'd climbed about five rungs. "Could be snakes up there."

Amy was back on the ground with the speed and dispatch of a cartoon character. "Snakes?" she croaked.

Harry took a manly stance for effect, then began to climb deftly toward the tree house, the picnic basket in one hand. There was a rustling sound, followed by a fallout of leaves and dirt, then Harry peered down at her from a crudely shaped, glassless window.

"All clear, rose petal," he called.

Amy ran her tongue over her dry lips and then stepped onto the first rung, gripping another with both hands.

Although there were no snakes in the tree house, it was clear enough that other things had been nesting in there. For all of that, it was a lot of fun, yet another thing Amy had never done before.

"Come here," Harry said, and Amy went straight into his arms. It did not even occur to her to resist.

His kiss was one of thorough mastery; the slow dance of their tongues soon became a duel of passion. Amy felt as though a sudden fever had set in, and by the time Harry had removed her T-shirt, then her bra, then the rest of her clothes, she was weak with the need to surrender.

He enjoyed her, like some juicy tropical fruit, for a long, torturously sweet interval, wringing response after response from her. When he finally made her his own, she came apart in his arms as uninhibited as a jungle tigress with her mate.

After her senses were restored, Amy found herself lying on the floor of the tree house, where Harry had spread a soft blanket taken from the picnic basket. While Harry caressed her—he was lying quietly beside her, still recovering from his own invasion of heaven—Amy felt strong enough to permit herself memories of lovemaking with Tyler.

Her late husband had been a tender, considerate lover always, and Amy had learned a woman's secrets in his arms. She had to admit, though, that there had never been the sense of wild abandon she felt with Harry. It was a different sort of passion, more mature and more intense.

And far more dangerous.

He slid down to kiss the flat of her stomach. "Stay with me, Amy," he said hoarsely. "Please."

Harry had never said "I love you," nor had he asked her to be his wife. Amy was pretty sure he was marriage-shy after his first experience, and a sophisticated man of the world like him would *expect* an uncomplicated relationship with no strings attached.

"I can't," she said, as a soft tropical rain began to patter on the roof of dried leaves. She'd loved being married; Tyler had shown her just how marvelous a physical and spiritual partnership could be. For the first time since his death, Amy felt ready to make a real and lasting commitment to someone new.

They ate their picnic lunch naked, cozy inside the dank and dusty tree house, talking quietly, but the day had lost some of its magic.

When the rain let up, late that afternoon, they returned to the boat and sailed back to Harry's island.

Harry made a fire on the living-room hearth, because the rain had returned and there was a slight chill in the air.

That night, for the first time since their adventure had begun, Harry and Amy didn't make love.

They spent the next two days walking the beaches, soaking up the medicinal Queensland sun, playing backgammon on the terrace. Lying next to each other at night, they were unable to resist the magnetism, and while their lovemaking was as ferociously satisfying as ever, there was a distance about it. A certain reserve.

Amy's heart was heavy when they left the island on the morning of the third day; she thought she knew now how Eve must have felt when she and Adam had been driven from the Garden.

Harry kept himself busy in the cockpit of the jet, while Amy wandered aimlessly around the cabin, wishing the dream never had to end.

They landed in Sydney a few hours later, and Harry returned from the controls.

"You'll need an evening gown if you brought one," he said, as though speaking to a casual acquaintance instead of a woman he'd made love to in beds of flowers and in a tree house.

They rode downtown in yet another limousine, over the famous bridge, and their hotel suite boasted a view of the Opera House and the harbor.

Still, the mood was subdued, and Amy couldn't help thinking that, glamorous surroundings or none, Cinderella time was over. The glass slipper wasn't going to fit.

Chapter 7

Harry Griffith was a man who planned his life years in advance. He knew details about his future other people wouldn't even begin to consider until they'd passed the age of sixty.

One thing he had definitely *not* planned on, however, was falling in love.

He turned from the window overlooking Sydney Harbor when he sensed Amy's presence, and the sight of her standing there in her light blue, sleek-fitting dress practically stopped his heart. Still, cool reserve was Harry's strong point; he'd relied on the trait for so long that it was second nature to him now.

Amy's eyes were bright with a peculiar mixture of defiance and hope, and Harry made up his mind in that moment that he would sacrifice anything to have her for his own. His pride, his fortune—anything.

He took her to see *Madame Butterfly* at the Opera

House, and then the two of them had dinner in an out-of-the-way restaurant Harry had always favored.

"What did you think of the opera?" Harry finally asked. The question came out smoothly, as the things he said nearly always did, but behind the facade his emotions were churning in secret.

Amy took a sip of her wine before answering. "I've seen it before, of course," she replied, looking uncomfortable. "I always cry and I always get angry because Pinkerton shows so little regard for Butterfly's feelings. He goes into the marriage planning to dump her later, for a 'real wife.'"

Harry felt a rhythmic, thumping headache begin behind his right temple. Only when it was too late, when they'd already taken their seats in the Opera House, had he realized that *Madame Butterfly* was probably a poor choice because it dealt with the subject of male treachery.

"All men aren't like Pinkerton, of course," he said quietly.

Amy didn't look convinced. "When a man travels a lot," she said distractedly, "there are temptations. I have a friend who used to be married to an airline pilot, and he had a playmate in every city between here and Buffalo, New York."

Harry arched an eyebrow. "Busy man," he allowed. "Amy, what is it? What's really troubling you?"

He saw the battle going on behind her beautiful hazel eyes and wondered whether he was winning or losing.

"I think I'm in love with you," she said, as though confessing that she'd contracted some embarrassing disease.

Staid, sedate Harry Griffith. It was all he could do not to leap onto his chair and shout the news to everyone in the restaurant. "That's a problem?" he asked.

"Yes!" she whispered furiously. "You're a rich man! You have your own jet and a private island!"

"I'll try to reform," Harry promised.

Amy's cheeks glowed pink, and her wondrous eyes were now glistening with tears. "I can't share you with all the other women you probably know. I won't!"

"You don't have to," he said reasonably.

She stared at him for a moment. "What?"

"Amy, you're not the only one who's fallen in love here."

She dropped her fork. "You're saying that you—that I—that we—"

"I love you, Amy. I thought you understood that when I kept asking you to stay with me—I believe I said something poetic about our starting a new world together."

She picked up her fork again and waved it like a baton. Her mouth moved, as though she would deliver a lecture, but no sound came out.

"I'm asking you to marry me," Harry said, figuring he'd better grab the opportunity to speak while her tongue was still tangled. "I'll sell the island and we'll spend all our time in the States. I'll wear baseball caps, drink beer and call you 'babe,' if that's what you want. And even though it goes without saying, I'm going to say it anyway—I'll never be unfaithful to you."

A tear scurried down Amy's cheek. "You'll get tired of us, Ashley and Oliver and me."

"No way," Harry answered, his voice sounding hoarse. "Amy, men *are* capable of making solid commitments. You know that. Tyler did."

She obviously had no argument. Tyler had made her happy, and Harry blessed his late friend for that, silently promising Ty, as well as himself, that he would never bring Amy anything but joy.

"I wouldn't want you to sell the island," Amy said after a long time. "If you did, we'd never be able to make love in the tree house again."

"Are you saying yes?" Harry inquired, leaning forward slightly in his chair.

"Yes," she replied, and then there were more tears. Happy ones, silvery in the candlelight.

Once again, Harry kept himself from shouting for joy, but just barely. He paid the check and, after the waiter had pulled back Amy's chair, helped her into her wrap. When they reached the waiting limousine, he opened the door for her and gave the driver very rational directions.

It was only when they reached the privacy of their hotel suite that he put his hands on either side of Amy's slender waist, hoisted her over one shoulder and carried her to bed for a proper celebration.

In the morning Amy and Harry went shopping. She bought a toy koala bear for Ashley and an outback hat for Oliver, and Harry bought an engagement ring.

He put it on her finger that afternoon, on board the jet, with Australia falling away behind them. Amy was pretty certain she could have flown home without an airplane, she was so happy.

Twenty-six hours later, they touched down in Seattle. Harry drove her home in his van.

"You're going to need some time to recuperate," he said, when they were standing in her kitchen. "I have some business to take care of in New York, but I'll call you when I get back."

Jealousy flared in Amy's heart, but she was too tired from all that traveling and lovemaking to nurture the flame.

If she was going to love Harry, then she had to trust him as well.

"I love you," she said.

He kissed her, weakening her knees and causing her heart to catch. "And I love you," he replied, his voice a low rumble.

The first thing Amy did was call the number in Kansas that Louise had given her. She talked to both Oliver and Ashley, who were having a grand time at the reunion, but said nothing about her own trip or the wedding awaiting her in the future. Those were subjects she wanted to bring up in person.

"We'll be home next Tuesday, according to Grampa," Ashley said. "I'm bringing you something really neat."

Amy smiled, picturing an ashtray in the shape of Kansas or maybe a plate bearing a painting of the state bird. "I'll be looking forward to that," she said.

After saying goodbye, Amy immediately dialed her friend Debbie. She would listen to her voicemail messages later.

"What do you *mean,* you went to Australia with Harry Griffith?" Debbie demanded, the moment the receptionist at the clinic put Amy through to her office.

Amy smiled, perched on the edge of her desk and wrapped the phone cord idly around one finger. "He asked me to marry him," she said. "And I said yes."

Debbie gave a delighted cry, then apparently had second thoughts. "Wait a minute. You don't know him all that well."

"I know him as well as I need to," Amy replied quietly. "And what happened to all those lectures you were handing out before I left? I think the general theme was,

'Amy, you've got to put your past behind you and get on with your life.'"

Debbie sighed. "It sounded good in theory. Do you love this guy?"

"With all my heart."

"I'm coming right over. We'll go out for pizza and talk this through—"

"I'm not going anywhere," Amy sighed. "Not tonight. I just traveled from one hemisphere to another and I'm exhausted. I'm planning to have some soup, take a bath and crawl into bed."

"All right, we'll talk tomorrow, then," Debbie said breathlessly. "You're not going to live in Australia, are you?"

"Only part of the year," Amy answered, half yawning the words. "Goodbye, Debbie."

Before her friend could protest, Amy hung up.

She could barely see to heat soup, but she knew she needed nourishment, so she made herself a bowl of chicken and stars. After eating about half of the impromptu meal, Amy stumbled upstairs, had the bath she'd promised herself, put on a cotton nightshirt and fell into bed.

"It's about time you got home," commented a disapproving male voice.

Amy's eyes flew open, and she sat bolt upright in bed, reaching feverishly for the lamp switch. The subsequent burst of lights showed Tyler standing at the foot of the bed, one foot balanced on the antique blanket chest.

The fact that this had happened before did nothing to ease the shock. In fact, by that time Amy had half convinced herself that she'd never seen Tyler's ghost at all.

"What are you doing here?" she managed, staring at him, blinking hard and then staring again.

Tyler shoved one hand through his curly brown hair and sighed. "I used to live here, remember? I used to live, period."

Amy tossed back the covers, meaning to scramble over to Tyler and see if she could pass her hand through him, like a projection from her father-in-law's old eight-millimeter movie camera.

But Ty stepped back, and the expression on his face, though a benevolent one, was unmistakably a warning. "Don't try to touch me, Amy," he said. "It dissipates my energy."

Kneeling in the middle of the bed that had once been theirs, Amy covered her face with both hands. "This is insane. *I'm* insane!"

"I told you before," Tyler sighed, "you're perfectly all right. Where have you been for the past week?"

Amy lowered her hands. "You don't know? That's weird. I thought you knew all, saw all."

"I'm confined to a certain area," Tyler explained somewhat impatiently. "And my time is running out. Where were you, Amy? And where are the kids?"

"Ashley and Oliver are in Kansas, with your parents," she answered, worried. "And I was in Australia, with Harry Griffith. What do you mean, your time is running out?"

Tyler turned away for a moment.

"Ty?"

He held up one hand. "It's okay, Amy. I knew you and Harry were going to hit it off—it was meant to be—but it's still a little hard to let go."

Amy's throat tightened, and her eyes filled with tears. "You're telling me. Losing you was the worst thing that ever happened to me, Ty. If I could have held on to you even a moment longer, I would have."

When he turned to face her again, his eyes were suspiciously bright. He started to say something, then stopped himself.

Amy drew a deep breath and held it for a moment, struggling to regain her composure. She adored Harry, and she knew marrying him was the right thing to do, but Tyler had been her first love, the father of her children, and saying goodbye to him would not be easy.

"Will I see you again—someday?" she asked, clasping her hands together in her lap.

"Our paths may cross at some point," he answered gruffly. "Whether or not we'll recognize each other is another question. Be happy, Spud."

He started to fade.

"Tyler!" Amy cried. "Don't go!"

Between one instant and the next, however, Tyler disappeared completely.

Amy switched out the lamp and cried herself to sleep, and when Harry called the next morning, her throat was scratchy and she felt as though she hadn't slept in a week. He told her he'd be back the following day, and that he loved her, but that was all Amy could remember of the conversation.

"I saw Tyler again last night," she told Debbie, when the two of them met for pizza and salad at a restaurant near the clinic.

Debbie took the announcement in stride, just as she had before. "Part of the grieving process, I'm sure."

"He was really there!" Amy insisted.

"I believe that you believe that," Debbie replied. "Tyler came to say goodbye, didn't he?"

Amy couldn't deny that. She knew her grudging nod

only confirmed her friend's theory that Tyler was some kind of subconscious manifestation.

"Do you still love him?" Debbie uttered the question subtly, spearing a cherry tomato from her salad bowl while she spoke.

"Tyler?" Amy searched her heart, and found a deep, sweet sadness there. "Not in the same way as before," she confessed, her voice barely audible.

"Separation complete," Debbie said.

"You think I'm crazy."

"I think you're a perfectly normal woman who loved her first husband to distraction. But you're young and you're healthy and now you care for somebody else."

Amy dried her eyes with a wadded napkin and sniffled. "Last night, you weren't quite so blithe about it."

"I was having a personal conflict," Debbie said matter-of-factly, every inch the professional. "You're my best friend, and I don't exactly relish the idea of seeing you move to Australia."

"I told you, it will only be for half the year."

"I'm not used to having to wait six months for a lunch date, Amy," Debbie pointed out. "This is going to create a serious gap in my social life. How do you think the kids will react to the news? And Tyler's parents?"

Amy sighed. "Ashley and Oliver adore Harry," she said. "The Ryans like him, too, of course, but I'm not sure how they're going to feel about being separated from their grandchildren for such long periods."

"They could visit," Debbie said practically.

"So could you," Amy pointed out.

Debbie beamed. "You're right. Will you introduce me to Hugh Jackman?"

"Why not?" Amy teased with a shrug. "I'll probably know everybody in Australia on a first-name basis."

Later, Amy stopped by the supermarket to buy milk, fresh vegetables, cat food and a magazine. When she arrived home, Mrs. Ingallstadt was there, feeding Rumpel.

"My goodness, you scared me!" the old woman said, laying one plump hand to her heart.

Amy smiled. "I'm sorry. I should have called, but I was so tired when I got home yesterday."

"That's all right, dear," Mrs. Ingallstadt said kindly. "You've got a very good cat here, though it seems to me the poor creature is a little on the jumpy side."

Amy had been taking groceries from the canvas shopping bag she always brought to the store with her, but she stopped. Something in Mrs. Ingallstadt's tone had put all her senses on the alert. "Jumpy?"

"Cats are generally unflappable, you know," the neighbor explained. "But every time I came over, she flung herself into my arms and meowed like there was no tomorrow. I could hardly get her to settle down to eat."

If the cat had seen Tyler, that would prove he was real and not a delusion. Wouldn't it?

"Maybe she saw a ghost," Amy said with a nervous giggle.

Mrs. Ingallstadt didn't smile. "I used to see my Walter sometimes—after he was gone, I mean."

Amy no longer made any pretense of being interested in the groceries. "Really? What was he doing?"

The old lady chuckled fondly. "Cleaning out the birdbath in the backyard," she said. "I saw him on and off for about three years, I guess. Then, once I knew I could make my way alone, he stopped paying me visits."

Pulling back a chair, Amy sank into it. "Do you think you really saw Walter, or was it just your imagination?"

"Oh, I think I really saw him," Mrs. Ingallstadt said confidently. "I may be old, but I know when I'm daydreaming. Walter was as real as you are."

Amy wanted to laugh and cry, both at once. Her emotions were so tangled she couldn't begin to sort them out. "Why do you think he came back?" she ventured after a few moments.

Mrs. Ingallstadt smiled. "He was looking after me the only way he could," she said. "Walter always promised he'd stand by me, no matter what." She approached and laid a hand on Amy's shoulder. "Are you all right, dear? You look a little peaky."

Amy couldn't tell her neighbor and friend about seeing Tyler, not then at least. But she was overjoyed to know she wasn't the only one who'd had such an experience.

That night she made herself a salad, ate and went to bed early.

In the middle of the morning, Harry arrived, carrying an enormous bag full of rose petals. He poured the cloud of white softness onto the living-room floor, laid Amy on top of them and made slow, exacting love to her.

While she was caught up in the last, fevered stages of response, he gently squeezed her bottom and spoke to her in low, soothing words.

She was drenched with perspiration when she finally lay still, caressing Harry's strong shoulders while he strained upon her and finally spilled his passion.

"I have a bed, you know," she said much later, when he was lying with his head on her breast. She entangled her finger in an ebony curl as she spoke.

He raised up far enough to look her in the eye. "Tyler's bed," he pointed out.

"Ty would approve of our getting married," Amy said. She was certain of that, since Tyler had told her so himself.

"I know," Harry agreed, caressing her intimately. "But a man's bed is sacred."

Amy gasped as his finger slid inside her. His thumb, meanwhile, was making slow revolutions of its own.

She used the last of her strength to rebel, to bait him. "You mean, if you—died—I couldn't bring my third husband to the tree house?"

Harry bent to nibble at a breast that was still wet from previous forays of his tongue. "Not a chance. I'd haunt you."

Amy's last coherent thought was *It wouldn't be the first time that had happened.*

Hours later, when she and Harry were eating homemade spaghetti in Amy's kitchen, she said boldly, "I want you to stay here tonight."

The swift flatness of Harry's answer surprised her. "No."

"We could sleep in the guest room," Amy said reasonably. She'd been alone for two years, and now that she had someone to share her life again, she didn't want to sleep solo.

Harry shook his head. "Tyler's house," he said.

Amy was frightened, although she couldn't have explained the sensation. "That didn't stop you from making love to me in the middle of the living room," she pointed out in what she hoped was an even voice.

"I was desperate," Harry replied. "We'd been apart."

"I don't believe this!"

"Believe it. I love you, Amy, and I'm convinced Tyler would be happy about our being together. But he was one of my best friends and making love to his widow, under *his* roof, is not my idea of a fitting memorial."

Now Amy understood why she was scared. Harry was going to think of Tyler every time they were intimate, and maybe it would get so it didn't matter where they were at the time.

"Suppose I told you I'd seen Tyler," she burst out, without thinking. "Suppose I said he'd *told* me you and I were going to be married and have two children!"

Harry pushed away his plate. "Then I'd say you weren't through grieving and the last thing you were ready for was a new relationship."

The room seemed to sway around Amy; she gripped the table's edge to steady herself.

"What's going on here?" she demanded. "Are you getting cold feet?"

"If anybody's entitled to ask what's going on, love, I am!" Harry roared, throwing down his napkin and shooting to his feet. "Are you over Tyler or not?"

Amy was stunned. Although she'd seen anger snapping in Harry's blue eyes, she'd never heard him yell before. She'd never even *imagined* him yelling. "Yes, I'm over him," she said in a small, stricken voice.

"But you've seen him?"

Amy wanted to say no, but she couldn't lie. Not to Harry. So she didn't say anything at all.

Harry bent and kissed her angrily on the mouth. Amy didn't know if he was mad at her or himself.

She followed him to the front door and stood on the step, watching him storm down the walk.

"I love you, Harry," she called after him.

"I love you!" he shouted back.

* * *

That weekend, he and Amy went to Vashon Island together, to get the lighthouse ready for occupancy. They washed windows and walls and bathtubs all day Saturday, and made love in front of the fireplace most of the night. On Sunday they chose furniture from the showroom of an exclusive Seattle department store.

Sunday evening, Amy broiled steaks for dinner, and they ate at the picnic table in her backyard.

She wanted to ask Harry to stay, but she didn't because she knew he'd say no. He'd been his old self at the lighthouse, but once they were back in Seattle, he acted as though Tyler were looking over his shoulder.

They indulged in a passionate kiss, there in the backyard, and Harry helped Amy carry the debris from their meal into the house. He rinsed their plates and utensils, and she loaded the dishwasher.

When that was done, Harry said good-night, promised to call the next day and left.

Amy was brewing a cup of decaf when Tyler put in another one of his appearances.

This time he was sitting at the kitchen table, his chin propped in one hand.

Amy set the coffee aside so she wouldn't spill it. "I'm not supposed to be here, actually."

"Then why—?"

"You're pregnant," he said, looking and sounding as pleased as if he'd accomplished the deed himself. "I just thought you might like to know that."

Instinctively, Amy put both hands to her flat stomach. "I can't be pregnant," she said. "I took precautions."

"Precautions don't mean diddly where The Plan is concerned," Tyler replied blithely. "It's a girl. Dark hair, blue eyes. She's going to run Harry's company someday."

Amy felt dizzy. She'd barely come to terms with her feelings for Harry as it was.

"Tyler, I'm imagining you. You're not here and I'm not seeing you!"

"I hope not," observed a third voice.

Amy whirled to find Harry standing in the kitchen doorway. The expression in his eyes was bleak, resigned, and Amy knew he couldn't see Tyler.

"Do something!" Amy ordered Tyler frantically. "Show yourself, make a sound, tip over the table—something!"

"It's no use, Spud," Tyler said with a philosophical sigh. "Nobody can see or hear me but you. And the cat, of course. To show myself to Harry would take so much energy that I'd probably short out or something."

Amy turned to Harry. "He's really here," she cried. "Harry, I swear I'm not having delusions—Tyler is *right here!*"

Harry looked sad. "It's obvious that you're not ready for a new marriage, Amy." He collected his sweater, which he'd left draped over the back of a chair. "I'll call you sometime."

"Harry!"

"Now I know why they told me not to come back," Tyler muttered.

"Oh, shut up!" Amy yelled. She'd finally found happiness, and it was walking out the door.

Harry paused on the front step. "Do you want me to call your doctor or something?" he asked.

Amy bit her lower lip, held back all the fevered denials and angry defenses that rushed into her throat. It was too late now, Harry had heard her talking to someone he couldn't see or hear, and he thought she was in the midst of some emotional crisis.

"I'll be fine," she managed to say.

Harry got into his van, closed the door and drove away.

The next day Ashley and Oliver returned from their trip, bearing gifts from every tacky souvenir shop between Seattle and Topeka, or so it seemed. Amy was delighted to see them; they were, at the moment, her only viable reasons for not going crazy.

"That's a pretty ring," Oliver told her that night, when he'd had his bath and his story, and she was tucking him into bed.

Amy looked at the diamond engagement ring she would have to return and sighed. "It is pretty, isn't it?" she said sadly. "I only borrowed it, though."

"I missed you a whole bunch, Mom," Oliver confided. "A couple of times I even thought I might cry." He whispered the final word, lest it fall on enemy ears. Ashley's, for instance.

Amy kissed her son on the forehead. "I missed you a whole bunch, too, and I *did* cry," she said.

"I know," Oliver replied. "Your eyes are all red and swelly, like they used to be after Dad died."

"I've got some problems," she told the child honestly, "but I'll work them out, so I don't want you to worry, all right?"

"All right," Oliver agreed, closing his eyes and settling into his pillow with a sigh. "'Night, Mom."

Amy went on to Ashley's room. Her daughter was sitting up in bed, busy writing in her diary.

"I guess that trip to Kansas must have been pretty exciting," Amy said gently, standing near Ashley's ruffly, stuffed-animal-mounded bed.

"It was," Ashley beamed, "but I'm glad I'm home. What did you do while we were gone, Mom?"

Amy kissed the little girl's warm cheek. "That's a long story, baby," she answered gently. "But someday I'll tell you all about it."

She switched out Ashley's light and left the room, and in the hallway Amy touched her stomach again, wondering.

If she was about to present Ashley and Oliver with a little sister, as Tyler claimed, she'd be doing that explaining sooner rather than later.

Chapter 8

Amy waited a full week for Harry to reach out and touch someone—namely, her. When he didn't, she tracked him down by calling the Ryans and asking for his office address and telephone number.

After summoning Mrs. Ingallstadt to look after the kids, Amy jumped into her car and set out for downtown Seattle.

Harry's investment firm was housed in one of the swanky, renovated buildings overlooking Elliott Bay. Clutching her courage as tightly as she clutched the handle of her purse, Amy took an elevator to the nineteenth floor.

A pretty receptionist greeted her from behind a tastefully designed desk when she entered the suite, and Amy felt another sting of envy. She was also more than a little nettled by the fact that she'd been going to marry the man and yet had had to call her former in-laws to find out where his office was located.

"I'd like to see Mr. Griffith, please."

The receptionist smiled. "I'll see if he's available. Your name?"

Amy swallowed, feeling at once foolish and belligerent. "Amy Ryan."

An exchange over the intercom followed, though Amy could only hear the receptionist's side.

"Go right in," the girl said, gesturing toward a heavy pair of mahogany doors.

Amy's bravado flagged a little, but she lifted her chin and squared her shoulders and walked boldly into Harry's inner office, closing the door behind her.

Harry sat behind an imposing library table desk, an antique from the looks of it, and he was as handsome as ever. His ebony hair gleamed in the subdued light coming in through elegantly shuttered windows, and he had taken off his coat to reveal a tailored white shirt and a gray silk vest.

"Amy," he said. He hesitated before standing, just long enough to rouse Amy's ire.

Eyes flashing, she stormed over to one of the sumptuous leather chairs facing his desk and sat down, practically flinging her purse to the floor.

"I haven't had a decent night's sleep in a whole week!" she announced.

One corner of Harry's mouth tilted slightly upward, but he didn't exactly smile. Which was a damn good thing, Amy figured, because she was in no mood to be patronized.

"Nor have I," he replied in a husky voice. Sinking back to his chair, he made a steeple with his index fingers and propped them under his chin.

Amy's pride was in tatters, but her temper sustained her. "If you want your ring back," she challenged, "that's just tough. I'm keeping it!"

Harry sighed. "It wouldn't fit me, anyway," he retorted quietly.

Amy rushed on, just as though he hadn't spoken. "And the reason I'm not giving it back is because I still love you," she blurted out, "and I think what we have together is too special to throw away!"

He rose from the chair again to stand at one of the windows, his back to Amy. "To have you for my own and then lose you," he said, "would be a thousand times worse than never having you at all."

She felt the wrench of his words to the very core of her soul, and before she realized what she was doing, she went to him and laid her cheek against his back.

"Harry, what if we visited my friend Debbie—she's a psychologist, and she could reassure you that I'm not crazy—"

He turned and took her shoulders gently in his hands. "I never said you were crazy, love. I said you needed some time to work things through. Having me around would only complicate the process."

Amy couldn't resist; she laid her hands against his smooth-shaven cheeks. "Okay, we don't have to get married next week or next month. But I want you in my life, Harry."

Harry sighed, pulled Amy close and propped his chin on the top of her head. She was practically drunk on the strength and substance and fragrance of him.

"You didn't say you needed me," he pointed out, after an interval of sweet, poignant silence.

Amy laughed, even though there were tears in her eyes. "It's not fashionable for a woman to say she needs a man. I could end up with people picketing in front of my house."

Harry kissed her forehead. "Well, I don't give a damn about fashion or any of that other rot," he said. "I'm perfectly willing to admit it, Amy—I need you, even if it's only to be my friend."

She drew back in his arms, feeling as if he'd given her a kidney punch. "Your—friend?"

He cupped her chin in his hand. "Yes, Amy, your friend. Things got too hot, too fast between us. I should have known better."

Amy swallowed, feeling wretched. She wanted Harry's friendship, of course, but she also desired him as a lover. The idea of never making love in a tree house again, or on a bed of rose petals, was a desolate one. "What do you mean, you should have known better?"

Harry smoothed her hair back from her cheek, and his smile was infinitely sad. "You're still grieving for Tyler, and I guess I am, too. It's impossible to tell whether what we feel for each other is real."

"Harry—"

He traced the outline of her mouth with one index finger. "Shh. We'll be mates, you and I. No need to complicate that with sex and marriage and all that."

Amy's cheeks were warm with color. "Were you trifling with me before?" she demanded.

He chuckled. "*Trifling?* You've been reading too many Victorian novels, Amy." He paused, seeing her ire, and cleared his throat. "It's because I love you," he concluded solemnly, "that I refuse to take further advantage of your emotional state."

She stepped back, because being so close to Harry made her ache in ways that would not be relieved in the foreseeable future. "I guess that's better than nothing," she concluded, speaking more to herself than to Harry. She turned and moved toward the door, as if in a daze.

Amy wondered how she was supposed to feel now. Happy? Sad?

She hadn't lost Harry exactly, but she hadn't really won him back, either. They were going to be *friends*.

Instead of going straight home, Amy drove across the Mercer Island bridge and made her way to her in-laws' gracious Tudor-style house. Louise met her at the door with a joyful hug.

"I'm relieved to see you're still speaking to me!" The older woman laughed. "After I let Ashley and Oliver buy you that awful Kansas ashtray, I thought your affection might cool a little."

They were in Louise's living room, about to have tea in delicate china cups that had belonged to Tyler's great-grandmother, before the older woman's expression turned serious.

"That's a very nice suntan you have," Louise said. "You didn't get that in Seattle."

Amy cleared her throat and looked away for a moment. Tyler was gone and she was an adult, free to do as she chose, but Amy still felt as though she were confessing to adultery. "While you and John and the kids were in Kansas," she finally said, "I went to Australia. With Harry Griffith."

Louise's smile was thoughtful, speculative, but not condemning. "I see."

Suddenly, without warning, Amy began to cry. She snuffled, and when Louise presented her with a box of tissue, blew her nose industriously.

"I take it you're in love with our Harry," Louise said with no little satisfaction. "Well, I think that's wonderful!"

Amy plucked a fresh batch of tissues from the box and blotted her mascara-stained cheeks. "You do?"

"Of course I do," Louise replied, reaching out to pat her daughter-in-law's hand. "You've been alone too long. All the better that it's Harry you've taken up with—for all practical intents and purposes, you'll still be our daughter-in-law."

"He wants to be my friend," Amy informed her gloomily. "He thinks I'm not ready for a new relationship."

"What gave him that idea?" Louise inquired in a calm tone, pouring more tea for herself and Amy.

Amy fidgeted in her chair. "It's—well—I just don't know how to tell you this!"

"How about just opening your mouth and spitting it right out?" Louise prompted matter-of-factly. She'd always been a proponent of the direct approach.

"I've seen Tyler—since he died, I mean. Several times."

To her credit, Louise didn't scream and run. She just drew her beautifully shaped eyebrows together for a moment in an elegant frown, then replied, "Oh, dear. I don't think that's very usual."

Amy shook her head miserably. "No, it isn't. But my neighbor used to see her late husband cleaning the birdbath, and Debbie says I'm not dealing with a ghost at all, but some projection from my deeper mind."

"Hmm," said Louise.

"Anyway," Amy went on, "Harry happened to walk in on one of my conversations with Tyler and now he thinks I haven't adjusted. For a whole week I didn't see Harry, and he didn't call. Now he wants to be—" she began to cry again "—*buddies.*"

"I think things will work out, dear. You and Harry just need a little time, that's all."

"You don't think I'm weird for seeing Tyler?"

Louise smiled sadly and shook her head. "There were times when I thought I caught a glimpse of him myself, just out of the corner of my eye. When you love someone, they leave a lasting imprint on your world."

Amy wanted to tell Louise there might be a baby, a dark-haired, blue-eyed girl who would one day run Harry's empire, but she figured she'd done enough soul baring for one day. Besides, if Tyler was really a figment of her imagination, then the baby was nothing more than wishful thinking.

"You've been a big help," Amy said, gathering up what seemed like a square acre of crumpled tissue and carrying it to the wastebasket.

"Why don't you bring the kids over for dinner tonight?" Louise said eagerly. "I'll be all alone if you don't come."

Assuming her father-in-law was out of town playing golf or overseeing some investment property he and Louise owned in the eastern part of the state, Amy didn't question Louise's statement. "Sure," she said. "Why not?"

"See you at seven," Louise replied, "and dress pretty."

When Amy returned to Mercer Island that evening, wearing her green silk skirt with a lightweight white jacket, she was surprised to find Harry's van parked in the Ryans' driveway.

"Harry's here!" Oliver crowed, bounding out of the car a second after Amy had brought it to a stop.

Ashley was more circumspect, but Amy could see that her daughter was just as pleased.

As for Amy, well, her mother-in-law's final words were echoing in her ears. *Dress pretty.*

"I should have known you were up to something," Amy accused pleasantly, when Louise answered the door. "Did you call him up the minute I agreed to come to dinner?"

After hugging their grandmother, Oliver and Ashley rushed inside in search of Harry.

"As a matter of fact, yes," Louise answered.

When Harry stepped into the entryway, wearing gray slacks and a blue summer sweater, Amy could have sworn the earth backtracked on its axis for a few degrees before plunging forward again.

"Hello, Amy."

She resisted an urge to smooth her hair and her jacket. "Hello," she replied.

"I'll just leave the two of you to chat while I go and put the chicken on the grill," Louise announced busily. A moment later she was gone.

Amy just stood there, as embarrassed as if she'd crashed a private party. Ashley and Oliver appeared behind Harry, anxious for his attention.

Harry held his hands out to his sides, and Ashley and Oliver each took one, on cue. "We're going for a walk down by the water. Want to go along?"

Since her emotions were as raw as an exposed nerve, Amy opted out. "I'll stay here and help Louise with the chicken," she said.

Harry's ink-blue eyes swept over her once, in a way that used to precede a session of lovemaking. "You're not exactly dressed for barbecuing, but I guess that's your choice."

Having made this cryptic pronouncement, Harry turned and walked back through the big house, taking Amy's children with him.

Amy took an alternate route to the big deck overlooking the water and found Louise there, busily brushing her special sauce onto the chicken pieces she'd already arranged on the grill.

The elder Mrs. Ryan looked at her daughter-in-law quizzically. "Didn't you want to join Harry and the children on their walk?"

"I think Ashley and Oliver need to have him to themselves for a little while," Amy answered.

Louise smiled, watching with a wistful expression in her eyes as the three figures moved down the verdant hillside behind the house. "Tyler was a good father," she said. "It's not surprising that his children miss the presence of a man."

"They have their grandfathers and their uncles," Amy pointed out.

"That's not quite the same," Louise said, meeting Amy's eyes, "and we both know it. Children need a man who not only loves them, but loves their mother as well. And Harry loves you passionately."

Amy went to the deck railing, helpless to turn away, and stood watching, listening to her children's laughter on the evening breeze. Watching Harry and shamelessly wanting him.

"Harry's not sure what he feels," Amy mused. "He told me that himself. He thinks we need time."

"Harry may very well not be sure what he feels," Louise replied without hesitation, "but he's wildly in love with you. He might as well have the fact tattooed on his forehead."

Amy smiled at that image, though she felt more like crying. It seemed to her, in her present fragile mood, that love should be simpler than it was. With Tyler, romance had been as natural as breathing, and their relationship had progressed without a hitch.

Finally remembering her original plan to help with the chicken, Amy turned and started toward the grill.

"Stay back," Louise warned, brandishing her barbecue fork. "You're not dressed for this."

The sun was starting to dip behind the horizon when

Harry, Ashley and Oliver climbed the wooden stairs behind the house to join the small party on the deck. Amy's heart started thumping painfully the minute Harry was within a dozen feet of her, and she wondered how on earth she was ever going to stand just being his friend.

Ashley and Oliver chattered nonstop, all through dinner, and Amy was relieved because that saved her from having to make conversation. The moment the meal was over, however, Louise enlisted the kids to help clear away the dishes, leaving Amy and Harry alone at the redwood picnic table Ty and his father had built one long-ago summer.

"I'm sorry," Amy said. She gazed at the city lights and their aura of stars because she still wasn't bold enough to look straight at Harry. "Louise seems to be throwing us together."

Their knees touched under the table, and Harry drew back as if he'd been burned. "She's a matchmaker at heart."

Amy swallowed. She'd made love with this man in a tree house, for heaven's sake, not to mention the bedroom of a fancy jet and on her own living-room floor. For all of that, she felt nervous with him, vulnerable and shy.

"Thank you for paying so much attention to the kids," she choked out. "They miss having a man around."

"It isn't an act of charity, Amy," Harry said quietly. She sensed that he was about to take her hand, but when she looked, he withdrew. "I love kids. I've always wanted a whole houseful of my own."

Amy considered telling him she might be pregnant, but decided against it. Her crazy confessions had gotten her into enough trouble. Besides, as much as she loved Harry, as much as she yearned to share her life with him, she didn't want him to marry her as a point of honor. When Harry became her husband, it had to be by his own choice, not by coercion.

"Let's go in," he said, when the silence grew long and awkward. "It's getting chilly."

"I noticed," Amy replied ruefully, but she wasn't talking about the weather.

For the next month Amy saw Harry only when she went to dinner at her in-laws' house, or when he could be sure Ashley and Oliver would be around to act as chaperons.

Right after Labor Day, school started, and Amy told herself it was time to start concentrating on her real estate deals again. Instead of putting on a power suit and going out to meet with a potential client, however, she jumped into the car and headed for the nearest drugstore the minute the school bus turned the corner.

In the end, though, Amy didn't have the nerve to go into that familiar neighborhood establishment and buy what she needed. She drove on until she found another one, where the proprietors were strangers.

Even then, Amy wore sunglasses and a big hat while making her purchase.

At home again, she tore open the box and rushed into the downstairs bathroom to perform the pregnancy test.

The process took twenty minutes, and the results were positive.

Amy sat on the edge of the bathtub, unable to decide whether she should mourn or celebrate. Her relationship with Harry was clearly over, except for his playing doting uncle to the kids, and nobody knew better than Amy did how hard it was to raise a child alone.

On the other hand, she had wanted another baby for a

long time. In fact, she and Tyler had planned to have at least two more little ones—until fate intervened.

Amy needed desperately to talk to someone. After throwing away the paraphernalia from her test and washing her hands, she wandered out into the living room.

"Tyler?"

Nothing.

Struck by another impulse, Amy brushed her hair, applied fresh lip gloss and snatched up her purse and keys. Within minutes she was on the road again.

When she reached the cemetery where Tyler had been buried, she parked the car and sat behind the wheel for a while, struggling to contain her emotions.

Finally she walked up the hill to Tyler's grave. His grandparents and another Ryan son who'd died in childhood shared the well-maintained plot.

After looking around carefully and seeing nobody but a gardener off in the distance, Amy touched Tyler's marble headstone lovingly, then sat down on a nearby bench.

Five minutes passed, then ten, then fifteen. Amy wiped away a tear with the back of one hand.

"Oh, Ty, what am I going to do? You were right about the baby—I'm pregnant, and Harry's going to know the child is his. He'll insist on doing the honorable thing, and we'll have one of those terrible, grudging marriages—"

A breeze, warm because it was still early in September, ruffled the leaves of the trees and wafted through Amy's hair.

"Tyler, you started all this," Amy went on. "You've got to help me. You've got to tell me what to do."

There was no answer, and yet Amy thought she could sense Tyler's presence. Maybe it was only a silly fancy.

"I'm open to suggestions!" Amy said, spreading her hands wide in a gesture of acceptance.

An older couple stopped to look at her, probably wondering if they should scream for help, then hurried on, hand in hand.

"You're no help at all!" Amy whispered, bending a little closer to the headstone so her voice wouldn't carry. But it did help to sit there, talking to Tyler. Only when she was driving away did Amy realize that she'd said a goodbye of her own, final and complete.

She just wished there were a way to convince Harry that she'd turned the corner, that she was ready to love him with her whole heart. As for her body, well, that was *more* than ready to love Harry.

"Harry's living at the lighthouse now," Tyler's sister, Charlotte, announced that night, when she came to have supper with Amy and the kids.

Amy thought of the child growing within her and ached to share the news, but, much as she dreaded telling Harry, she knew he had to be the first to know.

"Oh?" Amy tried to sound unconcerned as she assembled a salad. "Is he dating anybody?"

Charlotte shook her head. "You're not fooling me with the casual act, Amy. You can hardly keep your hands off the man. What's going on between you two, anyway?"

"I wish I knew," Amy sighed. "He thinks I'm not over Tyler." She gazed out the kitchen window at the lilacs, withered now with the coming of fall, and felt sad because Ty had loved them so much.

Charlotte shrugged. "It's Friday," she said. "Why don't you go out to the lighthouse and talk things over with Harry? I'll stay here and look after the kids."

"I couldn't—"

"Why not?"

"It would be too forward."

Charlotte rolled her eyes. "Amy, you're not in junior high school. And you love this guy, don't you?"

Amy nodded. "I always thought it could only happen once."

"Well, don't blow it," Charlotte hissed happily. "Go! Get out of here!"

"What if he's with someone else?" Amy whispered. "I'd die."

"He won't be," Charlotte replied in a confident tone of voice, "but if you insist on being civilized, call first."

"No," Amy said resolutely. But when Charlotte and the kids were eating, she found she couldn't choke down a bite of the special eggplant dish she'd made.

Finally she went into the den and closed the door.

She didn't have to call information, or Louise, for Harry's new number. It was branded on her mind in steaming digits.

He answered on the third ring, with a gravelly and somewhat impatient "Hello?"

Amy wondered despairingly if she'd pulled him away from a glass of wine, a crackling fire and a willing woman. "Hello," she finally managed to say.

"Amy?" Her name echoed with alarm. "Are you all right? Has something happened to one of the kids?"

She cleared her throat. "No," she said as quickly as possible. "I mean, yes, I'm all right, and no, nothing has happened to Ashley or Oliver. I just...wanted to talk with you."

He was silent, waiting for her to go on, but she couldn't tell whether it was a receptive silence or an impatient, angry one.

"Do you think I could come out there? There's a ferry in half an hour, and I can catch it if I hurry."

It was agony, waiting for his answer. "All right," he finally said, and again, his tone betrayed none of his emotions.

Amy dropped her toothbrush into her purse, grabbed her coat and gave Charlotte the okay sign from the dining-room doorway.

After saying good-bye to Ashley and Oliver, carefully avoiding any explanation of her destination the whole while, Amy rushed out to her car.

She made the ferry with only seconds to spare.

Finding the lighthouse, once she reached the island, was easy. The structure's giant electric lamp was shining in the darkness, guiding her.

When she pulled up in front of Harry's spectacular house, he came out to meet her, his blue eyes searching her face worriedly in the glow from above. He took her arm and shuffled her inside and across a glistening hard-wood floor to the fireplace.

"What's this about?" Harry asked. "Are you all right?"

Amy could no longer carry the burden alone, and besides, her secret was going to be obvious enough in the months to come. She needed to tell Debbie and Louise and Charlotte, in order to enlist their support, and she couldn't do that until Harry knew.

"I'm going to have a baby," she said bluntly.

Harry's mouth dropped open. "I thought…?"

"That I was protected? So did I. But sometimes babies just decide they're going to be born, no matter what."

His hands closed on her shoulders, firmly but with a gentleness that touched her heart. He pressed her into the big leather chair they'd picked out together, that happy day before things had fallen apart.

"I'm not sick, Harry," Amy pointed out practically. "Just pregnant."

"When?" He croaked the word, paused to clear his throat, and started again. "When will the little nipper be joining us?"

"In the spring," Amy answered, wishing there truly could be an *us*.

Harry was completely beside himself. He paced and ran one hand through his usually impeccable hair, and Amy would have laughed if the situation hadn't had such a serious side.

She knew she was about to get everything she wanted, for all the wrong reasons. And those reasons might well poison her relationship with this man forever. He'd soon view her the same way he'd seen Madeline—as a manipulator and a schemer.

"We'll have to be married right away," he said.

"No," Amy replied. "We can't get married."

Harry was quietly outraged. "Then what the hell are we going to do? You're not going to bring *my* child into this world with no claim to his rightful name! And don't suggest living together, because that wouldn't be good for Ashley and Oliver."

"I wasn't going to suggest living together," Amy said. "I think we should just go on as we have been." *Even though it's torture,* she thought, *that's better than it would be to look into your eyes and see contempt, or boredom, or God help us both, hatred.*

He took her hand, pulled her easily to her feet. "I think I know how to convince you," he said. And then he slanted his mouth over hers for a commanding kiss, and Amy thought she'd faint with excitement and relief.

Chapter 9

The fact that he knew better didn't keep Harry from making love to Amy. Nor did the realization that she was carrying his child; *that* only made her more attractive.

No, Harry could no more have turned away from her than a starving man could resist hot cornbread dripping with butter.

They didn't even get as far as the bed, but instead sank to the Persian rug on the hearth. Their clothes melted away and their tongues mated and then, suddenly, their bodies were engaged in the ancient struggle, twisting and writhing and colliding with sweet, fevered violence.

Arched beneath him, Amy threw her head back and gave a long, guttural cry. Tendrils of her hair clung to the moisture on her forehead and cheeks, and her eyes stared sightlessly past him, past the ceiling and the night sky.

Harry's own climax was fast approaching when he saw surprise in her features, felt her sated body come alive once more under his hips, heard her murmur with joyous desperation, "Oh, God, Harry, it's going to happen—again!"

Harry drove deep inside her, and she came apart in his arms, chattering senselessly, enfolding him in her strong, slender legs. A sound that was half sob and half shout of triumph tore itself from Harry's throat, and he stiffened upon Amy, surrendering what she demanded of him.

For several long moments, his body spasmed violently in response to her gentle conquering. Then he collapsed beside her on the rug in front of his fireplace.

"We'll be married as soon as we can get the license," he said a long time later, when he had regained enough strength to speak.

She shook her head, which had been resting placidly on his shoulder until that moment.

"No, Harry, we won't. I don't want it to be like this."

Harry swallowed a growl of frustration; this was no time to be macho. He was proud of the fact that he spoke so calmly. "Tell me what you want, Amy, and I'll give it to you."

She raised herself on one elbow, and the firelight bathed her satiny, naked flesh, making Harry want her all over again. "I want you to want me, for *me*. Not because I'm carrying your baby, not because you feel obliged to look after your good friend's widow, but because you're absolutely wild about me."

He raised her fingers to his lips and kissed the knuckles lightly, one by one. "I thought I just proved that."

"You just proved that you wanted *a woman*, Harry. I refuse to buy the delusion that someone else couldn't have satisfied you just as completely."

Harry sighed. God, but women were a frustrating lot, always attacking a man's pure logic with their reasonable implausibilities. The bloke who figured out what in the hell they really wanted would make millions.

"I love you," he said. "You know that."

She laid her head on his chest again and started making circular motions on his belly with one hand. If she kept that up, he'd be out of his mind in about five seconds. "I know we have good chemistry," she argued sweetly. "I also know that you were perfectly willing to end everything between us until you found out about the baby."

With another sigh, Harry shoved splayed fingers through his hair. "All right, rose petal, jump to whatever conclusions that might look comfortable. But add this to the list of things you know—I have rights where this child is concerned and I *will not* sacrifice them."

He felt her shiver in his arms, but when she executed her special vengeance, her hand was damnably strong and steady.

"Oh, God," he rasped, closing his eyes.

Amy was kissing her way down over his chest, his rib cage, his midriff. "Even prayer won't help you now, Harry Griffith." She purred the words, but not as a kitten would. Oh, no. This was a lioness.

Harry gave a strangled gasp of pleasure when she claimed him.

The next morning, Amy awakened in Harry's bed. She'd spent the night in heaven, but now, as she sat there alone, she returned to earth with a painful thump. Nothing had really been resolved, nothing had changed.

She sat bolt upright and looked wildly around for her clothes.

With perfect timing, Harry entered the room, carrying a tray with a coffee cup, a covered plate and a news-paper on it.

"Where are my things?" Amy demanded, embarrassed to remember how she'd behaved the night before. Merciful heavens, this man could turn her into a harlot with a touch or a single kiss.

He grinned, setting the tray across her lap. "What clothes?" he asked innocently.

"The ones I was wearing last night, when I arrived," Amy answered tightly. She wanted to spurn the food he'd brought, but she'd had a world-class workout and she was hungry. She lifted the lid from the covered plate and nibbled at a piece of fresh pineapple.

"Oh," Harry replied, in a tone of great revelation, standing back from the side of the bed, "you're speaking of the garments you tore off, in your eagerness to surrender yourself to me in front of the fireplace last night." He paused, rubbing his chin. "I'm afraid I burned them."

Amy's fork clattered to the tray. *"You burned them?"*

Harry nodded. "Essentially, rose petal, you're a prisoner of love. Unless you want to make the trip back to Seattle in the altogether, of course."

She narrowed her eyes. "You're making this up!"

"See for yourself," Harry said, gesturing toward the door leading to the living room. "Of course, I feel honor bound to tell you that you'll be taking a big chance, just walking past me. There's something about impending fatherhood that makes me—well—eager."

Color flooded Amy's face, but it was a blush of chagrin and not anger. She'd just realized that she didn't mind the prospect of being Harry's toy for a while, and that insight embarrassed her greatly.

"What are the conditions for my release?" she asked after sitting there for a long time, staring at Harry like a fool.

He raised an index finger. "Oh, there is only one. You'll have to become my wife."

Amy closed her eyes, took a deep breath and let it out again. With that she was calm. She wouldn't scream and yell.

She opened her eyes and her mouth at the same time, and when she did she found that Harry was gone.

Furiously Amy stuffed down the rest of her breakfast. Then, wrapping herself in the bedspread, she got up and started going through Harry's bureau drawers.

She put on a pair of his briefs in place of underpants, but he didn't have anything that could be adapted to serve as a bra. After adding tailored wool slacks, a cinched belt, a striped, button-down shirt, socks and a pair of loafers that flippity-flopped when she walked, Amy stormed defiantly into the living room.

"I'm leaving," she said.

A corner of Harry's mouth quivered, but he didn't laugh. He didn't even smile. He closed the book he'd been reading and rose from his chair. "How? I've hidden your car, not to mention your purse, and if you try to walk to the ferry terminal in my clothes, the police will probably pick you up and haul you off to some shelter."

Amy stomped one foot. "Harry, this isn't funny."

His blue eyes swept over her. "That's your opinion, rose petal. I think it's hilarious." Another sweep of his eyes left her feeling weak. "Come here," he said.

Although reason and pride dictated that she must stand her ground, instinct prevailed. Amy stepped out of the loafers and walked slowly across the room to Harry.

Methodically, he untucked the shirt she'd borrowed, then

unfastened the belt buckle. The slacks fell straight to the floor, and Harry chuckled when he saw the briefs beneath.

Reaching smoothly, boldly inside the flap, he cupped her femininity in his hand, making a circular motion with his palm.

"Harry," she whimpered, helpless to twist away from him because he'd already made her need what he was doing to her.

"Open the shirt, Amy," he said. "I want to see your breasts."

She obeyed him, moving slowly and deliberately, like some creature under a spell. All the defiance she could come up with was "You can't make love to me in the living room in broad daylight, Harry."

"Watch me," he replied. Then, still caressing her, he plunged one finger deep inside her and, at the same moment, bent to take one of her nipples greedily into his mouth.

He brought her to the very edge of release, made her coast back to earth just short of satisfaction, then carried her high again.

Finally, sitting in his leather wingback chair, he positioned Amy on his lap, facing him, her knees draped over the arms. She was transfixed when he took her, letting out a long, low, primitive cry of pure animal pleasure.

His hands gripping the quivering flesh of her hips, Harry rocked Amy back and forth until she was literally out of her mind with passion. He sucked her breasts, first one and then the other, while she shivered again and again and again.

Finally Harry climaxed, too, and she was allowed to sag forward against him, her forehead propped on his shoulder.

"You didn't really burn my clothes," she managed, after some time.

"Oh, yes I did," he replied. "Marry me."

Amy trembled, still filled with him, her legs still balanced over the arms of the chair. "No."

He took her to the master bath, bathed her languid body thoroughly in the big marble tub, then, in his room, placed her atop a bureau and had her again.

If Amy had told Harry she didn't want to make love, he would have respected her wishes and left her alone. The trouble was, he was very good at arousing her, and by the time he'd gone through all the steps, she was more than ready to cooperate.

Her responses this time were just as wild, just as violent, as before. Harry had opened some well of need inside her, some region of surrender that had never been reached before.

"Marry me," he said intractably, kissing her shoulder blades, when she finally stopped howling in raucous appeasement.

"Absolutely not," Amy gasped with the last of her defiance.

Harry began to massage her bottom with both hands, although he did not withdraw from her depths because he had somehow stopped himself on the brink of satisfaction and he was still hard inside her.

Slowly, rhythmically, he began to move—in, out, in, out.

Amy groaned and clutched the edges of the bureau. "Oh, no," she whimpered, feeling the treacherous pressure begin to build inside her. "Oh, Harry, don't make me—"

He did make her, though.

More than once.

"Harry," she said, much later, huddled in his bed again, with the covers pulled to her chin, "I have children. I must get back to them."

"Louise and Charlotte are looking after the nippers," Harry replied. Fresh from the shower, he was wearing a dark blue terry robe with a hood, and his dark hair, only partially dry, was combed.

"What did you tell Louise?" Amy wanted to know.

"That I've made you my love slave and she shouldn't look for you to return to the city anytime soon," Harry replied, turning to stand in front of the dresser mirror.

"You didn't!" Amy cried in mortified disbelief, her cheeks hot with humiliation.

"Sure I did," Harry answered. "But don't look for the sheriff to come and save you, rose petal. Louise thought being a plaything might do you some good."

Amy snatched up a pillow and flung it at him, missing by a wide margin. "She did not. Louise is a very modern woman. She would never approve of this!"

Harry picked up the pillow and hurled it back with deadly accuracy. "She also comes from a generation where women married the men who made them pregnant. She thinks I should keep you here until I've made you see reason."

Amy swallowed, no longer sure what to believe. It was no small irritation to her pride that she secretly loved this game Harry was playing with her, and even though she was exhausted, she could hardly wait to see where he would make love to her next.

"You're a bastard, Harry Griffith," she sulked.

"And you're a hot little number who needs to be taken on a regular basis."

Again, it was the truth in Harry's statement that made Amy so angry.

"I hate you!" she yelled.

"Mmm-hmm," he answered distractedly. "It's going to

be a man-sized job keeping you properly pleasured. Of course, I'm—" he paused, cleared his throat "—up to the task."

Amy screamed in frustration. "Damn you, Harry, get me some clothes and take me home, right now!"

He wrapped her in a heavy bathrobe of navy velvet and led her out to the living room, where he settled her in a chair by the hearth, then built up the fire. He brought her food, fruit and bread, and a snifter of brandy, and for a while she thought Harry was beginning to see reason.

Instead, he was resting up for another round.

Once she'd eaten, he took her back to bed and made love to her again.

"Will you marry me?" Harry inquired implacably, when she was dangling from the edge of ecstatic madness.

"Yes!" Amy cried. "Oh, Harry—oh, God—*yes!*"

Her reward left her drenched with perspiration and weak from her own straining efforts.

Harry finished what he'd begun, and after a long time, he got up and found oil to rub into every inch of her skin. Finally, then, he allowed her to sleep.

The next day a judge arrived with a special license, and Louise, John and Charlotte appeared with the children. Louise had brought along a flowered sundress for Amy to wear, along with casual clothes, nightgowns and underwear for later.

"You're sure you're okay with this?" Amy asked her children, when the three of them were alone in one of Harry's guest rooms. She hadn't told them, of course, how Harry had burned her clothes and made love to her repeatedly. "You really want a stepfather?"

"We really want *Harry,*" Ashley clarified.

"We're going to live in Australia, on an island!" Oliver crowed, hardly able to contain his enthusiasm at this good fortune. "Wow!"

Amy was looking forward to becoming Harry's wife, but she was also reluctant. She couldn't get past the idea that none of this would be happening if she hadn't told Harry she was expecting his baby.

The wedding was to be held in Harry's living room, that evening, by the light of a hundred candles. All the rest of Tyler's family came over for the occasion, and since Amy's father couldn't take enough time off from being a world-renowned surgeon to make the trip, John Ryan gave away the bride.

Oliver was to be the best man, Ashley the maid of honor.

Amy went to the master bedroom to be alone and gather her thoughts before the ceremony, and what she found there practically stopped her heart in midbeat.

In the middle of the bed, fragrant and lacy and totally impossible, lay an armload of white lilacs.

Mentally Amy searched the lighthouse grounds, and she found no lilacs. They couldn't have come from the mainland, either, because there had been a hard freeze the last week in August and all the flowers were gone.

Slowly, her eyes filling with happy tears, Amy approached the bed and lifted one of the lovely fronds into her hands. She was drawing in its unforgettable scent when she heard the door open.

Harry was standing there.

"Did you have these shipped in from somewhere?" she asked, knowing the answer before he spoke. Harry had sent for caviar and champagne, but his contribution to the ceremony was a massive bouquet of pink roses, already in full bloom. Amy knew their petals would become her marriage bed and, for all the time she'd spent exploding in Harry's arms, she was ready to give herself again.

"No," Harry answered, coming to her side and taking up one of the boughs with a frown. "I thought these were gone for the year."

Someday, Amy thought, she would tell him that white lilacs had been special to her and Tyler. Someday, she would say that Tyler had found a way to offer his blessing on their marriage, but now wasn't the time for explanations and Amy knew it.

She made a wreath of the lush lilacs for her hair, and when it came time for the ceremony, she drew a deep breath, said a prayer and went out to be married. Somehow, she would find a way to make Harry love her, truly love her, for real.

In the meantime, she would take whatever happiness she could find, wherever she found it.

The Ryans took Ashley and Oliver back to Seattle after the wedding, and Harry drove Amy to the jet. When the plane was high in the air, bound for some mysterious honeymoon destination, he left the pilot to handle the controls and joined Amy in the main cabin.

"You are beautiful, Mrs. Griffith," he said in a hoarse voice, taking off his suit jacket and draping it casually over the back of one of the seats. As he loosened his tie, he went on. "If you would be so good as to go into our bedroom and take off your clothes, please."

Amy could hear her own heartbeat, thundering as loudly as the jet's engines. "You're incredible," she said.

He smiled easily. "Thank you," he said, with a slight bow of his head.

Amy went to the master suite as she'd been bidden. The bed was mounded with pink rose petals, just as she'd expected, and there was a bottle of sparkling cider on the nightstand, cooling in a silver bucket.

"I thought champagne might be bad for the baby," Harry said from the doorway.

Amy was touched, but she wished she could matter to Harry as much as this child she was carrying. "Where are we going?"

Harry closed the door and kicked off his shoes. "I'm taking you to the morning star and back again," he said.

She couldn't believe it, not after the marathon they'd already put in. "I meant, for our honeymoon," she retorted dryly.

"Wait and see," he answered.

Soon rose petals were drifting down off the edges of the bed like pink rain, and Amy had made more than one trip to the morning star before the plane touched down.

She looked out and saw an isolated airstrip, a lot of desert and cactus and a proud hacienda of white stucco.

"Mexico?" she asked, kneeling on the bed and peering through the porthole.

"Yes," Harry answered, pulling her back down beside him.

Later, they went into the house, which was clean, well furnished and vacant. The pilot refueled the jet, went through a flight check and took off again.

"Is this your place?" Amy inquired, amazed. There was a pool out back, filled with inviting crystal-clear water, and the main bedroom had air-conditioning, a terrace and its own hot tub.

Harry smiled. "Belongs to a friend," he answered, setting their suitcases down at the foot of the massive bed. "Not a bad place to be a prisoner of love, is it?"

Amy blushed furiously at the reminder. "I gave in to

your demands," she pointed out. "By all rights, I should no longer be classified as a captive."

"You may get a reprieve someday," Harry responded easily. "Time off for good behavior and all that. Louise is going to interview governesses for the kids so we can leave for the island soon."

Amy sat down on the bed. "You certainly are anxious to get back to Australia," she said, worried.

Harry stood near enough to touch the tip of her nose with an index finger. "Never fear, rose petal," he began. "I'm not planning to dump you and the nippers there and then go off and chase women. I want my baby to have the best possible start in life, and a calm, peaceful environment for its mother seems like a good beginning."

No protests came to mind. The kids, who would have been her best excuse for staying in Seattle, were eager to visit the island. Harry had promised them each a pony, and Tyler's folks were already making plans to visit.

The honeymoon lasted a week, though afterward those delicious days and nights ran together in Amy's mind, indiscernible from each other. She and Harry swam and made love, talked and made love, ate and made love, played tennis and made love.

Then they went back to Seattle, where Amy put her house on the market, said good-bye to her friends and family, packed summer things for herself and the children, put Rumpel into Mrs. Ingallstadt's loving care, and did her best to absorb the fact that her life had changed forever.

It wouldn't have been accurate to say she was unhappy—she was married to a man she loved desperately and was expecting his child—but there was an undercurrent of suspense. Harry was doing what he saw as his duty, and it didn't matter that he did such a damn good job at pretending to like it.

Amy's happiness was underlaid with a sense of urgency, of barely controlled anxiety.

The children thrived on the long, often-interrupted journey from Seattle to Australia. Both of them took their turns at the plane's controls, and when they stopped in Hawaii for a day, they explored their surroundings with energetic delight. The same thing happened in Fiji and Auckland, New Zealand and finally Sydney.

Once again, there was no problem with Customs. Ashley and Oliver were permitted into the country on the strength of Amy's passport and, she suspected, because Harry Griffith was their stepfather.

Returning to Harry's private isle, which Oliver promptly renamed Treasure Island, was like having the gates of Eden swing open again. It was a second chance.

The governess Louise had selected, a pretty brown-haired girl who had been doing graduate work at the University of Washington, was waiting when they arrived, as were Elsa and Shelt O'Donnell. Evidently, Amy thought testily, the nanny had taken a direct flight.

Although Amy's pregnancy was in its early stages, it had already begun to take its toll. She was exhausted from the trip to Australia, even though Harry had taken every opportunity to let her rest.

She hadn't been able to sleep on the plane, though she'd tried. Instead, she'd mindlessly read one book after another, and five seconds after she'd closed the last cover, she'd forgotten what the story was about. When she wasn't reading, she was in one of the swanky bathrooms, being violently sick.

Amy concluded that she just wasn't cut out to be a jet-setter.

When they finally reached their destination, she slept for two days straight, waking up only to eat and bathe and go to the bathroom, and although he was in bed beside her at regular intervals, Harry didn't once make love to her. She supposed the inevitable withdrawal had already begun, and for the first time in her life she was irrationally jealous of another woman.

Mary Anne, the governess, to be precise.

"You're just saying Louise hired her," Amy said pouting one night, when she and Harry were sitting on the terrace outside their room. The children were asleep and the sky was scattered with gaudy stars that were bigger and brighter than they had any business being. "You probably hand-picked Mary Anne yourself, because of her great body."

Harry bent over her chair, gripping the arms, his nose less than an inch from Amy's. "You're very fortunate that you're pregnant, rose petal," he said. "If you weren't, I'd turn you over my knee, bare your backside and paddle you soundly for saying that."

Amy stuck out her lip. "You wouldn't dare. Modern American men don't do such things."

"Maybe they don't," Harry replied softly, "but I'm not an American and I'm not especially modern, either. It would behoove you to remember that."

A tear slipped down Amy's cheek. "She's so pretty."

With a warm chuckle, Harry gathered Amy up, sat down in the chair she'd occupied before, and cradled her on his lap. "If I didn't know better, Amy-girl," he said soothingly, holding her close, "I'd think Tyler did you wrong. What on earth gives you the idea that I'm constantly on the prowl for other women?"

"You wouldn't really spank a grown woman," Amy said, ignoring his question. But she laid her head against his shoulder, feeling fat and frumpy and very worried.

"Don't test the theory," Harry warned. "Australian men are still a generation or two behind the times, love. I would never get myself into a drunken rage and beat you or anything like that, but a few smart swats on the bottom never hurt."

"That depends on whose bottom it is," Amy reasoned. She had an unsettling feeling that Harry was totally serious.

Harry laughed and kissed her soundly on the forehead. "I will never, ever, be unfaithful," he promised in a sincere tone of voice a few moments later. "So stop worrying."

"What about when I'm fat and cranky and I'm retaining water?"

"You're cranky now, love, and no doubt you're retaining water, too." He opened her robe, baring one of her breasts to the attentions of an idle index finger. "And all I can think about is taking you to my bed and having you, thoroughly and well."

A delicious shudder ran through Amy, and when Harry bent to take her nipple between his lips and tease it mercilessly, she gasped.

Both her breasts were wet, their peaks hard and tingling, when Harry carried his bride inside and arranged her gently on his bed.

He laid aside her robe, like the wrapping on a gift, and never took his eyes from her as he stripped away his clothes.

He made her body tell all its secrets over the course of that magical night, and he had Amy so thoroughly and so well that, a couple of times, she thought she glimpsed the far side of forever.

Chapter 10

The following week Harry left the island on business for the first time. Late that afternoon a tropical rainstorm blew in, hammering at the roof and tapping at the panes and making Ashley and Oliver rush, giggling with nervous excitement, from one window to another.

"Do you think it's a hurricane?" Amy asked Mary Anne, who was reading a book next to the fireplace. Amy had already come to terms with the fact that her children's teacher was a good person, not likely to engage in frolics with the master of the house, and the two women were becoming friends.

Mary Anne smiled. "Just a regular spring storm," she said.

It still seemed weird to Amy that mid-October could qualify as spring, but in Australia it did. "It doesn't appear to be bothering the kids."

Mary Anne closed her book, the pleasant expression lingering on her pretty face. "Kids are born adventurers," she agreed. "Is there anything I could get you, Mrs. Griffith? Some tea, maybe, or a glass of lemonade?"

Amy shook her head, feeling guilty for all the uncharitable thoughts she'd once harbored for this bright, intelligent young woman. "Thanks, no. I'm all right."

But she wasn't, and Mary Anne seemed to know that as well as Amy did. Amy was imagining Harry in cosmopolitan Sydney, dressed in one of his tuxedos, surrounded by sexy blondes, brunettes and redheads at some swanky party.

The next day, however, the storm blew out and Harry blew in. He brought fancy saddles for the kids, whose promised ponies had been waiting in the stable on their arrival, and for Amy there was a sketch pad and the biggest selection of colored chalk she'd ever seen.

She began to sketch the fabulous birds roosting in the trees just outside her walls. Startled at her own ability, Amy progressed to drawing images of Shelt and Elsa and Harry and the kids. When Ashley and Oliver were busy studying and Harry was either away or working, Amy's new interest in art positively consumed her.

Harry brought oil paints and canvases when he returned, and so many art books that Shelt had to make two trips to the landing strip to pick them all up.

In November, Amy and Harry went to Sydney on their own to take in a concert, have elegant dinners in gracious restaurants and do some preliminary shopping for the holidays. Amy visited her doctor, who pronounced her in good health, and she and Harry made love all of one afternoon and half the night.

When they returned to the island, Amy felt restored and renewed.

In early December they flew back to Sydney, this time taking Mary Anne and the kids with them. Although it was the height of summer, it was also Christmastime, and the clean, beautiful city was decorated for the holidays.

Harry and Amy took the kids and their governess to see *The Nutcracker* at one of the city's better theaters, then everyone shopped. Mary Anne sent presents to her family via airmail, and when they returned home, there were boxes galore awaiting them at the mainland post office.

They decorated a towering artificial tree, even though the sun was dazzlingly bright on the water. It seemed to Amy that there were presents hidden everywhere, and Ashley and Oliver were having the time of their lives.

Amy couldn't quite trust Harry's commitment—every time he left the island, she was on pins and needles until he returned. She had progressed by that point to making her own exquisite gift wrap, though, complete with hand-painted angels and other heralds of Christmas, and she did her level best to keep busy.

"Happy, love?" Harry asked, late Christmas Eve, when they'd filled the kids' stockings and played Santa.

Her emotions were complex and very confusing, and she supposed a lot of them could be ascribed to her pregnancy. For all of that, Amy was insecure as she had never been insecure before. Despite her art and her beautiful children and the much-wanted baby tucked away between her heart and her soul, Amy felt cut off from Harry. It seemed to her that the only time they were really close was when they were in the throes of lovemaking, unable to speak coherent words, flinging themselves at each other as if in battle.

Not being able to put her condition into words, Amy started to cry instead.

Harry put an arm around her and drew her close beside him in bed, one hand resting in a proprietary way on her rounded stomach. "There now, love," he said, his lips moving against her temple. "Your hormones are in a bit of a muddle, but it'll all come right in the end. You'll see."

Tell me you love me, Amy thought. "That's easy for you to say, Harry," she said aloud. "You're not pregnant."

"Darn good thing, too," he confirmed good-naturedly, "or we'd get nothing done for fending off photographers from all the tacky tabloids."

Amy laughed in spite of herself. "If I were you, I'd hate me," she said.

Harry rolled over to look deeply into her troubled eyes before he kissed her. "Hate you?" he countered hoarsely, after he'd left Amy dizzy from the intimacy of their contact. "Never."

Normally he would have made love to Amy then. Instead, he just cuddled her close, sighed contentedly and went to sleep.

The next day was a noisy riot of rumpled gift paper, food, presents and laughter.

On New Year's, Elsa and Mary Anne took the Christmas tree down and put it away, and Amy got out her oils and canvas and started to paint.

Harry took Amy to Sydney for another doctor's appointment at the end of the month and again in February.

The first week in March, just as winter was getting off to a fine Australian start, Amy went into labor.

This time she didn't go to the doctor, he came to her on board Harry's jet, bringing a nurse and an anesthesiologist with him.

Sara Tyler Griffith was born in her parents' bedroom, with a tropical storm threatening to make the seas run over onto the land. She was a lovely child, with the blue eyes all babies have, and a rich shock of dark, dark hair. Just as Ty had predicted.

Harry held his daughter, his beautiful eyes glistening with wondrous tears, while the doctor and nurse saw to Amy's care.

Amy looked at her husband and this innocent, trusting child, and couldn't help being happy, at least for the moment. She had practically everything she'd ever wanted, and so what if there were slight imperfections in the fabric of her life? So what if Harry didn't truly love her and she still wondered what he did when he was away from home? Nobody had everything.

A day later, when her milk came in, Amy nursed Sara, stroking her tiny, doll-like head, and told her, "You'll be more your daddy's girl than mine, I think, but I guess I can live with that." She smiled. "Just between you and me, Sara Griffith, you'll be running the family business someday. I have that on good authority."

There was a timid knock at the door, and Ashley and Oliver trailed in, drawn to their sister and at the same time wondering how her presence would affect their places in the scheme of things.

"I'm going to need lots and lots of help from the two of you," Amy told her older children solemnly. "Raising a baby is a very hard job, even if it is fun most of the time, and I'm counting on you."

"What about Harry? Is he going to help?" Ashley asked reasonably.

The words stung. Harry adored the baby, although he seemed to hold just as high an affection for Ashley and Oliver, but he'd already started drawing away from Amy. He slept in one of the guest rooms, and when he paid a visit, it was always to see his daughter, not his wife. Soon he was traveling as much as ever, and when Sara was two and a half months old, Amy's unhappiness rose to tremendous proportions.

It was time, she decided when Harry called from Brisbane to say he'd be staying over a few days longer on business, for a confrontation.

Boldly Amy called the mainland and ordered a helicopter, since Harry had taken the jet. She kissed Ashley and Oliver goodbye and, carrying Sara while Shelt hauled the heavy diaper bag, she boarded the whirlybird and was soon on her way.

The pilot obligingly landed the copter on the roof of Harry's hotel, and not one but two bellhops were waiting to carry baggage.

"I'd like you to deliver our things to Room 373," Amy said to one of the young men, feeling more and more nervous as the elevator swept from the roof to the third floor. What was she doing?

If she caught Harry with another woman, she was going to be devastated. And if she didn't, he would be furious with her for not trusting him.

She bit her lower lip, holding Sara a little too tightly, when one of the bellhops knocked at the door of Harry's suite.

There was no answer, so the gentleman opened the door himself, using a special key, and escorted Amy inside.

Harry's clothes were hanging in the closet, but only Harry's clothes, and the dresser drawers contained his things alone. The scent of his cologne lingered in the air, but there was no tinge of perfume.

By that time Amy was beginning to feel really foolish. "I need to join one of those self-help groups for clingy women," she muttered to herself after the bellhops had taken their tips and left. She wanted to flee, to pretend she'd never done this stupid, suspicious, sneaky thing, but Sara was hungry and Amy herself was tired to the core of her spirit.

She lay down on the bed to nurse Sara, and she was lying there, half-asleep herself, when the door opened and Harry came in. Amy felt a pang when she saw the realization that she didn't trust him register in his wonderful indigo eyes.

"Well, Amy," he said, extending his arms from his sides in a gesture of furious resignation, "have you looked under the bed and checked the medicine cabinet for lipstick?"

Tears welled in her eyes. "I'm sorry," she said.

Harry bent to kiss his sleeping daughter's downy head, then took the infant and laid her gently in her portable crib. He had no kiss for Amy, however, only quiet, well-controlled outrage.

"What a pity you didn't come here because you wanted to be with me," he said bitterly. "Damn! I suppose you'll be hiring a private investigator next and having me followed!"

Amy sat up, trying to close her blouse, but Harry held her hands away, kneeling astraddle of her hips on the bed. He stared at her breasts for a long time, then, with a helpless groan, fell to her.

Because he hadn't touched her in so long, Amy was instantly on fire. And the anger pulsing in the room only made the interval more exciting.

Harry enjoyed one nipple, then the other, until he had Amy tossing helplessly on the bed. Then, with no more foreplay than that, he lifted Amy's cotton skirt and took her in one powerful stroke.

Amy gripped the underside of the headboard in both hands and held on, her back arched so high that only her head, shoulders, and heels were touching the bed. Her release began as Harry delved into her, and she went wild when he grasped her hips and bid her take him deeper and deeper.

Finally, with a burst of rasped swearwords and an involuntary buckling of his body, Harry reached his climax.

Amy had been as thoroughly satisfied as he had, if not more so, and that was what made her next words so hard to say. "I'm leaving, Harry. I'm going back to the States."

Her husband was quiet for so long that Amy feared he hadn't heard her. On another level, she *hoped* he hadn't, so that she could back down, pretend she'd never voiced the decision.

Then, still inside her, he raised himself on his palms and glowered as he searched her eyes. *"What?"*

She tried to squirm out from under him, but he'd pinned her, and there was no going anywhere until he set her free.

"You were right before," she said with breathless misery. "We're not ready for marriage, either of us. You're angry and frustrated all the time, and I'm turning into a shrew. So I want to go home."

He searched her eyes with angry blue ones for a long, long moment. "You'll damn well leave Sara here if you do."

Amy shook her head. "I'll never walk away from my baby, Harry," she vowed.

Harry flung himself onto his back and glared up at the ceiling, his breathing ragged, his scowl black as clouds before a tropical storm. "Damn it all, woman, you would drive a saint to drink!"

"You're going to let us go?"

He turned to meet her eyes. "Not in a million years, love," he said, his voice totally void of all traces of affection, "but I will take you back to the lighthouse. Maybe a miracle will happen and you'll be the woman I married again."

His words hurt Amy almost as much as finding him in the middle of a romantic tryst would have. She turned onto her side and cried silently, her heart breaking as she listened to the roar of the shower, the familiar, once comforting sounds of a man dressing, the crisp closing of the door.

Sara, blissfully unaware that her parents were at war, slept undisturbed in her little bed.

Within the week, the family was back in the States and, a few days after their return, they were settled in the lighthouse. Ashley and Oliver were immediately enrolled in elementary school, and Mary Anne went back to her studies at the university. Harry spent all day, every day, in the city, throwing himself into his work, and sent a steady stream of aspiring housekeepers for Amy to interview.

She finally selected an English grandmother type, Mrs. Hobbs, because the woman reminded her of Mrs. Ingallstadt. If nothing else, it was a relief not to have to review résumés and ask questions anymore.

"Main problem with you, mistress," Mrs. Hobbs announced one afternoon, when Amy was curled up in Harry's big leather chair, Sara nearly asleep at her breast, "is that you're tired. Begging your pardon, ma'am, but you've got dark circles under your eyes and every time I look at you, I want to cry because you seem so sad."

Amy gently lowered her daughter, put her bra in place and closed her blouse.

"I have everything," she confided forlornly. "It's shameful for me to feel so discontented."

"Maybe you should see your doctor," the gray-haired woman ventured kindly. "There are them as gets gloomy because there's chemicals off balance in their brain."

Smiling at the housekeeper's phrasing, Amy carried Sara to her crib and looked out the bedroom window at the choppy gray waters of Puget Sound. "I'm pretty sure my brain's all right," she said. *It's my heart that might not hold up.*

Mrs. Hobbs was puttering with the bedspread, even though it was mid-afternoon and the master suite was always the first room to be cleaned, after the kitchen. "Mr. Griffith be home tonight?" she asked casually.

Amy stiffened. How astute this Englishwoman was. She'd only been in the house a few days and already she knew there was trouble. "No," she said, hugging herself because she felt a chill. "Mr. Griffith won't be home. He has a late meeting tonight and conferences all day tomorrow."

The weekend ahead looked desolate from Amy's viewpoint: Ashley and Oliver would spend it with the Ryans on the mainland, and Harry, of course, would be working.

The housekeeper picked up the pink-and-gray plaid woolen afghan at the foot of the bed and refolded it, even though it had been perfectly arranged in the first place.

"Forgive me, ma'am," she said, lowering her eyes when Amy looked at her directly, "but it wouldn't hurt if you was to doll yourself up a little and spend some time in the city, with your husband."

Amy looked down at her baggy gray sweat suit, and a grin tugged at the corners of her mouth, even though she wanted very much to cry. "Are you insinuating that I'm not on the cutting edge of fashion, Mrs. Hobbs?"

The woman's already ruddy face was flushed with conviction. "Yes, ma'am."

The idea of going to Seattle, of perhaps finding some common ground with Harry, some way to reach him, was appealing. But Amy couldn't forget the last time she'd paid him an unscheduled visit, back in Brisbane. He'd been furious at her for mistrusting him.

"I have a small baby," Amy reminded Mrs. Hobbs and herself.

"She's big enough to be left for a day or so, ma'am. It's not like I haven't looked after a nipper or two in my time, you know. You'd just have to leave some milk."

Amy sighed. She could speak honestly to Mrs. Hobbs, and that was a great relief, because Amy had felt alone for a long time. "My husband wouldn't appreciate a visit from me," she admitted sadly, at the same time yearning to shop and see a play and eat in an elegant restaurant, all without having to nurse her baby or change a diaper. "He'd think I was checking up on him."

"That's easy to remedy," Mrs. Hobbs said briskly, fussing with the pillow shams. "You just play hard to get, Mrs. Griffith. You check into another hotel—not his—and then you call and leave a message, saying you're in town. After that, you go out and buy yourself some fine new clothes, and if it's a while before you return Mr. Griffith's messages when he calls, so much the better."

The plan appealed to Amy, whose unhappiness was rapidly escalating into sheer panic. Her marriage was turning out exactly as she had feared it would. If the relationship was to have any chance at all, she would have to stop mooning around and *do something*.

"You're right," she said excitedly. Then, impulsively, she gripped the housekeeper's sturdy shoulders and kissed her soundly on the cheek. "God bless you, Mrs. Hobbs, you're right!"

Amy packed hurriedly and made sure there was an ample supply of milk for Sara, who was already living mostly on baby food, anyway. When it was time for Ashley and Oliver to cross to West Seattle to meet their grandparents at the terminal, Amy kissed her infant daughter goodbye, rallied all her willpower, and got onto the ferry with them.

It wasn't easy; she and Sara had never been separated before, and the pull of maternal instinct was very strong indeed. In fact, a couple of times Amy thought she might not be able to keep herself from diving overboard and swimming back.

On the other hand, she wanted to reach out to Harry, to try to make things right between them again. She closed her eyes against a sudden swell of tears, remembering how he'd said he hoped a miracle would happen and she would turn back into the woman he'd married.

Am I so different? she wondered miserably, watching through blurred eyes as Oliver and Ashley ran happily up and down the deck on the other side of the window.

She looked down at herself.

Amy was only about five pounds heavier than she'd been before her pregnancy, but she *had* been neglecting her exercise program. She hadn't had a good haircut in weeks, and she often went for days without wearing makeup.

She felt a stirring of hope, because clothes and exercise and makeup and haircuts were all things within the realm of her control. Amy had read enough pop psychology to know she could change nothing about Harry, much less his feelings toward her, but she couldn't help hoping that he might be willing to meet her halfway.

After the boat docked and the Ryans had collected Ashley and Oliver, Amy drove downtown. Since Harry was staying in a suite at the Hilton, she took a room in the Sheraton.

She called his office and left a message with the puzzled receptionist, who had offered to put her through to Harry immediately. "Just tell him I called," Amy said brightly, and then she hung up.

The phone was ringing fifteen minutes later when she was leaving the room, but Amy didn't stop to answer it. She knew Mrs. Hobbs wasn't calling about Sara because she'd just talked to the woman, and that left Harry.

Let him wonder, Amy thought, closing the door on the insistent jangling.

She walked to the nearby Westlake Center, an urban answer to the shopping mall, boasting several levels of good stores, and bought bath salts and special soaps and lotions. After that, Amy entered an upscale lingerie boutique and purchased a sexy floral nightgown and some silky lingerie.

Down the street from the mall, at Nordstrom, her favorite department store, Amy selected a black crepe sheath and a glittery jacket to match.

When Amy returned to her room to drop off her packages and hang up the dress and jacket, the message light on her phone was blinking. She dialed the registration desk and was told that Mr. Griffith had called twice, once from his office, once from his hotel. He'd left both numbers, as if Amy wouldn't know them.

"Thank you," Amy said with a smile. Then she took the elevator down to the lobby, had her hair cut and styled in the swanky hotel salon and charged the whole obscene price to Harry's American Express card.

On her return, Amy found two message envelopes just inside the door. Both were from Harry.

Feeling better all the time, and blessing Mrs. Hobbs for being a genius, Amy yawned, set the messages aside and rustled through the bags for her soap and bath salts. She indulged in a long, luxurious soak in the tub, ignoring the telephone when it rang. She and Mrs. Hobbs had worked out a system earlier; if the housekeeper needed to reach Amy for any reason, she would ring twice, hang up and ring twice again.

Amy must have fallen asleep for a little while, because the bathwater got cold. She was just reaching out to turn the spigot marked Hot when she heard the outer door open.

"Thanks, mate," she heard Harry say.

"Thank *you,* sir," a bellhop replied, obviously receiving a big tip for letting Harry into the room.

"I think I'll complain to the management," Harry announced, stepping into the bathroom just as Amy was rising, towel wrapped, from the tub. "I could have been anybody, but all I had to do was tell them I was your husband."

Amy smiled, though she felt almost as nervous as she had the first time she'd met Harry Griffith. "I told the concierge to keep an eye out for you," she admitted. Then she made a shooing gesture with one hand. "Get out of here, please. I want to dress."

"It's not like I've never seen you naked," Harry reasoned, frowning. He was leaning back against the sink counter, his arms folded, his dark brows drawn together. "What are you trying to do, Amy?"

She put a hand to his arm and eased him through the doorway. "I'm planning to have a luxurious dinner and see a play. Tomorrow I plan to shop."

Amy closed the door and locked it.

"You're doing all this alone?" Harry called from beyond the barrier.

"Yes," Amy answered, smiling at her reflection in the mirror. She liked her sleek new haircut; it made her look both sexy and mischievous. She waited a few beats before adding, "Unless, of course, you'd like to accompany me. I wouldn't want you to think I was crowding you, or checking up on you, or anything like that."

"Amy, this is silly. Open the door!"

Amy reached for a makeup sponge and a new bottle of foundation and leaned toward the mirror. "I'm busy," she chimed. "Maybe you could come back later."

"Damn it, I'll break this thing down if you don't let me in."

"You wouldn't do that," Amy reasoned, blending her foundation skillfully with the sponge. "Trashing a hotel room would definitely be unHarrylike. Besides, the management would be furious."

She heard him sag against the door, probably in exasperation, and her heart took wings. Maybe he didn't love her in the classical sense, maybe his attachment to her was largely sexual, but there was no denying that Harry cared.

When she turned the knob, he practically fell into the bathroom. Staring at her in angry bewilderment, he said, "I don't like being kept from my own wife."

"Tough," Amy replied, bending close to the mirror to begin applying her eye shadow. "I'm through walking on eggshells, Harry. I'm going to live my life, with or without your approval."

He filled the doorway, glowering, a human storm cloud. "What about Sara? Where does she fit into your plans, Mrs. Griffith? And where is she, by the way?"

"Sara is with Mrs. Hobbs. She's going to be one of those modern babies who goes everywhere with her mommy. I'll buy a carrier of some sort."

"Right. And when she gets hungry, you can just whip out a breast in the middle of a board meeting!" Obviously Harry was losing his perspective as well as his temper. He shoved a hand through his hair, making it unperfect. "Damn it, Amy, you can forget the whole crazy idea! You're not dragging my daughter through the corporate world like a rag doll!"

Amy finished shadowing her right eye and started on her left. "Actually I was thinking in terms of attending art school. I've got real talent, you know, and in this day and age, a woman needs to know how to support herself."

Harry, the cool, the calm, the collected man of the twenty-first century, looked as if he were going to pop an artery. His voice, when he spoke, was low and lethal. "Even if you didn't have me to look after you, Amy, you would never need a job. Between what Tyler left you and the proceeds from selling the house—"

"There are other reasons to work besides money," Amy said, reaching for a green kohl pencil and starting to line her eyes. "Like knowing you mean something, knowing you're strong and you're interesting and you're worth something all on your own. The subject isn't open to debate, Harry— I'm going to art school, whether you like it or not."

Out of the corner of her eye, Amy could see that her husband's jaw was clamped down tight, as though he'd just bitten through a piece of steel. "Fine," he said. And when the door of the hotel room slammed, Amy wondered if her wonderful plan had backfired.

Chapter 11

Harry paused in the doorway of his office, his hand still on the light switch, thinking he'd finally lost his mind, once and for all.

He blinked, looked again and, sure as hell, Tyler was there, sitting in Harry's leather chair, feet propped on the tidy surface of his antique desk.

"You're really seeing me," his friend assured him with a sigh. Ty's hands were cupped at the back of his head, and he looked pretty relaxed for someone who'd been dead in the neighborhood of three years.

Harry rubbed his eyes with one hand. It was the problems with Amy that had pushed him over the brink, he was certain of that. "This is ridiculous," he said.

Tyler sighed again and hoisted his feet down from Harry's desk. He was wearing clothes Harry vaguely remembered: jeans and a University of Washington sweatshirt. "Look, old buddy, I don't have all night here, so listen up. I had to get special permission from the head office to make this appearance, and this is positively the last time they'll let me come back. You're blowing it, man."

Harry went to his private bar and poured himself a brandy. A good, stiff drink might jump-start his brain circuits and blast him back to reality.

When he turned around, however, Tyler was as substantially *there* as ever. He was leaning against the edge of the desk now, his arms folded, his eyes full of pitying fury.

"Do you realize what you have?" the apparition demanded. "Amy is wonderful and sweet and bright, and damn it, she loves you! There must be a million guys out there—" Tyler gestured toward the bank of windows behind the desk "—just wishing to God they could meet somebody like her! She adores you, you lucky bastard!"

Harry shoved one hand through his hair, thinking what a remarkable mechanism the human mind is. He would have sworn his dead friend was really standing there, every bit as real as Amy or the janitor downstairs dust mopping the lobby, or the doorman out on the street.

"Wrong," he said forcefully. "Amy's planning to leave me and become some kind of barefoot Bohemian, painting pictures and carrying my daughter around on her back like a papoose."

Tyler laughed, and the effect was remarkably authentic. It gave Harry a pang, remembering the old days, when he and Ty had thought the whole world was funny. "Oh, the art school thing," Tyler said. "As you Aussies say, 'No worries, mate.'"

The game was becoming alarmingly easy to play, and Harry put his brandy aside, unfinished. "You mean, she's going to change her mind about art school?"

"Hell, no," Tyler answered with a cocky grin. "You really

started something when you gave her those art supplies—
even Amy didn't know she had a talent for painting. In three
years she'll be having her own shows in some of the best
galleries in the country."

Harry sagged into a chair. Damn, but this was elaborate.
He hadn't known he was harboring so many possibilities in
his subconscious mind. "And that's supposed to keep me
from worrying?" he muttered. He'd already had a sample of
the new Amy, the woman who was bent on living her life to
the fullest, with or without him, and he wasn't sure he liked
her. One thing he had to admit, though, she was exciting.

"Relax," Tyler said. He crossed the room to touch one of
the crystal liquor decanters on Harry's bar. Harry figured
a genie would probably come out of the thing, thus laying
to rest all doubt that Harry had lost his sanity. "Amy's becoming the person she's supposed to be, and you'll be a
world-class fool if you try to stand in her way."

"How," Harry began raggedly, closing his eyes, "am I
supposed to live without her? Tell me that."

"You won't have to live without Amy if you'll just quit
trying to drive her away," Tyler replied without missing
a beat.

Harry's eyes flew open. "I haven't been trying to drive
her away!" he hollered.

Tyler grinned indulgently. "Sure you have, Harry. You're
afraid to let go of your emotions and really care about Amy
and the kids because of what happened before, in your first
marriage."

A sense of bleakness swept over Harry, practically
crushing him. He'd had such high hopes back then, for
himself and Madeline and little Eireen, before he'd learned
just how cruelly unpredictable life can be.

"I see you're not trying to deny that," Tyler observed,

pacing back and forth a few feet in front of Harry, his hands clasped behind his back. Except for the clothes, this was probably the way his friend had looked in the courtroom, authoritative and confident.

But not dead, of course.

"You're not here."

"Amy kept saying that, too. Did you like the white lilacs I sent for the wedding?"

Harry's mouth dropped open, but he didn't speak because he couldn't.

"Look," Tyler said, beginning to summarize, "I don't really give a damn whether you believe I'm here or not, because what you think about me doesn't matter. But you and Amy have to make it work—there's a lot riding on it."

For the first time since his friend's death, Harry thought he might actually break down and weep. He loved Amy, thoroughly, totally, as he'd never loved another human being, but Tyler had been right earlier. He was terrified of letting his guard down completely where Amy was concerned, because losing her would kill him.

"You'll find her in front of the Fifth Avenue Theater," Tyler said. He was standing at the windows now, looking through the shutter slats at the city lights. "She's carrying an extra ticket in her purse and hoping against hope that you'll have the good sense to show up. Don't drop the ball, Harry. Don't lose her."

"Next," Harry sighed, "you're going to offer to show me how the world would be if I'd never been born, right?"

Tyler chuckled. "Sorry, that's a Christmas bit. Good-bye, Harry, and good luck."

Before Harry's very eyes, Tyler vanished. He was there, then he wasn't. It was weird.

Harry got his coat and wandered out of the office,

through the swanky reception area and over to the elevators. He rubbed his chin as he waited, then looked at his watch.

It was seven-ten, and curtain time at the theater was usually eight o'clock. His hotel was connected with the theater by a walkway—

She *had* said she was going to the theater.

That was how he knew, Harry was sure of it. He'd only imagined Tyler because he was so stressed out, so lonesome for his wife. It was a spiritual longing, as well as a physical one, intense enough to explain his hallucinations.

He went back to the Hilton, glanced at the telephone— the message light wasn't blinking—and then took a hot shower. He shaved and put on fresh clothes, and when he passed through the underground shopping center and climbed the stairs to the Fifth Avenue Theater, Amy was standing there on the sidewalk.

She was so beautiful, in her clingy black dress, sexy jacket and high heels, that Harry was momentarily immobilized by the sight of her. He just stood gaping at her, his hand gripping the stair railing.

Amy must have felt his gaze, because she turned and smiled, and Harry tightened his grasp on the railing, as much off balance as if he'd been punched in the stomach.

"Hello, Harry," she said gently.

"You really mean it, about this art school thing?"

Worry flickered in her hopeful eyes. "I really mean it," she confirmed softly.

He finally broke his inertia and joined her in the line of theatergoers waiting to be admitted.

"You look fantastic," he said, not quite meeting her eyes.

He could feel her smile, warm as sunlight. "Thanks, Harry. You look pretty good yourself."

He turned, unable to resist the pull anymore, and went tumbling, head over heels into her eyes.

She linked her arm with his. "I love you, Harry," she said.

Harry felt something steely and cold melt within him. "And I love you," he whispered raggedly.

They went into the theater with the crowd, and sat there in their seats, holding hands. Harry was never able to remember, without a reminder from Amy, what play they saw that night, because his mind was everywhere but on the stage.

After the final curtain, they had a late dinner at an expensive, low-key restaurant.

Harry felt as nervous as a kid on his first date.

He wondered what she would say if he told her she wasn't the only one who'd ever had a delusion, that he'd seen Tyler, too.

"I think I'm going round the bend," he finally confessed, because he wanted to be honest with Amy. Completely honest.

She arched one delicate brow and took a sip of her wine. "Oh? Why is that?"

"Because when I went back to the office after our conversation in your room, fully intending to lick my wounds and whimper a little, Tyler was there."

Amy set the wineglass down, very slowly. Her cheeks were pale, and although her throat worked visibly, no sound passed her lips.

"Not that I believe I saw a ghost or anything like that," Harry was quick to clarify.

Amy reached for her wineglass again, her hand shaking as she extended it. She closed her eyes and took three or four gulps before looking at Harry squarely again and agreeing, "Of course not."

Harry sighed. "The human mind is a fascinating thing," he ruminated, hedging.

"What did Tyler want?" Amy asked in a small voice.

"He delivered a lecture, essentially," Harry said, frowning, "and I must confess that he was pretty much on target. Obviously my subconscious mind had worked the whole thing out beforehand."

"Obviously," Amy said in a whisper. Her beautiful eyes were very wide, and Harry could see the pulse at the base of her throat.

It made him want to kiss her there, as well as a few other places.

"I've been a fool, Amy," he went on, after clearing his throat and shifting uncomfortably in his chair. "I thought I could keep myself from loving you, and thereby keep my heart from being broken to bits, but it didn't work. Practically every stroke of good fortune in my life can be traced back to you—not only did you give me yourself, but Ashley and Oliver and Sara, too. God in heaven, Amy, I love you more than I ever believed could be possible, and it hurts—and I'm scared."

Tears brimmed in her eyes, and she reached across the table to grip Harry's hand. "Me, too. Everything just sort of fell into place with Tyler—we met, we got married, we had kids. I was happy, and I think he was, as well. Then I met you and suddenly everything was complicated."

Harry lifted her hand to his lips and kissed the knuckles lightly. A bittersweet sense of homecoming filled him. It was not like returning after an hour's absence, or even a week's. No, it was as though an eternity had passed, during which he'd been deprived of this woman he needed more than air, more than light, more than water.

"Give me a second chance," he said. "I'm a chauvinist, but I can reform."

Amy laughed softly. "Don't reform too much. There are things I like about the caveman approach."

Harry raised his eyebrows. "Such as?"

"Such as being your love prisoner," Amy said, leaning closer and uttering the words in a breathless tone that made Harry's loins pulse and his heart start to hammer.

"Is it warm in here?" he inquired, tugging at his collar.

Amy's smile was slow and hot and saucy. He felt her toe make a slow foray up his pant leg. "Steaming," she answered.

Harry practically tore his wallet from his inside pocket, fished out a credit card, and threw it at the first waiter to pass by. They were out of the hotel and onto the bustling night streets within minutes.

"My place or yours?" Amy teased.

"Which is closer?"

"Mine."

"Yours it is."

They entered Amy's room a few minutes later, and she snatched up a shopping bag and immediately disappeared into the bathroom again.

Harry paced, listening as the water ran and the toilet flushed and various things clinked and rattled. Finally he paused outside the door. "Amy?"

"Be patient, Harry."

He tried, he honestly tried. He went to the telephone and ordered champagne, then called the hotel florist for a dozen of whatever flower they happened to have on hand.

Both the carnations and the champagne arrived before

Amy came out of the bathroom, but the wait was worth it. She was wearing a gossamer floral nightgown, of the very thinnest silk, and it clung to her womanly curves in a way that made Harry's heart surge into his throat.

"My God," he rasped.

Amy walked past him, her hips swaying, her soft skin exuding the scent of lavender. The bellhop had opened the champagne before leaving the room, and Amy poured a glass for herself and one for Harry.

"Let's offer a toast," she said, holding out his glass.

He accepted it with a slightly unsteady hand.

"To us," she said. "To you and me and Ashley and Oliver and little Sara—and whoever else might happen to come along in the next couple of years."

Harry swallowed. "You mean, you're willing to have another child? But you've been so tired, and there's art school—"

"Other women have done it. I'll manage, Harry, with a lot of help from you and Mrs. Hobbs."

Now it was Harry who had tears in his eyes. He set his champagne aside and laid his hands on Amy's waist, pulling her close to him. "God, Amy, how I love you," he breathed.

She put down her glass, slid her arms around his neck, and drove him crazy by wriggling against him.

"Prove it," she said.

"Oh, I will," he answered.

Harry was as good as his word. He buried his fingers in Amy's hair and gently but firmly pulled her head back for his kiss. When his mouth crushed hers and his tongue gained immediate entry, Amy nearly fainted. It had been so long.

She peeled off Harry's jacket while their tongues battled,

then wrenched at his tie and ripped open his shirt, sending little buttons flying in every direction.

Amy didn't care about shirt buttons. She pushed the fabric savagely aside, sought a masculine nipple with her tongue and nibbled until Harry was moaning under his breath.

"This time," she said, "you're *my* prisoner. You have to do everything I tell you, and give me everything I want."

Harry moaned as she unfastened his belt buckle. "Amy—"

"I want to hear you crying out, for once," Amy said, kissing her way down his belly, baring his navel. "I want to hear you beg, the way I always do."

"Ooooh," he rasped, as she knelt and pushed down his slacks, her hands moving strong and light on his buttocks, molding and shaping him, pushing him into the pleasure she so willingly offered.

Amy enjoyed her husband, and the beautiful, angry, hungry sounds he was making, and she was greedy about it. His firm flanks began to flex under her palms and, with a gasp, he leaned forward to brace himself against the dresser.

Amy granted him no quarter.

"Amy..." he pleaded, a man in delirium. "Oh, God, Amy, I'm going to—"

She stopped, just long enough to finish the sentence for him, and then she was insatiable again.

Harry stiffened, with a low, primitive cry, and she made him experience every nuance, every degree of sensation, every shade of ecstasy. When she finally released him, it was clear that he could barely stand.

Their clothes were mysteriously gone. Amy didn't remember shedding her own garments or stripping away

Harry's, but when they fell onto the big bed in the center of the room, they were both naked.

"I'll have to have vengeance for that," Harry said, after a long time, rolling onto his side to begin kissing Amy's stomach.

"For what?" Amy teased, but a little gasp of anticipation betrayed her as Harry's mouth drew dangerously near the center of her femininity.

"For turning me inside out," Harry answered in a rumbling voice, then took her boldly into his mouth.

She cried out, but it was only the beginning. Harry teased her unmercifully, for what seemed like hours.

Amy was wild, untamed, primitive in her responses. She cried, she pleaded, she moaned and groaned and cursed, and finally, in a long, shattering spasm, she lost all control.

Although he had what he wanted, Harry was not a benevolent captor.

He folded her close, and held her, and stroked her, until she was ready again. When he entered her, it was a sudden, fierce invasion, and her eyes rolled back in her head.

"Look at me, Amy," he ordered.

She opened her eyes and stared up at her husband dreamily.

"I want to see you responding to me," Harry said. "I want to see you belonging to me…"

Amy dug her heels into the bed and rose and fell under Harry with graceful desperation. She needed him, wanted him, so much, that giving herself was heaven. "Put a baby inside me, Harry," she choked out. "Please—give me your baby."

At her words, he seemed to lose control. He groaned and threw his head back, as fierce as a stallion having his mare. "I love you, Amy," he struggled to say.

She ran her hands up and down the straining muscles of his back, soothing, tormenting, urging him on. "I love you," she answered breathlessly, meeting him thrust for thrust, heartbeat for heartbeat, dream for dream.

Finally, in one blinding, spectacular collision, the joyous miracle happened and their two souls mated, just as their bodies did.

Later, much later, Amy lay with her head on Harry's shoulder, exhausted, nibbling at his heated skin.

"We never made love in the tree house again," she said, as he entwined one finger in a lock of her hair.

Harry drew in a deep breath, let it out slowly. "If ever I've heard a good reason for going back to Australia, that's it. We'll leave as soon as Oliver and Ashley are out of school."

Amy smiled in the cozy darkness and kissed Harry's shoulder. "And come back before classes start at my art school," she negotiated.

"Deal," he said, after a lengthy and very philosophical sigh.

Down on the sidewalk, beside the hotel, stood Tyler, unseen by the city dwellers hurrying past him, looking up at one certain window. He was about to return to a place where there was no darkness and no pain, but during those few precious moments, he was a living, breathing man again.

He could hear the noise of passing cars, a plane overhead, people chattering as they rushed along. He felt the solid cement of the sidewalk beneath his feet and smelled the peculiar mix of salt water, pine and exhaust fumes that was Seattle. He also felt no small measure of satisfac-

tion because he knew Harry and Amy had a long, rich life
ahead of them.

Tyler had accomplished his mission. Amy and Harry
would live and love, laugh and cry. They would decorate
Christmas trees together and balance checking accounts
and shop for snow tires. They would fight sometimes, but
they would have a glorious time making up.

It was all written in the book.

Tyler sighed and lifted one hand in farewell. "Goodbye," he whispered. And then he walked away, into the
waiting light.

One year later...

The tree house was just as Amy remembered it, dusty
and primitive and wonderful. Harry gave her a mischievous pinch on the bottom as she climbed the last rung and
scrambled inside.

It had taken them a little longer than they'd expected to
reach this very special, very private place—Amy had completed her classes at the art school, and she worked on her
painting for several hours every day.

Sitting there, with her blue-jeaned legs drawn up, she
made a mental note to draw a sketch of the tree house. She
would frame the picture, and when she and Harry and the
kids were far away in the States, she could look at the drawing and remember.

"I think you're crazy, wanting to spend the night here,"
Harry remarked, dusting off his pants. "If the mosquitoes
don't eat us alive, the rain will come through and give us
our deaths."

Amy laughed. "Me, Jane," she said. "You, Tarzan. And
don't you forget it, buster!"

Harry opened the canvas bag he'd brought along, taking out food, a blanket and a small sterno-powered stove. "Alas," he said, "all we need now is a monkey."

Amy's smile was broad; she could feel it stretching her face. She waited for Harry to look up and see her kneeling there, beaming, and laid her hands to her flat stomach. "We already have three monkeys," she answered. "I guess one more won't hurt."

Harry's befuddled expression made her shriek with laughter, scaring all the beautiful birds from their roosts in the tree.

When the beating of wings finally died down, he said, "You mean, you're—?"

"Again." Amy nodded. "I think it's a boy this time."

Harry swallowed visibly, scrambled over to her and covered both her hands with one of his own, as though by doing that he could somehow make contact with this new child. His indigo eyes glistened with tears of wonder.

Amy rose up on her haunches to kiss Harry's eyelids, first one and then the other. She tasted his tears.

"Do you know how much I love you, Harry Griffith?" she asked, one hand on either side of his handsome face.

His voice was gruff. "How much?" he asked.

Her answer was a kiss, deep and fiery. "That much," she said, when it was over.

Harry broke away to spread the blanket on the floor of the tree house. His motions were graceful and quick, and when he reached for Amy, she came to him willingly, with laughter and love and the purest joy.

He kissed her, subjecting her to a tender invasion of his tongue, and then laid her on the blanket and began removing her clothes with deft, methodical hands.

"I can't wait, Amy," he said, tossing her jeans aside and

bending her knees and pushing her legs wide of each other. "I've got to be inside you, part of you, now."

She opened his jeans, pushed them down, along with his briefs. "Come in, Mr. Griffith," she whispered.

In the depths of the night, the rain came.

Harry lay awake on the floor of the tree house, listening, holding a sleeping Amy close by his side. He supposed he should wake her and insist that they go back to the shelter and safety of their house on the other island, but he didn't have the heart to awaken his wife. She was tired and she'd given him everything and she looked like an angel, lying there.

Idly, he caressed her. Soon, her beautiful body would ripen, her breasts would grow heavy with milk to nourish his child. He smiled, even though his vision was suspiciously blurred. He wondered if Amy would be as crabby this time around as she'd been while she was carrying Sara.

He decided he didn't care.

She moved against him, inadvertently setting him on fire again. Some men were put off by pregnancy, he knew, but knowing Amy was going to bear a child—his child—made him yearn for her in a way that went beyond the physical into a realm he didn't begin to understand.

"Harry?"

He kissed her temple. "Shhh, it's all right. Sleep."

She played with his nipples and the hair on his stomach. "Harry?" Her tone was serious.

"Mmm?"

"Are you happy about the new baby? Really happy?"

"Ecstatic," he answered.

"Oliver says if he doesn't get a brother pretty soon, he's joining the Foreign 'Region.'"

Harry laughed. Oliver was a miniature version of Ty, and Harry loved the boy as much as if he'd been his own, by blood. "Promises, promises," he said.

"You've been so good to them, Harry—Ashley and Oliver, I mean. Anyone would think they were as much yours as Sara is."

"They *are* as much mine. In a funny sort of way, I think Tyler gave them to me. He knew I could be trusted to love his children as deeply as he did."

She sniffled against his shoulder. "I really saw him," Amy said half to herself after a long moment had passed.

"So did I," admitted Harry, who had long since come to terms with the fact that Tyler had really been in his office that night, when Harry's and Amy's marriage had been in crisis.

"Do you think Ty's happy, wherever he is?"

Harry thought the question through, even though he'd done as much many, many times before.

"Yes, rose petal," he said sincerely. "He's happy."

Amy raised her head far enough to plant a row of tantalizing kisses along Harry's jawline. "I think I just felt a raindrop land on my backside," she said.

Harry chuckled and gave said backside an affectionate squeeze. "I love a sophisticated woman," he replied.

Amy nudged him with one elbow, pretending to be angry. "Oh, yeah?" she joked. "What's her name?"

* * * * *

Also by Brenda Jackson

HQN

Visit her Author Profile page at Harlequin.com,
or brendajackson.net, for more titles!

STONE COLD
SURRENDER

Brenda Jackson

Happy is the man that findeth wisdom,
and the man that getteth understanding.
—*Proverbs* 3:13

To my husband, the love of my life
and my best friend, Gerald Jackson, Sr.
And to everyone who asked for Stone's and Storm's
stories, this book is for you!

Chapter 1

The woman had a death grip on his thigh. The pain was almost unbearable but her hands touching him felt so damn good.

No longer satisfied with looking at her out of the corner of his eye, Stone Westmoreland slowly glanced over to stare at the woman, studying every single element about her. She was strapped in her seat as if the plane would crash unless she grabbed hold of something. Her eyes were shut tight and her breathing was irregular and it reminded him of the breathing pattern of a woman who'd just experienced the most satisfying orgasm. Just thinking about her touch aroused him....

He leaned back in his seat as the plane leveled off in the sky and closed his own eyes. With back-to-back book deadlines, it had been a long time since he'd been with a woman and a mere touch from her had sent his libido into overdrive.

He opened his eyes and took a shaky breath, hoping the

month he would spend at his cousin's ranch in Montana, getting his thoughts together for a new book, would do him some good. At thirty-three, he and Durango were only a few months apart in age and had always been close. Then there was his uncle Corey who lived not far from Durango on a ranch high up in the mountains. Corey Westmoreland was his father's youngest brother who, at fifty-four, had retired as a park ranger after over thirty years of service.

Stone had fond memories of the summers he and his one sister, four brothers and six male cousins had shared visiting Uncle Corey. They had gained a great appreciation for the outdoors, as well as for wildlife. Their uncle always took his job as a park ranger seriously and his love for the wilderness had been contagious.

The one thing that stood out in Stone's mind about his uncle was that he never planned to marry. In fact, other than the women in the family, no other woman's foot had ever touched the soil of Corey's mountain. His uncle always said it was because he was so ornery and set in his ways that marriage wasn't for him. He much preferred living the life of a bachelor.

Stone's thoughts shifted to his brothers. This time last year all of them had been happy-go-lucky, enjoying every single minute of playing the field. Then the next thing you know, Dare, the eldest, got married and less than six months later, last month to be exact, his brother Thorn was marching down the aisle. Everyone in the family began ribbing Stone, saying since he was the third Westmoreland brother he would probably be next.

And he had been quick to tell them that hell would freeze over first.

He enjoyed being a bachelor too much to fall for any type of marriage trap. And although he would be the first to admit that the women his brothers had married were the best and more than worthy of their undying love and affection, he had decided a long time ago, just like Uncle Corey, that marriage wasn't for him. Not that he considered himself ornery or set in his ways; he just did not want to be responsible for anyone other than himself. He enjoyed the freedom to come and go whenever he pleased, and being a national, award-winning, bestselling author of action-thriller novels afforded him that luxury. He traveled all over the world to do research, and whenever he did date it was on his time and no one else's. For him women were a necessity, but only at certain times, and usually it wasn't difficult to find one who agreed to an affair on his terms.

To be completely honest, Stone had no issues with the concept of marriage, he just wasn't ready to take the plunge himself. He'd made a decision long ago to remain single after watching a good friend, who was also a bestselling author, become hopelessly in love and besotted with a woman. After getting married, Mark had decided that writing was not a priority in his life anymore. His focus had switched. He much preferred spending time with his wife instead of sitting at a computer all day. It was as if Mark had become Samson who'd gotten a hair cut. Once married, he had been zapped of his identity.

The thought that he could lose his desire to write over something called love totally unnerved Stone. Since publishing his first book at twenty-three, writing had become his life and he didn't intend for that to change. Doing so would mean losing control and the idea of losing that type of control on his life was something he couldn't handle.

Stone decided to check out the woman sitting beside him once more. Even with her eyes closed, he immediately liked what he saw. Shoulder-length dark brown hair and skin the color of dark coffee. She had a nice set of full lips and her nose was just the right fit for her face. She had long lashes and her cheeks were high. If she was wearing makeup, it was not very much. She was a natural beauty.

He glanced down at her hand, the one gripping his thigh. She was not wearing an engagement or wedding ring, which was good; and she had boarded the plane in Atlanta, which meant she either lived in the area or had come through the city to catch this connecting flight. Since they were on the same plane, unless she had another connecting flight, she was also bound for Montana.

His body tensed when he felt her grip tighten on his thigh. He inhaled deeply. If her hand moved even less than an inch, she would be clutching the most intimate part of him and he doubted she wanted to do that. Chances were she assumed her hand was gripping the armrest, so he decided he'd better let her know what was going on before he embarrassed them both.

He noticed that the sun, shining through the airplane window, hit her features at such an angle that they glowed. Even her hair appeared thick and luxurious and fanned her face in a way that made her look even more attractive.

Leaning over quietly, so as not to startle her, he breathed in her scent before getting a single word out of his mouth. It was a fragrance that turned him on even more than he already was. The aroma seemed entrenched into her skin and he was tempted to take his tongue and lick a portion of her bare neck to see if perhaps he could sample a taste of it.

Stone shook his head. Since when had he developed a fetish for a woman's skin? He enjoyed the art of kissing, like most men, but wanting to taste, nibble and devour a woman all over had never been something that interested him.

Until now.

He pushed the thought to the back of his mind, deciding it was too dangerous to even go there; he leaned closer and whispered softly in her ear, "The plane has leveled off so you can let go of me now."

She snapped open her eyes and quickly turned her head to meet his gaze. A part of him suddenly wished she hadn't done that. He found himself staring into the most beautiful set of brown eyes he had ever seen. They were perfect for the rest of her features and something in their dark depths made his body almost jerk in the seat.

She was simply gorgeous, although in truth there wasn't anything simple about it. She literally took his breath away. And, speaking of breath, he watched as she drew in a long, shaky one before glancing down at her left hand. She immediately snatched it off his thigh.

Awareness flashed in her eyes and total embarrassment appeared on her face. "Oh, oh, I'm so sorry. I didn't mean to touch you. I thought my hand was on the armrest. I—I didn't mean to act so improperly."

When Stone saw the degree of distress on her face he decided to assure her that he would survive. The last thing he wanted was for her to come unglued and get all flustered on him. And he really liked her accent. It was totally different from his Southern drawl and had the unmistakable inflection of a northeasterner. She was definitely someone from one of those New England States.

"Hey, no harm's done," he tried to say casually. "My name is Stone Westmoreland," he said, introducing himself and presenting his hand to her.

She still looked embarrassed when she took it and said, "And I'm Madison Winters."

He smiled. "Nice meeting you, Madison. Is this your first flight?"

She shook her head when he released her hand. "Nice meeting you, too, and no, this isn't my first flight, but I have a definite fear of flying. I try using other means of transportation whenever I can, but in this particular situation time is of the essence."

He nodded. "And where are you from?" he couldn't help but ask, her accent affecting him just as much as her touch had. Just listening to how she pronounced her words was a total turn-on.

"I'm from Boston. I was born and raised there."

He nodded again. "I'm from the Atlanta area," he decided to say when moments passed and she hadn't taken the liberty to ask. Whether it was from shyness or disinterest, he wasn't sure. But as far as he was concerned it didn't matter if she wasn't interested in him. He was definitely interested in her.

"I love visiting Atlanta," she said moments later. "I took my class on a field trip there once."

He raised a brow. "Your class?"

She smiled and his stomach flipped. "Yes, I'm a teacher. I teach music to sixth graders."

Stone smiled, surprised. He would never have figured her to be the artsy type. He remembered taking band when he was about eleven and learning to play the clarinet. His band teacher had looked nothing like her. "Must be interesting."

Her smile widened. "It is and I enjoy what I do."

He chuckled. "Yes, in this day and time it's good when a person can enjoy their work."

She stared at him for a second then asked, "And what type of work do you do?"

He hesitated before answering. As a bestselling author he used a pseudonym to ensure his privacy, but for some reason he felt comfortable being truthful with her. "I'm a fiction writer."

A smile tilted her lips. "Oh, how wonderful. Sorry, but I don't recall ever reading any of your books. What exactly do you write about?"

Stone chuckled. "I write action-thriller novels under the pseudonym of Rock Mason."

She blinked and then gasped. "You're Rock Mason? *The* Rock Mason?"

He smiled, glad that she had at least heard of Rock Mason. "Yes."

"Oh, my gosh! My mother has read every single book you've written. She is an avid fan of yours."

His smile widened. "What about you? Have you read any of my books?"

She gazed at him with regret. "No, I usually don't have time to read for pleasure, but from what I understand you're a gifted author."

"Thanks."

"A few of my girlfriends are in book clubs and they select your books to read and discuss whenever they hit the bookstores. You have quite a following in Boston. Have you ever visited there?"

"Yes, I did a book signing in Boston a couple of years ago and thought it was a beautiful city."

Madison beamed. "It is. I love Boston and can't imagine myself living anywhere else. I even attended Boston University because I didn't want to leave home."

At that moment they were interrupted as the flight attendant stopped to serve them drinks and a snack.

"So are you headed for Montana on business?" Stone asked. He remembered her saying something earlier about needing to get there rather quickly. He watched as she took

a bite of her muffin and immediately felt his libido register the single crumb that clung to the side of her mouth. If
that wasn't bad enough, she took a long sip of coffee and
closed her eyes. Seconds later, as if the coffee was the best
she'd ever tasted, she reopened her eyes. He saw the play of
emotions across her face as she thought about his question.

"No, my visit to Montana is strictly personal." Then she
studied him for a moment as if making a decision about
something and said, "I'm going to Montana to find my
mother."

Stone lifted a brow. "Oh? Is she missing?"

Madison leaned back against her seat, seemingly frustrated. "Yes. She and a couple of other women from Boston
flew to Montana two weeks ago to tour Yellowstone National Park." She looked down and studied her coffee before adding in a low voice, "All the other women returned
except my mother."

He heard the deep concern in her voice. "Have you heard
from her?"

She nodded her head. "Yes. She left a message on my
answering machine letting me know that she had decided
to extend her vacation another two weeks."

A part of Madison wondered why she was disclosing
such information to Stone, a virtual stranger. The only
reason she could come up with was that she needed to talk
to someone and Stone Westmoreland seemed like a nice
enough guy to listen. Besides, she needed an unbiased ear.

"She left a message that she's extending her vacation yet
you're going to Montana to look for her anyway?"

Stone's question, and the way he had asked it, let her
know he didn't understand. "Yes, because there's a man
involved."

He nodded slowly. "Oh, I see."

Frankly, he really didn't see at all and evidently his expression revealed as much because she then said, "You might not think there's reason for concern, Mr. Westmoreland, but—"

"Stone. Please call me Stone."

She smiled. "All right." Then she started explaining herself again. "There is good reason for my concern, Stone. My mother hasn't done anything like this before."

He nodded again. "So you think that perhaps there has been some sort of foul play?"

She shook her head, denying that possibility. "No, I think it has something to do with her going through some sort of midlife crisis. She turned fifty a couple of months ago, and until that time she was completely normal."

Stone took a sip of his coffee. He remembered what happened when his mother turned fifty. She decided that she wanted to go back to school and start working outside of the home. His father almost had a fit because he was one of those traditional men who believed a woman's work was in the home raising kids. But his mother had made up her mind about what she wanted to do and nothing was going to stop her. Since his baby sister, Delaney, had gone off to college and there weren't any kids left at home to raise, his father had finally given in.

He shifted his thoughts to Madison's mother. Personally, he saw nothing abnormal with a woman disappearing in the wilds of Montana with a man, if that's what she wanted to do. However, from the worried expression on Madison's face, she evidently thought otherwise.

"So what do you plan on doing when you find her?" he asked curiously. After all, she was still the daughter and her mother was still the mother. He had learned from experience that parents felt they could do whatever pleased them without any interference from their children. At least that had always been the case with his mother and father, and he thought they were the greatest parents in the world.

"I'm going to try and talk some sense into her, of course," Madison said, her lips tightening in determination. "My father died of a heart attack over ten years ago, and my mother has been a widow since that time. She is the most staid, levelheaded and sensible person you could ever meet."

She sighed deeply then added, "Taking off with a man she doesn't know, whom she only met one night at dinner, doesn't make sense and it's so unlike her."

Stone's action-thriller mind went to work. "And you're positive she went off with this man willingly?"

He watched a clearly frustrated Madison take another sip of her coffee before answering. "Yes, there were witnesses, including the ladies who accompanied her on the trip. They said she simply packed one morning and announced that the guy was coming for her and she would be spending the rest of the time with him and to let me know she had decided to extend her trip. Of course I couldn't believe it and had all but called in the FBI before I got her phone call. Unfortunately, I wasn't at home when she called so we didn't talk, but her message clearly said that she was all right and was extending her vacation another two weeks and not to worry about her. But of course I'm worried."

Stone thought that was pretty evident. "Can she take additional time off from her job like that?" he asked, curious with everything Madison was telling him.

"Yes. My mother retired as a hospital administrator last year and owns a day-care center for the elderly. She has an excellent staff. Over the past couple of months she's been spending less time at the office and doing a lot of charity work in the community. She's really big into that."

Stone leaned back in his seat. "Do you have an idea where you plan to look? Montana is a huge place."

"I've made reservations at this dude ranch outside of Bozeman called the Silver Arrow. Have you ever heard of it?"

Stone smiled. Yes, he had. In fact, the Silver Arrow Dude Ranch was only a short distance from Durango's place. He was rather pleased that he and Madison would be in close proximity to each other. "I know exactly where it is. In fact, it's not far from where I'll be staying. The two of us will practically be neighbors."

She smiled like the thought of that pleased her. Or maybe it was wishful thinking on his part, Stone thought as his gaze centered on her lips.

"I've made plans for a tour guide to take me up into the mountains after I'm settled," she said, breaking into his thoughts.

Stone lifted a brow. "Up into the mountains?"

"Yes, that's where the man has taken my mother."

He paused in the act of taking a bite of his muffin. "This man took your mother up into the mountains?" At her nod he then asked, "Why?"

"Because that's where he lives."

After chewing a morsel of the muffin, Stone inquired, "The guy actually lives in the mountains?" He took a swallow of coffee, thinking he'd always thought his uncle Corey was the only man brave enough to forgo civilization and live high up in the mountains. While he worked as a park ranger, Corey Westmoreland stayed in the lowlands, making the trip into the mountains on his days off.

"Yes, according to the information I was able to find, he

lives on this huge mountain," Madison said, interrupting his thoughts. "The man is a retired park ranger. I don't have his full name but I understand he's well known in those parts and goes by Carl, Cole, Cord or something like that."

A portion of Stone's coffee went down the wrong pipe and he began coughing to clear his throat.

"Stone, are you all right?" Madison asked in concern.

Stone looked at her, not sure if he was all right or not. The man she had just described sounded a lot like his uncle Corey.

But a woman on Corey's mountain?

He cleared this throat thoroughly before asking his next question. He met her gaze, hoping he had not heard her correctly. "Are you saying that some guy who is a retired park ranger and who owns a ranch high up in the mountains is the person your mother ran off with?"

After wiping her mouth with a napkin, Madison nodded her head. "Yes. Can you imagine anything so ridiculous?"

No. In all honesty I can't, if we're talking about the same person. Stone thought about what she had told him. He then considered everything he knew about his uncle, especially how he felt about a woman ever setting foot on his beloved mountain.

He then answered Madison as honestly as he knew how. "No, I can't imagine anything so ridiculous."

She must have talked the man to death, Madison thought, glancing over at Stone a short while later. Conversation between them had dwindled off and he was leaning back in his seat, his head tipped back against the headrest, his eyes closed either in sleep or deep thought.

She couldn't help but take this opportunity to examine him.

If a man could be described as beautiful, it would be him. He was more handsome than any man had a right to be. She could easily tell that he had broad shoulders and although he was sitting down there was no doubt in her mind that he probably had pretty lean hips. But what captivated her most about him were his dark almond-shaped eyes and she wished they weren't closed so she could gaze into them some more.

They were as dark as midnight and, when he had looked at her, it was as if he could see everything, right deep into her very soul. Then there was his neatly trimmed curly black hair that was cut low, his high cheekbones and his beautifully full lips that had almost melted her in her seat when he had smiled. And the healthy texture of his chestnut skin tempted her to touch it to see if it was really soft as cotton.

For the first time, her mind was not focused on the fact that she was on a plane, but on the fact that she was sitting next to the most gorgeous man she had ever seen. Ordinarily, she would be the last person to notice a man after what Cedric had done to her a couple of years ago. Finding out the man you were about to marry was having an affair was painful to say the least. Since then she had decided that no man was worth the trouble. Some people were just meant to be alone.

She settled back in her seat, frowning as she wondered if the reason her mother had taken off with a man was because she had been tired of living alone. Abby Winters had been widowed for over ten years, and Madison knew her father's death had not been easy on her. She'd also known, even though her mother had refused to discuss it, that her parents had not had a happy marriage. All it had taken was a weekend spent in the home of a high school friend, whose

parents were still very much in love, to notice things she
didn't see at home. Her father had never kissed her mother
before leaving for work, nor had they exchanged funny
looking smiles across the dinner table when they thought
no one was watching.

Her parents had been highly educated people: Harvard
graduates. Somehow over the years they had become absorbed in their individual careers. Although there was no
doubt in her mind that they had loved her, it was clearly obvious that at some point they had stopped loving each other.

It seemed they had pretty much accepted a loveless marriage. Even after her father's death, her mother still didn't
date, although Madison knew several men had asked her
out once or twice.

That's what made Abby Winters' actions now so baf-
fling and unacceptable. What was it about the man that had
captured her mother's interest enough to do something as
outrageous as going off with him to his mountain? As she
had told Stone, her mother was the most rational person
she knew, so it had to be some sort of midlife crisis. There
was no other explanation for it.

And what would she say to her mother when she saw
her? That was a question for which she had no answer. The
only thing she knew for certain was that she was determined to talk some sense into her. Fifty-year-old women
just did not run off with men they didn't know.

Madison shook her head. She was twenty-five and she
would never take up with some man she didn't know, even
someone as good looking as Stone. She quickly glanced
over at him and had to admit that taking off with him was
definitely a tempting thought.

A *very* tempting thought.

She pushed the thought aside, thinking that one Winters woman acting impulsive and irrational was enough.

What if the man Madison Winters had described was really Uncle Corey?

With his eyes closed, that question continued to plague Stone's mind. At the moment he was pretending to be asleep, not wanting Madison to see his inner turmoil. Since the plane was at an altitude where he could use a mobile phone, he considered calling Durango to find out if Corey had abducted the woman. Durango, who was also a park ranger, had moved to Montana to attend college and joined the profession that their uncle had loved so much.

Durango had lived with Corey until he had saved up enough to purchase his own land. But calling Durango was not an option, not with Madison sitting next to him. Although she would try not to eavesdrop, there was no way she would not overhear his every word. He had no choice but to wait until the plane landed to question Durango. He hoped like hell that he was wrong and there was another retired park ranger who lived high in the mountains and whose name began with the letter C.

Stone breathed in slowly. Madison's scent was getting to him again. If he were completely honest he would admit that his blood had begun stirring the moment she had sat next to him on the flight. He had tried ignoring her by concentrating on the activities outside the plane window as the airline crew prepared for takeoff, and had pretty much dismissed her from his mind until she had touched him.

Aroused him was a much better word.

He sighed deeply. This would definitely be one flight he would not forget in a long time. He couldn't help but open his eyes and glance over at her. Her eyes were closed, her lips were parted and she was breathing at an even pace. Unlike before, she was now resting peacefully and had somehow taken her mind off her fear of flying, and a part of him felt good about that. He didn't want to dwell on the protective instincts he was developing for her. Perhaps he felt this way because she reminded him of his baby sister, Delaney.

A lazy smile touched his lips. As the only girl constantly surrounded by five older brothers and six older male cousins, Delaney had been overprotected most of her life. But after graduating from medical school she had pulled a fast one on everyone and had sneaked away to a secluded cabin in the North Carolina mountains for rest and relaxation, only to discover the mountain retreat was already occupied. A visiting desert sheikh, who'd had the same idea about rest and relaxation, had been ensconced in the cabin when she'd arrived. During the course of their "vacation," the two fell in love and now his baby sister was a princess living in the Middle East.

Delaney was presently in the States with her family to finish her residency at a hospital in Kentucky. He enjoyed seeing his one-year-old nephew Ari and had to admit that his sister's husband, Sheikh Jamal Ari Yasir, had grown on him and his brothers, and now he was as welcome a sight as Delaney. Stone knew Jamal loved his sister immensely.

He looked around the plane, wishing there was some way he could walk around and stretch his stiff muscles, but knew that would mean waking Madison to reach the aisle, and he didn't want to do that for fear she would start talking again about the man who could be his uncle. Until he got some answers from Durango, the last thing he wanted to do was come across as if he were deceiving her.

He glanced over at her once more and admired her beauty. To his way of thinking, Madison Winters was a woman no man in his right mind would want to deceive.

Chapter 2

The landing was smooth and as the plane taxied up to the terminal, Madison breathed a sigh of relief to be back on the ground. She unbuckled her seat belt and watched as the other passengers wasted little time getting out of their seats and gathering their belongings from the overhead compartments. Some people were moving quickly to catch connecting flights, while others appeared eager to be reunited with the loved ones waiting for them.

"Do you need help getting anything?"

She turned and met Stone's gaze. His voice was low, deep and seductive, and reminded her of the husky baritone of the singer Barry White. The rhythm of her heart increased.

"No, I can manage, but thanks for asking. If you don't mind, I'll wait until the plane empties before getting off. If you need to get by I can move out of your way."

"No, I'm in no hurry, either. I doubt my cousin is here

to pick me up since he's never on time." He smiled. "But then he just might surprise me this time."

His smile did funny things to her insides, Madison thought, glancing around to see how many people were left to get off the plane. The best thing to do would be to get as far away from Stone Westmoreland as soon as she could. The man messed with her ability to think straight and, for the moment, finding her mother needed her full concentration.

"Do you have transportation to the Silver Arrow ranch?"

Again she met his gaze. "Yes. I was told they would be sending someone for me."

Stone nodded. "Too bad. I was going to offer you a ride. I'm sure Durango wouldn't mind dropping you off since it's on the way."

Madison lifted a brow. "Durango?"

Stone smiled. "Yes, my cousin Durango. He's a park ranger at Yellowstone National Park."

Stone watched her eyes grow wide. "A park ranger? Then there's a chance he might know the man my mother took off with," she said excitedly.

Durango might know him better than you think, Stone wanted to say but didn't. Although the man she had described sounded a lot like Corey, it was still hard for Stone to believe that his uncle had actually taken a woman to his mountain. Stone never knew the full story why Corey had written off any kind of permanent relationship with a woman, he only knew that he had. "Yes, there is that possibility," Stone finally said.

"Then, if you don't mind, I'd like to ask him about it."

"No, I don't mind." Stone only hoped that he would get the chance to speak to Durango first.

"The way is clear to go now."

Madison's words recaptured his attention. He watched as she stood and eased out into the aisle. Opening the overhead compartment, she pulled out an overnight bag, a brand he recognized immediately as being Louis Vuitton. He smiled, remembering that he had given his sister Delaney a Louis Vuitton purse as a graduation present when she had earned her medical degree. He had been amazed at how much the item had cost, but when he had seen how happy the gift had made Delaney, the amount he'd spent had been well worth it.

Delaney had once explained that you could tell just how polished and classy a woman was by the purse she carried. If that was the case, Madison Winters was one hell of a polished and classy woman because she was sporting a Louis Vuitton purse, as well. He stood up and followed her into the aisle.

Madison looked ahead and thought the aisle of the plane seemed a hundred miles long. When they had to stop abruptly for the line of people moving slowly ahead of them, Stone automatically placed his hands at her waist to keep her from losing her balance.

She turned and gazed over her shoulder at him. "Thanks, Stone."

"My pleasure."

She smiled thinking it wasn't his pleasure alone. She felt his hard, solid chest pressed against her back and, when he placed his hands on her waist, she was acutely aware of the strength in his touch. He was a tall man. She wasn't conscious of just how tall until he stood up. He towered over her and when she tilted her head back to thank him, he met her gaze. The look in his eyes nearly took her breath away.

Although he wasn't wearing a wedding ring, there was

no way a man who looked this good could be unattached, she thought. A probing query entered her mind. He'd said his cousin Durango would be picking him up. Would there be a special lady waiting for him, as well? In her opinion, Stone Westmoreland had a magnetic, compelling charm that made him an irresistible force to reckon with.

When they left the plane, the two of them walked side by side through the ramp corridor toward the arrival area. "So, how long do you plan to stay in Montana?" Stone asked.

Madison could tell he had shortened his stride to stay level with her. She glanced over at him, met his gaze and tried to ignore the way her breasts tingled against the fabric of her blouse. "I'll stay until I find my mother and talk to her. I'm hoping it won't take long. According to Mr. Jamison, who owns the Silver Arrow, the cabin where my mother is staying is not far, but since it's located in the mountains getting there will be difficult. He's arranging for someone to take me by car as far as possible, then the rest will be done on horseback."

Stone lifted a brow and scrutinized her with an odd stare. "You ride?"

Madison's lips curved into a smile. "Yes. Growing up I took riding lessons. I'm sure climbing up a mountain will be far more challenging than just prancing a mare around a riding track, but I think I'll be able to manage."

Stone wasn't so sure. She seemed too refined and delicate to sit on a horse for a trip into the rugged mountains.

"That's something I don't understand."

Her words interrupted his thoughts. "What?"

"How my mother got up the mountain. I don't think she's ever ridden a horse. My dad tried getting her to take riding lessons when I took mine but she refused."

Stone nodded. "They probably rode double. Although it

might be strenuous, it's possible on a good, strong horse," he said. He could just imagine Madison sitting behind him on horseback. He took a deep, calming breath as he thought about her arms wrapped around him when she hung on to him, and the feel of her breasts pressed against his back while her scent filled his nostrils.

He winced. He had to stop thinking about her like this. He was in Montana to research a book, not to get involved in a serious affair or a nonserious one for that matter. However, he had to admit that the thought of it, especially with Madison as a partner, was a damn good one.

Together they walked to the area where they needed to claim their luggage. Stone scanned the crowd for Durango and wasn't surprised when he didn't see him. He assisted Madison in pulling her luggage off the conveyor belt before getting his bags.

"Thanks for making my flight enjoyable. Because of you I was able to take my mind off my fear of flying."

He decided not to say that, on the same note, thanks to her, he was reminded just how long it had been since he'd had a woman. "Do you see the person who's supposed to be picking you up?" he asked glancing around.

"No. Maybe I should call. Will you excuse me while I use that courtesy phone over there?"

"Sure."

Stone watched her walk to the phone. In a tailored pantsuit that fit her body to perfection, she looked totally out of place in Bozeman, Montana. All the other women were wearing jeans and shirts, and she was dressed like she was attending a high priority business meeting somewhere. He appreciated the sway of her hips when she walked and how her hair brushed against her shoulders with every step she took.

"You can't be left alone one minute before you're checking out a woman, Stone. Even one who has 'city girl' written all over her."

Stone switched his attention from Madison to the man
who had suddenly appeared by his side: his cousin Durango. "I sat by her on the plane from Atlanta. She's nice."

Durango chuckled as a wide grin covered his face. "All
women are nice."

Stone shook his head. Everyone in the family knew that,
like his brother Storm, Durango was a ladies' man, a player
of the first degree and, like Stone and their uncle Corey,
Durango had no intention of ever settling down. And speaking of Corey....

"When was the last time you saw Uncle Corey?" Stone
decided to cut to the chase and ask. He knew that Durango
kept up with their uncle's comings and goings. If there was
some woman on Corey's mountain, Durango would know
about it.

The grin suddenly disappeared from Durango's face;
not a good sign as far as Stone was concerned. "Funny you
should ask," Durango said frowning. "I haven't seen him
for a week and I know for a fact he has a woman up there
on his mountain."

That wasn't what Stone wanted to hear. "Are you sure?"

"Yes, I'm sure. I saw her myself when they were passing
through. She's a nice-looking woman, probably in her late
forties and talks with one of those northern accents. They've
been up on that mountain for almost a week now and Corey
won't answer the phone or return my calls. It makes me
wonder what's going on up there and how this woman got
such special privileges. I couldn't believe he broke his long-
standing rule about a woman on his mountain."

Stone leaned back against the railing. His mind was reeling and he needed to make sure he had heard everything Durango was telling him correctly. "You're saying that Corey actually has a woman on his mountain?"

"Yes, and she's not a long-lost relative, either, because I asked. Besides, it was obvious she wasn't related by the way they were acting. He couldn't wait to leave my place to head into the mountains and it doesn't appear he's bringing her down anytime soon."

Stone rubbed a hand down his face. "And you're sure you don't know who she is?"

Durango's frown deepened. "No, I don't know who she is, Stone, other than the fact he was calling her Abby. But you better believe that this Abby woman has hooked him in good, and I mean real good."

When the crowd standing directly behind Durango shifted, Stone noticed that Madison had finished her call and had walked up. From the expression on her face it was obvious that she had pretty much overheard most of what Durango had said.

Aw hell!

Durango noticed that Stone's gaze was fixed on something behind him and turned around. He smiled when he looked into the face of the woman Stone had been checking out earlier. He grinned. No wonder his cousin was taken with the woman, she was definitely a looker. Too bad Stone had met her first, because she was definitely someone who would have interested him.

He started to speak and introduce himself, since it seemed Stone had suddenly lost his voice. But something made him pause. Durango had dealt with enough women to know when they weren't happy about something and it was obvious this woman was angry, royally pissed off. And her words stopped him dead in his tracks.

"I believe the woman the two of you are discussing is my mother."

It wasn't hard to tell the two men were related, Madison thought, glancing up at them. Both were tall, extremely handsome and well built. Then there were the similarities in their facial features that also proved a family connection. They possessed the same close-cropped curly black hair, chestnut coloring, dark intense eyes and generous, well-defined mouths.

And both of them could wear a pair of jeans and a chambray shirt like nobody's business.

Madison inwardly admitted that, had she met the other man before Stone, she probably would have felt the same attraction to him, the same pull. However, she thought there was a gentleness and tenderness in Stone's eyes that she didn't easily see in the other man's.

She could tell her statement took the other man by surprise but when she glanced over at Stone, it was obvious that what she'd said hadn't surprised him, which meant he had known or at least suspected the identity of her mother's abductor all along.

She lifted a brow and leveled a pointed gaze at Stone. She had trusted him enough to discuss her mother with him openly, because she had needed someone to talk to, and talking to him had calmed her fears of flying and had also helped her to think through her mother's situation. If Stone had suspected the people she had been talking about were his uncle and her mother, why hadn't he said something?

Stone read the questions in Madison's eyes. "I didn't know, Madison, or at least I wasn't a hundred percent certain," he said in a low and calm voice. "And although I thought there was a possibility the man was my uncle Corey, I didn't want to upset you any more than you already were by adding my speculations."

Madison released a deep sigh. His reason for not telling her did make sense. "All right," she said softly. "So, what do we do now?"

Durango lifted a confused brow and looked at Stone and then back at Madison. "Why should we do anything? When they're ready they'll come back down the mountain."

Stone stifled a grin at the angry look Madison gave Durango. His cousin, the player, didn't have a snowball's chance in hell of winning this particular woman over. He doubted Madison got upset about anything or with anyone too often, but he could tell Durango was making her break her record. Durango had a rather rough way of dealing with women. He wasn't used to the soft and gentle approach. Yet the way women were still drawn to him defied logic.

"This is my cousin, Durango Westmoreland, Madison," Stone decided to say when silence, annoyance and irritation settled between Durango and Madison.

"And when Durango gives himself time to think logically, I'm sure he'll understand your concern for your mother's well-being. And although Durango and I both know that our uncle Corey would never do anything to harm your mother, we can certainly understand your desire to see for yourself that she's fine."

Stone watched a slow smile touch Durango's lips. From childhood they had always been able to read between the lines of each other's words. Stone was letting Durango know, in a subtle way, that he wanted him on his best behavior and to clean up his act.

"I apologize if what I said upset you, Madison," Durango said, offering her his hand in a firm handshake. "I wasn't aware that you thought your mother was in harm's way. If that's the case, we'll certainly do whatever needs to be done to arrest your fears. And let me be the first to welcome you to Montana."

Stone rolled his eyes. No one, he thought, could go from being a pain in the ass to irresistibly charming in a blink of an eye like Durango. Stone watched the warmth return to Madison's eyes and she smiled. Although that smile wasn't directed at him, a riot of emotions clamored through him nonetheless.

"Now that we have all that settled," he decided to speak up and say, "how about the three of us going somewhere to talk? Durango, you mentioned that you had met Madison's mother when Uncle Corey made a stop at your place."

A smile was plastered on Durango's face when he said, "Yes, and I even talked to her for a few minutes while Corey was loading up on supplies. I could tell she was a real classy, well-bred lady."

Madison nodded. She appreciated his comments although her mother's actions were showing another side of her. "Stone is right. I'd like to get to the Silver Arrow and unpack and freshen up, but as soon as I can, I'd like to meet with you and ask you a few more questions."

Durango quickly glanced over at Stone and Stone deciphered the message in his eyes. There were some things Madison was probably better off not knowing about her mother and their uncle.

Stone nodded and Durango caught his drift and returned his attention to Madison and said, "Sure, that will be fine, Madison. Is someone coming to pick you up from the Silver Arrow or can I give you a lift?"

"I don't want to put you to any trouble, Mr. Westmore-land."

Durango grinned again. "Just call me Durango and there's no trouble. The Silver Arrow is on the way to my ranch and is nicely situated between Bozeman and Yellowstone, and only a stone's throw away from the Wyoming line."

Madison nodded. "Thanks, I'll be glad to take you up on your offer. The man who answered the phone at the Silver Arrow said the guy who usually picks up his guests was ill and he was trying to find a replacement."

Durango reached out to take the luggage out of her hand. "Then consider it done."

Madison sat in the vehicle's back seat. Although she hated being in Montana, she couldn't overlook the beauty of this beautiful June day, as well as the vast country surrounding her. It was magnificent and left her utterly speechless. The Rocky Mountains were all around and the meadows were drenched with wildflowers: Red Indian Paintbrush and an assortment of other flowering plants. She had always heard about the beauty of being under a Montana sky and now she was experiencing it firsthand.

They were traveling down a two-lane stretch of highway; she knew they were a stone's throw away from Yellowstone National Park and hoped that she could tour the park before returning to Boston.

At the airport, after Stone and Durango had helped with her luggage, they had walked out to where Durango's SUV was parked in a "no parking zone" with its caution lights flashing. She smiled when she saw he was driving a nice, sleek, shiny black Dodge Durango.

Stone leaned over and whispered in her ear that Durango owned a Dodge Durango because he was conceited enough to think Dodge had named the vehicle after him. Durango, she knew, had heard Stone's comment and had merely laughed it off, and she could immediately feel the closeness between the two men.

"So how long do you think you're going to stay in Montana after meeting with your mother, Madison?" Stone asked, glancing at her over his shoulder. It was easy to see how captivated she was with the beauty of the land surrounding them. Earlier, she had said that she would probably only be in Montana long enough to talk to her mother, but he knew that Montana had a way of growing on you. And he had to admit that there was something about Madison that was growing on him. It was obvious that she had some real concerns about her mother and more than anything he wanted to help her resolve them.

He watched as she switched her gaze from the scenery to him. "I know what I said earlier, but now I'm not sure. I had planned to leave as soon as I had talked to my mother but I might decide to hang around awhile. This place is beautiful," she said, taking a quick glance out of the window again.

She turned back to him to add, "Since school is out for the summer I can enjoy myself. I seldom take vacations during the summer months. Usually I give private music lessons, so this is a really nice break, although I wished it was a planned trip rather than an unplanned one."

Stone really didn't care about the reason she was in Montana, he was just glad that she was. He hoped things worked out between her and her mother but it seemed that Madison had never heard of anyone acting out of character. He had a feeling that, in the world she was used to, things went according to plan and as expected.

He smiled inwardly. In that case, his family would take some getting used to if she ever met them. His father had two brothers. Of the three siblings, their uncle Corey was the only single one. Never having been married and the youngest of the three, he had been a surrogate father to his eleven nephews and one niece.

Corey had left Atlanta to attend Montana State University and fell in love with the land. Once he had a job as a park ranger with Yellowstone National Park, he made the state his permanent home. By the time he retired a year ago, he had been president of the Association of National Park Rangers for the past five years and had accumulated a vast amount of land.

"Well, if you decide to stick around I'd like to show you the sights. I spent a lot of time here as a kid while visiting my uncle Corey and know my way around pretty well."

A smile touched the corners of Madison's mouth. "Thanks. I might take you up on that." She then asked quietly, "Just what type of person is your uncle Corey? I know Durango said he was harmless and trustworthy, but I'm trying to come to grips with what there is about him that made my mother act so unlike herself."

Stone glanced over at Durango and saw the smile that tilted his cousin's lips; he was grateful that Durango, for once, had the decency to keep quiet. The rumor that Uncle Corey could make even the First Lady stop being a lady was something Madison didn't need to know. Chances were, if she asked anyone working at the Silver Arrow about Corey they would gladly enlighten her since his reputation was legendary.

Stone didn't really know what he could tell her; her mother being on his uncle's mountain didn't make much sense to him, either. He couldn't wait to get Durango alone to get the full story.

"I guess there are times when things happen that defy logic, Madison, and it appears this is the case with your mother and Uncle Corey. Just like your mother's actions are unusual, his actions are unusual, too. For as long as I've known him, which has been for all of my thirty-three years, he's been pretty much of a loner; preferring not to marry and spending most of his time when he wasn't at Yellowstone up on his mountain. And he's always had a rule about taking women up there."

Madison lifted a brow. "And what rule is that?"

Stone smiled. "That it would never happen. Other than female family members, there has never been a woman on his mountain. There must have been something about your mother to make him change his way of thinking about that."

A thought crossed Stone's mind. "Is there a chance that my uncle and your mother knew each other before?"

Madison frowned. That thought had crossed her mind but she didn't see how that could be. "I guess anything is possible. That would certainly explain things somewhat if it were true. But I don't see how that could be possible unless your uncle had visited Boston. My parents dated all through high school and college, and married right after graduation. I was born two years later." She decided not to mention the unhappy marriage her parents had shared even though they had tried to pretend otherwise.

"Then there could be another reason for their madness," Stone said softly, reclaiming her attention, casting a sideways glance.

She looked at him, squinting against the sun that shone through the vehicle window. "And what reason is that?"

"Instant attraction."

Stone watched as Madison immediately parted her lips to refute such a thing was possible, then she closed them tight. She had to know that such a thing was possible because the two of them had experienced that same attraction on the plane, so to deny such a thing existed would be dishonest.

Moments later she said, "I'm sure that's possible but can it be that powerful to make a levelheaded person become impulsive and irrational?"

Stone chuckled. "Trust me, Madison, I've seen it happen." One day he would prove his point by telling her about his two brothers who'd recently married. He didn't count his sister's marriage as anything unusual, since Delaney had always looked at things through rose-colored eyes, which was the main reason he and his brothers had been so overprotective of her during her dating years.

But his brothers Dare and Thorn had been dead set against marrying anytime soon, if ever. He clearly understood why Dare had wed since Shelly had been Dare's true love. When she had returned to town after having been gone ten years, and with a son Dare hadn't known existed, it had been understandable that the two would get back together and make a home for their child. But a sense of obligation had nothing to do with Dare's marriage to Shelly. His brother loved Shelly, plain and simple.

Now there hadn't been anything plain and simple about Thorn's marriage to Tara. Thorn was the last Westmoreland anyone expected to marry and he was a prime example of what instant attraction could do to you if you weren't careful.

"Well, I can't imagine anything like that happening with my mother," Madison said defiantly, recapturing Stone's attention. "Does your uncle have a phone up on his mountain?"

Stone nodded his head. "Yes."

"Then I need the number. I want to call my mother and let her know I'm on my way up there."

Durango, who had been quiet all this time, ended his silence with a chuckle. "You might have a problem reaching them," he said, not taking his eyes off the road.

"Why?" Madison asked curiously. "Are the phone lines down or something?"

"No, but I've tried calling Uncle Corey for the past several days to remind him that Stone was coming for a visit and he's not answering his phone."

Madison arched a dark brow. "He's not answering his phone? But—but what if something has happened to them and they can't get to the phone. What if—"

"They don't want to be disturbed, Madison?" Stone suggested. He saw her eyes shift from the back of Durango's head over to him. He could tell from her expression that his comment had conjured up numerous possibilities in her mind, but there was no hope for it. At some point she needed to accept that her mother had decided to extend her vacation by two weeks because she had wanted to, and not because she had been forced to. As far as Stone was concerned, the same held true with Madison's mother being on that mountain. It didn't seem that his uncle had forced the woman, so chances were she was just where she wanted to be. Sooner or later Madison would have to realize that.

She didn't answer his question. Instead she turned back to the car window and looked out at the scenery again. Stone inhaled deeply and turned back around in his seat. At least he had her thinking and for the moment perhaps that was the best thing.

Chapter 3

*W*hat if Mom doesn't want to be disturbed like Stone suggested?

That thought ran through Madison's mind as she studied the mountains and the ripened green pastures they passed. She couldn't help but think of all the things she knew about her mother.

The two of them were close and always had been, but there were some things a mother didn't share with a daughter and Madison was smart enough to know that. It came as no surprise that she had never thought of her mother as a sensual being. To her, she was simply Mom, although she had always thought her mother was a very beautiful woman.

Stone's comment was forcing her to see her mother through different eyes. One thing she knew for certain was that, since her father's death, her mother hadn't shown any interest in a man, and Madison had never given any thought as to whether that was a good thing or not. Usually, when Abby Winters went to social functions, she attended with Ron Carmichael, a widower who had been her father's business partner, or she would attend with some other family friend.

Although both Durango and Stone had been too polite to state the obvious, it seemed pretty clear that her mother and their uncle Corey were on his mountain engaging in some sort of an illicit affair. And if that was the case, Madison was determined to find out how Corey Westmoreland had tempted her mother to behave in such a manner.

She also knew that, although neither men had voiced it, they probably thought she had taken things a little too far in coming after her mother, and especially when she'd been told her mother was fine. But a part of her had to see for herself. She had to talk to her mother.

And she had to understand, or at least try to understand. What had possessed her mother to do what she did? She had to believe there had to be a good reason.

She licked her lips as they suddenly felt dry. When Stone had talked about instant attraction, she had known just what he'd meant. From the moment she had opened her eyes on the plane to gaze into the dark depths of his, she had been attracted to him in a way she had never experienced before. And she was still attracted to him. Every time he looked at her, she felt a funny feeling inside that started in her breastbone and quickly moved down her body to settle right smack in the center between her legs. She was drawn to Stone. It was Stone who had her breathing fast just thinking how she had touched him intimately on the plane without knowing it. She felt a sudden tingling in her hand when she thought about just where it had been. And the first time he had spoken to her, she had immediately become mesmerized by the sound of his voice.

She sighed deeply. Considering her current state, she needed to get to the Silver Arrow, check into her cabin and pull herself together as soon as possible. She had to remember that she was here for one reason and for one reason only. It had nothing to do with Stone and everything to do with her mother.

But…once the issue of her mother's state of mind was resolved, she couldn't help but think of all the very tempting possibilities.

"You and Durango didn't have to help with my luggage, Stone," Madison said as she watched him place the last piece next to her bed. Once they had arrived at the Silver Arrow, the two men had been adamant about helping her instead of letting the ranch hands do it.

The ranch consisted of numerous rustic cabins that were located some distance away from the main house for privacy. Guy Jamison, the owner, had said he would give her a tour of the ranch once she got settled. He also told her the time dinner would be served and said he was waiting to hear back from the man who'd agreed to be her tour guide up to the mountains.

The cabin she had been given was tucked beneath a cluster of trees and appeared more secluded than the others. Durango bid her goodbye and left after helping Stone with her bags. He went to wait outside in the SUV.

She glanced around, trying to get her mind off Stone and how good he looked standing in the middle of the room. In an attempt not to notice him, she let her gaze float across the décor and furnishings of the cabin. There was a dark oak bureau, dressing table and two nightstands on either side of the biggest bed she had ever seen. It appeared larger than king size and the printed covers made it look very welcoming and comfortable. She also took note of the matching curtains at the windows and frontier-printed rugs on the floor.

"Would you like to join me and Durango for dinner later?"

Madison met Stone's gaze. The attraction that had been there from the beginning was overcharging the room, blazing the distance between them and making her heart pound faster in her chest. Should she have dinner with him? He had indicated they wouldn't be alone since Durango would be joining them. And what if Durango wasn't joining them? Should she hesitate in accepting his offer just because he turned her on? But then she had more questions for Durango about her mother and Corey Westmoreland, and he'd said she could come over to his place.

She took a deep breath, deciding to be upfront with Stone since she couldn't deny the obvious. "The only reason I'm here is because of my mother, Stone, and when I resolve that issue, I'll decide if I want anything out of this trip for myself. Chances are I won't and will return to Boston as soon as I can."

He nodded, understanding what she was saying. "All right," he said and slowly crossed the distance separating them. "If that speech was to let me know you need time to figure things out, that's fine. Take all the time you need."

He needed time to figure things out, as well. Why did she turn him on like no other woman he knew and why at that very moment was the need to taste her about to make him lose his mind? In the past, his writing had always taken center stage in his life. He had lived more or less through his characters, knowing their fears, conflicts and deep-rooted and often chilling adventures. Transferring his thoughts from his mind to paper had been all consuming and the need to block off everything and anyone had been essential. His only goal had been to deliver, on every occasion, what readers expected from a Rock Mason book and he, without exception, had happily obliged them. The last thing he had to spare while working on a book was time for a woman, and in the past that was something he understood and accepted. But he knew he would be hard pressed to understand and accept anything about this situation with Madison Winters other than the fact that he wanted her. Pure and simple.

"Can I leave you with something to think about?" he asked quietly. The afternoon light that was flowing in through the only window in the cabin was casting a shadow on her features, but instead of dimming her allure, the light brought Madison's beauty even more into focus. He swallowed hard, steeling his resolve, only to discover that when it came to this woman he didn't have any.

Madison met Stone's gaze, holding it tightly. Intensely. She wondered what he was giving her time to think about. Did he have words of wisdom to share or was there something else? Her mind began whirling at all the possibilities and, heaven help her, but a part of her wished there was something else. She contemplated him for a long moment, wondering how she should respond if what he had in mind was the latter. Any physical contact, no matter how casual, wasn't a good idea since they had just met that day. Then she remembered that the first phase of physical contact had taken place the moment she had touched him on the plane, although the contact hadn't been intentional. But still, contact had been made and she hadn't been the same since.

And she could be honest enough with herself to admit that her mind had been made up about Stone the moment she had stepped off the plane with him. There was something about him that denoted a sense of honor, something rarely seen in a man these days.

He was the silent type with the word sexy oozing out of every pore on his body. She had never met a man like him before and doubted that she would again. For some reason she felt she could trust him, although blindly placing her trust in a man had been precisely how her heart had been broken two years ago. But with Stone she felt safe.

"Yes, you can leave me with something to think about," she finally said softly, after gathering her courage for whatever was to come. She didn't have long to wait to find out.

He reached out and cupped her chin in his hand, letting her know his intent and giving her every opportunity to put a stop to what he was about to do if that was what she wanted. When she didn't move or say anything, but continued to meet his gaze, while her breathing became just as erratic as his, he lowered his head to hers.

Madison felt the pull of her insides the moment their mouths touched, and immediately she felt the heat of his skin as his jeans-clad thigh brushed against her when he brought her closer into his arms. And when he settled his hands at her hips, and with it came the deep, compelling sizzle of desire, she thought she was certainly going to lose it.

Nothing prepared her for the onslaught of emotions that rammed through her when her lips parted and he entered her mouth and proceeded to kiss her in a way she had never been kissed before. It was a gentle kiss. It was tender. But on the flip side, it contained a hunger that made the pressure she felt in her chest too intense, almost unbearable.

And when he deepened the kiss, capturing her tongue with his, she was grateful that he had the mind to hold her tighter because she would surely have melted to the floor. She savored the hot sweetness of his mouth as he carried her to a level where sophistication, poise and what was proper had no place. As their tongues mingled, dueled and mated, feelings and emotions she had never felt before clashed into her, smothering her in a sexuality she hadn't known existed.

And when he finally broke the kiss, she drew in a long shuddering breath and gazed up at him. His eyes were intense and she knew that she and Stone had shared more than just a kiss. They had also shared an understanding. What was happening between them was probably no different than what his uncle and her mother had experienced.

Instant attraction.

The kind that hit two people from the first so you were compelled to do the unthinkable and act on it.

She sighed deeply and unconsciously licked her lips, tasting the dampness, a lingering reminder of his taste. Sharp coils of desire raced through her and she knew that Stone Westmoreland was a dangerous man. He was dangerous to her common sense. Although she needed to talk to Durango, she couldn't do it today. She needed time to clear her mind and think straight. At the moment the only thing she could think about was romancing Stone. In less than twenty-four hours he had unearthed another side of her, a side even she hadn't known existed and the thought of that frightened her somewhat.

"I don't think joining you and Durango this evening for dinner would be a good idea, Stone," she decided to say.

No matter how desperately she needed to know about her mother and their uncle, she also needed space from this man who caused emotions to grip her that were so foreign and unfamiliar. "I want to get settled in here first and think about a few things. Is there any way we can meet tomorrow, possibly before noon? I'd like to try and contact my mother to let her know that I'm here."

Stone held her gaze. "Tomorrow's fine, Madison. Just tell the lady at the front desk to phone Durango's ranch. They have the number and I'll be glad to come and pick you up."

"All right."

He stared at her for a few minutes then, without saying anything else, he turned and walked out of the door.

Pushing back from the kitchen table, Stone stood to help Durango clear the dishes. "I tell you, Stone, it was the strangest thing seeing Uncle Corey act that way, like a love-smitten twenty-year-old. And I didn't want to say anything in front of Madison, but her mother wasn't acting any better, although it would be clear to anyone that she was a lady with a lot of class."

Stone shook his head. "Well, Madison is determined to find answers. I think I gave her food for thought earlier and she's pretty much accepted the idea that her mother and Uncle Corey are involved in an affair, but she still needs to understand why."

Durango raised a brow as he leaned against the table. "What's there to understand? Lust is lust."

Stone rolled his eyes upward. Durango definitely had a way with words. "Well, with her mother being such a classy, well-bred lady and all, lust as you see it is something Madison just can't seem to understand."

Durango grinned. "Then I guess it's going to be up to you to explain it all to her then. Now if you need my help in—"

"Don't even think about it," Stone responded quickly in a growl.

Durango chuckled. "Hey, I was just kidding. Besides,

you know how I feel about city women anyway." Even with the laughter in his voice, his words echoed with bitterness.

Unfortunately Stone did know how he felt. "Need help with the dishes?" he asked after walking across the kitchen and placing them on the counter.

"Nope, that's what dishwashers are for. If you want we can try reaching Uncle Corey again, but take my word for it, it'll be a waste of time. He and his lady friend aren't accepting calls. I truly believe they turned the damn thing off."

Stone decided to try calling anyway and hung up later when he didn't get an answer. He shook his head emphatically. "You would think Madison's mother would have tried to reach her daughter."

Durango raised a brow. "I thought she had. Didn't Madison say on the drive over to the Silver Arrow that her mother had called to say she was fine and was extending her vacation for two weeks?"

"Yes, but she left the message on the answering machine. I'd think she would have made a point to talk to Madison directly to allay her fears."

Durango raised his eyes heavenward. "And I'd think— which is probably the same way Madison's mother is thinking—that at fifty years of age she doesn't have to check in with anyone, not even a daughter, especially if she's assured her daughter that she's okay." He grabbed an apple out of the basket and bit into it like he hadn't just eaten dinner. "Do you know what I think, Stone?"

Stone shrugged, almost too afraid to ask. "No, Durango, what do you think?"

"I think the reason Madison is so busy sticking her nose into her mother's love life…or lust life, is because she doesn't have one of her own."

A hint of a smile played at the corners of Stone's lips. "She doesn't have what? A love life or a lust life?"

"Neither of either. And I think that's where you need to step in."

Stone crossed his arms over his chest and met his cousin's direct gaze. "And do what exactly?"

Durango smiled. "Give the lady a taste of both."

Stone snorted. Only someone like Durango who had a jaded perception of love and marriage would think that way. Although Stone didn't have plans to ever settle down and marry, he did believe in love. His parents' marriage was a prime example of it, so was his sister Delaney's and his brothers Dare's and Thorn's marriages.

"I think I'm going to spend a few hours in your hot tub if you don't mind," he said to Durango.

"By all means, help yourself."

Less than twenty minutes later, Stone was sitting comfortably in the hot tub on Durango's outside deck. A good portion of Durango's land was the site of natural hot springs and the first thing he had done after building the ranch had been to take advantage of that fact and erect his own private hot tub. It was large enough to hold at least five people and the heat of the water felt good as it stimulated Stone's muscles.

He closed his eyes and immediately had thoughts of Madison. Maybe Durango was right about her failure to take her mother's words at face value that she was okay. But in just the short amount of time he had gotten to know Madison he could tell she was a person who cared deeply about those she loved. She probably couldn't help being a consummate worrier. And then maybe Durango was right again. Perhaps Madison needed something or someone in her life to occupy her time so she could stop worrying about her mother.

Stone inhaled deeply. For all he knew she might very well have someone already, some man back in Boston. He immediately pushed that thought from his mind. Madison Winters was not the type of woman who would belong to one man and willingly kiss another. And she had kissed him. Boy, had she kissed him. And he had definitely kissed her. The effects of their kiss still lingered with him. Even now he could still taste her. Durango's beef stew hadn't been strong enough to eradicate her taste from his mouth.

"Hey, Stone, you just got a call."

Stone cocked one eye open and looked at Durango who was standing a few feet away with a cold bottle of beer in his hand. "Who was it?"

"Your city girl."

Stone quickly opened both eyes and leaned forward, knowing just whom Durango was talking about. "Did she say what she wanted?"

Durango leaned against the door with a smirky grin on his face. "No, but I got the distinct impression that she wanted you."

Madison nervously paced her cabin as she waited for Stone to return her call. Deciding she had walked the floor enough, she dropped down into the nearest chair as she recounted in her mind what Frank, the husband of a good friend of hers who owned an investigative firm, had shared with her less than an hour ago. In addition to that, she couldn't help but replay back in her mind the communication she had picked up from her mother when Madison called her apartment in Boston to replay her messages.

She jumped when she heard a knock at her door and

wondered who it might be. It was late and she would think most of the guests and workers at the ranch had pretty much retired for the night. She had to remember this wasn't Boston and that she was practically alone in an area where the population was sparse.

She eased her way to the door. "Who is it?"

"It's me, Madison. Stone."

She let out a sigh of relief when she heard the familiar sound of Stone's voice and quickly opened the door. "Stone, I was waiting for your call. I didn't expect you to come over here," she said, taking a step back to let him in. She was glad that, although she had showered earlier, she had slipped into a long, flowing caftan that was suitable for accepting company.

Stone entered and closed the door behind him. "Durango said you sounded upset when you called so I thought I'd come over right away." His gaze took in her features. They appeared tense and worried. "What's wrong, Madison?"

She inhaled deeply and nervously rubbed her hands together. "I don't know where to start."

Stone studied her for a moment, concerned. "Start anywhere you like. How about if we take a seat over there and you can tell me what's going on," he suggested in a calming voice.

She nodded and crossed the room to sit on the edge of the bed while he sat across from her in a wingback chair. "All right, now tell me what's wrong," he said, his tone soothing.

Madison folded her hands in her lap. A part of her was grateful to Stone for coming instead of calling, although she hadn't expected him to. She lifted her chin and met his gaze; again, like before, she felt that powerful current pass through them and wondered if he'd felt it, too.

She put the thought of the sexual chemistry that was

sizzling between them to the back of her mind and started talking. "I called my apartment in Boston to retrieve my phone messages and discovered that my mother had called and left another one."

Stone lifted a dark brow. "Really? And what did she say?"

Madison sighed. "She said she regretted that we keep missing each other but that she wanted to let me know she was doing fine and…"

Stone waited for her to finish and when she seemed hesitant to do so he prodded. "And?"

Madison inhaled deeply once again before saying, "And she plans to extend her trip by an additional two weeks."

For a moment there was not a sound in the room, just this long pregnant silence. Then Stone slowly nodded as he continued to study her. He could tell the message had been upsetting to Madison. "Well, at least you know that she's okay."

Madison shook her head and Stone watched as her hair swirled around her shoulders with the movement. "No, I don't know that, Stone. I'm more worried about her than ever. There's something else I think you should know."

Stone gazed across the few feet separating them. "What?"

Madison slowly stood then nervously paced the room a few times before coming back to stand in front of Stone. "I know that you and Durango tried to reassure me that your uncle is a decent man—honest, trustworthy and safe—but I had to be sure. I had to find out everything I could about him to help me understand why my mother is behaving the way she is. A friend of mine, another teacher at the school where I work, well, her husband owns an investigation firm.

After you left here today, I contacted him and gave him your uncle's name."

Stone sat back in the chair, his gaze locked with hers as he rubbed his chin. "And?"

Madison swallowed nervously. "And, according to Frank, when he entered your uncle's name into the database, he discovered another investigative firm, one that's located somewhere in Texas, was checking out your uncle's past, as well. For some reason it seems that I'm not the only one who wants information about him."

Stone frowned and sat up straight in his chair. Anger suddenly lined his features. "Are you trying to accuse my uncle of—"

"No! I'm not accusing him of anything. Even Frank indicated that he's clean and doesn't have a criminal record or anything. I just thought it was strange and felt that you should know."

Stone stared at Madison for a long moment then stood in front of her. "I don't know what interest another investigative company has in my uncle but, whatever the reason, it has nothing to do with his character, Madison. Corey Westmoreland is one of the finest men I know. I admit he can be somewhat ornery at times and set in his ways, but I would and do trust him with my life."

Madison heard the defensive anger in Stone's voice although he tried to control it. She crossed her arms over her chest and gazed up at him. "I wasn't insinuating that he wasn't a—"

"Weren't you? I also think that until you talk to your mother and see her for yourself to make sure she's not up there with some crazy mountain man, you won't have a moment of peace."

Unable to help himself, Stone reached out and brushed

a strand of hair back from her face. There were tension lines around her eyes and the mouth he had kissed earlier that day was strained, agitated and on edge. "And I intend to give you that peace. I will take you up Corey's Mountain myself."

His words had an immediate effect on Madison and she released her arms from across her chest. Her heart began beating a mile a minute. "You will?" she asked in a rush.

"Yes. I would head up there first thing in the morning, but unfortunately you don't have the proper attire to make such a trip. We need to take care of that as well as getting the supplies we'll need. If all that works out then we can leave the day after tomorrow, bright and early. We'll take a truck as far as Martin Quinn's ranch, then borrow a couple of his horses to go the rest of the way on up."

Madison tried to mask her relief. She hated admitting it but Stone was right. She wouldn't have a moment of peace until she saw and talked to her mother herself. "I'll make sure I get all the things I need."

Stone nodded. "I'm going to make sure you get all the things you need, too. I'll be picking you up in the morning to drive you into town and take you to the general store. We should be able to purchase everything we'll need from there."

Madison nodded. Uncertain what to say next she knew the one thing that she *had* to say. "Thank you, Stone."

Her heart lurched in her chest when she saw that her words of thanks had not softened the lines around his eyes. He was still upset with her for what she'd insinuated about his uncle.

"Don't mention it. I'll see you in the morning." And without saying anything else, he crossed the room and walked out of the door.

Chapter 4

Whoever said you can take the girl out of the city but you can't take the city out of the girl must have known a woman like Madison Winters, Stone thought, as he sat silently in the chair with his long legs stretched out in front of him and watched her move around the cabin packing for their trip.

That morning they had gone to the general store to purchase the items they would need. Getting her prepared for their excursion had taken up more time than he figured it would. When he had inventoried what she'd brought with her from Boston, he hadn't been surprised to discover her stylish clothing—mostly with designer labels—included nothing that would be durable enough to travel up into the mountains. When they'd driven into town she had agreed with his suggestion that she buy several pairs of jeans, T-shirts, flannel shirts, a couple of sweaters, a wool jacket, heavy-duty socks and, most important, good hiking boots. He had also strongly suggested that she buy a wide-brimmed hat. He'd explained to her that the days would be hot and the nights would be cold.

He had taken care of the other things such as the food they would need, the sleeping bags they would use, as well as the rental of the truck that would carry them as far as the Quinns' ranch.

Stone's lips broke into an innately male smile as he continued to watch her. She was definitely a gorgeous woman but, more than that, he found her downright fascinating. He would even go so far as to say that she intrigued him, especially now when she was frowning while glancing down at herself, as if the thought of wearing jeans and a flannel shirt was nothing she would ever get used to.

Hell, it was something he doubted he would get used to, either. He had seen plenty of women in jeans in his lifetime but none, and he meant none, could wear them like they'd been exclusively designed just for their bodies. Another man might say that she was built and had everything in all the right places, but the writer in him would go further than that and say she was…*a summer pleasure and a fall treasure whose beauty was as breathtaking and captivating as a cluster of tulips and daffodils under a spectacular Montana sky.*

"Do you think I packed enough, Stone?"

Her words intruded on his musings and he glanced at the bed. To be quite honest she had packed too much, but he knew that was the norm for any woman. Somehow they would manage even if it meant leaving some of it at the Quinns' ranch once they got there. The back of a horse could handle only so much on what would be a treacherous climb up the mountain.

"No, you're fine," he said coming to his feet. "I contacted Martin Quinn and he's expecting us by noon tomorrow.

We'll sleep overnight at his place then head up the mountain right after breakfast. If our timing is right, we won't have to spend but one night out under the stars."

Madison raised a brow. "It will take us two days to get to your uncle's ranch?"

"Yes, by horseback. At some point during the daylight hours it will be too hot to travel and we'll need to give the horses periodic breaks."

Madison nodded. She then cleared her throat. "Stone, I want to thank you for—"

"You've thanked me already," he said, picking up the Stetson that he had purchased that day off the table.

"Yes, I know, but I also know that taking me to your uncle's place is intruding into your writing time."

He looked at her and the liquid heat that had started flowing through his bloodstream from the moment he had met her was still there. "No, you're not," he said, forcing himself to ignore how good she smelled. "I had planned to go visit Uncle Corey anyway while I was here, so now is just as good a time as any."

"Oh, I see."

Stone doubted that she saw anything. If she did she would have second thoughts of them spending so much time together over the next three days. If she really had her eyes wide-open she would see that he wanted her with a passion so thick he could cut it with a knife. The clean scent of the mountains had nothing on her. She had a fragrance all her own and it was one that reminded him of everything a woman was supposed to be. She was more than just a city girl. She was sensuality on legs and a gorgeous pair of them at that.

He couldn't believe it had only been yesterday when he had first looked into eyes that were so mesmerizing they had taken his breath away. And since then, undercurrents of sensual tension had surrounded them whenever they were together, leaving them no slack but a whole lot of close encounters of the lush kind. He had never been this incredibly aware of a woman in his life.

"Well, I guess that's it until tomorrow morning."

Her words cut into his thoughts, reminding him that he had stood to leave yet hadn't moved an inch. "Yes, I think that's about it except for your attitude about things."

She lifted her chin just a bit. "What do you mean?"

He rather liked when she became irritated about something. She became even sexier. "I mean," he began slowly, deciding that no matter how sexy she got when she was mad, he didn't want to get her pissed off too much. "Before we head up toward Uncle Corey's mountain, you need to come to terms with what we might find when we get there, Madison."

He watched as she averted her eyes from his briefly and he knew she understood exactly what he meant. She tilted her head and their gazes connected again. "I hear what you're saying but I don't know if I can, Stone. She's my mother," she said quietly.

Stone held her gaze intently. Logical thinking—which he knew she wasn't exemplifying at the moment—dictated that he have something to say to that. So he did. "She's also a full-grown woman who's old enough to make her own decisions."

She sighed and he could just feel the varied emotions tumbling through her. "But she's never done anything like this before."

"There's a first time for everything." He of all people should know that. Until yesterday, no woman had taken hold of his senses the way she had. He wasn't exactly happy about it and in some ways he found it downright disturbing. But he was mature enough to accept it as the way things happen sometimes between a man and a woman. Unlike his brother Thorn who liked challenges, he was one of those men who tried looking at things logically without complications and definitely without a whole lot of fuss. He accepted things easily and knew how to roll with the flow.

Madison was a very desirable woman and he was a hot-blooded male. He had conceded from the first that getting together with her would be like pouring kerosene on a fire. The end result—total combustion. The only problem with that picture was that, no matter how hot they could burn up the sheets, on some things he had made up his mind with no chance of changing it. Getting involved in a permanent relationship with a woman was one of them. It wouldn't happen.

Seeing the look of uncertainty on her face, he knew she was a long way from accepting the possibility that her mother and his uncle were lovers. As strange as it seemed, he had come to terms with it and eventually she would have to do the same. "I suggest that you get a good night's sleep," he said, moving toward the door. He intended to open it and walk out without looking back.

But he couldn't.

He turned and reached out and pulled her to him, encircling her waist and resting her head on his chest. Some inner part of him just knew that she needed to be held in his embrace. And that same inner part of him also knew that she needed a kiss, as well.

A tenderness fed by a burning flame of desire raced through him, making his heartbeat quicken and his body go hard. She must have felt his arousal and lifted her head. Their gazes locked. Words weren't needed, sexual chemistry had a language all its own and it was speaking to them loud and clear.

She parted her lips on a sigh and he lowered his head and captured the very essence of that moan with his mouth. The taste of her was tempting, and he immediately thought of silken sheets, burning candles and soft music. He thought of touching her all over, loving her with his mouth and his hands until she groaned out his name, then placing her beneath him, entering her, thrusting in and out in the same rhythm he was using at that very moment on her mouth. All during the previous night he'd had a hard time sleeping because his body had silently yearned for her. And he knew tonight, tomorrow night and all of the nights after that wouldn't be any different.

After a long moment, he broke off the kiss and rested his forehead against hers. Kissing her was exhausting as well as stimulating. He could have continued kissing her forever if he hadn't needed to breathe.

"Stone?"

He inhaled and tried to get his body to relax, but her scent filled his nostrils making regaining his calm downright difficult. "Yeah?"

"This isn't good, is it?"

He chuckled against her ear. "You don't hear me complaining, Madison."

"You know what I mean."

Yes, he knew exactly what she meant. "If I go along with your way of thinking, that we should place our full concentration on your mother and Uncle Corey and not on each other, then I would have to agree that it isn't good because the timing is lousy. But if I adhere to my own thoughts, that I feel whatever is going on between my uncle and your mother is their business and that you and I should place our full concentration on each other, then I would say it is good."

He said the words while a barrage of emotions raced through him. They were emotions he wasn't used to dealing with. A part of him suddenly felt disoriented. Totally confused. Fully aware.

The woman he held in his arms was as intoxicating as the most potent brand of whiskey and she had his senses reeling and his body heated. "I'm going to leave the decision as to how we should handle things up to you, Madison. I suggest you sleep on it and let me know what you decide in the morning."

Leaning down, he kissed her again; this kiss was tender but just as passionate as the one before. He pulled back and released her, opened the door and walked out into the cool Montana night.

Clinging to the strength of the decisions she had made overnight, Madison opened the door for Stone the next morning. The eyes that met hers were sharp, direct and she immediately felt herself wavering on one decision in particular as she inwardly asked herself: *how can I stand behind my decision to make sure that nothing happens between us?*

Of the two decisions she'd made, that had been the hardest one and, as she glanced at the strong, vital and sexy man standing in the doorway, she knew it would be the hardest one to keep. Stone wasn't a man any woman could ignore and being alone with him for the next few days would definitely test her resolve. If she were smart she would put any thoughts of a relationship between them out of her mind completely. She had never been involved in any sort of casual affair before and wasn't sure that type of relationship would suit her. But then she had to remember that she had thought her relationship with Cedric had been anything but casual and look where it had gotten her.

"You're earlier than I expected," she somehow found her voice to say. In the predawn light that encompassed him, she searched his eyes for any signs of decisions that he himself might have made and only saw the heated look of desire that had been there from the very first. And she knew if she was ever undisciplined enough to risk all and take a chance, this man would and could introduce her to passion of the hottest kind.

He was standing before her so utterly handsome in his jeans, flannel shirt, boots and Stetson. He looked nothing like an action-thriller author but everything like a rugged cowboy who made the unspoiled land surrounding Montana's Rocky Mountains his home. But she knew there was something else about him that was holding her interest. It was what she saw beyond the clothes. It was the man himself. There was a depth to him that was greater than any man she'd ever met. There was a self-confidence about him that had nothing to do with arrogance and a kindness that had nothing to do with a sense of duty. He did things out of the generosity of his heart and concern for others and not for show. And she felt loyalty to him. He would be true to whatever woman he claimed as his. Cedric could certainly have taken a few lessons from Stone Westmoreland.

He smiled. "I thought we could grab something to eat on the way," he said, interrupting her thoughts. She sighed, grateful that he had. She could have stood there and stacked up all his strong points all day.

She offered him a smile. A part of her was tempted to offer a lot more. He had just that sort of effect on her. "All right. I just need to grab my luggage."

"I'll get it," he said, entering her cabin, immediately filling the space with his heat and making her totally aware of him, even more than she had been before. She watched as he glanced over at the luggage she had neatly lined up next to her bed. Then he looked at her and she heard him swear under his breath before moving—not toward the luggage but toward her.

"I don't know what decisions you made about us," he said in a low, husky voice. "But I thought of you all last night and I swore that as soon as I saw you this morning I would do something."

"What?" she asked, trying to ignore the seductive scent of his aftershave as well as the intense beating of her heart.

"Taste you."

Madison's breath caught and, before she could release a sigh, Stone captured her mouth in his. As soon as their tongues touched she knew she would remember every sweet and tantalizing thing about his kiss. Especially the way his tongue was dueling with hers, staking a claim she didn't want him to have but one he was taking anyway as he tried kissing the taste right out of her mouth. His tongue was dominating, it was bold and it left no doubt in her mind that when it came to kissing, Stone was an ace, a master, a perfectionist. She placed her arms around his neck, more to stop from melting at his feet than for support. He had a way of making her feel sexy, feminine and desirable; something Cedric had never done.

Moments later, when he broke off the kiss and slowly lifted his head to look down at her, she couldn't help asking, "Got enough?"

"Not by a long shot," he said hotly against her moist lips. Then he leaned down and kissed her again and Madison quickly decided, what the heck. Once she had told him of her decision about them he wouldn't be kissing her again anytime soon, so she would gladly take what she could for now.

Her common sense tried kicking in—although it didn't have the punch to force her to pull from his arms just yet. Her practical side was reminding her that she'd only met Stone two days ago. Her passionate side countered that bit of logic with the fact that in those two days she probably knew him a lot better than she'd known Cedric in the three years they had dated. Stone was everything her former fiancé was not—including one hell of a kisser.

Desire surged through her and she knew if she didn't pull back now the unthinkable might happen. But then a rebel part of her that barely ever surfaced hinted that the unthinkable in this case just might be something she should do.

She didn't have much time to think about it further when Stone lifted his mouth again and she, regretfully, released her arms from around his neck and took a step back, putting space between them.

"I guess I better grab that luggage so we can leave," he said, keeping his gaze glued to her face.

"That's a good idea and I don't think there should be any more physical contact between us until we talk," she said softly, trying to hold on to the resolve she'd had that morning. The same resolve his kiss had almost swiped from her.

She watched as he arched a dark brow. "You've made decisions?"

Her gaze held on to his. "Yes."

He nodded then walked across the room for her luggage.

"Tell me about yourself, Stone, and I would love hearing about all of your books."

Stone briefly glanced across the seat of the truck and met Madison's inquiring gaze. They had been on the road for over an hour already and she'd yet to tell him of any decisions she'd made. Even when they had stopped at a café for breakfast she hadn't brought their relationship up. Instead she had talked about how beautiful the land was, how much she had enjoyed teaching last year and about a trip to Paris she had taken last month. She was stalling. He knew it and knew that she knew it, as well.

"Do you want to know about Stone Westmoreland or about Rock Mason?"

A bemused frown touched her face. "Aren't they one and the same?"

"No. To the people I know I'm Stone Westmoreland. To my readers, the majority of whom don't know me, I'm Rock Mason—a name I made up to protect my privacy. I should correct that and say it's a name my sister Delaney came up with. At the time she was eighteen and thought it sounded cool."

She nodded. "And which one of those individuals are you now?"

"Stone."

She nodded again. And although she had made her mind up not to go there, she couldn't help but ask. The need to know was too strong. "And each of the times you kissed me, who were you?"

He glanced over at her. "Stone." He then pulled off the road, stopped the truck and turned to her. "Maybe I need to explain things, Madison. I don't have a split personality. I'm merely saying that a lot of people read a book a person writes and assume they know that individual just because of the words he or she puts on paper. But there's more to me than what is between the pages of my novels. I write to entertain. I enjoy doing so and it pays the bills in a real nice way. Whenever I finish a book I feel a sense of accomplishment and achievement. But when all is said and done, I'm still a normal human being—a man who has strong values and convictions about certain things. I'm a man who's proud to be an African-American and I'm someone who loves his family. I have my work and I have my privacy. For my work I am Rock Mason and for my private life I am Stone. I consider you as part of my private life." With that said he started the truck and pulled back on the main road.

Madison blew out a breath. The very thought that he considered her part of his life at all made her heart pound and parts of her feel soft and gooey inside. "So tell me something about the private life of Stone Westmoreland."

Her request drew his brows together as he remembered the last time a woman had asked him that. Noreen Baker, an entertainment reporter who'd wanted to do an interview on him for *Today's Man* magazine. The woman had been attractive but pushy as hell. He hadn't liked her style and had decided when she'd tried delving into his personal life that he hadn't liked her. But she was determined not to be deterred and had decided one way or another she would get her story.

She never got her story and found out the hard way that, although on any given day he was typically pretty nice and easygoing, when pissed off he could be hell to deal with. Instead of giving her the exclusive she had desired, he had agreed to let someone else do a story on him.

"I'm thirty-three, closer to thirty-four with a birthday coming up in August, single, and have never been married and don't plan on ever getting married."

Madison lifted a brow. "Why?"

"It's the accountability factor. I love being single. I like coming and going whenever I please and, with being a writer, I need the freedom of going places to do research, book signings, to clear my mind, relax and to be just plain lazy when I want to. I'm not responsible for anyone other than myself and I like it that way." He decided not to tell her that another reason he planned to stay single was that he saw marriage as giving up control of his life and giving more time to a wife than to his writing.

Madison nodded. "So there's not a special person in your life?"

"No." But then he thought she was special and he had pretty much accepted that she was in his life…at least at the present time.

"What about your immediate family?"

"My parents are still living and doing well. My father works with the construction company my grandfather started years ago. He's a twin."

Madison had shifted her body in the seat to search her pockets for a piece of chewing gum and glanced over at Stone. "Who's a twin?"

"My father. As well as my two brothers, Chase and Storm, and my cousins, Ian and Quade. They are Durango's brothers."

"Are they all identical twins?" she asked fascinated. She'd never heard of so many multiple births in one family before.

"No, everyone is fraternal, thank God. I can't imagine two of Storm. He can be a handful and considers himself a ladies' man."

Madison smiled, hearing the affection in his voice. "How many brothers do you have?"

"Four brothers and one sister. Delaney, who we call Laney, is the baby."

Madison frowned. "Delaney Westmoreland? Now where have I heard that name before?"

Stone chuckled. "Probably read about her. *People* magazine did a spread on her almost a year and a half ago when she married a prince from the Middle East by the name of Jamal Ari Yasir."

A huge smile touched Madison's face. "That's right, I remember reading that article. *Essence* magazine did an article on her, as well. Wow! I remember reading it during…"

Stone glanced over at her to see why she hadn't finished what she was about to say. Her smile was no longer there. "During what?"

She met his gaze briefly before he returned it to the road. "During the time I broke up with my fiancé. It was good reading something as warm, loving and special as the story about your sister and her prince; especially after finding out what a toad my own fiancé was."

"What did he do?"

Madison glanced down at her hands that were folded in her lap before glancing over at Stone. His eyes were on the road but she knew that she had his complete attention and was waiting for her response. "I found out right before our wedding that he'd been having an affair. He came up with a lot of reasons why he did it, but none were acceptable."

"Hell, I should hope not," Stone said with more than a hint of anger in his voice. "The man was a fool."

"And she was a model."

Stone lifted a brow. "Who?"

"The woman he was sleeping with. He said that that justified his behavior. He believed he was actually using her so as not to wear me down. He wanted to preserve me for later."

A dark frown covered Stone's face. "He actually said that?"

"Yes. Cedric was quite a character."

Stone didn't want to get too personal, but he couldn't help asking, "So the two of you never, ahh, never slept together?"

Instead of looking over at him he watched as she quickly glanced out the window. "Yes, we did but just twice during the three years we were together."

Stone shook his head. "Like I said before, he was a fool."

Madison leaned back comfortably in her seat. She was glad Stone felt that way. Cedric had tried to convince her that just because he'd been involved in one affair was no reason to call off their wedding. A model, he'd tried to explain, was every man's fantasy girl. That didn't mean he had loved her less, it only meant he was fulfilling one of his fantasies. She guessed fulfillment of fantasies came before fidelity.

"Tell me some more about you, Stone," she said, not wanting to think anymore about Cedric and the pain he had caused her.

She listened for the next few miles while Stone continued to tell her about his family. He talked about his brother Dare who was a sheriff and Chase who owned a restaurant in downtown Atlanta. Once again she was surprised to discover that he had another well-known sibling—Thorn Westmoreland, the motorcycle builder and racer who had won the big bike race in Daytona earlier that year.

"I've seen your brother's bikes and they're beautiful. He's very skillful."

"Yes, he is," he said. "He got married last month and is in the process of teaching his wife how to handle a bike."

By the time they had reached the Quinns' ranch, Madison felt she knew a good bit about Stone. He had openly shared things about himself and the people he cared about. She knew he never, ever wanted to marry but was proud that his parents' marriage had lasted for such a long time. And he was genuinely happy for his sister and brothers and their marriages.

When they pulled the truck up in front of the sprawling ranch house, Madison caught her breath. It was breathtaking and like nothing she had ever seen before. "This place is beautiful," she said when Stone opened the truck door for her to get out.

He laughed. "If you think this place leaves you gasping for air, just wait until you see Uncle Corey's place. Now that place is a work of art."

Madison couldn't wait to see it. Nor could she wait to see her mother. Stone must have read the look in her eyes because he gently squeezed her hand in his, giving her assurance. "She's fine and you'll see her soon enough."

She nodded. Thankful. Before she could say anything a woman, who appeared to be in her middle fifties, came out the front door of the house with a huge smile on her face. She was beautiful and it was quite obvious she was Native American. Her dark eyes were huge in her angular face. She had high cheekbones and long, straight black hair that flowed down her back. "Why, if it isn't Stone Westmoreland. Martin said you were coming and I decided to cook an apple pie for the occasion. I'll share if you autograph a few books for me."

Stone laughed as he swept the woman off her feet into his arms for a hug. "Anything for you, Mrs. Quinn. And you know how much I love your apple pie." When he had placed her back on her feet he turned her around so he could introduce her to Madison.

"Madison, this is Morning Star Quinn, Martin's wife. They are good friends of my uncle Corey and their son McKinnon is Durango's best friend."

Madison smiled. It was easy to see that the woman had Stone's affection and respect. She offered Morning Star Quinn her hand to shake, liking her on the spot. She seemed like such a vibrant person who blended in well with her surroundings. "It's nice meeting you."

"It's nice meeting you, as well. And I've prepared a place for the two of you to stay overnight. I understand you are on your way up to see Corey."

Stone nodded. "Yes. Mr. Quinn mentioned when I spoke with him on the phone yesterday that the two of you haven't seen Uncle Corey in a while."

Morning Star Quinn shook her head. "It's been weeks. He's missed the Thursday night poker game for almost three weeks now, and you know for your uncle that's unusual. But we know he's all right."

"How do you know that for certain?" Madison couldn't help but ask.

Morning Star Quinn raised a curious brow as if wondering why she was interested then smiled at her and responded. "He came down off the mountain a couple of days ago to use the phone. It seems something is wrong with his telephone, which is the reason no one has heard from him. Martin and I had gone to town so we didn't get a chance to see him, but McKinnon was here and had a chance to talk to him. He assured us that Corey was fine."

Mrs. Quinn then switched her gaze to Stone. "McKinnon also said he had a woman with him; a very nice-looking woman at that. Of course that surprised all of us because you know how Corey feels about a woman being on his mountain."

Stone shook his head, smiling. "Yes, I know. In fact that's one of the reasons we're going up to see him."

Tapping her finger to her bottom lip, Morning Star

Quinn gazed thoughtfully at Stone. "Then you know her? You know who this woman is?"

Madison knew that, out of consideration for her mother's reputation, Stone would not say. But she knew that Morning Star Quinn was a person that she could be honest with; and was a person that she *wanted* to be honest with. "Yes, we know who she is," Madison finally answered. "The woman up there on the mountain with Corey Westmoreland is my mother."

Chapter 5

Nothing, Madison thought as she walked outside on the huge porch, could be more beautiful than a night under a Montana sky. Even in darkness she could see the outlines of the Rockies looming in the background and was starkly amazed at just how vastly different this place was from Boston.

She turned when she heard the door open behind her and wasn't surprised to see it was Stone. She smiled as she took a couple of minutes to calm the rapid beating of her heart. The more time she spent with him, the more she appreciated him as a man...a very considerate and caring man. Even now she could feel the warmth of his eyes touching her.

Earlier he had helped her unload her luggage and had placed it in the bedroom that Mrs. Quinn had given her to use. Then later, after she had gotten settled, he had come for her when Martin Quinn and his son McKinnon had come home. She had blinked twice when she saw McKin-

Stone Cold Surrender

non. The man was simply gorgeous and had inherited his mother's golden complexion. After introductions had been made, Stone had asked her to take a walk with him to show her around the Quinns' ranch before dinnertime.

On their stroll, he had shared stories with her about how, while growing up, he and his brothers and cousins would visit this area every summer to spend time with their Uncle Corey. It was a guy thing, which meant Delaney was never included in those summer retreats. She usually came to Montana during her school's spring breaks. Stone also shared with her the little escapades the eleven Westmoreland boys and McKinnon and his three brothers had gotten into. He had made her smile, chuckle and even laugh a few times, and for a little while she had forgotten the reason she had come to Montana in the first place. At dinner she had met Martin's other three sons, who were younger than McKinnon, but who had also inherited their mother's Blackfoot coloring, instead of the light complexion of their Caucasian father.

"You okay?" Stone asked quietly, coming to stand beside her.

She tipped her head to look up at him. When he placed his arms around her shoulders as if to ward off the chill in the air, she became very aware of how male he was. And the nice thing about it was that he didn't flaunt it. In fact he seemed totally unaware of the sensuality oozing from him. "Yes, I'm fine. Dinner was wonderful, wasn't it?"

"Yes. Mrs. Quinn always knew how to cook and her apple pie has always been my favorite," he answered.

Madison grinned when she remembered the number of slices he'd eaten and said, "Yeah, I could tell." She then thought of something. "They didn't say a lot about your uncle at dinner." She felt his fingers inch upward to caress the side of her neck, sending a glimmer of heat through her.

"There wasn't much to say. They know the man Uncle Corey is and know that your mother isn't in any danger."

She shot him a quick look. "I know she isn't in any danger with him, Stone. I just don't understand what's going on. And I'm beginning to understand a bit about instant attraction if that's what it was, but still I have to talk to her anyway."

"I understand," he said, giving her shoulders a quick squeeze.

A part of Madison wondered if he did understand when there were times when she didn't.

"Tell me about your parents, Madison."

His question caught her off guard. "My parents?"

"Yes. What sort of marriage did they have?"

She frowned, not sure why he was asking and whether or not she was willing to disclose any details of her parents' relationship as she had seen it. But this was Stone. He had stopped being a stranger to her that first day on the plane and she figured there must be a reason that he wanted to know. "It was nothing like the Quinns' marriage, that's for sure," she said in a rush.

The sound of his chuckle filled the night air. "It wasn't?"

She leaned back and looked up at him as she thought of the two adults with four grown sons. Even with visitors sitting at the dinner table with their sons, they still exchanged smiles filled with over thirty years of intimacies. "No, it wasn't. Is your parents' marriage like theirs?"

Stone looked down at her and she could actually see the smile that touched both corners of his mouth. "Umm, pretty much. I'm proud of the fact that my parents have shared a long marriage, but even prouder that they are still very much in love after nearly forty years."

He shifted his body to lean against the porch rail and took her with him, letting her hip rest along the strength of his. "They claim it was love at first sight after meeting one weekend at a church function. Within two weeks they were married."

He decided not to tell her that his parents' had predicted that their six children would also find love that way—at first sight. So far Delaney claimed that's how it had been for her and Jamal, although realizing it had been the tough part for her, as well as for Jamal. And everyone knew the moment Dare had gotten zapped. Stone and Shelly were friends in high school and working on a project together when Dare had come home unexpectedly from college and walked into the living room. He had taken one look at the sixteen-year-old Shelly Brockman and fallen in love with her then and there.

Then there was Thorn. Tara had been his challenge, as well as the love of his life from the moment she had stormed out of their sister Delaney's kitchen one night to give the unsuspecting Thorn hell about something. She had taken him aback and had also taken his heart in that same minute. Again, love at first sight.

He released a deep sigh. That may have been the way things had happened for his sister and two brothers but it wouldn't happen that way for him. He wouldn't let it.

"Your parents like touching, Stone?"

Madison's question interrupted Stone's thoughts and he couldn't help but chuckle again when he thought of the many times he'd seen his father playfully pat his mother on her behind. "Yes, and they also occasionally kiss in front of us. Always have. We're used to it. Nothing real passionate but enough to let anyone know that they still love each other. I'm sure they leave the heavy-duty hanky-panky stuff in the bedroom," he said grinning, not at all bothered by the fact that his parents might still have an active sex life. He pulled Madison closer to him. "Didn't your parents ever touch?"

After a brief moment she shrugged. "I'd never seen them touch. And I'd never thought anything about it until I went away for the weekend to spend some time at a friend's house. Her parents were like the Quinns...and probably a lot like your parents. It was easy to see they loved and respected each other and it suddenly hit me what was missing at my house, between my parents. Then I started watching them closely and I began to realize that, although they liked and respected each other, they were two people who were not in love but locked in a marriage anyway."

Stone lifted a brow. "Why would they stay married if they didn't love each other?"

She sighed deeply. "I can think of several reasons. Me for one. They would have stayed together just for me. I know in my heart that my parents loved me. I was my daddy's girl and my mother's daughter. I had a great relationship with them both. My father's death was hard on me."

Silence stretched between them; then she said, "Another reason they would have possibly stayed together is for religious reasons. They were both devout Catholics who didn't believe in divorce. It was til-death-do-you-part."

Stone nodded, taking in everything she'd said. "Didn't you say that your father has been dead for ten years?"

"Yes, he died when I was fifteen."

"And during that time, since his death, your mother has never been romantically involved with anyone?"

"No."

"Don't you think that's odd?"

She heaved a sigh. "I never thought about it before. I always assumed she just wanted to bury herself in her work after my father's death. I never assumed she was lonely and in need of companionship."

"Well, that might be the reason she took off with Uncle Corey. There are some things a man or woman can't control at times. Passion. Especially if they haven't shared it with anyone in a while. Hormones are known to get the best of you if you aren't careful."

Madison wondered if he was speaking from experience? She hadn't slept with anyone since Cedric and she definitely didn't feel like she was missing out on anything. He had been her first lover and she really didn't care if he was her last.

But then, standing so close to Stone with the feel of his warm breath on her cheek, she knew she had to rethink that declaration. Any time he had held her in his arms against his broad chest, her temperature had had a tendency to go up a notch. And whenever she had leaned into his aroused body while they kissed, it always amazed her that he had wanted her. And she would have to admit she had spent the last couple of nights in bed wondering how it would feel if he were to make love to her; for him to climb on top of her and—

"Are you cold, Madison?"

She was jerked out of her racy thoughts. She cleared her throat. "No, why do you ask?"

"Because you were shivering a few moments ago."

"Oh." She met his gaze when he looked down at her. She hoped he didn't have a clue as to why she had been trembling.

"What about you and your fiancé?" Stone asked, pulling her closer so that her cheek rested on his shoulder.

"What about us?"

"I know you said the two of you weren't intimate often, but did you do a lot of touching?"

She sighed deeply. There was an inner urgency within her to share with Stone how things had been with her and Cedric. She'd already told him that they had slept together only a couple of times but now he needed to hear the rest.

"Cedric and I didn't do a whole lot of anything, Stone. I mentioned earlier today that we were intimate two times, but even then it wasn't for enjoyment. It was done only to make sure we were compatible."

Stone shook his head, not sure he'd heard her right. *They'd been intimate a couple of times not for enjoyment but just to make sure they were compatible?* Now he had heard it all. How in the world could you be compatible without enjoyment? "What about passion?"

She shrugged. "What about it?"

Nothing, if you have to ask, he thought. But then he decided that he needed to appease his curiosity anyway. "Weren't there ever times when the two of you lost control?"

She chuckled as if the thought of his question was ridiculous. "No, and to be quite honest, I never experienced real physical attraction until I met you."

Damn, Stone thought. He wished she hadn't told him that mainly because it was the same way with him. He, too, had never experienced real physical attraction until he had met her. Oh, sure, he'd felt lust for a woman before but for some reason the attraction with Madison was totally different. He thought about her during some of the oddest times and, whenever he did, unexplainable warmth would flood his insides. He never, ever remembered actually hungering for a woman until he had met her. And now she was a constant craving and that didn't bode well.

After a few moments, he said, "I guess we're going to have to come up with some ground rules once we leave here and head up into the mountains."

It took Madison a moment to realize what he meant. But she decided to pretend otherwise and ask just to make sure. "Ground rules?"

"Yes, about us, Madison. About this attraction we can both honestly admit that we have for each other. About these hormones of mine that don't want to behave worth a damn. And about the fact you haven't told me what decisions you've made."

Madison forced a lump down her throat. She quickly remembered the decisions she had made overnight; the ones she'd been determined to stick to when she'd woken that morning. She knew that doing things her way was for the best.

She released a long, resigned sigh and said, "I think we should only concentrate on the situation with your uncle and my mother. At the present time my mind isn't free to dwell on anything else. I'm not sure how you may feel about it but I prefer that any thoughts about anything between us be placed on the back burner to be analyzed and discussed later, after I see my mother."

Stone shook his head. Back burner, hell! Did she think things would be that easy? Did she actually think two people could turn off sexual chemistry like it flowed from a faucet or tuck it away like an agenda item to be looked at and discussed later? Didn't she realize how difficult it would be for them once they were alone together in the mountains, in constant close proximity to each other?

No, he quickly concluded. She didn't know. She didn't have a clue because, from what he'd gathered tonight from their conversation, her parents had not been passionate beings. And, to make matters worse, her fiancé had been a damn poor excuse for a man. Instead of introducing the woman he was engaged to marry to fiery passion and red-hot desire, the bastard had been too busy doing it with a model.

A part of Stone was glad he had discovered the reason behind Madison's irrational thoughts on the situation involving his uncle and her mother. She couldn't see passion and desire for what they were if she had never experienced them before. It was obvious that she had never felt toe-curling, scream-til-your-throat-becomes-raw passion. Those sensations were something everyone should experience at some point in their lives. He couldn't imagine anything worse than having to suppress your desires—especially for a long period of time.

He quickly made a decision. He would introduce Madison to the pleasures of sex. She would soon discover that the attraction between them was something neither of them could ignore. He wanted to show her what it meant to have uncontrollable hormones zap the very sense out of you. He wouldn't do anything in particular, just sit back and let nature take its course and, considering everything, he had all the confidence in the world that it would.

Stone Westmoreland was convinced that by the time they reached his uncle's cabin, his city girl would have a clear understanding of how easy it was for a person to lose control to passion of the strongest, most potent kind.

"And you're sure that's the way you want things?" he asked after a long moment of silence.

"Yes. It will be for the best."

He nodded as a slow smile touched his lips. What Madison didn't know was that the best was yet to come. He would give her a summer night in the mountains that she would remember for a long time.

The next morning Stone glanced over at Madison as she sat patiently on her horse. He actually envied the animal's back. He would just love to have her sitting on him with her legs flanking him on both sides while she rode him to sweet oblivion.

He had not gotten much sleep last night, thinking of her and their trip up into the mountains together. He hadn't changed his mind. Before they reached his uncle's place he intended to have taught his city girl a few things. She would see how it was to deal with a real flesh-and-blood man. A man who appreciated everything a woman stood for.

He glanced up at the sky. The sun hadn't quite come up yet which meant it was a good time to start their trip. He could hardly wait. Anticipation was eating away at him, fueling his desire for her even more. "You okay?" he decided to ask her.

She smiled over at him. "Yes, I'll be fine just as long as you're not expecting an experienced cowgirl. I can do okay with a horse but, like I told you, even with the lessons I took, I'm not much of a rider."

He nodded. All that would be changing. She might not be much of a rider now but by the time they reached his uncle's cabin she would be pretty proficient at it. He would definitely teach her how to ride an animal of the two-legged kind.

"Do you think we will come across any wild animals?"

Her question made him stop what he was doing with his saddle and glance over at her. A smile tilted his lips.

"You mean which kind of wild animals do you hope that we won't encounter?"

She chuckled and the sound made his stomach clench in desire. It was such a sexy sound and was like a caress to his already sensitized flesh. "Yeah, that's it."

He took the time to get on his horse before answering her. "Namely bears, wolves and mountain lions."

"Oh."

He grinned over at her when he saw the look of fear that appeared in her eyes. "Don't worry. The path I plan to take is one that's well used and most wild animals know to avoid it." He decided not to tell her that he would be taking another route that would delay their arrival at his uncle Corey's ranch by a full day. Madison Winters needed an education in wildlife of the human kind.

But first he had to get his libido under control, which wasn't easy. She looked so desirable sitting on the horse with her face tipped up to the sun. She had pulled her hair back in a ponytail and was wearing the big wide-brimmed hat on her head. But still, he could see her beautiful dark skin glowing in the predawn light. She was a natural beauty and he wondered how he would be able to keep his hands off her until she made the first move. And she would make the first move. He would see to it. He would lay temptation at her feet, then wait for her to act on it.

"Ready?" he asked, looking over at her.

"Yes."

"Okay then, let's go." They started at a slow pace since he wanted her to get the feel of the animal beneath her. He wanted her to be aware of everything around her; the way the sun was beginning to rise over the mountains, the rustle of the wind through the trees, and the sound of pine needles snapping under their horses' feet. And he wanted to make sure she was aware of him; the man who wanted her.

If she wasn't aware of it now, she would definitely be aware of it later.

They rode in silence for the first few hours, only engaging in conversation when he pointed out something of interest to her. He liked the way she appreciated her surroundings. She might be a city girl, but it was apparent she was enjoying embarking on their journey.

"Thirsty?" he asked, wondering if the ride had taken a toll on her yet. The sun had come up fully now and the heat of it was beaming down on them. He was grateful he was wearing his hat and that she had followed his suggestion and had worn hers.

"Yes, I'm thirsty."

"How about a drink of water?"

"That would be nice," she said, as he brought the horses to a stop.

"Just sit tight while I get the canteen. Mr. Quinn told me before we left that during this past year he and McKinnon built a cabin that's located halfway to Corey's place. They use it when he and his sons go hunting in these parts. He said that we could use it if we liked. So if we make it there before nightfall, we won't have to sleep outside after all."

He idly stroked the back of his horse, wishing it were Madison's body. He then added, "And there's a place up ahead where we can camp for a while and eat lunch. If we continue at this pace, we should be able to make it there before it gets much hotter."

The look on Madison's face indicated that she hoped they would. He grinned. She was being a real trooper. A lot of women would be whining and complaining by now. He remembered the first time his father had decided to take

Delaney camping with him and his brothers. He shook his head at the memory. That had been the first and the last time.

He got off his horse and, after making sure both of their mounts' reins were securely tied to a nearby tree, he went to her saddlebag and pulled out the canteen, then walked over and handed it to her.

She quickly took it from him. "Thanks."

He watched as she opened the top and tipped the canteen up to her mouth. Some of the water missed her lips and drizzled down her chin. He was tempted to lap it up with his tongue. He had thought about tasting her that way a lot lately and intended to get his chance real soon.

He continued to watch her; getting turned on just from seeing how her throat moved as the cool liquid flowed down it. His eyes were so focused on her throat that he didn't notice that she had stopped drinking.

"Stone, you can have this back now."

He blinked. "Oh," he said, reaching for the canteen.

"Thanks again. The water was delicious."

"You're welcome. It's natural spring water," he said, thinking that she was delicious, too. Instead of putting the canteen away, he pulled the top back off and began drinking some of the water, deliberately tasting where her mouth had been.

When he finished he licked his lips, liking the hint of a taste of her that he had gotten from the canteen. He glanced up to see her watching him. She didn't say anything but just continued to look at him. And he looked at her. Then he felt it, that deep, hard throb in his gut that made him want to snatch her off the back of the horse and tumble with her in the grass. His body was already hot and was beginning to get hotter, in need of physical contact with her.

He saw how her cheeks darkened and he saw the moment desire filled her eyes. He also saw how fast the pulse was beating in her neck and the way she took out her tongue to moisten her already damp lips. His gaze slowly dropped to her blouse and saw how the nipples of her breasts were straining against the material. Her breathing, as well as his, was erratic. He heard it. He felt it. He wanted to taste it.

"You had enough?" he forced his gaze back to her eyes, as he tried like hell to get his thoughts and mind, and especially his body, back under control.

"Enough of what?" she asked, her voice soft, somewhat husky and definitely sensual. Her gaze was still holding his.

"Water."

She blinked and he saw that her features relayed both her confusion, as well as her longing for something she didn't quite understand yet. But she would in time. He would see to it. "Yes, I had enough," she said, after drawing in a deep breath.

He smiled. She hadn't had enough of anything yet. After putting her canteen back in her saddlebag he went around and got back on his horse. He leaned over and handed her reins to her. "Come on," he said huskily. "Let's continue our ride."

Chapter 6

Up until a half hour ago Madison thought she was hungry, but now something was affecting her appetite…or rather someone.

Stone Westmoreland.

She tilted her head as she watched him. He was standing some distance away tending to the horses. She was sitting on a stump eating one of the sandwiches Mrs. Quinn had packed for them and drinking a cold can of cola, while her eyes were glued to Stone.

She was attracted to him. There was no use denying it since that fact had already been established a few days ago. But what she couldn't understand was why she couldn't get past it. Why did a part of her want to act on it?

It seemed that although her mind was definitely on him, his mind was on the horses. He hadn't looked her way since they had stopped for lunch. She should have been grateful, but she couldn't deny being bothered by the fact that he could dismiss her so easily. But then, hadn't she laid out the ground rules last night? And hadn't those ground rules included a statement that anything developing between them was to be placed on the back burner? Evidently he had taken her at her word and intended to adhere to it.

She let out a deep sigh and the sound must have caught his attention. He lifted his eyes to hers, holding it for several long moments, saying nothing but looking at her. She met his gaze without flinching while desire stirred in her stomach, hot, thick, the likes of which she'd never experienced before. Without a sound, without a touch, and over the distance of twenty feet, she actually felt the heat of his gaze as tiny shocks of warmth began inching all the way up her spine to flow through her body. She even felt heat forming between her legs. Especially between her legs. And the appetite forming in her stomach had nothing to do with regular food. She continued to look at him while trying to cling to her composure, her resolve and her sanity.

Her throat tightened when he began walking toward her and the heat surging through her got hotter. She had never appreciated a Western shirt and tight jeans on a man until she had met him. She couldn't imagine his tall, muscled body wearing anything else…unless it was nothing at all.

Her breath caught. She wished she could strike that thought from her mind, call it back, and not think about it. But the deed was done. That wicked thought went right along with the dreams she'd been having about him lately. The man exuded raw sex appeal without trying and she was fully aware of him, more so than she needed to be.

"You okay?"

Madison shook her head. Not sure words would come out of her mouth even if she wanted them to, but she forced herself to speak anyway. "Yes, I'm fine, Stone."

He nodded as he continued to look at her. "Can I use some of that?" he asked indicating the small bottle of liquid hand sanitizer she had brought along.

"Sure, help yourself."

She watched as he uncapped the small bottle and poured some in his palm and then began rubbing his hands together in slow motion. She immediately thought of him rubbing those same hands all over her...in slow motion. She glanced at her soda can wondering if there was something inside it other than soda that was making her dizzy with such wanton thoughts.

"This is a beautiful spot, isn't it?"

His question got her attention. She shifted her gaze away from his hands to take in the beauty of their surroundings. "Yes, it is. I wish I had thought to bring a camera along."

He lifted a brow. "I'm surprised that you didn't."

She was surprised, too. "I had other things on my mind." And those *other things,* she told herself, were what she should be concentrating on and not on Stone. She continued to watch him as he recapped the hand sanitizer and placed it back in her gear. Then he walked over to his saddlebag to pull out his own sandwich and drink. She sighed. Maybe if she got him talking about his uncle she just might be able to clear her mind of hot, steamy thoughts. She figured it was worth a try.

"Do you have any idea who in Texas is trying to locate your uncle, Stone?" she asked, after she had finished off the last of her sandwich.

He walked back over to her and sat down on the stump beside her. "No, I have no idea. I mentioned it to Durango and he didn't have a clue, either. We decided to turn it over to Quade and let him solve the mystery."

Madison lifted a brow. "Who?"

Stone smiled. "Quade. He's one of Durango's brothers—the one I mentioned was a twin. He used to be a secret service agent. Now he works for the government in some behind-the-scenes capacity. We don't have a clue exactly what he does. We see him when we see him and don't ask questions when we do. But we know how to contact him if we ever need him and usually within seventy-two hours we'll hear back from him."

Madison nodded. "And you think he can find out what's going on?"

"He'll find out."

Madison sat quietly for a moment thinking that Stone seemed pretty sure of his cousin's abilities. Her thoughts then shifted back to the man her mother had run off with. "Tell me about Corey Westmoreland," she said, feeling the need to know as much about him as she could since she would be coming face-to-face with him soon.

Stone glanced over at her after taking a sip of his soda. "Exactly what do you want to know?"

She shrugged. "What I'm really curious about is why everyone thinks it's strange for him to have a woman on his mountain."

Stone's lips lifted into a smile. "Mainly because as long as I can remember Uncle Corey claimed it would never happen. He's been involved with women before but none of them have ever been granted access to this mountain. He's always drawn the line as to how much of his life he's been willing to share with them."

Madison mulled this over for a second then said, "Yet he brought my mother here?"

"Yes, and that's what has me, Durango and the Quinns baffled."

Madison let out a deep sigh. "Now I'm beginning to wonder if perhaps they did know each other before."

Stone stared at her. "There is that possibility, but if I were you I wouldn't try to figure it out. Tomorrow you'll see them for yourself and can ask all the questions you want."

He reached across the distance and caught one of her hands in his and squeezed it gently. "But don't feel bad if she doesn't want to give you any answers. Maybe it's time for you to let your mother enjoy her life, Madison. After all, it's her life to live, isn't it?"

Although a frown appeared on Madison's face, she didn't say anything. Nor did she withdraw her hand from Stone's. All along he had given her food for thought and all along her mind had refused to accept what was becoming obvious.

"So when I see Corey Westmoreland, what should I expect?"

When he didn't answer right away, Madison assumed he was getting his thoughts together. "What you should expect is a fifty-four year old man who's been like a second father to his niece and eleven nephews. He's a man who believes in family, honor, respect and love for nature. For as long as I've known him, he has preferred solitude in some things and a vast amount of companionship in others. He won't hesitate to let you know how he feels on any subject and deeply respects the opinion of others."

A smile touched the corners of Stone's lips when he added, "And I learned early in life that he's also a man with eyes in the back of his head. You can't ever pull anything over on him."

The affection Madison heard in Stone's voice caused her to think just how different Corey Westmoreland was from her father. Her father had been an only child. He did have a cousin who'd also lived in Boston, but the two had never had a close relationship, so she hadn't developed a close relationship with that cousin's children who were all around her age.

Her father had been born in the city, raised in the city and lived in the city. They'd never owned a pet while she was growing up and the thought of leaving the city to go camping wasn't anything he would have been interested in doing. And Larry Winters had preferred socializing to solitude, especially when it benefited him. He'd been a financial adviser. He would often host lavish parties for his clients with her mother acting as hostess. She remembered her father being excited each and every time they'd given a party, but now as she thought about it, her mother hadn't particularly cared for entertaining. She had merely accepted it as part of her role as the wife of a successful businessman. She tried to think of one single thing her parents had in common and couldn't think of anything. Last night Stone had asked her why two people who possibly didn't love each other would stay together. Now her question was why had they gotten married in the first place?

She came out of her reverie when Stone removed his hand from hers. She sat quietly and watched him finish off the rest of his sandwich and down the last of his soda. He then glanced over at her and studied her as if she was going to be his dessert. Visibly feeling the heat of his gaze and not able to sit and take it any longer, she stood and glanced around.

Stone studied Madison for a long moment then asked, "How are you holding up so far?"

She shrugged. "I'm fine. Usually I have an overabundance of energy. It takes a lot to wear me out."

Stone's gaze drifted down the length of her body. He

would definitely remember that later. He watched as she picked up her hat and placed it back on her head.

"Don't you think we should move on if we plan to make it to that cabin before nightfall?" she asked.

He stood and flashed her a slow, sexy grin. "Yeah, Miss Winters, I think that you're right."

The cabin was not what either Stone or Madison had expected. What they assumed they would find was a small one-room structure. But what Martin Quinn and McKinnon had built in the clearing—nestled between large pine trees with a breathtaking view of the mountains and valleys for a backdrop, as well as a beautiful stream running at the back of it—was a cabin large enough to be used as a home away from home.

Stone and Madison took a quick tour of the place. The outside of the cabin featured an inviting wraparound porch. Inside, there was a huge living room with a fireplace, two bedrooms connected by a large single bathroom, and an eat-in kitchen with an enormous window that overlooked the stream out back. It didn't take long for Stone to discover that they would have electricity once he fired up the generator and the linen closets had fresh sheets and coverings for the bed.

Stone sighed, grateful that they had made it to the cabin before nightfall. They still had a few hours of daylight left and he would use the time to feed and care for the horses and start the generator.

He glanced over at Madison who was silently standing beside him. Like him her gaze was on the two bedrooms and he could swear he'd heard her deep sigh of relief.

"I've got a few things to do outside," he said, breaking the silence between them.

She nodded. "Okay and I can work to get the fireplace going. I have a feeling it's going to be rather cold tonight."

Stone met her gaze, deciding not to tell her that he would be more than happy to provide her with all the heat she would need. "All right, I'll be back later."

It was a full hour or so before Stone returned. Madison had taken advantage of his absence to take a shower. He inhaled the soft, seductive and arousing scent of her the moment he walked into the cabin and came to a dead stop when she walked out of the bedroom.

She had changed into a pair of sweatpants with a tank top; something she must have found more comfortable than jeans. No matter what the woman put on her body, it looked elegant as hell on her. Madison Winters was definitely one class act. Her hair was no longer pulled back in a pony-tail but its silky, luxurious strands flowed in sexy disarray about her shoulders. He growled deep in his throat, resisting the urge to cross the room and pull her into his arms and get a real good taste of her; something he'd been dying to do all day.

She glanced up and saw him staring at her. She stared back at him for a moment without saying anything, then a nervous smile touched the corners of her lips. "Although I was tempted, I didn't use up all the hot water. There's plenty left if you want to go ahead and take your bath."

"That sounds rather nice," he said, his voice sounding hoarse. He wanted to take a bath and soak his tired, aching muscles but something had him rooted in place and he couldn't seem to move from that spot.

He continued to stare at her while his insides ached, throbbed. A long period of silence suspended every sound, except for his breathing...and hers. They both jumped when a piece of burning log crackled in the fireplace. Stone shifted his gaze from hers to the fire. "It feels real good in here. Thanks for getting the fire started," he said, although his mind was on another type of fire altogether.

She shrugged. "It was the least I could do while you were outside taking care of the horses and getting the generator started. And I took the liberty to unpack dinner. Mrs. Quinn sent a container of beef stew for us to eat. It's warming now."

Stone nodded and sniffed the air. There was the faint smell of the stew. He hadn't picked up on it when he'd come inside. The only scent his nostrils had caught had been of her. "Smells good."

"It should be ready by the time you have finished your bath."

He nodded. "All right. I guess I'd better get to it then." Seconds passed and he still didn't move. He continued to look at her. Absorb everything about her.

"Stone?"

He blinked. "Yes?"

"Your bath."

A slow smile touched his lips. "Oh, yeah. I'll be back in a minute." He crossed the floor into the other bedroom and closed the door.

As soon as Stone pulled the door shut behind him, he leaned against it and hooked his fingers into the belt loops of his jeans as he tried to get his body under control. He felt blood surge through his body, making him swell in one particular area. He needed to get out of his jeans real quick-like or the force of his arousal that was straining against his zipper would kill him or at least injure him for life.

Part of his plan had been to lay temptation at Madison's feet but she was unknowingly laying it at his. He'd thought with all the chores he'd had to do outside that he would have worked off some of his nervous energy. But as soon as he'd seen her, the only thing he'd managed to do was to work up an oversize case of sexual need.

A prickle of unease made its way up his spine. For Madison to be someone who knew nothing about passion, she definitely looked like a woman who could deliver. And he had a feeling that that delivery would be so much to his liking that he might start getting crazy ideas about wanting to keep her around.

He closed his eyes and clenched his jaw tight. The last thing he needed was to think of any woman in permanent terms. And he refused to let a beautiful, proper-talking, brown-eyed, delectable-smelling city woman come into his life and change things. All he needed to do was remember that episode with Durango a few years ago to screw his head back on tight. The first time his womanizing cousin had let his guard down and fallen for a city woman, he'd been left with scars for life.

But then Stone knew Madison was nothing like the woman who had ripped out Durango's heart. Madison Winters wasn't like any woman he knew. He'd been so hell-bent on introducing her to sexual pleasures that he'd outright forgotten how long it had been for him. He hadn't slept with a woman in over a year after practically shutting off his social life to complete his last book. And the last few women he had been involved with had been downright bores. The need for physical intimacy was tugging at his insides, making him feel things he normally didn't feel; making him want something he usually didn't think twice about doing without.

But still, when all was said and done, no matter what torture he was going through, the woman in the other room was his main concern. Her needs outweighed his and more than anything she needed to understand how it felt to be driven to lose control, to act impulsively and to be spontaneous. She deserved to experience reckless pleasure and uncontrollable passion at least once. And as he moved away from the door and walked toward the connecting bathroom, he knew he wanted that one time to be with him.

Madison placed her hand on her forehead, feeling her skin and wondering why she was beginning to feel so hot. But deep down she knew the reason why. Anytime she was within close proximity to Stone, her temperature went up a few degrees. There was no way she could deny that she wanted him. And hearing the sound of the bath running and knowing that he was in the bathroom naked and wet wasn't helping matters.

Ninety-six hours was the equivalent of four days. That's how long she had known him and here she was thinking all kinds of naughty thoughts. There were still some things about Storm Westmoreland that she didn't know, but she felt certain there was a fair amount that she did know. She had a feeling that the same description he had given his uncle earlier that day could also be used to describe him.

During the ride up the mountain he talked about his family and she knew he was close to them and that all the Westmorelands had a special relationship. And she knew that he also had a love and deep appreciation for nature. That was evident when he had pointed out various plants and trees, as well as telling her about the different types of wildlife that was found in these parts. And she had a feeling there were times in his life—possibly while working on one of his novels—that he sought solitude more often than others. But at the same time he would feel comfortable in any type of social gathering if that was where he wanted to belong.

And she knew that although he would be the last person to brag about his work, she'd heard her girlfriends say countless times that he was an excellent storyteller. She even remembered one of her friends staying overnight at her place after reading one of his thriller-chiller novels, because she was frightened. That was one of the reasons Madison had decided never to read his books. She lived alone in her apartment and the last thing she needed was to start looking over her shoulder or waking up during the night at the slightest sound.

Madison had discovered after reading the newspaper at breakfast yesterday morning that Stone's latest book, *Whispers of a Stalker,* was still on the *New York Times* bestseller list even after twelve weeks. During the ride today, Stone had also shared with her information about his involvement on a national level with the Teach the People to Read program—a program aimed at fighting illiteracy.

Another thing she believed with all her heart was that he was someone who could be trusted. She had felt comfortable with him from the first and the thought of them alone in this cabin, miles from civilization, didn't bother her.

Yes, she decided to admit, it *did* bother her, especially when it stirred something inside her each and every time he looked at her with promises of untold pleasures in his eyes. Pleasures she'd never had before.

She walked to the window and looked out. It was dark and everything around them appeared black and still. She had actually seen a bald eagle fly overhead, but she might have missed the experience if Stone hadn't pointed it out to her.

"What are you thinking about, Madison?"

Madison quickly spun around, holding shaking fingers to her chest. She hadn't heard Stone approach. In fact she had been listening to the sound of the water running during his bath and wondered at what point he'd turned it off.

He was standing in the middle of the kitchen wearing another pair of jeans and a T-shirt with the words, The Rolling Stone, boldly displayed across his large, muscular chest. His hair was damp and she felt like crossing the distance separating them and rubbing her hand over his head. And that wasn't the only thing she wanted to rub her hands over, she thought as he held her gaze. His eyes blazed with a deep heat. She may not be experienced in some things, but she could definitely recognize sexual desire in a man; especially this man. It had been in his gaze the first time his eyes had met hers.

"So, you want to keep whatever it was you were thinking a secret?" he asked with a rueful smile.

Madison sighed, turned back to the window. "I was just thinking how quiet things seem outside and yet I know there are plenty of animals out there that make this area their home. In a way I feel as if we are invading their territory."

She felt the heat of him when he came to stand beside her. "Invasion is fine as long as we don't do anything to destroy their natural environment."

She nodded and turned and almost collided with him. She hadn't been aware that he had been standing so close.

"There's something else I've discovered about invasions," he said, holding her gaze.

Madison knew her control was about to be tested. "What?"

"It can make some people rather uncomfortable. Like right now. I am invading your space, aren't I?"

Madison nodded. Yes, he was invading her space but she didn't feel uncomfortable or threatened by it. Instead she felt an incredible magnetism, an intrinsic sensual pull to him.

"Madison?"

She inhaled, pulling air into her lungs before answering, "Yes, but I don't mind sharing my space with you, Stone. Are you ready for dinner?"

She watched as a smile curved his sensuous lips. "I'm ready for a lot of things."

She didn't want to read between the lines but did so anyway. Visions of just what those other things might be danced around in her head. She tried holding on to the decisions she had made yesterday morning about their relationship and discovered she was having a hard time doing so. She cleared her throat. "I'll put the food on the table."

Without giving him a chance to say anything else, she walked off toward the kitchen cabinets to take down a couple of bowls.

"The stew's good, isn't it?"

The sound of Stone's husky voice drifted across the table and was as intimate as a caress. Madison glanced up from eating her stew and met his gaze. A part of her shivered inside from the visual contact. More than once she had caught him staring at her, and against her will her body had responded, each and every time.

Common sense demanded that she fight her interest in him, but it was hard to dredge up will power or common sense around a man like Stone. "Yes, it's delicious," she said trying not to feel the warmth that was spreading through her belly.

Stone pushed his bowl aside, licking his lips. "Too bad we don't have anything for dessert."

Madison swallowed, eyeing his lips with interest. Oh, she could think of a few things she had definitely developed a sweet tooth for over the last few days. His kisses topped the list. "Yes, it is, isn't it?" she decided it was safer to say.

"I'll help you with dishes," Stone said, getting to his feet.

Madison considered his offer and quickly decided that it wouldn't be a good idea. Earlier she'd told him that she didn't mind him in her space but at the moment she needed him out of it to get her mind focused. "There's no need. I only have a few items to take care of anyway."

"You sure?" he asked.

"Yes, I'm positive. I'd think you'd want to retire early. Today has to have been an exhausting one for you."

Stone's throaty chuckle swirled over her like a sensual mist, absorbing her, snarling her and making desire ripple through her. "No, usually I have an overabundance of energy. It takes a lot to wear me out."

She recognized his words as similar to ones she'd spoken earlier that day. She came to her feet and gathered their dishes off the table. Deep down she was aware of the electrical tension that was beginning to short circuit in her body, however she was determined not to go up in smoke.

She walked over to the kitchen sink, feeling the heat of Stone's stare; she tried hard to ignore it. His very presence and the scent of him taunted her with the unknown and, although her back was to him, she was aware of every move he made and every breath he took.

Her pulse rate increased when she heard him get up from the table and cross the room to stand less than two feet behind her, and for a few moments he stood silently, not saying anything, not doing anything. Then he took another step, reducing the distance separating them and she quickly turned around.

Their gazes collided. His was so intense the force of it ripped through her, sending a sharp sexual longing to her belly, between her legs and to her breasts; making her nipples harden in immediate response.

Then she felt herself moving, taking a step forward and reaching out to drape her arms around his neck. She heard the growl he made, deep in his throat, just moments, mere seconds, before he claimed her mouth with a kiss that seduced any resistance she may have had out of her.

The heated, yet gentle thrust of his tongue as it slipped between her lips had her whimpering in pleasure, and he toyed and teased with her tongue while sharing his taste and the intensity of his hunger. She was trying hard to understand what was happening to her. Then she decided, why bother. Who could possibly understand how Stone was making her feel? Who could understand why her heart was beating five times its normal rate and how the heat of him was branding her all over, especially in the area between her legs to the point that she felt her panties getting wet. And when he pressed his body up against her, bringing her closer and letting her feel the magnitude and strength of his arousal, she emitted a soft moan. He was stoking a flame within her and she was a willing victim. She didn't want to dwell on the decisions she had made yesterday morning. The only thing she wanted to think about was how he was making her feel.

She felt him pulling his mouth away and thought, *no, not yet* and tightened her arms around him, keeping their mouths locked, as her tongue became the aggressor, doing what his had done to her earlier. She licked the insides of his mouth from point A to point Z, exploring, tasting, consuming as much of him as she could, but still feeling it wasn't enough. Her body had broken free of any restraints and was raging with an intense sexual need that only he could fill.

He broke free from their kiss and she whimpered in protest until she felt him lift her top and his mouth latch on to one of her nipples. She had forgotten she hadn't worn a bra and the touch of his tongue to her breast, sucking, flicking and licking, was like he was getting the dessert he talked about earlier. She moaned deep in her throat as coils of sexual need tightened deep within her.

He pulled back slightly and she felt herself being lifted effortlessly into his arms. "I want you," he whispered, his voice hot next to her ear.

She wanted him, too, and reached out and pulled his mouth back down to hers. Tonight they were in a cabin deep in the wilderness and succumbing to the call of the wild. She felt out of control with him and knew whatever he wanted to do she wanted to do, too. Never in her life had she wanted or needed a man with this much intensity. She hadn't known such a thing was possible.

He lifted his mouth from hers and she felt herself being carried swiftly out of the kitchen and straight into one of the bedrooms; the one he had planned to use. He placed her on the bed and immediately went to her clothes, pulling the top over her head and easing her sweatpants down her legs.

Heat soared through her as he removed her panties and she knew he was aware just how wet they were. But he didn't say anything, merely tossed them aside. His gaze was still on her, penetrating and compelling. Then he reached out and skimmed his hand across her femininity, as if using his fingers to test her readiness and the degree of her need. She groaned, threw her head back and opened her legs to give him access and he took it.

"Damn, you're hot and wet," he murmured hoarsely against her ear as his tongue moved over her face to lick the perspiration off her throat and he worked his way up to her chin. He inched his way farther upward and his tongue parted her lips, seeking her taste once again.

But after a moment, that wasn't enough for him. His mouth began moving lower like he was obsessively hungry for her. His tongue worked its way past her breasts and down her chest to her navel, torturing every inch of her in the process. Then he reached the very essence of her heat and used his mouth and tongue to drive her mad in a very intimate French kiss.

She screamed as her body shook with a force that had her digging her fingers into his shoulders to stop the room from spinning, the earth from shaking and her body from splintering in two. The feel of his mouth on her touched off an explosion but still he wouldn't let up. It was as if he was determined to have it all and, in the process, give her everything. Her body was thrown into an orgasm of gigantic proportions that had her nearly sobbing in pleasure and before she could recover from that first orgasm, his mouth and tongue were busy sending her whirling into a second as he once again pushed her over the edge.

Moments later, while she lay there trying to learn how to breathe all over again, he stood back away from the bed and began removing his shirt. She barely had enough strength to prop her elbows on the bed to watch him, studying how well defined his chest was and how a thin line of dark hair led a path downward, past the waistband of his jeans.

She continued to watch, fascinated, and knew at that moment she had never seen a more perfectly made male body. She could stare all day and not tire of seeing it. She held her breath as he slowly eased down his zipper. Then he pulled off his jeans and briefs, letting her see all of him. Her gaze immediately went to his shaft, thick, large and hard, protruding like a statue from the bed of dark curls that surrounded it. She almost swallowed her tongue.

"I want you," he said huskily, coming back to join her on the bed after putting on the condom he had taken from the pocket of his jeans. "Come here, baby, and let me show you how much."

She eagerly went into his arms and felt her body shudder when her bare skin made contact with his. He took her into his arms and kissed her again. It was as if she hadn't had two orgasms already. Her body was getting aroused all over again. The ache began throbbing between her legs and she knew it would take more than his mouth and tongue this time to satisfy what ailed her there.

He evidently knew it, too. She heard his low groan as he eased her back against the pillows. "I want it all. I want to give you something you've never had before," he whispered huskily in her ear.

She opened her mouth to tell him that he'd already given her something she hadn't ever had before, twice. But he kissed her, silencing her words, drugging her senses and stirring up a need within her that demanded more. Their gazes held, locked and she became ensnarled by the heat in his eyes.

Stone inhaled deeply as he struggled to maintain control. He couldn't last much longer without getting inside of her, needing to be there as much as he needed his next breath. He had tasted her and now he wanted to mate with her, become a part of her, thrust deep and stay forever if there was any way that he could. He moved his body over hers, not breaking eye contact.

"Let me ease inside," he whispered huskily, and she

shifted her body to accommodate his request. Then he leaned forward, captured her mouth and kissed her again, wanting to convey without words just how he felt. He rotated the lower part of his body, letting his shaft caress her, seek her out and he found her wet, slick and hot.

He lifted his mouth as his hands gripped her hips. When she began closing her eyes he knew he wanted her to look at him, he wanted to see the expression on her face the moment their bodies joined. "Open your eyes. Look at me, Madison. I want to see you when you take me in."

Her gaze held his and her fingers began stroking his shoulders as she parted her legs for him. Not able, nor willing to hold back any longer Stone eased inside of her. He sucked in a deep breath and his hands held her hips in a firm grip as he continued going as deep as he could, feeling the muscles of her body clench him, take him, claim him.

And then he established a rhythm, slow and easy; then fast and hard thrusting in and out in an urgency that enveloped them. He groaned deep in his throat as he gave her all of him and took all of her in the process. He felt the tremors that began radiating through her body when he increased his rhythmic pace, stroking her, as well as himself into an explosion. He threw his head back and felt the muscles in his neck strain, and when she screamed his name, he lifted her hips to lock her legs around him to share in the orgasm that was overtaking her.

He growled out her name between clenched teeth and when the shudders began racking her body, he felt it; something he had never felt before. Passion yes. Satiated hunger— that, too. But there was something else he felt and when he buried his face against her neck, he pushed out of his mind whatever it was. The only thing he wanted at that moment was to share in the aftereffects of such a beautiful mating.

He shifted his weight off her and pulled her into his arms. He somehow found the strength to lean up and look at her. A smile, a deep, satisfied smile, drifted across her lips and the gaze holding his was filled with joy and wonder. Utter satisfaction. And he knew they had shared something special and unique. They had shared passion of the most unbridled and the richest kind, and he knew that before they left this cabin they would do so again, and again and again....

Chapter 7

Stone lay propped up on his elbow as he gazed down at the sleeping woman beside him in the bed. What Madison had said yesterday had been true. She possessed an over-abundance of energy and it took a lot to wear her out.

He couldn't help but smile when he thought of the number of times they had made love during the night; her body taking him in, clenching him, satisfying him and demanding from him all that he could give. And he had given a lot; all he had and they had made love until exhaustion had racked their bodies. It was only then that she had fallen asleep in his arms, her limbs entwined with his. He'd managed to get some sleep in, as well, but now he was wide-awake and fully aroused. He wanted her again. He glanced down at their bodies, seemingly joined at the hips and liked what he saw. He liked it too much.

Taking a deep breath, full realization hit him and he accepted that he had shared something with Madison that he had never shared with any other woman. A lot of himself. No, he had shared *all* of himself. For her he had let his guard down.

His gaze dropped back down to her and latched on to her bare breasts. This attraction he had for her was nothing but lust, he tried convincing himself, but then he remembered how he felt emotionally, each and every time she had screamed out his name while swept up in the throes of ecstasy. Okay, he admitted he would always remember last night, but he refused to get hung up on it and start reading more into it than was there. He had wanted to introduce her to passion, and he had. No big deal. He had wanted to show her how two levelheaded individuals could suddenly become overtaken with desire, a desire so consuming that it could stir uncontrollable passion between them. And he'd done that, too. The only thing left was for them to find her mother and Uncle Corey.

He frowned when he thought what would probably happen after that. Once Madison saw her mother and was reassured that she was fine, she'd probably return to Boston. He, on the other hand, would go back to Durango's place and do what he'd intended to do from the beginning. He would get a little R and R before starting work on his next book.

Why did the thought of them going their separate ways begin to gnaw on his insides? Why did the thought of her sharing her newfound passion with another man bother the hell out of him? He had made love to other women and never felt troubled by the thought of them sleeping with someone else after their relationship ended. In fact, he'd always been grateful that his ex-lovers wanted to move on.

He inhaled deeply. He needed distance from Madison to think straight and to get his head back on right. She was making him feel things no other woman had made him feel and he didn't like it worth a damn.

Easing from her side, he slipped out of bed and quickly pulled on his jeans, not bothering to put on his briefs or a shirt. He didn't want her to wake up for fear that he wouldn't know how he would handle things.

Before walking out of the bedroom he glanced back and wished that he hadn't. His gaze roamed over her. She was curled on her side with a satiated smile on her lips while she slept. She looked like a woman made for passion and every muscle in his body ached to make love to her again.

He forced his gaze away as a thickness settled in his throat at the same time as one formed in his midsection. Stone slowly shook his head. He needed distance and he needed it now. Quickly walking out of the room, he closed the door behind him.

Madison stirred awake and squinted her eyes against the bright sunlight that was coming in through the window. She stretched and immediately felt the soreness in muscles she hadn't used in a long time. She smiled. She had definitely used them last night.

Pulling herself up in bed she glanced around, wondering where Stone had gone. She knew they had planned to get an early start to reach his uncle's place before nightfall but now she felt downright lazy. She didn't want to do anything but stay in bed and wait for his return.

She drew in a shuddering breath when she remembered all the things they had done the night before. He had introduced her to passion of the most sensual kind. She had felt emotions and had done things with Stone that she had never felt or done with her former fiancé. A blushing heat stole into her features when she thought how Stone had touched her all over, tasted her all over, made love to her all over. Even now his scent was drenched into her skin. Her nostrils were filled with the aroma of him: manly, robust and sexy.

What was there about Stone Westmoreland that had made her throw caution to the wind and do what she'd done? What was there about him that made her eager to do it again?

When moments passed and Stone didn't return to bed, and she didn't hear any movement or sound from the opposite side of the bedroom door, she wondered where he had gone and decided to find out. What was he thinking this morning? Did he regret what they'd done? Did he think she assumed that now that they'd made love she expected something from him? She remembered distinctly him saying that he wasn't the marrying kind. He believed strongly in the institution but also believed that marriage wasn't for him. He had no plans ever to settle down. He had told her that he liked his life just the way it was. He enjoyed the freedom of coming and going whenever he pleased and not being responsible for anyone but himself. He didn't want any worries, no bothers and definitely no wife.

She sighed deeply as she slipped out of bed. She glanced around for the clothes she had discarded the night before and decided that, instead of putting them back on, she would slip into Stone's shirt. It hit her midthigh and she liked the way it looked on her because it symbolized that she was his and he was hers.

She shook her head, wondering where that thought had come from and decided not to think that way again. Stone wasn't looking for a serious relationship and neither was she. Opening the door she knew she had to pull herself together before seeing him. The last thing she needed was to put more into her relationship with him than was really there.

* * *

Madison searched the house and found no sign of Stone. She stepped outside onto the porch. Then she saw him. He was in the distance, shirtless and riding without a saddle. Instead, a blanket covered the animal's back.

She leaned against the column post and watched him. He had told her that he knew how to handle a horse and she'd seen firsthand how well he did so on their trek up the mountains. He had explained that his uncle had made sure his eleven nephews and one niece learned how to ride and had taken the time to teach each one of them how to handle a horse when they came to visit. She had to admit that those lessons had paid off. It was evident that Stone was a skilled horseman. He even shared with her that he owned a horse that was stabled at Highpoint Manor, a place where he could go and enjoy the Georgia Mountains on horseback. From Atlanta it would take him less than two hours to reach the Blue Ridge Mountains where he would get on the back of his horse for an excursion into the wilderness.

Something made him look her way and her breath caught when he saw her. He trotted the horse over to her, coming to a stop by the porch. "Good morning, Madison."

"Good morning, Stone."

Some part of her felt she should be embarrassed after how she'd acted last night and everything they had done together. But she felt no shame. In fact she wasn't even feeling self-conscious that she was standing before him wearing his shirt without a stitch of clothing underneath. It seemed that all her proper Boston upbringing had gone back up North without her, leaving her doing and thinking all sorts of naughty things.

She tipped her head back to look at him. He was sitting on the horse looking sexier than any man had a right to look. Their gazes locked, held and she felt a quickening in her stomach. She also felt a stirring heat between her legs and as he continued to gaze down at her, she saw the color of his eyes darken as desire flooded their depths.

"Come ride with me," he said throatily. His voice was so husky it sent a sensuous chill down her spine.

Without asking where they were going or bothering to bring to his attention the fact that she wasn't appropriately dressed to go riding, she accepted the hand he reached out to her. He leaned over and, with one smooth sweep, gathered her into his arms. However, instead of placing her on the horse behind him, he placed her in front of him turning her to face him. When she lifted a brow in surprise, he said, "You're beautiful and I can't help but want to look at you this morning."

Madison smiled, touched by his comment. "But how will you see to lead the horse with me blocking your view?"

A grin touched the corners of his mouth. "You won't be blocking it. Besides, I get the feeling this horse has been up here several times and knows his way around. I pretty much let him lead the way."

Madison nodded, then held on as Stone urged the horse into a trot. When they got a little distance from the cabin he slowed the horse down to a walking pace. At first she had felt uncomfortable facing him while sitting on the back of a horse, especially with the way he was looking at her, but another feeling was taking over. It didn't help matters when the horse came to a complete stop and began nibbling on the grass. Stone decided to use that time to nibble on her. He leaned forward and captured her lips, kissing her with an intensity that set her body on fire. She encircled his neck with her arms for support while enjoying their kiss.

"Aren't you afraid that we're going to fall off this horse?"

she asked him when he pulled his mouth away moments later.

"No. It's just like anything else you ride," he responded, his tone breathy and hot. "You have to keep your balance."

She wondered how a person could keep their balance when their mind was spinning. Stone's kiss had rocked her world and she was dizzy from the impact. He had stroked her tongue with his, causing the heat that was already settled inside of her to go up another degree.

"You look good in my shirt," he said, before reaching out and undoing the top button. Then the second and third.

"Stone, what are you doing?" she asked in a startled gasp, barely getting the words out when he had eased buttons four and five free. She brought her hands up to cover his.

"Undressing you."

Madison could clearly see that. She glanced around. "But, but, we're outside in the open."

"Yes, but we're also alone. No one is here but you, me and this horse, and he's too busy filling his stomach to worry about what we're doing."

"Yes, but—"

That was as far as she got when Stone recaptured her mouth and at the same moment gently slid off the horse with her in his arms, snagging the blanket in the process.

When he ended the kiss and placed her on her feet, she met his gaze and he thought about how different she was from all the other women he had been with. With Madison, he had no control and he wondered if she knew just how seductive she was. He had a feeling that she didn't have a clue.

Stone had left her alone in the cabin because he'd needed distance to think, but all he'd done while out riding was think about her. He couldn't erase from his mind how she had made him feel when she had run her hands over him, sending shock waves of pleasure through his body. Nor could he forget how she had smiled at him after they had both reached their pleasure, snuggling closer to him, resting her head against his chest and going to sleep in his arms like it was just where she wanted to be. Just where she belonged.

With that memory firmly imbedded in his mind, he reached up and began stroking her hair, needing to touch her, to feel connected. He watched with penetrating attentiveness as her breathing quickened, her eyes darkened and her lips parted.

He gently cupped the back of her neck and drew her closer to his face. Bringing her lips just inches from his, he whispered, "I want to make love to you, here, under the Montana sky."

He watched as her eyes drifted closed and when she reopened them, the eyes that looked at him were filled with desire, as well as uncertainty. He wanted to keep the former and remove the latter. He reached for her hand and began slowly stroking her wrist in a slow seductive motion and watched as the uncertainty in her gaze faded.

"I want to make love to you under the Montana sky, too," she whispered when only desire shone in the depths of her dark eyes. Her voice was so low he could barely hear the words.

Stone drew in a sharp intake of breath as the intensity of just how much he wanted Madison hit him. Taking her hand in his, he led her through a path that was shrouded with lush green prairie grass. When he found what he thought was the perfect spot, he spread the blanket on the ground, sat down and pulled her on to his lap.

His mouth captured hers and with a shaking hand, he

removed his shirt from her body. Moments later, he pulled back and stood to remove his jeans; taking a condom pack from the pocket before tossing them aside. His hand continued to shake as he sheathed himself.

He is a beautiful man, Madison thought as she watched what Stone was doing. A sheen of perspiration covered his chest; a chest she knew was broad and muscular. Then there were those strong thighs, firm buttocks and the huge erection that promised more of what they'd shared last night.

She inhaled deeply. A slow throbbing ache had started low and deep in her stomach, inching its way through every part of her body. She actually felt a climax building and Stone hadn't done anything but kiss her…but the look in his eyes promised everything. And she wanted it all.

She wanted Stone Westmoreland.

She didn't want to think about the implications of what that might mean. At the moment she couldn't give herself that luxury. The only thoughts she wanted flowing through her mind were intimate ones. She forced the lump in her throat away, as a little voice in the back of her mind whispered, *live for the moment. Enjoy this time with him to the fullest.*

After Stone finished putting on the condom he paused as his gaze held Madison's. Last night while making love, he had never felt so connected, so joined, so linked to a woman. It was as if they had formed a kinship, an unshakable attachment, a special bond that he couldn't dismiss even if he wanted to.

Maybe it was pure insanity on his part to think that way. In that case, he might as well call himself crazy because the thoughts were in his head and there wasn't a damn thing he could do about them now. He would have to figure things out later because what he wanted more than anything, even more than his next breath, was the woman who was sitting on the blanket watching every move he made with so much desire in her eyes, it only made his body harder.

He let out a deep breath and wondered how he could have gone through life for thirty-three years and not known of her existence. She was beautiful, exquisite and, for now, right this minute, she was his.

His.

He swallowed deeply, knowing he had to say something and that he needed to choose his words carefully. He wanted her to know, he *had* to let her know, that this wasn't just another coupling for him. What they shared all through last night, as well as what they were about to share now were special to him and totally out of sync with how he usually did things. He wanted her to know she had touched him in a way that no woman had done before.

When he moved his mouth to say the words, Madison leaned forward, reached out and placed her fingers to his lips. She wasn't ready to hear what he had to say, especially if it was something that would break the romantic spell between them. She didn't want to hear him stress once again the kind of man that he was. She knew that he was not looking for a serious involvement and she respected that, but neither of them could turn their backs on the passion that was now raging between them. Right now, all she wanted to think about—all she cared about—was that this wonderful man had given her a real taste of passion, something she had never experienced before. He'd also shown her how it felt to fall for someone.

And she had fallen helplessly and hopelessly in love with Stone Westmoreland.

He pulled her fingers from his lips and leaned forward, brushing those same lips against hers before letting the fullness of his mouth settle over hers, kissing her with an intensity that sent heat soaring through her veins. The same wanting, longing and desire that she had encountered from the moment she'd met him took over and she pulled him down to her, determined to make this morning a repeat of last night.

He broke off the kiss and his hands and mouth went to work to drive her insanely out of her mind. She twisted and moaned beneath him sighing his name and reaching out to capture in her hands that part of him she wanted so badly.

When she held his thick arousal in her hand she folded her fingers around him, squeezing him in her palm. She looked up, met his gaze and asked, "Ready?"

The heat from his gaze nearly scorched her insides and when he smiled she became entrenched in passion so intense she could barely breathe. "Ready," he replied.

She let go and the solid length of him probed her feminine folds as he rolled his hips, finding the rhythm he intended for them to share. Sweat appeared on his forehead and she knew he was just as over the edge as she was, just as hungry for this.

Lowering his head, he captured her mouth, sought out her tongue at the same exact moment that he entered her, swallowing the moan that came from deep in her throat. He lifted her hips and wrapped her legs around him as he went deeper. She felt all of him, every single inch of his intimate flesh. He thrust back and forth inside her as he deepened the kiss they were sharing.

Stone released her mouth when a growl erupted deep in his throat. Sensations spiraled through him. He increased their rhythm and his body began moving faster, his thrusts became harder and went deeper. All of him worked tirelessly to satisfy this woman he was making love with and when he felt her body begin shuddering in an orgasm that made her cry out, he knew he had again succeeded.

He threw his head back as his thrusts quickened even more and he knew that, for as long as he lived, he would have memories of the time he had made love to her under a Montana sky. When he felt her body explode in another climax, he was there with her and continued to pump into her until he had nothing left to give.

"Stone!"

"Madison!"

Everything transformed into one sensuously dizzy moment and he captured her mouth, needing to be joined with her from the top all the way to the bottom. And she returned his kiss the same way he was giving it to her, responding to every delicious stroke of his tongue.

Moments later, Stone slid from her body and gathered her into his arms to hold her as she slumped against him. She tucked her face into the warmth of his neck, and he couldn't help but wonder just how he would handle things when she returned to Boston.

"Are you sure that you won't mind staying here another night?"

Madison looked across the kitchen table at Stone. They had made love once again after returning to the cabin and drifted off to sleep. Hunger had awakened them a few hours later and after dressing—or half-dressing, since she had put his shirt back on and he was wearing only his jeans—they had stumbled into the kitchen. For two people who prided themselves on possessing endless energy, they were definitely wearing each other out.

Surprisingly, the kitchen cupboards weren't bare. There

were a number of cans of soup and they decided to share some tomato soup.

"Yes, I'm sure, as long as we have something to eat." She smiled. "Besides, it would be dangerous to travel if we were to leave now. Soon it will be dark."

Stone nodded then reached across the table and captured her hand in his. "Do you regret that we didn't head out first thing this morning as we'd planned?"

She met his gaze. "No."

They went back to bed and made love again and later, after dressing fully, they decided to take a walk around the cabin. "Have you prepared yourself for tomorrow?" Stone asked, holding her hand as they walked along the stream.

Madison glanced up at him. A beautiful sunset was emerging before them and she had a beautiful man to share it with.

"No, I've been so caught up in what we've been doing that I haven't had a chance to really think about it. And maybe that's a good thing."

"Why?"

"Because sharing this time with you has opened my eyes to a lot of things. I hate to think of my parents' love life, but what if my mother never experienced anything as rich and profound as the passion we've shared in the whole time she was married to my father?"

Stone hugged her tighter to him. "Maybe your parents were passionately in love at one point." But he knew what she meant. He also knew that his uncle had a way with women and he couldn't help but wonder if perhaps, when he saw Abby Winters, he had detected untapped passion in her in the same way Stone had detected it in Madison.

"But I plan to do as you suggested, Stone."

Her words intruded on his thoughts and he glanced down at her. "What is that?"

"Keep an open mind about things and not be judgmental."

He nodded. "I'm sure your mother would appreciate that. She'll probably be surprised as hell to see you. The last thing she needs is for you to become the parent and make her feel like a naughty child."

Madison sighed deeply. "Do you think I made a mistake by even coming?"

He put his hand on her wrist to stop them from walking any farther, knowing he had to be honest with her. "At first I did, but now I know it's just your nature. You were concerned about her. I think she will understand that."

Madison hoped so. The closer the time came to seeing her mother, the more she began to feel nervous about her motives in pursuing her. What right did she have to interfere in her mother's life? Her mother was a fifty-year-old woman and if she was going through a midlife crisis then it was her business. She shook her head. Her mother was the only family she had so anything her mother was going through was both of their businesses. She would just have to adjust her way of thinking about things and practice understanding. And thanks to the man standing in front of her, she believed that she could. Stone had shown her the true meaning of passion and the pleasures of making love. And he had also introduced her to the joys of loving and Madison now knew that she truly loved him.

Once things were settled with her mother, she would leave immediately for Boston. The memories she would have of the time she and Stone had spent together would keep her warm on those lonely nights when she would long to have him naked in bed beside her; those times when she would yearn for her dreams of him to become reality. Already the thought of leaving him caused pain to pierce her heart, but she would survive…she had no other choice.

Chapter 8

Wow! That was the one word that immediately came to Madison's mind when they reached the top of the mountain where Corey Westmoreland lived.

Coming to Montana had certainly opened her eyes to the beauty of an area she had never visited before. Seeing the spacious and sprawling ranch house in the distance, set among a stand of pine trees and beneath the beautiful Montana blue sky, forced a breathless sigh to escape from her lips.

"Why would one man need a place so huge?" she turned and asked Stone.

His mouth twitched into a grin. "Mainly because of his family, especially his nephews. When it became evident that the number of male Westmorelands was increasing and this place would be their summer home, Uncle Corey decided he needed lots of space and a huge food budget."

Madison blinked. "You mean, while growing up, all eleven of you would visit at the same time?"

Stone chuckled. "Yeah, we would all be here at the same time. But you'd better believe that, although everyone thought Uncle Corey was nuts for having all of us here, they knew him well enough to know that he would keep us in line and keep us busy. He did and we loved it. My fondest childhood memories were of the times I spent here. That's why me and my four brothers and six cousins have such a close relationship. Each summer we did some serious male bonding and learned how to get along with each other. Once in a while, we'd let Delaney come with us during the summer, but she preferred coming during her spring breaks."

Madison nodded. "Your uncle must really like kids."

Stone smile wavered some. "He does. It's unfortunate that he never married and had any of his own."

She gazed at him. "Do you like kids?"

He cast her a sideways glance. "Yes. Why do you ask?"

"Because I think it's unfortunate that in a few years you're going to find yourself in the same situation as your uncle."

He held her gaze for a long moment, then said in a low voice, "Yeah, I guess you're right. Come on. Chances are Uncle Corey knows we're coming."

Madison lifted her brow as the horses moved forward at a slow pace with Stone traveling slightly ahead. "How will he know that?"

Stone turned and looked back at her and the chuckle that poured from his lips seemed to echo in the wind. "Because Uncle Corey knows the moment anyone sets foot on his mountain. He may not know it's us who's coming but he knows that somebody is on his property."

And as if to prove how well Stone knew his uncle, Madison watched as the front door of the huge ranch house swung open and a bear of a man—who looked to stand at least six-five—stepped out onto the wraparound porch. He was wearing a Stetson on his head and peered at them as if trying to make out the identity of his trespassers. When moments passed and it became obvious that he'd figured out that at least one of them was his nephew, he smiled, tugged at the brim of his Stetson and stepped off the porch to come and meet them.

When he came closer the first thing Madison saw was that he was definitely a Westmoreland. Upon first meeting Durango she had immediately known that he and Stone were related and the same held true for Corey Westmoreland. He had the same dark eyes, the same forehead, chin and full lips.

The next thing she noticed was that, at fifty-four, he was a very good-looking man. Like his two nephews, he was magnificent. When he removed his hat she saw that his dark hair had streaks of gray at the temple, making him seem distinguished, as well as handsome. And he appeared to be in excellent physical shape. This was definitely a man who could still grab female interest and she could see why her mother had evidently found him attractive and irresistible.

As soon as Corey reached them Stone brought his bay to a stop and was off his horse in a flash, engulfing his uncle in a huge embrace. "Well, my word, Stone, it's good seeing you. I almost forgot Durango had mentioned that you would be visiting these parts. The phone's been down for a couple of weeks and I've been cut off from civilization."

Corey Westmoreland then turned his attention to Madison who was still sitting on the back of her horse staring at him. He tipped his hat to her. "Howdy, ma'am," he said walking over and offering her his hand in a friendly handshake. "Welcome to Corey's Mountain and who might you be?"

Madison saw the look of amusement in Corey Westmoreland's dark eyes and knew he had immediately jumped to the conclusion that she was there because of Stone and that the two of them were lovers. She could give him credit for being partly right.

She accepted his assistance when he reached up to help her off her horse and knew the exact moment that Stone came to stand beside her. "Hello, Mr. Westmoreland, I'm Madison Winters and I've come to see my mother."

There was complete silence for a few moments, then Madison watched as the look in Corey Westmoreland's eyes became tender and, when he spoke, his tone of voice matched that look. "So you're Madison? I've heard a lot about you. Abby will be glad to see you."

Madison nodded as she tried reading signs in the older man's features that indicated otherwise. "She doesn't know I'm coming."

He chuckled. "That won't mean a thing. She hoped you had gotten the messages she'd left so you wouldn't worry. With the phones being down, she couldn't leave any more. I'm hoping Liam will be feeling well enough to do the repairs."

Madison lifted a brow. "Liam?"

"Yes, he's another rancher who lives on the opposite mountain. He's also the area's repair man and electrician." Corey Westmoreland put his hat back on. "But enough about that. I'm sure you're eager to see your mama."

"Yes, I am." Madison glanced around. "Is she still here?" She watched as the man's mouth lit into a huge smile.

"Yes, she's here. Go on up to the house and open the door and go right on in. When I walked out she was in the middle of preparing dinner."

Madison blinked. "Dinner? My mother is actually cooking?"

"Yes."

Madison frowned. She couldn't remember the last time her mother had cooked. She turned to Stone. "Are you coming?"

He shook his head. "I'll be in later. I need to talk to Uncle Corey about something."

She nodded. Although she knew he probably did need to talk to his uncle, she also knew that he was hanging back to give her and her mother time alone. "All right." And without saying anything else, she walked the short distance to the house alone, wondering what she would say to her mother when she saw her.

Madison opened the door and cautiously walked inside the impressive house. She heard the sound of a woman humming and immediately knew it was her mother's voice. Quickly glancing around she scanned her surroundings. The inside of Corey's ranch house was just as huge as the outside. The heavy furnishings were made of rich, supple leather and were durable and made to last forever. The place looked neat and well-lived-in and several vases of fresh flowers denoted a feminine touch.

"Dinner's almost ready, Corey. I think a soak in the hot tub would be nice afterwards, what do you think?"

Madison swallowed as the sound of her mother's voice reached her. Evidently she had heard the door open and assumed it was Corey Westmoreland returning. Sighing deeply, Madison crossed the living room to the kitchen and came to a stop in the doorway. Her mother, the prim-and-proper Abby Winters, was bending over checking something in the oven. She was wearing a pair of jeans, a short

top, was barefoot and had her hair untied and flowing down
her back. Her mother had always been weight conscious
and had a nice figure; the outfit she was wearing clearly
showed just how nice that figure was.

Madison blinked, not sure if this sexy looking creature
in Corey Westmoreland's kitchen was actually her mother.
She looked more like a woman in her thirties than someone
who had turned fifty earlier that year. And Madison found
it hard to believe that the woman who normally wore con-
servative business suits, high-heeled pumps and her hair
up in a bun was the same person standing less than ten feet
away from her.

"Mom?"

Abby Winters snatched her head up and met Madison's
uncertain gaze. She blinked, as if making sure she was really seeing her daughter, and then a huge smile touched
both corners of her lips and she quickly crossed the room.
"Maddy, what are you doing here?" she asked, mere seconds before engulfing Madison in a colossal hug.

"I wanted to make sure you were all right," Madison
said when her mother finally released her.

Her mother lifted a worried brow. "Didn't you get my
messages saying I was extending my trip?"

"Yes, but I had to see for myself that you were okay."

Abby pulled her daughter back to her. "Oh, sweetheart,
I'm sorry that you were worried about me, but I'm fine."

Madison sighed. What she needed to hear was a little more than that, but before she could open her mouth
to say anything, she heard the front door open and Stone
and Corey Westmoreland walked in. She watched the expression on her mother's face when she looked up and saw
Stone's uncle. If there was any doubt in Madison's mind, it
vanished with the look the two of them exchanged. It was

a good thing they were already in the kitchen because she could certainly feel the heat simmering between them. It was quite obvious that her mother and Corey Westmoreland had a thing going on.

Madison cleared her throat. "Mom, this is Stone, Mr. Westmoreland's nephew and my friend. Stone, this is my mother, Abby Winters."

She saw Stone blink and knew the prim-and-proper picture she had painted of her mother was definitely not the one Stone was seeing. He took a step forward and took Abby's hand in a warm handshake. "Nice meeting you, Ms. Winters."

Abby Winters smiled warmly. "And it's nice meeting you, Stone. Corey speaks highly of you and I've read every book you've written. You're a gifted author."

"Thank you."

"And please call me Abby." She glanced back at Madison. "How do the two of you know each other?"

"We met on the plane flying out here," Stone said before Madison could respond.

Abby's smile widened. "Oh, how nice. I'm glad that Madison had some company for the flight. I know how much she detests flying."

The room got quiet and then Abby spoke again. "Corey and I were just about to have dinner. He can show you where the two of you can stay and then we'll sit down and eat. I'm sure you must be hungry."

Madison was more curious as to what was going on between her mother and Corey Westmoreland than she was hungry, but decided she and her mother would talk later. That was a definite. "That's fine."

Sighing deeply, she and Stone followed Corey Westmoreland out of the kitchen.

* * *

"So you have no idea who's trying to find you, Uncle Corey?" Stone asked later as he stood with his uncle on the porch. Dinner had been wonderful. For someone who Madison thought couldn't cook, her mother had prepared a delicious feast. Madison and her mother were inside doing dishes and no doubt Madison was grilling her mother on her relationship with Corey. As yet, his uncle had not explained anything to him. Corey acted like it was an everyday occurrence for Stone to show up on his mountain and find a woman cooking and serving as hostess as if she had permanent residence there.

Corey leaned against a column post. "No, I don't know a living soul who would be looking for me," he said shaking his head in confusion. "You said Quade is checking things out?"

"Yes. Durango contacted him."

Corey nodded. "Then there's nothing for me to do but wait until I hear from him." He then looked over at his nephew. "Madison is a pretty thing. She reminds me of Abby when she was young."

Stone turned and gazed at his uncle. "You knew Abby Winters before?"

Corey chuckled as if amused. "Of course. Do you think we just met yesterday?"

Stone shook his head as if to clear his brain. "Hell, Uncle Corey, I didn't know what to think and Madison is even more confused."

Corey nodded again. "I'm sure Abby will explain things to her."

Stone crossed his arms over his chest. "How about if you explain things to me."

A few moments later, Corey sighed deeply. "All right. Let's take a walk."

The two of them walked down a path that Stone remembered well. It was the way to the natural spring that was on his uncle's property. He remembered how he and his brothers and cousins had spent many hours in it having lots of fun. The sun had gone down but it wasn't completely dark yet. The scent of pine filled the air.

"Abby and I met when I was in my last year at Montana State. She had come with her parents to visit Yellowstone as a graduation gift before starting college. I was working part-time at the park and will never forget the day I saw her. She was barely eighteen and I thought I had died and gone to heaven. When I finally got the chance to talk to her without her parents around, I knew she was the person I had fallen in love with and someone I would never forget." Corey smiled. "And she felt the same way. It was love at first sight and the attraction between us was spontaneous."

The smile then vanished from Corey's face. "It was also forbidden love because she was about to become engaged to another man, someone attending Harvard. He was a man her well-to-do family had picked out for her, one of those affairs where two families get together and decide their kids will marry. And no matter how we felt about each other I knew Abby wouldn't change her mind. She was raised not to defy her parents. Besides, I was not in a position to ask her to stay with me. Her fiancé's family had money and I barely had a job. When she left I never saw her again and she took my heart with her. I knew then that I would never marry, because the one woman I wanted was lost to me forever."

Stone nodded, wondering how he would feel if the one

woman he wanted was lost to him forever. "There was never another woman over the years that you grew to love?"

Corey shook his head. "No. There was one woman I took up with a year or two later, when I worked for a while as a ranger in the Tennessee Mountains. I tried to make things work with her, but couldn't. We stayed together for almost a year but she knew my heart belonged to someone else. And one day she just took off and I haven't seen her since."

Stone nodded again. "So when you saw Abby three weeks ago, that was the first time the two of you had seen each other in over thirty-two years?"

Corey smiled. "Yes, and we recognized each other immediately and the spark was still there. And after a few hours of conversation—she told me her life story and I told her mine—we decided to do what we couldn't do then, all those years ago. Steal away and be alone. After talking to her it was plain to see she had lived a lonely life just like I had, and we felt we owed it to each other to start enjoying life to the fullest and to be happy. She's only been here three weeks but Abby has brought nothing but joy and happiness to my life, Stone. I can't imagine my life without her now and she's assured me that she feels the same way."

Stone stopped walking and stared at his uncle. "What are you saying?"

A huge grin spread across Corey Westmoreland's face. "I've asked Abby to marry me and she's accepted."

Madison stared at her mother in shock. "Marriage? You and Corey Westmoreland?"

Abby smiled at her only child as she handed her a dish to dry. "Yes. He asked and I accepted. Corey and I met and fell in love the year before I entered Harvard. My parents had already decided my future was with your father and I was the obedient daughter who wouldn't defy their plans."

Madison continued to stare at her mother. "So I assumed right. You and Dad never loved each other."

Abby reached out and took her daughter's hand in hers, knowing that Madison was probably confused by a lot of things. "In a way, your father and I did love each other but not the way I loved Corey. As long as your father was alive, I was determined to make our marriage work, and I did. I was faithful to your father, Madison, and I was a good wife."

Madison knew that was true. "So you came out here hoping that you'd run into Corey Westmoreland again?"

Abby smiled as she shook her head. "No. For all I knew Corey had gotten on with his life and was married with a bunch of kids. I knew he had wanted to become a park ranger, but I didn't even know if he still lived in this area. Imagine my shock when I went out to dinner that night and he walked into the restaurant. He looked at me and I looked at him and it was as if the years hadn't mattered. I knew then that I still loved him and I also knew that the most joyous part of my life was the summer I met him."

Her hand tightened on Madison's. "But that doesn't mean your father didn't bring me joy. It means that with Corey I can be someone I could never be with your father."

In a way Madison understood. During the past two days, she had behaved in ways with Stone that she had never behaved with Cedric. "So when is the wedding?"

"In a few months. We decided to wait until after his nephew Thorn's next race. That way Corey can make the announcement to all of his family at one time. The entire Westmoreland family always attends Thorn's races."

Madison sighed deeply. "What about you? What about your life back in Boston?"

Abby smiled. "I plan to keep Abby's Manor since there's definitely a need for day-care facilities for the elderly. And it will continue to be managed the same way it's being managed now. Everything else I can tie up rather quickly. My friends, if they are truly my friends and love me, they will want me to be happy. I haven't been involved with anyone since your father's death over ten years ago. I'm hoping everyone will understand my need to be with him."

She then stared for a long moment at her daughter. "What about you, Madison? You are the person who concerns me the most. Do you understand?"

Madison met her mother's gaze. Yes, she understood how it felt to want to be happy, mainly because she also knew how it felt to be in love. As unusual as it seemed, her mother still loved Corey Westmoreland after all these years. Their love had been strong enough to withstand more than thirty years of separation. She knew her mother was waiting for her answer. She also knew that her response was important to her. Abby Winters had been right. The people who truly loved her would understand her need to be happy.

Madison reached out and hugged her mother. "Yes, Mom, I understand and I'm happy for you. If marrying Corey Westmoreland makes you happy, then I am happy."

Abby's arms tightened around her daughter. "Thank you, sweetheart."

Stone Westmoreland glanced at the clock on the nightstand next to the bed. It was after midnight and he couldn't sleep. He had Madison on his mind. She and her mother had joined him and Uncle Corey on the porch and she had congratulated his uncle on his upcoming marriage to her mother and had even gone a step further and hugged Uncle Corey and welcomed him to the family. Uncle Corey had done likewise and welcomed her to his. Then Madison had indicated to all that she was tired and would be going to bed early. He of all people knew of her overabundance of energy and figured that it wasn't exhaustion that had made her escape to her room. She was trying to come to terms with her mother's marriage announcement.

Getting out of bed he slipped into his jeans. Quietly opening the door he entered the darkened hallway. He had walked this hallway many times and knew his way around, even in the dark. The room Madison had been given was only a couple of doors from his. He wondered how she felt knowing his uncle and her mother were probably sharing a bed tonight. He doubted they would change their routine because of their unexpected guests, especially since they intended to marry.

He opened the door and quietly slipped into Madison's bedroom. As soon as he entered and closed the door behind him, he saw her. She was standing across the room gazing out of the window. From where he stood he saw she was wearing a nightgown and the light from the moon that shone through the window silhouetted how the sleepwear sensuously draped her figure.

He breathed in deeply. As much as he wanted her, he hadn't come to her for that. He wanted to hold her in his arms because whether she admitted it or not, she *was* having a problem coming to terms with her mother's upcoming marriage to his uncle.

"Madison." He whispered the name softly and she quickly turned around.

"Stone?"

Without answering, he quickly crossed the room and

pulled her into his arms and kissed her, needing the taste of her and wanting to give her the taste of him. Her response made him deepen the kiss and when his tongue took control of hers, the soft moans that flowed from deep within her throat nearly pushed him over the edge.

He gently broke off the kiss. "You were quiet after dinner. Are you all right?"

She nodded against his chest and his arms around her tightened. "They are happy together, Madison," he said, trying to reassure her.

She pulled back from him and glanced up. "I know that, Stone, and that's what's so sad. They went all those years loving each other but not being able to be together."

Stone nodded. "Yeah, my uncle told me."

Madison sighed. "They fell in love from the first. According to Mom, she fell in love with your uncle the first time she saw him although she knew her life was destined to be with someone else."

Stone stared down at her for a moment then asked, "And how do you feel about that, Madison?"

She knew why he was asking. The man her mother had married instead of Corey Westmoreland had been her father. "My heart aches for the three of them. What if there was someone who my father would have preferred to love. I think it's ridiculous for parents to plan their children's future that way. I won't ever do that to my kids."

Stone had been rubbing her back. He suddenly paused. "Kids? You plan to have kids?"

She looked up at him and smiled. "Yes, one day."

He nodded. That meant she also planned on getting married one day. Hellfire. He sure didn't like the thought of that. "You need to get into bed and try and get some sleep."

He saw awareness flash in her eyes when she suddenly

realized he wasn't wearing a shirt. "I'll only get into bed if you get in with me."

He shook his head. "With your mother and Uncle Corey at the end of the hall, I don't think that's a good idea." He didn't want to bring up the fact that he doubted he could lie beside her for any period of time without wanting to make love to her, and their lovemaking tended to be rather noisy.

"Please. I promise to behave. Just stay with me for a little while."

He looked down at her and knew she had no intention of behaving. He would stay but would somehow dredge up enough control to behave for the both of them. "All right, into bed you go. I'll stay with you for a little while."

"Thanks, Stone."

He walked her over to the bed and pushed the covers aside. She slid in and he slid in beside her and pulled her into his arms. She automatically shifted her body in a spoon position against him and he knew she felt his arousal through his jeans. "Wouldn't you be more comfortable if you were to take off your pants?" she asked in a soft voice.

He tightened his arms around her. "Go to sleep, Madison," he growled in her ear.

"Are you sure you want me to do that?"

"Yes, I'm sure. Now go to sleep." He knew he didn't want her to do that but under the circumstances he had no choice. He hadn't missed the looks his uncle had given him at dinner. Corey and Abby were curious about his relationship with Madison. Although they hadn't asked anything, they had gone quiet when Madison had innocently mentioned they had stayed at the Quinns' cabin for two days.

A few hours later, the only sounds Stone heard were Madison's soft even breathing and a coyote that was howling in the distance. He leaned over and kissed her lips then slipped from the bed to return to his room. Before opening the door he glanced back over to look at her and knew that, if he had been in his uncle's shoes thirty some years ago and Madison had been her mother, there was no way he would have let her go and marry another man.

There was no way on God's green earth that he would have allowed that to happen.

Chapter 9

The next two weeks flew by and Madison's heart swelled each and every time she saw her mother and Corey Westmoreland interacting together. It was quite obvious the two were in love and were making up for lost time. She had never seen her mother smile so much and it seemed that Corey had brought out a totally different woman in Abby Winters. Her mother enjoyed cooking, baking and thought nothing of helping Corey do chores around the ranch.

The days of the prim-and-proper Abby Winters were over—but not completely. She still set the table like she was expecting guests for dinner and occasionally Madison would hear classical music on the disc player. Madison liked the change in her mother and more and more she was accepting Corey's role in her life.

Madison then thought about her own love life or lack of it. Stone still came to her room every night and held her until she went off to sleep. In respect for her mother and his uncle, he refused to make love to her although she always tried tempting him into doing so.

She had looked forward to today. Her mother and Corey had mentioned a few days ago that they would be gone from the ranch most of the day to visit another rancher who lived on the other side of the mountain. That meant that she and Stone would have the entire house to themselves and she intended to make good use of it.

She was aware that it had been hard for him to keep his hands off her and it had been just as hard for her to keep her hands off him. All it took was a look across the table into his dark eyes to see the longing and desire, and to know what he was thinking and feel the sexual currents that radiated from his gaze.

He stayed away from the house most of the day helping his uncle do various chores around the ranch. Corey had decided that, with Stone there, now was a good time to start constructing a new barn. When Stone came in each afternoon he would take a bath before dinner and usually retired to his room to work on his book after sitting and talking with everyone for a while. But no matter how tired he was, he always came to her room every night to spend time with her. They would sometimes sit and talk for hours. He would tell her about the book he was working on and the scenes he had plotted that day. Once or twice he even read some of them to her and she was amazed how his mind worked to come up with some of the stuff he'd written.

Madison sighed with disappointment as she sat at the kitchen table and looked out. It seemed that she and Stone wouldn't have the ranch to themselves today after all. Corey had announced at breakfast that he and Abby had changed their minds and would visit the Monroes another time. She had glanced across the table and seen the same disappointment in Stone's eyes that she knew had been in hers.

"It's a beautiful day for a picnic, don't you think?"

She glanced around and met her mother's smiling face, then shrugged her shoulders. "I suppose so."

"Then why don't you find Stone and suggest that the two of you go to Cedar Canyon? You can take the SUV and not worry about traveling by horseback. It's simply beautiful and there's a lake so you may want to take your bathing suit with you."

Madison perked up. The picnic sounded nice, but… "I don't have a bathing suit."

Abby chuckled. "You can certainly borrow one of mine. That's one of the first things Corey made sure I had when I came here. With so many hot springs and lakes around, it would be a waste not to have one."

Madison glanced back out of the window. She saw Stone in the distance standing next to the corral gate as he watched his uncle rope a calf. "Stone may be too busy to want to take off like that."

Abby chuckled again. "Oh, I don't know. Something tells me that he'll like the idea."

Stone definitely liked the idea and when Madison suggested it he didn't waste any time going into the house to shower and change. He was dying to be alone with her away from the ranch. And the way he was driving the truck indicated that he was in a rush to get to their destination.

"We will get there in one piece, won't we, Stone?"

He glanced over at Madison and even though she was smiling, she was hinting that he slow down. He had made a couple of sharp turns around several curves. "Sorry. I guess I'm kind of eager to get there."

She gave him an innocent look. "Why? Are you hungry? Is what's in that picnic basket tempting you?"

He met her gaze and decided to be completely honest. "Yes, I'm hungry but my hunger has nothing to do with what's in that damn basket. You're what's tempting me. Aren't you?" He watched the smile that spread across her lips; lips he was dying to kiss. He had noticed each and every time she had inched her skirt up her legs, although he should have been keeping his eyes on the road.

"Yes. I just wanted to make sure you wanted me," she said grinning.

He brought the car to a screeching stop. Taking a deep breath, he turned to face her. "I want you, Madison, don't doubt that. I want you so bad that I ache. I want you so bad that if I don't get inside of you real soon, I might embarrass myself."

She glanced down at his midsection and nodded when she saw what he meant. "Then I guess we'd better be on our way again, because I wouldn't want that to happen."

"No."

She lifted a brow. "No?"

"No, I don't think I can wait now."

Her brow lifted when she saw he was unbuttoning his shirt. He removed it and tossed it in the back seat of the SUV. She swallowed hard. She had seen him shirtless numerous times but still her midsection filled with heat each and every time she saw him that way. And she didn't want to think about how turned on she got whenever she saw him naked.

"Uhh, would you like to tell me what's going on here?" she said in a low voice. Desire was making it almost impossible for her to speak.

His smile widened into a grin. It was a smile so hot she

felt heat center between her legs in reaction to it. "We're what's going on. And the one thing I really like about this SUV is that it's very roomy. My brother Dare owns one and he let my brother Storm borrow it when his car was in the shop. He later wished that he hadn't. Storm discovered just how roomy it was when he used it to go out on a date."

Stone chuckled as he shook his head. "Needless to say, Dare learned his lesson when he found a pair of women's panties under the seat the next day and he swore never to let Storm borrow his truck again."

Madison grinned. "Sounds like your brother Storm is quite a character."

"Yeah, for some reason the women think so and around Atlanta he's known as 'The Perfect Storm.' Of course none of us think there's anything perfect about him but evidently the women do. I don't know who's worse, him or Durango."

After unzipping his jeans, he lifted his hips to pull them off. Madison, he noticed, was watching him intently. "Instead of paying so much attention to me, you might want to start stripping."

She blinked in pure innocence. "Surely you're not suggesting that I get naked?"

"Yeah, that's exactly what I'm suggesting since seeing you naked is definitely one of my fantasies today. I want you naked and stretched out beneath me. Then I want to get inside you and stroke you until you can't take any more," he whispered huskily across the cab of the vehicle.

Madison swallowed. Her heart began pounding. The heat between her legs broke out into a flame. She began burning everywhere, but especially there. "Okay, you've convinced me to cooperate," she said, lifting her skirt and pulling down her panties. She held the scrap of black lace up in her hand. "I need to make sure I put these back on.

I don't want your uncle to find these in his truck like your brother Dare found those in his."

Stone reached out and plucked them out of her hand and stuffed them in the pocket of his jeans before pulling out a pack of condoms. "I'll try to remember to give them back to you," he said grinning. He then tossed his jeans in the back seat to join his shirt. He glanced over at her. "Need help removing that skirt and blouse?"

Madison smiled. "No thanks. I think I can manage."

"All right." And he got an eyeful while he saw her doing so. He was glad she hadn't needed his help. In his present state he might have been tempted to rip her clothes right off her. His breath caught when he saw she hadn't worn a bra and, when she removed her top, her breasts spilled free and his shaft reacted by getting even harder.

Madison glanced over at Stone. God, she wanted him. Bad. All his talk about wanting her and needing to get inside of her and stroking her had set her on fire. And she didn't feel a moment of embarrassment sitting with him naked in the truck. She was beginning to discover that with Stone she could be prim and proper and she could also be bad and naughty. She felt him ease the bench-seat back and the SUV became roomier.

She licked her lips when she gazed down at him— especially a certain part of him. "And you're sure no one will surprise us and come along?" There was a husky tone to her voice that even she didn't recognize.

"Yeah, I'm sure. I'd never risk exposing you like that. I intend to be the only man ever to see you naked."

She opened her mouth to tell him that sounded pretty much like a declaration that he intended to be with her for a while, but before she could get the words out he had captured her mouth in his and pulled her across the seat to him.

His kiss reflected all the want and desire he'd claimed he had for her; all that he'd been holding back for the past weeks. Now he was letting go and the moan that erupted deep in her throat was letting him know that she appreciated it.

She had missed this, a chance to moan and groan to her heart's delight without having to worry about anyone hearing her. But she knew that Stone had something else in store for her, too. Today he intended to make her scream.

In a smooth and swift move, he had her on her back and the leather felt warm against her naked back and his body felt hot to her naked front. And then there was that hard part of him that was insistently probing trying to get inside of her. She decided the least she could do—since she was more than eager for this pleasure—was to help him along. She reached out and held him in her hand. He felt hot, hard and thick.

"Take it home, baby."

Stone's words, whispered in a deep, husky tone, sent sensuous chills all through her body and she adjusted her body when he lifted her hips to place her legs on his shoulders. She guided him home and when he entered her and went deep, his growl of pleasure mingled with her sigh of contentment.

He gazed down at her and the look of desire in his eyes touched her in a way she had never been touched. He smiled and so did she. "I know this vehicle is roomy, now let's see how sturdy it is."

Before she could figure out what he meant he began thrusting inside of her at a rhythm that had her groaning and moaning. The seat rocked and she thought she felt the entire truck shake as his body melded into hers over and over again.

"I can't get enough of you, Madison," he groaned throatily as he continued to mate with her, stunned by the degree of wanting and desire he had for her. His jaw clenched and he hissed through his teeth when he felt her muscles tighten around him mercilessly. He reacted by thrusting into her even more. He felt her body shudder and when she let out a scream that was loud enough to send the wildlife scattering for miles, he threw his head back as his own body exploded. At that very moment he thought that he had to be stone crazy, especially when he felt another orgasm rip through her.

"Damn!" Never had he felt such a mind-blowing experience. It was a wonder the truck hadn't flipped over. The windows had definitely gotten steamy.

Moments later they collapsed in each other arms. Stone raised his head to gaze down at the woman still beneath him; the woman he was still intimately connected to; the woman he wanted again already. And he knew without a doubt that he wasn't stone crazy, but he was stone in love.

"So how was the picnic?" Corey asked as he sat down to the kitchen table for dinner.

"It was nice," Madison quickly said, glancing across the table to Stone. She was glad he didn't lift his head to look at her because if he'd done so, it would definitely have given something away. After making love in the truck a second time, they had continued on to Cedar Canyon. They spread a blanket next to the lake and ate the delicious snack her mother had packed for them. Then they had undressed and made love again on the blanket before going swimming. Then they had made love several more times before coming back to the ranch. To say the picnic had been nice was putting it mildly.

After dinner the four of them were sitting on the porch listening to Corey talk about the progress he and Stone were making on the barn, when one of the dogs barked. Corey glanced in the distance and saw riders approaching.

"Looks like we have visitors," he said, standing. He used his hand as a shield as he squinted the brilliance of the evening sun from his eyes. A smile touched his lips when he said, "It looks like Quade and Durango, and they have two other men with them."

Everyone watched the riders approach. Madison blinked when she saw the men, surprised that Corey didn't recognize the other two since it was crystal clear all of them were Westmorelands. The four could pass for brothers. She glanced over at Stone, but he was looking at the other two men intently, as well. The four riders dismounted and walked toward the porch.

"Durango, Quade, good seeing you," Corey said, grabbing his nephews in bear hugs. He then turned to the other two men. "I'm Corey Westmoreland and welcome to Corey's Mountain." He then frowned, as if seeing them had him confused. He stared at them for a second. "Do I know you two? Damn, I hate staring, but the two of you look a hell of a lot like my nephews here."

Quade Westmoreland cleared his throat. "There's a reason for that Uncle Corey."

Corey glanced over at Quade and lifted a brow. "There is?"

"Yes," Durango said quietly. "I'm sure Stone told you that someone was looking for you."

Corey nodded. "Yeah, that's what I heard. So what has that to do with these two?"

When everyone went silent, Corey crossed his arms over his chest. "Okay, what the hell is going on?"

One of the men, the taller of the two, spoke up. "Do you remember a Carolyn Roberts?"

Corey's arms dropped to his side. "Yes, I remember Carolyn. Why? What is she to you?"

The other man, who was just as tall as Corey, then spoke. "She was our mother."

"Was?" Corey asked softly.

"Yes, she died six months ago."

Corey shook his head sadly as he remembered the woman he'd dated a full year before they'd gone their separate ways, never to see each other again. "I'm sorry to hear that and you have my condolences. Your mother was a good woman."

"And she told us just moments before she died that you were a good man," the taller of the two said.

Corey sighed deeply. "I appreciate her thinking that way."

"That's not all Mrs. Roberts told them, Uncle Corey. I think you need to hear the rest of it," Quade Westmoreland said.

After glancing over at his nephew, Corey turned to the men. "All right. What else did she tell you?"

The two men looked from one to the other before the taller answered. "She also told us that we were your sons."

It was evident that the two men's statement had shaken Corey, Madison thought. But then all you had to do was to look at the other three Westmoreland nephews to know their claim was true. Quade was a good-looking man and reminded her a lot of Stone. He was quiet and didn't say much, but when he spoke people listened. And there was a dangerous look about him like he enjoyed living on the edge and wouldn't hesitate to take anything into his own hands if the need arose. Then there were the other two men, who until a few minutes ago were virtual strangers. The only names they'd given were their first ones, Clint and Cole. They said they would explain everything once they were seated at the table where they could talk.

Now it seemed everyone was ready. Her mother, being the ever-gracious and proper hostess, had made coffee and served Danishes when the men declined dinner. Abby was now seated beside Corey and, understanding her mother's presence but thinking this was a family matter and her presence wasn't warranted, Madison was about to leave to go to her room when Stone grabbed her arm and almost tugged her down in his lap. "Stay," he said so close to her lips she thought he was going to kiss her.

She glanced over at his cousin Quade who smiled mysteriously. She looked at Stone and nodded, "All right," and sat down in the chair beside him.

"Now, will the two of you start from the beginning?" Corey Westmoreland asked Clint and Cole.

Clint, the taller of the two men began speaking. "Twenty-nine years ago Carolyn gave birth to triplets and—"

"Triplets!" Corey exclaimed, nearly coming out of his seat.

Clint nodded. "Yes."

Corey shook his head. "Multiple births run in this family, but…hell, I didn't even know she was pregnant."

"Yes, she said she left without telling you after the two of you broke up. She moved to Beaumont, Texas, where an aunt and uncle lived. She showed up on their doorstep and fabricated the story that she had married a man who'd been a rodeo bronco and that he'd gotten killed while competing. She claimed that man's name was Corey Westmoreland and she was the widowed Carolyn Westmoreland. She'd even obtained false papers to prove it. We can only assume she did that because she was twenty-four and her aunt and uncle, her only relatives, were deeply religious. They wouldn't look down on her if she told them she was married instead of a girl having a child out of wedlock."

A few moments later Clint continued. "Anyway, she found out she was having triplets and, since she was using the Westmoreland name, the three of us were born as Westmorelands and no questions were asked. We were raised believing our father had died before we were born and never thought any differently until Mom called us in just seconds before she passed away and told us the truth."

Cole took up the story. "She said our father was Corey Westmoreland but he wasn't dead like she'd told us over the years. She said she didn't know where you were and would leave it up to us to find you. She told us to tell you, when we did find you, that she was sorry for not letting you know about us. If she had told you about her pregnancy she thought you would have done the honorable thing and married her, although she knew you didn't love her and that your heart still belonged to another. We promised her just seconds before her eyes closed that we would do what we could to find you and deliver that message. I believe that she was able to die in peace after that."

For a long moment no one at the table said anything and Madison felt the exact moment Stone took her hand in his and held it like the story had touched him deeply. She understood. It had touched her, as well.

Corey Westmoreland cleared his throat but everyone could see the tears that misted his eyes. "I thank her for wanting me to know the truth after all these years." He then cleared his throat again. "You said there were triplets. Does that mean there's a third one of you?"

A smile touched Clint's lips. "Yes, I'm technically the oldest, Cole's in the middle and Casey is the last."

Corey Westmoreland swallowed deeply. "I have three sons?"

Clint chuckled as he shook his head. "No, you have two sons. Casey is a girl and, just so you know, the reason she's not here is because she's having a hard time dealing with all of this. She and Mom were close and for years she thought you were dead and now to discover you're alive and that Mom kept it from us has her going through some changes right now."

Once again there was silence at the table and then Stone spoke. "Damn, another Westmoreland girl and we thought Delaney was the only one." He turned and smiled at the two men, his newfound cousins. "Delaney is my sister and we thought she was the only female in the Westmoreland family in this generation. Did the two of you catch hell being big brothers to Casey as much as my four brothers and six cousins caught hell looking out for Delaney?"

Clint and Cole exchanged huge grins. "Hell wasn't all we caught being brothers to Casey. Wait until you meet her, then you'll understand why."

Madison cuddled closer into Stone's embrace as they lay in bed together. "In a way, today's event had a happy ending to a rather sad beginning. At least Clint and Cole got to meet Corey and Corey found out he had two sons and a daughter."

"Umm," Stone said, placing a kiss on Madison's lips. "Uncle Corey is going to make history in the Westmoreland family. He'll become a father and a groom within months of each other. He was so excited that he picked up the phone to call everyone but then remembered the phone was dead.

I can't wait until the family gets the news." He chuckled. "And when Clint and Cole told Uncle Corey what they did for a living, he was as proud as could be." Both Clint and Cole were Texas Rangers. According to the brothers, Casey owned a clothing store in Beaumont.

Less than an hour later, when Madison had fallen asleep, Stone slipped out of her bedroom and ran smack into Durango. Durango placed his arms across his chest and had a smirk on his face. "Making late night visits, I see."

Stone frowned. "You see too much, Durango? Why aren't you in bed like everyone else."

"Because, Cuz, I was looking for you. When you weren't in your room I assumed you had gone outside to take a dip in the hot spring. Evidently I was wrong."

Stone glared at him. "Evidently. Now why were you looking for me?"

Durango reached into his pocket and pulled out an envelope. "To give you this. I almost forgot because of the excitement. This telegram came for you a few days ago. I assume it might be important."

Stone took the envelope from Durango, tore it open and scanned the contents. "Damn!"

Durango lifted a brow. "Bad news?"

Stone shook his head. "It's from my agent. I sold another book and the offer is eight figures and a Hollywood studio has bought an option on it. He wants me in New York in two days to announce everything at the Harlem Book Fair."

Durango smiled. "Hey, Stone, that's wonderful news and I'd think announcing the deal at that book fair would be good publicity."

"Yeah, but I don't want to go anywhere right now."

Durango lifted a dark brow in confusion. "Why not?" When Stone didn't respond he said, "Oh, I see."

Stone frowned. "And just what do you see, Durango?"

"I see that a city girl has wrapped herself around your heart like one wrapped herself around mine a few years ago. Take my advice and be careful about falling in love. Heartache is one hell of a pain to bear."

Stone sighed deeply as he met his cousin's gaze. "Your advice comes too late, Durango. I think I'm already there." Without saying anything else, he walked off.

Stone glanced at his watch as he waited for Madison to come to breakfast the next morning. He would be leaving with Durango and Quade when they left in less than an hour. Clint and Cole would be staying awhile to spend time with Corey and Abby.

"Stone? Mom said you wanted to see me."

Stone glanced up and smiled when he saw Madison enter the room. She was dressed in a pair of jeans and a Western shirt and looked feminine as hell. He took her hand in his. "Durango gave me a telegram last night. My agent wants me in New York for an important media announcement regarding a recent book deal. I need to leave for New York as soon as possible."

Madison's features filled with disappointment. "Oh." Then, after taking a deep breath, she met his gaze and said, "I'm going to miss you."

He pulled her into his arms. "I'm going to miss you, too. I'll be back as soon as it's over. Will you be here when I return?"

She met his gaze. "I'm not sure, Stone, I—"

"Please stay until I get back, Madison. You haven't been to Yellowstone and I'd like to take you there."

She smiled. "I think I'd like that."

Not caring who might walk up on them at any moment,

he pulled her into his arms and kissed her deeply, needing to take the taste of her with him and wanting to leave the taste of him with her. He planned for them to have a long talk about their future when he returned.

"I'll be back as soon as I can," he whispered against her moist lips.

She nodded. "I'll be counting the days."

He pulled her closer into his arms. "So will I."

Chapter 10

At any other time Stone would have enjoyed attending a gala thrown in his honor, but at this moment he didn't appreciate that his agent, Weldon Harris, had planned the surprise event. Even the media had been invited and he cringed when he saw that the one reporter he detested, Noreen Baker, was among the crowd.

He was even more mad that what was supposed to have been a weekend affair in New York had stretched into a full week including unscheduled interviews and parties that his agent had arranged for him to attend. He hated that his uncle's phone still wasn't working. He had no way to let Madison know why he hadn't returned to the mountains.

He saw Noreen Baker glance his way and knew an encounter with her was the last thing he wanted. He turned to make his escape, but when she called out to him, he decided it would be rude not to acknowledge her. He sighed deeply when she approached.

"Congratulations on your achievements. You must be proud of yourself."

"I am," he said curtly, deciding not to engage in small talk.

She glanced around. "And I must say that this is a real nice party for the prolific Rock Mason."

"I'm glad you like it, Noreen. Now if you will ex—"

"Are you still trying to be a recluse?"

He had turned around to leave but her question ticked him off. "I've never tried to be a recluse. If you would catch me when I'm doing my Teach the People to Read functions you would know that. Instead you prefer attending those affairs that promote dirt instead of positive functions."

Noreen looked at him and smiled. "How about telling me something that's positive?"

"Try doing an article on the Teach the People to Read program."

"No, I want to do an article about you. After the announcement a few days ago, you are definitely big news and being young, single and rich, you will be in demand with the ladies. Any love interests? What about marriage plans?"

Stone immediately thought about Madison. He would gladly announce to the world that she was the woman he loved and the one woman he wanted to marry, but information like that in this particular barracuda's hand might be hurtful to Madison. Noreen would never give her a moment's rest in the process of fishing for a story. She would camp outside Madison's home if it meant getting a scoop.

"How can I consider marriage when there's no special woman in my life?"

Noreen's lips quirked. "What about a special man?"

Stone narrowed his eyes. "You've kept up with my past history long enough to know better than to ask that."

"Okay, so that was a cheap shot and I admit it. So are you telling me that there's no woman that Rock Mason is interested in at the moment? There is no woman you would consider marrying?"

Stone frowned. "I think I've made myself clear on several occasions that Rock Mason enjoys the freedom of being a bachelor too much."

"Is that why you've agreed to do that four-month promotional tour in Europe?"

Stone frowned again, wondering how news of that got leaked to the press. He hadn't made a decision on whether or not he would go on that damn tour and he had told his agent that. A lot depended on Madison. He would only go if she went with him. He had no intention of leaving the woman he loved behind.

He met Noreen's curious gaze and said, "No comment. Now if you will excuse me, there's someone over there that I need to see." Stone then walked off.

Three days later Stone was in his hotel room, finally packing to return to Montana. He had spoken with his family in Atlanta several times over the past week. They had heard from Quade and were excited that there were now three additional Westmorelands. He had also spoken with Durango who indicated that he hadn't seen or spoken to Corey since he'd left.

Stone was anxious to get back to Madison. He missed her like hell. He glanced over at the television when he heard his name and stopped what he was doing as Noreen Baker's face appeared on the screen during a segment of *Entertainment Tonight*. He crossed the room to turn up the volume.

"As we reported last week, national bestselling author

Rock Mason accepted an eight-figure deal from Hammond Publishers and with it came movie options, as well as a four-month book tour in Europe. I spoke with Rock a few nights ago at a New York bash given in his honor and he squashed any rumors that he is romantically involved with anyone, and went on to assure me that he still prefers bedding women to wedding them. He also plans to leave for Europe in a few weeks. So any of you women out there who're holding out for the attention of Mr. Money Maker himself, don't waste your time. Rock Mason is as hard as they come when the discussion of marriage comes up and he intends to maintain his bachelor status for quite a while."

Stone switched off the television, shaking his head. Of course, as usual, Noreen had reported only part of the truth. At the moment he hadn't made a decision about Europe. And of course she had put her own spin on what she had gleaned from their conversation.

He crossed the room to finish packing. The cab would be arriving shortly to take him to the airport. Right now the only thing on his mind was getting back to Madison.

Hundreds of miles away, Madison was also packing. She had watched *Entertainment Tonight* and had heard everything the reporter had said. Stone had been gone for ten days and she hadn't heard from him. Although the phone lines were down, if he had wanted to contact her he could have sent her a letter or something. The postal plane delivered mail to the residents in the area at least twice a week.

He still prefers bedding women to wedding them…

She closed her eyes, fighting back tears. Why had she allowed things to get serious with Stone when he had told her from the very beginning what his feelings were on the subject of marriage? He didn't want to be accountable for anyone but himself and he was going to prove it by taking off to Europe for the next four months. Any pain she was suffering was nobody's fault but her own so she couldn't feel betrayed in any way. He had been totally upfront and truthful with her. She had been the one to assume she had meant something to him and that each time they'd made love it meant more than just having sex. She had actually thought that—

"You're leaving?"

She turned at the sound of her mother's voice. After meeting her mother's gaze and nodding, she continued packing. Her mother and Corey had been in the living room with her when *ET* had come on and had also heard everything the reporter had said.

"Running away won't solve anything, Madison. You told Stone you would be here when he returned and—"

"What makes you think he's going to return, Mom? You heard what that lady said. He's made plans to do a book tour in Europe. I made a mistake and put too much stock into what I thought he and I were sharing. End of story."

Abby crossed the room and took her daughter's hand in hers. "It's never the end of the story when you love someone. The end of the story only comes when the two of you are together."

Madison pulled her hand from her mother. "That may have worked for you and Corey, but then the two of you love each other and deserve a happy ending. I know how I feel about Stone but at no time did he ever tell me that he loved me, and at no time did he lead me to believe we had a future together. I made a mistake by assuming too much. I never expected to fall in love with him so quickly and so hard, Mom, but I did. Even now I don't regret loving him. The only thing I regret is that he doesn't love me back, but

I'll get over it. I'm a survivor, and someway, somehow, I'll eventually forget him."

Abby reached out and pulled Madison into her arms. She knew that now was not a good time to tell her daughter that she knew from firsthand experience a woman could never truly forget the man she loved. She'd been there, had tried doing that and it hadn't worked.

She sighed as she released Madison and stepped back. "So, when do you plan to leave?"

"In the morning. I've already talked to Corey and he said the postal plane will arrive tomorrow with the mail and he's sure they won't mind giving me a lift down the mountain and back to the Silver Arrow ranch. When I get back to Boston I'm going to contact the Institute about helping to provide students with summer lessons."

Abby reached out and stroked her daughter's cheek gently, feeling her pain. For her to even think about getting on a small plane showed how desperate she was to leave. "I had hoped you would stay with Corey and me for a while, at least until the end of the summer."

Madison nodded. She had hoped that, too, but knew the best thing for her was to return to Boston. School would start soon and she would go and get prepared for that. "I'll be back in December for your and Corey's wedding."

Even thinking about that brought her pain, knowing Stone would probably be there for the wedding, too. He would just have returned from Europe. "Besides, you did say you're coming home for a while in September to take care of business matters."

Abby smiled. "And when I do, we'll have to do a play or something. Definitely a concert."

Madison smiled through her tears. "That would be nice, Mom. That will really be nice."

* * *

"What do you mean she's not here?"

Corey Westmoreland crossed his arms over his chest and met his nephew's glare. "I mean just what I said. She's not here. Did you actually expect her to stick around after what she heard on that television show?"

Stone frowned. "What television show?"

Corey's frown matched Stone's. "The one where that reporter announced to the whole world that you preferred sleeping with women instead of marrying them. I guess Madison felt she fell within that category."

Frustration racked Stone's body and he rubbed his hand down his face. "How could she think something like that?"

Corey leaned back against the porch's column post. "Why wouldn't she think something like that? Have you ever told her anything different?"

Stone inhaled deeply. "No."

"Well, then. She acted just like any woman would act considering the circumstances. And that reporter also mentioned you had agreed to do some European tour and I guess Madison figured if you were planning to do that then she didn't mean a damn thing to you."

Stone met his uncle's stare. "Madison means everything to me. I love her so much I ache."

Corey rubbed his chin as he eyed his nephew. "And what about all that talk you've done over the years about wanting to have your freedom, seeking adventure and not being responsible for anyone but yourself? Not to mention your fear of losing control of your life?"

"My views on all that changed when I fell in love with Madison."

For the longest moment neither man spoke, then Stone

said. "There's no need for me to unpack since I'm leaving as soon as I can grab something to eat."

"Where're you going?"

Stone felt his pocket where he'd placed the diamond ring that he had purchased before leaving New York. "I'm going after Madison."

Stone saw her the moment she came out of the Hoffman Music Institute and began walking down the sidewalk. Abby had told him that, since Madison lived only a few blocks from her school, she preferred walking to work on nice days instead of driving. Besides, on any given day, parking in downtown Boston was known to be limited, as well as expensive.

Today was a fair day. The wind was brisk but the sun overhead added a ray of beauty to the city on the Charles; the city that was the origin of the American Revolution and where buildings, parks, fields and churches echoed the city's patriotic past. He remembered Madison once saying how much she loved Boston and he would gladly make this place his home if that's where she wanted to be. He would move anywhere just as long as they were together.

His heart swelled with love when he continued to watch as she came to Downtown Crossing with its brick streets. He wondered if she intended to go into Macy's and decided that now was the time to make his presence known. He hurriedly crossed the street when she stopped to admire the fruit on display at a sidewalk produce stand.

"Madison?"

Madison quickly glanced up. She pressed her hand to her chest and for a moment she forgot to breathe, she was so startled at seeing Stone. "Stone, what are you doing here?" she asked, amazed at how good he looked. It hadn't been quite two weeks since she had seen him last; twelve days exactly if you were counting and she had been unable not to do so. Seeing him reminded her how wrapped up in him she had gotten and how quickly. He was casually dressed in a pair of khaki pants and a polo shirt and she was hard pressed not to let her gaze travel the full length of him.

He was looking at her with an intensity that made her flesh tingle and a shiver moved down her spine. "You said you would stay at Uncle Corey's until I returned," he said, in a deep, husky voice that only added to her dilemma.

She licked her lips nervously and, when she remembered all the things that the reporter had said, she immediately decided that she didn't owe him an explanation, just like he didn't owe her one. "I decided to return home since Mom was okay," she said, as she went back to studying the fruit.

"I think we need to talk," he said and she looked back at him and wished she hadn't. She studied his features. There was a stubble of beard that darkened his chin and tired lines were etched under his eyes. He looked downright exhausted.

"When was the last time you had a good night's sleep?" she asked, as she continued to stare at him for a long moment. She wondered if his lack of sleep was due to all the partying he had done while in New York.

He shrugged. "Not since trying to get back to you. I was too wired up to sleep on the plane from New York to Montana and then when I arrived at Uncle Corey's and found you'd gone, I immediately left again and flew here."

She lifted an arched brow. "Why?"

"Because I have to talk to you."

She sighed. "Where are your things?"

"I checked into a hotel." He glanced around. "Is there someplace we can go and talk?"

Madison swallowed immediately. She had a feeling she knew what he had to say and thought that the last place she wanted him was in her home where she would always have memories of him being there. But it was the closest place and the least she could do was offer him a cup of coffee. "Yes, my condo is not far from here if you'd like to go there."

"Sure."

They walked side by side on the brick streets with little or no conversation between them. Occasionally, she would point out a historical landmark or some other note of interest. Moments later when she stopped in front of the elegant Ritz-Carlton Towers he met her gaze. "I live in the Residences, a portion of the tower that has private condos," she said, after saying hello to the doorman. "The entrance is through a private lobby that is separate from the hotel."

He nodded as he followed her inside to the lavishly styled lobby that led to a private elevator. "How long have you lived here?" he asked as they stepped onto the elevator.

"Ever since I finished college at twenty-one. My father left me a trust fund and I decided to invest a part of it in a place that I knew would increase in value. It's located within walking distance from my job and I like the ultimate amenity of having the hotel as an extension of my home. We use the same hotel staff and any packages, dry cleaning and other deliveries I get are held until I get home. I have access to all the restaurants in the hotel, as well as all the hotel's facilities like their spa and pool." She smiled. "And on those days that I come home too tired to cook, I can even order room service."

Stone liked what he saw the moment he walked into her condo. It was spacious and elegantly decorated. He could tell the furniture was expensive and added soothing warmth to the interior of the room. "I have one bedroom, one and a half baths, a living room with a fireplace, a kitchen and a library, and it's just the size I need," she said, crossing the room to open the blinds. The floor-to-ceiling window provided a breathtaking view of Boston.

His attention was drawn to the beautiful white piano in the middle of her living room. She saw where his gaze had gone and said, "That was the last Christmas gift my father gave me before he died. And for me, at fifteen, it was like a dream come true. Sauter pianos are renowned for their outstanding sound, fine touch and unique expressiveness." She brushed some curls back from her face and added, "And as you can also see, it's pleasing to the eye. There's not a day that goes by that I don't admire it whenever I look at it. It's brought me hours of joy."

He nodded. "Do you play it often?"

"Yes. Playing the piano relaxes me." She decided not to tell him that when she had returned from Montana two days ago, it had been the sound of the music she had played on her piano that had brought solace to her aching heart. "If you'd like to have a seat, I'll fix us a cup of coffee."

"Thanks, I'd appreciate it." He watched her leave the room. He had played out in his mind what he was going to say to her and now that the time had come for him to say it, he wondered if he would have trouble getting the words out. He was a master at putting words down on paper but now that it was a matter of the heart, he was at a loss for words. He needed to let her know just how much he loved her and how much she meant to him and that, more than anything, he wanted her in his life. Loving her was more than a stone cold surrender. It was a lifeline he needed to make his life complete.

He sat down on the sofa, liking the softness of the

leather. The entire room had her scent and he was engulfed in the pleasantly sweet fragrance of her. He leaned his head back and decided to close his eyes for a second. He could hear her moving around in the kitchen and in the distance he could hear the sound of boats tooting their horns as they passed in the harbor and the faint sound of an airplane that flew overhead. But his mind tuned out everything as he slowly drifted into a deep sleep.

"I forgot to ask how you want your—"

Madison stopped talking in midsentence when she saw that Stone had literally passed out on her sofa. Quickly walking over to the linen closet she pulled out a blanket and crossed the room back to him. She touched his shoulder. "Stone, you're tired," she said softly. "Go ahead and stretch out on my sofa and rest for a moment."

Glazed, tired eyes stared at her. "But we need to talk, Madison," he said in a voice that was heavy with sleep and weighty with exhaustion.

"And we *will* talk," she said softly, quietly. "As soon as you wake up from your nap. Okay?"

He nodded as he stretched out on her sofa. She placed the blanket over him and moments later his even breathing filled the room. She sighed. He was intent on talking to her and she didn't want to think about what he had to say. He probably thought, considering the affair they'd shared, that he owed her the courtesy of letting her know that things were over between them and he was moving on.

She didn't want to think about it and decided to take a shower and relax and try to forget he was there until he woke up and made his presence known. But as she looked down at him she realized that, even if he didn't make a sound, she would know that Stone was within reaching distance and for her that was not good. It was not good at all.

Stone slowly opened his eyes as soft music drifted around him. He immediately recognized it as a piece by Bach. When Delaney had been around eight or nine, she had taken music lessons for a short time and he distinctly remembered that same classical number as being one she had relentlessly hammered on the piano as she prepared for her first recital. He slowly sat upright and gradually stood, folding up the blanket Madison had placed over him.

He sighed deeply. He had come all this way to talk to her and instead he had passed out on her. He stretched his muscles then decided to go look for her. He needed to let her know how he felt about her and hoped she felt the same way about him.

Stone found her standing on a balcony that extended from her bedroom. She had changed out of the slacks and silk shirt she'd been wearing to a long flowing skirt and a matching top. She was standing barefoot, leaning against the rail with a glass of wine in her hand as she looked at the city below. He was sure he'd been quiet, that he hadn't made a sound, but still she turned and looked straight at him. Their gaze held for several moments and when a small smile touched her lips, his stomach tightened in response to that smile. "How was your nap?" she asked.

He covered the distance separating them and came to stand beside her. "I didn't mean to pass out on you like that."

"You were tired."

"Yes, I guess I was."

"And you're probably hungry. I can order room ser—"

"We need to talk, Madison."

She turned back to look out over the city. "You know you really didn't have to come, Stone. I understood how things were from the beginning so you don't owe me an explanation."

Stone lifted a brow, wondering what she was talking about. "I don't?"

She turned and met his gaze. "No, you don't. You never misled me or implied that anything serious was developing between us. In fact you were very honest from the beginning in letting me know how much you enjoyed your freedom and that you never planned to marry." She inhaled deeply. "So you're free to go."

He gazed at her for a moment as if enthralled by all she had said, and then asked, "I'm free to go where?"

She shrugged. "Back to New York, Montana, on your European book tour or anywhere you want to go. I guess you figured that, with your uncle marrying my mom, we should end things between us in a proper way so there won't be any hard feelings and I just want to assure you that there won't be. No matter what, Stone, I will always consider you my friend."

Stone took the glass of wine from her hand after suddenly deciding that he was the one who needed a drink. He looked at the glass and made sure that he placed his mouth on the exact spot that showed the imprint of her lips. The white wine tasted good and felt bubbly as it flowed down his throat. He emptied the glass then set it on the table next to where they were standing. He then met Madison's curious gaze. "So you think that's the reason I'm here? To bring our intimate association to a proper close?" he asked, managing a soft smile.

She met his gaze. "Isn't it?"

Her question, asked in a quiet, soft voice, stirred something deep inside Stone and he regretted more than ever that he had never told her that he loved her. She needed to know that. She needed to know that each and every time he had made love to her had meant more to him than just satisfying overzealous hormones. Yes, he had taken her with a hunger that had almost bordered on obsession, and he had always been acutely aware of everything physical about her. But he had also been aware of her emotional side. That had been what had first touched his heart. Her love and concern for the people she cared about.

Knowing he needed to get her out of the vicinity of her bedroom, he took her hand in his. "Come on. Let's go into the living room and talk."

He led her through the bedroom and into the living room. When she started to sit beside him on the sofa, he pulled her into his arms and placed her in his lap. He smiled at the look of surprise that lit her features.

"Now then, I think I need to get a few things straight up front," he said.

She lifted a brow. "Such as?"

"The reason I'm here and the reason I hadn't gotten any sleep in over forty-eight hours. First let me start off by saying I'm not going back to New York or Montana, and I'm sure as hell not going on some European book tour—unless you go to all of those places with me."

Madison blinked, confused. "I don't understand."

Stone chuckled. "Evidently. And in a way it's entirely my fault. I failed to make something clear to you each time that we made love."

He saw how her throat tightened when she swallowed. "What?"

He met her gaze and held on to it, locked it with his. "That I love you."

She pulled back and stared at him in disbelief. "But, but, I—I didn't know," she said, her words coming out in a stream of astonished puffs of air.

He skimmed a fingertip across her lips. "That's why I'm here, Madison, to let you know. I think I fell in love with you the moment I saw you on the airplane, although it took me a while to come to terms with it. I should have told you before I left for New York, but I was in a rush to leave and decided to wait and tell you when I got back. The trip took longer than I expected. I watched that television show, just as you did, but I didn't think when you heard what the reporter said that you would believe it had anything to do with my relationship with you. When she interviewed me I didn't want to mention you or tell her how I felt about you, mainly because I wanted to keep things between us private. Besides, I wasn't sure how you felt about me since we hadn't talked."

He leaned over and replaced his fingers with his lips and brushed a kiss across her mouth. "And I still don't know. I've told you how I feel about you, but you've yet to say how you feel about me."

Madison snuggled closer into Stone's arms and reached up and placed her arms around his neck. The same happiness that shone in her heart was reflected in her eyes. "I love you, Stone Westmoreland, with all my heart. I think I fell in love with you the first moment I looked into your eyes on the airplane, too. And I was so embarrassed when I realized where my hand had been and how close I came to touching a certain part of you. But now I know it went there for a reason," she said, shifting her body and reaching down to actually touch him.

She smiled upon realizing how hard he was and what that meant. "I didn't know at the time that that part of you, all of you, was destined to be mine and I feel like the luckiest and the happiest woman in the world."

Stone groaned out her name as he captured her mouth and deepened the kiss when she sank into him, returning his kiss the way he had taught her to do, enjoying the passion that would always be there between them. Moments later he pulled back and cupped her face in his hands.

"Will you marry me, Madison? Will you agree to spend the rest of your life with me and be my soul mate? I know how much you love Boston and that you don't ever want to leave and that's fine. We can make our primary home here and—"

Madison quickly touched her mouth to his to cut off his words. "Yes, I'll marry you, Stone. I love you and my home will always be wherever you are. I know how much you like to travel and now, after visiting Montana and seeing so much beauty there, I see what I've been missing by not traveling. Now I want to go to those places with you."

Her words touched him and he reached out, pulled her back into his arms and again kissed her, long and deep. When he lifted his head, he stood up with her in his arms. "I love you," he told her again as he carried her into the bedroom. He gently placed her on the bed and stood back. He then reached into his pocket and pulled out a small white velvet box.

"I bought this for you while in New York. I had every intention of asking you to marry me when I got back to Montana." He leaned forward and handed her the box.

With tears misting her eyes, Madison nervously opened it to find a beautiful diamond engagement ring. It was so lovely that it took her breath away. She gazed back at Stone. "I—I don't know what to say."

Stone chuckled. "Baby, you've already said everything

I wanted to hear. The only thing left is for us to set the date. I don't want to seem like I'm rushing things, but I want us to get married as soon as possible.... I'll understand if you prefer to wait until next June and have a huge wedding here."

Madison shook her head. "No, I had planned a big wedding with Cedric and I don't want that for us. We don't need it. We can go before the justice of the peace and I'd be happy. I just want to be your wife."

Stone's smile widened. "And more than anything, I want to be your husband. Before leaving Montana, Uncle Corey suggested the Westmorelands get-together at his place the second week in August. He wants everyone to meet Abby, as well as his sons and daughter. I know that's only six weeks from now but what do you think of us having a wedding then, there on Corey's mountain?" he asked, taking the ring and placing it on her finger. He liked the way it looked. He could tell that she liked the way it looked, too. She held her hand out in front of her and kept peeking at it, smiling.

She then glanced up at him. "I think August will be a wonderful time. When do you leave for Europe?"

He shook his head. "I haven't agreed to that book tour, Madison. Everything hinges on what you want to do. I know how much you like teaching and—"

She leaned up and placed a finger to his lips. "Yes, I've always enjoyed teaching because that's what I limited myself to do. I appreciated those nights when you came into my bedroom at Corey's and shared your writing with me. And, because of it, I now have a burning desire to do something I've always wanted to do but was never brave enough to try."

"What?"

A wishful thought flashed across her face. "Compose my

own music. I once shared a few pieces I'd composed with a friend at school and she told me how good she thought they were and that it was something I should do. And I think I will."

He pulled her into his arms. "I think that's a wonderful idea and is one that I wholeheartedly support." He nuzzled her neck, liking her scent and thinking he would never get enough of it.

Madison looped her arms around his neck and pulled him down on the bed with her and he kissed her slowly, deeply and began removing her clothes. When he had her completely naked, he sat back on his haunches and stared at her, a deep look of love in his eyes.

"It's your turn, Stone. Take off your clothes," she said softly, pulling at his shirt.

He stood, appearing more than happy to oblige. She watched as he removed every stitch of clothing and, when he rejoined her on the bed, she reached out and ran her finger down his chest. "This is nice," she said, leaning forward and flicking her tongue across his hardened nipples.

When she felt his shudder, Madison felt confident, loved and, thanks to Stone, passionate. She moved her hand lower and let her fingers travel past his waist and stroke that part of him she had almost touched on the plane. She heard his breathing increase and felt his body harden even more beneath her hand. He also felt hot and ready.

"You want me," she said softly, marveling at how much he did.

"Yes, and I'll always want you." He gently pushed her back on the bed to touch her everywhere, kiss her everywhere, taste her everywhere; and when she couldn't take any more and was thrashing about beneath him, he covered her mouth with his the same moment that he parted her legs, lifted her hips and eased inside of her. She shifted her body to welcome him and, with one quick thrust, he was bedded deep inside her.

He held himself still in that position as his mouth mated relentlessly with hers, filled with emotions of every kind. And when her muscles began clenching his heated flesh, he slowly began moving, establishing a rhythm that would bring them both pleasure.

Moments later when they both went spiraling off the edge, lost in passion of the richest kind, Stone knew his parents' prediction of love at first sight had been right. Loving Madison was something he would look forward to doing for the rest of his life.

Epilogue

When Stone and Madison returned to Montana they discovered that Corey and Abby had decided not to wait for a Christmas wedding but wanted to marry sooner. So the four of them—Corey, Abby, Stone and Madison—decided to have a double wedding on Corey's Mountain in August. Martin Quinn, a former judge, agreed to perform the ceremony.

Now the day of the wedding had arrived and, as Madison glanced around, she knew that only Abby Winters-Westmoreland could bring such style, grace and elegance to the rugged mountains of Montana for the mother-and-daughter wedding. Almost everyone had arrived by plane on the airstrip that several ranchers in the area shared. Her mother had even had a band flown in for the affair, as well as a well-known catering company from Boston. Every time she glanced over at her mother and Corey she saw just how happy they were together. It had taken thirty-two years but they were finally together and she knew it was meant to be this way.

"Ready?"

Madison glanced up at her husband of less than an hour and knew it was time to meet the rest of his siblings and cousins. She had met his parents, his sister Delaney, her husband Prince Jamal Ari Yasir and their son Ari last night. Almost everyone else had arrived an hour or two before the wedding was to take place, so she hadn't had the chance to meet them beforehand.

"Yes, I'm ready," she said, inhaling deeply.

Stone leaned down and kissed her lips; then, taking her hand in his, he led her over to an area where a group stood talking. A couple of people she recognized, but others she did not.

First he introduced her to his married brothers, Dare and Thorn, and their wives, Shelly and Tara. Madison could immediately feel the love flowing between the couples and hoped that her and Stone's marriage would be just as strong and loving.

Stone then introduced her to his brother, the one he said the ladies called "The Perfect Storm." She could see why. He was drop-dead gorgeous and she had a strong feeling that he knew it. Then she met Storm's fraternal twin, Chase, and he was just as gorgeous. In fact she was discovering that all the male Westmorelands were good-looking men.

Next came the cousins: Jared, Spencer, Ian, Quade and Reggie. She had already met Quade and Durango, and Durango pulled her into his arms and gave her an astounding, welcome-to-the-family kiss on her lips and said he liked her even if she was a city girl. She gave Stone a questioning look and the response in his eyes indicated that he would explain things later.

She then got the chance to see the newest Westmoreland cousins again; Clint and Cole, as well as the daughter Corey Westmoreland never knew he had: Casey.

Casey Westmoreland was shockingly beautiful and Madison thought it amusing to see how all the single men present who weren't Westmorelands were giving her their undivided attention. Now she understood what Clint and Cole had meant when they'd insinuated that it hadn't been easy being Casey's brothers.

After all the introductions were made, Stone pulled Madison into his arms. They would be leaving the mountain in a few hours to spend a week in San Francisco. Her mother and Corey were headed in the opposite direction to spend a week in Jamaica.

Madison had never been to the Bay area and Stone, who'd been there several times, had planned a special honeymoon there for them.

They would be leaving the country within the month for Stone's four-month European book tour. They would return just weeks before Christmas and had decided to make Atlanta their primary home.

"I can't wait to get you all to myself," Stone whispered to his wife moments later, when her mother had indicated it was time to cut the cake and to take more pictures.

"I can't wait to get you all to myself, too," Madison said smiling and meaning every word. She had a surprise for him. She had composed a song just for him. And she knew as she gazed lovingly at her husband that it was a song that would stay in her heart forever.

* * * * *

We hope you enjoyed reading

Wild About Harry

by *New York Times* bestselling author

LINDA LAEL MILLER

and

Stone Cold Surrender

by *New York Times* bestselling author

BRENDA JACKSON.

Both were originally Harlequin® series stories!

From passionate, suspenseful and dramatic
love stories to inspirational or historical,
Harlequin offers different lines to
satisfy every romance reader.

New books in each line are available every month.

**Luxury, scandal, desire—welcome to the lives
of the American elite.**

SPECIAL EXCERPT FROM

mira

Read on for an excerpt from
Linda Lael Miller's historical novel
The Yankee Widow

ONE

Chancellorsville, Virginia

May 3, 1863

JACOB

The first minié ball ripped into Corporal Jacob Hammond's left hand, the second, his right knee, each strike leaving a ragged gash in its wake; another slashed through his right thigh an instant later, and then he lost count.

A coppery crimson mist rained down on Jacob as he bent double, then plunged, with what felt like a strange, protracted grace, toward the broken ground. On the way down, he noted the bent and broken grass, shimmering with fresh blood, the deep gouges left by cannonballs and boot heels and the lunging hooves of panicked horses.

A peculiar clarity overtook Jacob in those moments between life as he'd always known it and another way of being, already inevitable. The boundaries of his mind seemed to expand beyond skull and skin, rushing outward at a dizzying speed, hurtling in all directions, rising past the treetops, past the sky, past the far borders of the cosmos itself.

For an instant, he understood everything, every mystery, every false thing, every truth.

He felt no emotion, no joy or sorrow.

There was peace, though, and the sweet promise of oblivion.

Then, with a wrench so swift and so violent that it sickened his very soul, Jacob was back inside himself, a prisoner behind fractured bars of bone. The flash of extraordinary knowledge was gone, a fact that saddened Jacob more deeply than the likelihood of death, but some small portion of the experience remained, an ability to think without obstruction, to see his past as vividly as his present, to envision all that was around him, as if from a great height.

Blessedly, there was no pain, though he knew that would surely come, provided he remained alive long enough to receive it.

Something resembling bitter amusement overtook Jacob then; he realized that, unaccountably, he hadn't expected to be struck down on this savage battlefield or any other. Never mind the unspeakable carnage he'd witnessed since his enlistment in Mr. Lincoln's grand army; with the hubris of youth, he had believed himself invincible.

He had assumed that the men in blue fought on the side of righteousness, committed to the task of mending a sundered nation, restoring it to its former whole. For all its faults, the United States of America was the most promising nation ever to arise from the old order of kings and despots; even now, Jacob was convinced that, whatever the cost, it must not be allowed to fail.

He had been willing to pay that price, was willing still.

Don't miss
The Yankee Widow,
coming soon from Linda Lael Miller and MIRA Books!

MIRABooks.com

HARLEQUIN
DESIRE

Luxury, scandal, desire—welcome to the lives
of the American elite.

Save **$1.00**

on the purchase of ANY
Harlequin Desire book.

Available wherever books are sold, including
most bookstores, supermarkets, drugstores
and discount stores.

Save **$1.00**

on the purchase of ANY Harlequin Desire book.

Coupon valid until September 27, 2021. Redeemable at participating outlets in the
U.S. and Canada only. Not redeemable at Barnes & Noble stores. Limit one coupon per customer.

52617137

Canadian Retailers: Harlequin Enterprises ULC will pay the face value of this coupon plus
10.25¢ if submitted by customer for this product only. Any other use constitutes fraud. Coupon is
nonassignable. Void if taxed, prohibited or restricted by law. Consumer must pay any government taxes.
Void if copied. Inmar Promotional Services ("IPS") customers submit coupons and proof of sales to
Harlequin Enterprises ULC, P.O. Box 31000, Scarborough, ON M1R 0E7, Canada. Non-IPS retailer—
for reimbursement submit coupons and proof of sales directly to Harlequin Enterprises ULC, Retail
Marketing Department, Bay Adelaide Centre, East Tower, 22 Adelaide Street West, 40th Floor, Toronto,
Ontario M5H 4E3, Canada.

U.S. Retailers: Harlequin Enterprises ULC will pay the face
value of this coupon plus 8¢ if submitted by customer for
this product only. Any other use constitutes fraud. Coupon is
nonassignable. Void if taxed, prohibited or restricted by law.
Consumer must pay any government taxes. Void if copied.
For reimbursement submit coupons and proof of sales directly
to Harlequin Enterprises ULC 482, NCH Marketing Services,
P.O. Box 880001, El Paso, TX 88588-0001, U.S.A. Cash value
1/100 cents.

5 65373 00076 2   (8100)0 12503

® and ™ are trademarks owned by Harlequin Enterprises ULC.

© 2021 Harlequin Enterprises ULC

BACCOUP40619MAX

 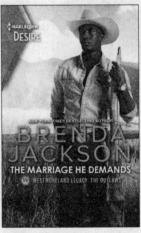